HAZARDOUS MONEY

HAZARDOUS MONEY

Alastair Gibbons

ISBN: 978-1-08918-816-2

To my family

Lynwen,
Joe, Elen, Dan, Siân

Gone, the merry morris din;
Gone, the song of Gamelyn;
Gone, the tough-belted outlaw
Idling in the "grenè shawe;"
All are gone away and past!
And if Robin should be cast
Sudden from his turfed grave,
And if Marian should have
Once again her forest days,
She would weep, and he would craze:
He would swear, for all his oaks,
Fall'n beneath the dockyard strokes,
Have rotted on the briny seas;
She would weep that her wild bees
Sang not to her — strange! that honey
Can't be got without hard money!

So it is: yet let us sing,
Honour to the old bow-string!
Honour to the bugle-horn!
Honour to the woods unshorn!
Honour to the Lincoln green!
Honour to the archer keen!
Honour to tight little John,
And the horse he rode upon!
Honour to bold Robin Hood,
Sleeping in the underwood!
Honour to maid Marian,
And to all the Sherwood-clan!
Though their days have hurried by
Let us two a burden try.

John Keats

Chapter One   James

Money begat power and on the seventh day, rich men replaced God and his laws with their own. James Tait dissented.

News footage of refugees fleeing a war zone loomed above the heads of baristas. Cascading red figures ticked along the bottom of the giant screen. 8am and the stock-market was plunging. James watched from the glum breakfast queue in *City Express Café* wearing a wry grin. A shame he couldn't share his secret. Today would be a good day.

The kitchen door swung open, and a pair in mauve aprons and oven-gloves, line-danced their way to glass counters, holding aloft metal trays of steaming pastries. Wafts of melted butter, sugar and chocolate teased him. He swallowed saliva as he eyed a feast of croissants, sweet pastries and muffins. His stomach groaned to the aroma and grind of coffee beans and the hollering of counter staff twisting customer orders in multiple accents.

He shuffled forward in line and heard a jangle of coins behind him. He swiveled, catching a stench of stale sweat. A dark faced man with a soiled blanket over his shoulders, jiggling a polystyrene cup, appeared at his side. James held his breath and dug into his pocket. As his fingers felt for change, the manager arrived with a coffee and coaxed the man to the exit. Everyone in line watched for a moment, then resumed their silent communion.

He reached the front and grinned. Isabella, the chattering Spanish girl fluttered her eye-lashes and flashed her immaculate white teeth. Their early morning ritual had begun. Who would be the first to chime, "Americano, extra shot, hot milk and a blueberry muffin?" Her thick Spanish accent tripped her sometimes but this morning she got in first. Her black pony-tail flicked like a whip as she turned to order his coffee from a gang of baristas. She was possibly half his age, was probably paid a fraction of his old investment banking salary, and plainly spoke twice the number of languages.

The bustle behind him and chaos before him, drowned out their routine chat. He ordered an extra muffin in a separate bag. Her finger tips brushed his, when she handed him the carry-out bags, and mouthed "Enjoy". They traded smiles and with, "same time, same place, tomorrow," he ended their habitual rite. Onlookers could smirk at his trite valediction, but the daily act nourished and starved him. It had been too long since his last proper relationship, too long to remember.

Outside on the pavement, James found the man, sat on a battered suit-case against a low wall, crowned with frost. He was sipping his coffee and scratching his grey stubble. He looked mid-thirties, which James reckoned made him mid-twenties; too old. James dangled a carry-out bag in front of him. The man looked up, sweeping matted black hair from his forehead, exposing bushy eye-brows knitted in confusion. His eyes darted between James's face and the bag.

"Breakfast." James let the bag drop gently on to the man's lap.

The man wiped a drip from his thick nc his hand, peered in the bag and grinned w stained teeth. " Shukraan. Thank you."

James stooped and stuffed a crumpled t into the polystyrene cup by his foot. The mar him, open mouthed. James patted him on the shoulder and smiled.

"Good luck my friend." Then he turned and joined the bustle of business executives pouring from Southwark tube station. He weaved through the fuming traffic, and sped across Shakespeare Square, a paved esplanade, towards the revolving glass doors of the capital's latest tower, soaring above the river. Pigeons, plump from tourist tit-bits skittered from his path, surprised by his feverish pace.

He crossed the airy planted atrium to the lift pods. His mind had already turned to the transformative deal he expected to clinch by lunchtime. He felt light-headed as he squeezed in amongst baggy-eyed, tight-lipped executives, burdened with gym packs. They were doused in perfume, deodorant and body spray; bore paper bags of pastries, bacon sandwiches and buttered toast; and gripped branded cardboard coffee cups. He murmured an apology as he leant forward, slid his security card into a slot and tapped the keypad for level fifty. A voice, eerie and androgynous, confirmed his choice. Like shop-window mannequins, nobody moved, spoke, or shifted grim, glacial stares. The stainless-steel corporate cell accelerated up. He stepped out of an empty lift, onto polished marble tiles of LifeChance Trust's reception area.

"Morning Lisa."

"Good morning James. Good journey?" It was always the same. The new mother from Morden, immaculate make-up, awash in floral scent, high-lighted fair hair adorned with headset microphone, beamed from behind a vast walnut

... To her rear, the wall was decked with digital screens, ~oling with twenty-four-hour news and business channels. As he dashed past, she called after him. "I've brought those photos in." Her child was a few weeks old.

James twisted round and smiled but kept walking. "Great. Love to look at them later." He disappeared through smoked-glass doors which had slid open before him.

He exchanged stares with the bulbous, blueberry muffin, which lay unwrapped on his desk. He knew he shouldn't, it broke the rules of his endless dietary regime. He broke off a lump and popped it into his mouth, savoring its sugariness. Caro, his 'adopted' big sister, would tut, pinch his flesh and tease him about his love-handles. How ironic, he thought, given his sporadic on-line dating debacles. But he took the jibes, and everything else from her in good humour. He'd call her in a while with the good news, seek her approbation.

He peered through the tinted glass of his corner office, down river towards the City's dazzling towers. A pale-yellow sun hovered low on the horizon of a blue sky, spotless but for a single cloud, drifting up river. A single dash of green, 'WMS 97 +5' flickered near the foot of his desktop screen teeming red figures. WebMaster Services plc's share price had surged five per cent in the first few minutes of the day's trading. God and several of James's closest associates were smiling on him.

James knew only the barest facts about WMS. He knew it was an on-line marketing services group, but that could mean anything. He knew that the company was based in London, was growing rapidly, served a global customer base and had a market value of over one billion pounds. He knew the chief executive was an American, Brad Jensen, forty-six. But then everyone else in the market knew all that and much else was speculation. But the market was unaware that Jensen had been having an affair with a young executive within WMS. He had begged James's associate not to send video footage of the pair having sex in a sterile budget hotel room to his wife, and mother of their three children. So, they had reached a mutually beneficial arrangement and today would witness its formal unveiling.

At eleven that morning, WebMaster Services plc would announce to the market that it had conditionally agreed a sale of the company to XinBuzz, a global US media group. The price, needed to obtain the board's recommendation, was a thumping forty per cent premium to the prevailing market value of the company. Evidently, with its share price rising, the news was leaking out. LifeChance stood to make a killing, and James intended to lock in the gains shortly after the announcement when the share price would soar. He would accept a small discount to get his hands on the cash now.

James clicked open an excel spreadsheet containing a financial model fed in real time by price updates from the market. At the current pre-announcement share price, it showed the stake he had carefully built over the past three months in WMS would yield a profit of three million pounds. He tapped his keyboard, entering the share price he knew had been agreed between the two companies. He knew it would generate a further eight million, but he wanted to see it confirmed one last time. The 'Aggregate Profits' cell flashed eight green figures.

"Beautiful," he muttered. A rewarding outcome from a simple operation, tried and tested several times in the past. No-one would suffer, no marriage would be wrecked, and the institutions which had sold him the shares had done so willingly. Above all else, the profits would be ploughed into

LifeChance, his charity for refugee children, where the money would do some good. Not that the Financial Conduct Authority which regulated City affairs, would share his view. What James referred to as privileged information gained from his investigations, the FCA defined as insider information. Acting on insider information was a criminal offence, carrying a prison sentence of up to seven years.

James gorged on a chunk of muffin, licked his fingers and picked up the phone to call Caro. He knew that Caro would already be at her office in the City, even if officially she could not be there in a management capacity. Caroline Noble owned WoMan Investments, which had been one of the UK's largest hedge fund companies, with eighty billion dollars under management. That was before she was found guilty of breaching money laundering regulations and sentenced to nine months in an open prison. She served only a few months, according to the popular press, because of the plight of her four young children. How she hated the media she once loved. They had used each other. She had built her business, in part on the back of extensive coverage of her personal profile.

Caro had been portrayed as a leading role model for women. The girl from humble beginnings, raised in a series of foster homes, graduated from Oxford, juggled a family with running a thriving financial services business and featured in the Times Rich List. Politicians from the left and right sought her out for photo opportunities. Feminist groups lauded her. Requests to speak at schools and universities piled up on her desk. She was treated to VIP status at celebrity parties and concerts. She had even received an invitation to tea, subsequently withdrawn, from the Prince of Wales.

Then came the televised raid by the Serious Fraud Office, with uniformed officers seen carrying out computers and files from her shiny new headquarters of cascading dark glass, a stone's throw from The Bank of England. Next a mob of reporters, camera crews, and prurient freaks, lodged out in front of her Notting Hill mansion, lenses and microphones jostling for a snatch of breaking news. The kids got a few days off school. Caro went to work as usual and gave the mob nothing more than a curt smile before she vanished behind the dark tinted windows of her driver's silver S-Class saloon.

The weekend newspapers had covered the raid and the allegations in detail. She had hated the photographs of her fish-eyed, jowly face almost as much as the cartoons. The media had been briefed, no doubt in Caro's view, by the Financial Conduct Authority. They had been on her case for a couple of years, prompting her to improve the firm's internal control procedures, to upgrade its Compliance department and to maintain adequate client records. She had always been civil to the morons she met from the FCA and promised in a vague way to deal with their concerns. But she preferred to be out in the markets with clients, accumulating more assets under management or driving the firm's growth into new more exotic areas of business to drive ever increasing returns for investors.

They had finally got her on a charge of not reporting suspicions about money laundering by one the firm's large Central American investors, a rich family, who were involved in a drugs related case in Colombia. Technically, she acknowledged that according to a strict interpretation of the law, the firm was in breach and that she as chief executive should take ultimate responsibility. But with almost a thousand employees she reasoned, how could it be judged fair that she alone be personally accountable. She expected slapped wrists, a sizeable fine for the firm, a warning about

7

future breaches and specific requirements for improvement in the firm's management procedures. That is what her lawyer told her to expect, the man she now called the Weasel.

Her instinct had been to plead guilty to her unwitting transgression and negotiate a more lenient settlement, but her lawyer had been adamant they should fight the case. He was a leading expert in his field and so she had trusted his categorical advice. His judgement, buoyed by a surfeit of arrogance founded on success, failed her. The judge had been particularly loathsome, going out of his way to pillory Caro as an exemplar of greed and the unacceptable face of unbridled capitalism.

Now, several months after her release, she still burned with a grievous sense of unfairness. She knew others had breached the same regulations but had received lighter treatment, out of the media's glare. She was convinced that she was guilty of just one thing – beating the men at their own game. WoMan Investments had been voted Hedge Fund of the Year by the respected *Acquisitions International* for an unprecedented third time. But following the trial's publicity, her assets under management had dwindled to a third of their former size. All state-owned funds had withdrawn capital at the first whiff of trouble. Others wilted under pressure from special interest groups. But not everyone had deserted her. She was no longer a role model and she was glad of it; she had learned a lesson. And she was determined to beat them all over again. She now had no doubts who were her friends, who were her enemies, and who were the nobodies. She never had doubts about her oldest, closest and most trusted friend, James Tait. And he needed her as much as she needed him.

"Morning Caro," James bellowed, still chewing on his muffin. He could hear the din of a trading floor in the background. It sounded just like the Royal Opera House minutes before the curtain rose; chattering waves mingling with dissonant notes as the orchestra warmed up. She would be doing her morning walk around, showing her face, revving up her troops. He recalled the frantic activity back in his day whenever the market swung sharply, up or down.

"Breakfast on the go, James?"

"No rest for the truly wicked. Hey look, I know you're busy but I wanted you to be the first to know about our good fortune with Project Rise." James adored his project names, a habit formed during his fifteen years of investment banking. Another was circumspection whenever using the phone – you could never be sure who might be listening in. This morning, the line was free of crackling. "Fingers crossed but it looks like our intensive research has paid off."

"That's good. You won't be needing me anymore then." Caro was the charity's biggest donor by a long way and had supported James's 'mad plan' to set up the charity five years ago. She thought his mid-life crisis would burn out, that he would return to the lucrative world of deal-making in the City. He had been a managing director in Goldwyn Morson's mergers and acquisitions department, working relentlessly, accumulating wealth, and living alone in an elegant Georgian Square in Chelsea. Occasionally, he would nod to his neighbours, as he passed them. More often he would spot the young families through the window, and watch them, laughing and exuberant as they crammed everything into Range Rovers and Mercedes. He sensed he was watching a lifestyle advertisement, not intended for him. And increasingly he felt his life was a piece of frivolous fiction written by a hack.

Goldwyn Morson had reluctantly granted his request for a sabbatical. A handful of colleagues, peevish about his success which they put down to excessive risk-taking, were not sad when he never returned. The rest still missed him, had benefited personally from his deal-doing, and regularly tried to lure him back.

"We'll always need you Caro. I have another plan to extend our services. It means we'll be able to reach many more children." Caro grunted. She'd heard it all before, and her bank account had paid for it.

"How's the dossier on the Weasel coming along?"

"Just about there. It's taken us longer than I'd hoped. We've kept digging, but so far, no definitive dirt; some speeding offences, a couple of clients disgruntled by excessive fees, gossip about an affair at work, muted allegations about sexual harassment, and some neighbours upset about a property extension he forced through. He's got a pool under his garden in Putney, and a double-level basement." He heard Caro's groan and imagined her rueful look.

"I bloody well paid for that. Outrageous how much he earns for doing an appalling job. Deserves to get booted out. Bloody Weasel."

James allowed her anger to settle for a few seconds, before reluctantly picking up. "I have one idea, if you are sure you want to go down this path." James had been deliberately dawdling with the dossier, hoping that time would heal Caro's fever for revenge. But since her release, it had festered. He did not share Caro's conviction about the Weasel's culpability, but then he had not suffered her sentence, her public humiliation and her family separation.

10

"I do. Come round for supper tonight. Bruce is cooking something veggie which the kids will hate, so there'll be plenty going spare. Bring the dossier."

"Okay, we can chat about my new idea as well." James needed her money for his bold plans. But he also genuinely valued her hard-headed, objective analysis. He would consult her before taking important issues to the non-executives on LifeChance's board.

"Fine. We have a deal. Nine as usual. Got to go, mayhem out there. The market's leapt off the edge. Time to dive in." With a click, the line went dead.

He was used to Caro's brusque manner on the phone and the abruptness with which she terminated calls. They had talked about it, but it had made no difference. He now felt foolish. All he had sought was a simple 'well done' from her; recognition of his achievement with Project Rise in pulling off the biggest single gain in the charity's history. It had always been like that, since they were children in the McManus' foster home, when he strove to earn the approval of the girl two years older than him.

James put down the receiver and dug two fingers into the soft dough of his muffin. It broke apart, and he jammed a giant piece in his mouth. He took a gulp from his coffee, its bitterness blending with the muffin's sweetness. He glanced guiltily over to his gym bag in the corner, where it had sat for three days. He would definitely make it to the gym, after the announcement and the sale of the WMS shares. He unglued the remaining morsel from its greasy blueberry-smeared paper and tossed it into his mouth.

He stood, stretched with his hands above his head, then picked up his coffee. He stepped over to the window. A police car, its blue light flashing, shot past traffic crawling near

Temple, sacred heart of bewigged barristers, London's leading lawyers. Below, the brown river flowed fast and relentless, ferrying its spoil towards the City. In the distance, commuters poured out from a ferry boat, on to the quay, and were soaked up by the narrow winding streets of the ancient capital. He wondered if any of them worked for LifeChance's broking firm, whether they would play any part in the trade which would transform the charity.

He heard his door open and swung around.

"Morning Megs." She closed the opaque glass door behind her. Something was wrong. Her face matched the solemnity of her black skirt-suit. "Whose funeral is it today?" He hated hearing bad news, always tried to quip it away.

"Ours, if we don't sell our WMS shares, right now." Megan, his younger 'adopted' sister, Operations Director of LifeChance, moved to perch on the seat by James's desk.

"But the announcement -"

"There won't be one. The deal is off." James's mouth froze. For a split-second, the roar of the air-con sounded like a bear-market hurricane as investors scrambled out, fear battering greed. His stomach gyrated. He felt faintly sick.

"How do we know?" He moved back to his chair to check the screen. If the deal was off, the news would leach out rapidly, and the share price would sink.

"Akhtar just got a call from his operative who got a text from Jensen. It just said, 'deal off sell'. That's all."

"But it might just be temporary, a hiccup in negotiations." The price on the screen had not moved.

"And it might be permanent."

James paused a beat, his mind swirling with possibilities. "We should check with Jensen."

"He's not responding. He must be manic if the deal is off. He's done what we agreed in case of an abort."

"But we need that money. We've committed half of it already on new centres." He peered at the screen and frowned at the sight of the price falling by a penny.

"James. Think. What if XinBuzz has discovered a problem at WMS? A profit warning would send the shares plummeting, and we borrowed to build our stake. We need to repay it before we make losses."

"We may be walking away from a ten-million-pound profit." But it was his last lament, the final flickering flame of his illusory giant gain and his image of ten new learning centres for the children; after school and weekend teaching, all free, small groups and even one to one tuition. He blinked at the screen, as the share-price fell another penny. Megan slapped her palms on the desk, her polished red fingernails arraigned against him.

"We cannot afford to take a loss. If we get out now, we could still make a couple of million." James nodded. He was already logged into his dealing page and began tapping on the keyboard the details to execute the sale order.

"You're right. I'll go for best price." He hit the green 'execute' button and then checked the price again – it was now back to 92, where it had started the day. Given their sizeable stake, James reckoned they would probably need to accept a discount on that price. He pressed a finger on to the muffin's wrapper, mopping up the crumbs. He sucked his finger and started to think about how to solve the problem, find another way to raise the cash needed for the new centres. He always had options running through his mind, none of them easy, all carried risk, took time he didn't have.

"You should call the broker as well – just in case our order is sitting at the end of a queue. You told me he owes you." Megan picked up James's phone and handed him the receiver.

James stood up and dialled the number as he moved to the white lacquered sideboard. He'd noticed that one of his deal tombstones had fallen on its back. Two dozen acrylic blocks and assorted deal toys lined the glossy surface-top, chronicling his decade and a half of deal fever. Engraved with the roll-call of corporate names and elongated numbers, each commemorated multi-million and some billion plus dollar deals he had led at Goldwyn Morson. He'd almost thrown them away so many times, but he clung to them like a toddler to his mother. They defined a major part of him, gave him the skills he was using to build LifeChance, and validated his achievements. And they impressed potential donors when he sat in his office regaling them with his grand vision for LifeChance.

But they also mocked him. The size of the deals loomed over any of his achievements at the charity. Just the fees earned on the larger deals dwarfed LifeChance's annual income. He picked up the fallen tombstone and wiped the dust off its smooth transparent surface with his fingers: 'Texman Resources Inc. - $1,700,000,000 Acquisition of North Sea Energy Partners plc. December 2007. He remembered the frantic on-off deal, the overnight sessions in lawyers' offices, the squabbles frustrating his drive to get the deal across the line pre-Christmas, to generate massive year-end bonuses for his team. Now, for LifeChance, he worked harder, risked more, and gambled his own reputation for just a tiny percentage of the deal's value, a mere smidgeon, an investment banking rounding error. The futility of ceaseless fund raising struck him sharp. The phone switched to voicemail. James sighed, and glanced at Megan, her facial muscles taught with insistence.

"He's not there. I'll keep trying." James walked back to his desk and slapped the handset back in its cradle.

"And we'll try to get hold of Jensen...just in case." James felt Megan's eyes on him, detecting the disappointment pinched by his lips and knitted in his brow: the look of the little boy whose father failed to show.

James slumped into his seat, sighed, and stared at her, unblinking for several seconds. His pulse was racing. "Megan. We're going to have to do something big, something that puts us on a firm footing for the long term. We can't keep lurching from one small deal to another. And donor fund-raising is a slow death." Megan stood up and gripped the edge of James's desk.

"We also need to be careful, otherwise there won't be a LifeChance for anyone." She sounded like every foster-parent he'd ever had, repeating the same lesson, straining to seem reasonable, and failing.

"I'm going to chat with Caro about the gaming company idea."

Megan smiled, small and tight. "She won't like it."

"Well I'll mention it, just casually."

Megan clattered over spotless ash wood flooring to the door, gripped the handle, then spun around on her black patent heels. "I'll start revamping the budget for next year. We'll have to cut back. We'll have a hole to fill, several million, hopefully no more. We need to keep Caro on side." Everything she said was right, James thought. Megan had a frightening tendency for telling him the truth. But it would never achieve the scale of his ambitions for LifeChance.

"I'm going over for dinner this evening."

Megan heaved open the door to leave. "Good luck." And she was gone, apart from the sound of her stride in the corridor until the swing-door clicked shut.

Her demurral and disappearance broke his spell of disappointment. In his dream, billionaire philanthropists showered him in regular dollops of largesse for his refugee children. Bill Gates and Warren Buffett contributed to his network of centres going global. Hundreds of thousands, if not millions of refugee children, had excelled in life. He had devoted his life to their cause and they loved him for it.

He scrunched up the muffin wrapper and threw it into the wire paper basket by his desk. He picked up the phone. Time to figure out a new plan of action. Time to stop the dreaming

Chapter Two   Caro

Caro was an ebullient, confident five-year old when James peeped at her from behind the legs of a social worker. He was scared and timid. This was to be his new home having survived three months in local authority care. The McManus's were seasoned foster parents used to handling traumatised children. They reckoned they could squeeze a toddler into their end of terrace house. Two teens shared one bedroom, and James was to join Caro in her small room with the new bunk beds. She was bubbling over with excitement, having bagged the upper bunk, and yanked at James's hand. A promise of a treasure-trove of sweeties finally loosened his grip on the social worker's skirt and allowed Caro to haul him upstairs. For several years, he clung to Caro like a climber to a precipice and she was his rock.

He trailed her everywhere, like a shadow, always seeking her approbation and sometimes irritating her with his relentless presence. She would scream at him to go away, but he would always lurk nearby, spying from behind the Hydrangea in the back garden as she played hop-skip-jump with her gang. Even then, she had to win, every game, every argument, everything. Sometimes even now, when he felt stung by her whiplash of words, he would rub the side of his head subconsciously, reliving the one occasion when she had clouted him for daring to win a game of monopoly.

Then at eight years old, his world was turned upside-down for a second time. Mrs McManus contracted breast cancer and underwent chemotherapy and radiotherapy, draining her of energy and her husband of hope. The burden of looking after all the children was now too much. Someone decided that James and Caro should be placed together with a new foster family, in the same area so that they could remain at the same school. James still remembered that promise. But he remembered even more the morning they came to take him away. Away from Caro. They promised it was only for a short time whilst they searched for a family able to take them both.

He had screamed and kicked and bitten the social worker who bundled him into a car. He called out for Caro, but he didn't know that a routine dental check-up had been booked for her at that precise time. His protestations grew wilder in the journey across London to his new foster family. He didn't give them a chance. Within hours, he had run away. He was found later that night, wandering around a park, shouting for Caro. She never replied and he never stopped screaming inside and out, whilst he moved through a series of foster homes unable to cope with his aggressive behaviour.

Half a life-time later, mild-mannered with a chilled glass of Sauvignon in hand, James sat at a sleek granite table in Caro's enormous kitchen chatting to her husband. Bruce filled him in on the design of their new bespoke, hand-crafted, German kitchen. To James, it looked like a chess-set, clean-lined, symmetrical, and ordered. Polished nickel handles protruded from everywhere. Bruce prattled about the Brechtian influence and the post-modern theatre concept he had insisted upon. Apparently, the recessed lights under glazed cupboards presented an ambience of 'Showtime'.

James nodded and smiled between sips of wine, as Bruce wittered on about his latest favourite celebrity chef who had endorsed the Mayfair kitchen design firm he had chosen without regard to price. One of a pair of dishwashers, heard but not seen, rumbled away somewhere upstage left whilst a gigantic fridge's ice-maker clunked centre stage right. Filtered fizzy water whooshed from a jet over a central island displaying a supporting cast of plum tomatoes, aubergines, carrots and peppers, all organic. A stainless pan sizzled on a ceramic hob. James stole a glance at his watch. He had already been there twenty minutes. Caro was upstairs reading a story to Olly, their five-year-old.

Bruce fussed about the counter top, putting the finishing touches to his culinary show, freshly made pasta from the local Italian deli, with almond, basil and pecorino, created from a recipe which he had torn out of the Times' weekend lifestyle section. He'd had enough of being an architect even before Caro's incarceration. That gave him the excuse he was secretly looking for, to become a house-husband. The children were young enough to consider it cool to play with their father and he was basking in the starring role as the sensitive, metropolitan man outside the school gates. He chatted to all the women, flirted with the nannies and au-pairs, and regularly joined a group-gossip over coffee after drop-off. He struggled to make headway with two other drop-off dads. They worked in tech start-ups and talked jargon he barely understood. Bruce was more at home with recipes.

"You guys need to slow down, take it easy," said Bruce, messianic still about his new life. It helps if your wife is worth a couple of hundred million and you have an army of eager immigrants in support, thought James. He liked Bruce even though he regarded him as a nearly man. He had nearly started up his own firm, had nearly thrown it all in to retrain as a doctor, had nearly started his own political party. But at least he had completed on his promise to marry Caro after she had proposed, the best decision of his life. He was good for her, calmed her, and never competed. And his genes had over-ridden hers in the creation of their beautiful children, two of each. James was god-parent to the lot and never missed a birthday.

"Too much to be done," said James yawning and reaching across the candle-lit table for an olive. He took a bite. "Greek?"

"Italian, from Umbria. Organically grown. A taste of grass and almond, kind of buttery wouldn't you say. I get them at Franco's, the deli around the corner. It's good to shop local." Maybe he had a point, reflected James. His olives from the local *Tesco* across from his apartment block in Southwark, never tasted of anything much. He rarely cooked these days, and he ingested food on the go rather than savouring the taste, delighting in its presentation, or simply dwelling in the moment. He was always leaving for appointments when he should have already arrived. Except when he had to meet Caro.

"How are the kids doing?" said James between swigs of wine which soothed his over-active mind. He undid his top button, yanked off his tie and lunged for the 'Economist' to flip through. He liked the directness and brevity of magazine articles. Books were for bed-time. At no other point in the day, could he sit in one place, concentrating, for long enough.

"All good, now Caro's back. Except Olly, he still has nightmares and wets the bed." Don't all children? thought James. He'd suffered the same nightmare, again and again since being a toddler.

"Your old trick. I was always bloody glad to be in the top bunk," Caro hooted at him as she marched into the room, carrying a book and making a beeline for the wine. Her hair was wet, and she smelt of a mixture of meadow and bubble-gum.

"Thank you for sharing. I'm sure you've enriched Bruce's life with that little nugget." She had always retained an appetite for the barbed comment, a put-down to let you know who was in charge, James reflected. He recalled her first words when they tumbled into each other at his college ball, St Hugh's in Oxford. By then, Alon Jäger had become James Tait. It was the summer term of 1993 and they had not seen or heard of one another since the day he had been hauled out of the McManus's.

"God, they'll let anyone into this dump." She was at Magdelen, better financially endowed and academically superior than St Hugh's. He responded by blubbing and hugging her. A concerned friend had to extricate her from his grip. They got drunk together that night and swore never to desert one another. That's what other people did. He alone during their university years got the occasional glimpse through a crack in her hard shell. Taken into care aged three, irregular visits from her parents dwindled to nothing in her mid-teens. When her drug-addled mother died several months after her heroine addicted father, all she'd said to James was, "about time." Then they downed a bottle of vodka and tearfully toasted the McManus's.

Caro slapped a tome on the table in front of him. "It's Le Carré's latest. I know how you like all that spy stuff. Just came out today, so the chap at *Waterstones* said. Thought you could do with some bedtime reading unless you've got something more interesting to tell us about your nocturnal activities."

21

"Nothing to report, I regret," said James with a smile.

"Well, I'm off in that case. I have Origami to read up on. Jess is doing this project at school," said Bruce placing two plates of pasta, and a steaming bowl of ratatouille in front of them. "I may have gone a bit mad with the butternut squash but it's good for you anyway. It's a new recipe. Hope you like it." He slipped out of his apron and skipped out of the kitchen, crooning 'Simply the Best'.

"I think everyone should have a Bruce," said James to the back of the disappearing figure.

"Well, keep your hands off mine. He's even better in the bedroom," Caro said with a chuckle." What was it with married people he knew, thought James? They invariably love to engage in smutty innuendos and feel it their right to debate his sex life and preferences in public. Unless of course, one of them has run off with the tennis coach, in which case everyone gravely stared at the floor at anything remotely risqué.

"The dossier you wanted, on the Weasel," said James, removing a slim folder from his briefcase. "It's pretty thin. Other than some speculation about his wandering eyes and hands, frankly it's rather dull. But we have dug deeply."

Caro grunted and started to leaf through the investigative report on Mark Phillips, partner at law firm Bone, Cumberbatch and Smith. He specialised in white collar crime, defending those who had fallen foul of regulations governing financial probity. With more regulations being added to the statute book every year, the work was lucrative in the City of London, the world's leading financial centre. Mark had earned a gilded reputation to justify his one thousand pounds per hour charge-out rate to clients. So Caro had hired him. She had been impressed by his clarity of thought, his clinical analysis and his assured manner.

Caro flicked through the pages, skim-reading sections about Mark's background, career, family, financial assessment and publicity surrounding other cases he had led. His clients evidently rated him highly. There was no prior example of losing a major case. Everyone seemed to view him as a leading practitioner in his field who had achieved success owing to his innate intelligence and hard work. Even professionals at the FCA, the opposing camp, rated him highly though some found him arrogant.

She settled on the final section which speculated about his personal behaviour with women at work. It contained gossip, unattributed tittle-tattle and innuendos. Interpretations ranged from annoying flirtation to an allegation of sexual favours being rewarded. Rumours about liaisons with junior female staff. But no names, no dates, no places. No substantiated facts. Perhaps some people at his firm, known for its extreme competitiveness, had an interest in spreading muck about him.

Caro sighed. She was still as embittered as the day she had been sentenced, torn from her family and transported miles away from home. She could not forget the first week she had to endure in a Category A prison somewhere in Surrey. One hundred and seventy hours of shock and terror that time would never erase. Outside, she had been the hunter, roving global capital markets in pursuit of profitable prey. Inside, the currency was fear and she became the hunted. Shipped off to an open prison anywhere down in Kent, she felt lucky to have escaped with a bruised eye and bloodied nose. The threats had been much worse. She spared Bruce the details and shared the worst with James. She ended up serving four months of her sentence, but it felt to her like four years. She was fined two million pounds personally and her firm paid out ten million. And she was pilloried throughout the media.

Mark got almost a million pounds in legal fees and sympathy from his profession that he had been a victim of a change in policy at the FCA following the appointment of a new head. Caro had no doubt that her ex-lawyer still dined with his chums at the FCA, the SFO and the City of London Police. He had sent a postcard, encouraging her to keep her spirits high in prison, whilst he was working hard for her early release. The glossy photo, shot in Disneyland, showcased the Weasel surrounded by his smiling family and Mickey Mouse.

"He must have a weakness. Everyone does. He must have enemies for God's sake." Caro's eyes appealed to James as she speared a piece of pasta with her fork. Caro's plaintive appeal pleased James. It was proof she needed him. He finished chewing, took a slurp of wine, inhaling zesty lemon-grasses, and leaned across the table for Caro's hand.

"We can create a weakness. We know something of his passions and motivations, and so we can set traps to make him fail. He hates losing." James paused to allow the thought to settle. "If you're sure that's what you want."

"Go on."

"Well, for example, he has a passion for running. He's been training hard for the London marathon next month. He has a professional coach. We've shot some of their sessions on Wimbledon Common, if you're interested. He is up there at six in the morning, five times a week. He has a charity website. It sets it all out – says he's been training for almost a year, and that he expects to break three-hours. Pretty impressive for a forty-year old."

"So what?" said Caro.

"Well he's gone public on achieving his goal. We stop him. He fails."

Caro grimaced. "So he gets a bit upset. Is that it?"

"It will hurt him. It'll batter his massive ego. You've said that he can't acknowledge failure, only success."

"After my case, he simply blamed everybody else," Caro snapped with a sneer.

"There won't be anyone else to blame here."

Caro sighed. "So this embarrasses him a bit. Hardly damaging."

"Trust me. This means an awful lot to him. He hates to fail at anything. And this would be a very public failing. He's so confident, he's encouraging sponsors to commit only if he beats three hours. He'd have to tell hundreds of people who have sponsored him that he failed to even complete the course."

"How do you propose to do that?"

"Well –"

"No, don't tell me. I've no intention of being detained at Her Majesty's pleasure again."

"Fair enough," said James with a half-smile, knowing full well she would insist on knowing at some point.

"And you really think he'll feel humiliated?"

James considered Caro's sceptical face. He'd hoped his relatively innocuous plan would be sufficient to satisfy her craving for vengeance.

"Well, let's try it and see how you feel afterwards. If you want to go further, then we could think again. I mean, ultimately one could ruin his life, if that is what you really want. But I don't think it is." James was hoping he was right.

Caro rose to fetch another bottle from the fridge. She unscrewed the cap and refilled their glasses. James could hear the babble from a television drifting out from Bruce's study.

"Okay," Caro said finally, "but I cannot be seen to be anywhere near this. No link. My name must be nowhere in sight. Keep me informed though."

James smiled at these contradictory orders driven by her urge to control. Throughout his banking career he had succeeded by leading, being bold, and taking risks whilst others hesitated to act. And at LifeChance, against the odds and Caro's predictions, he had succeeded. How ironic that he had broken laws to achieve his ethical goals, yet she was the convicted criminal. The paths of fortune and justice crossed over occasionally but more often diverged.

"Understood. You can pull it any time you like."

"Cheers," Caro said, clinking her glass with his. James watched as the cool wine trickled down her throat. Despite the bags under her brown eyes, her skin glowed, refreshed by the rush of alcohol. "At least, the Weasel will have to suffer something. Now, LifeChance. You wanted to talk about one of your ideas."

She had heard so many of his ideas before and dissuaded him from pursuing most of them. Her favourite judgements echoed in his head - 'laudable but impractical', 'it'll never work' or 'not with my money.' She and a few of her well-heeled cronies ended up footing the bill for a significant share of the charity's activities. Usually, having reflected, he agreed with her viewpoint. More recently she appeared to acknowledge his success in diversifying the revenue streams. She gathered that sometimes involved dubious means. So, she kept her distance from the detail and insisted he keep his so called 'research projects' to himself. But this latest idea just wouldn't leave him alone.

James finished chewing the last of his fusilli, wiped his mouth with one of Bruce's silver satin napkins, and took a gulp of water. He had rehearsed what he intended to say, that morning and then again in the taxi. Gaining Caro's support was vital. It would be the first question the non-executive board members would ask.

"We've reached crisis point with the level of unaccompanied migrant children reaching the country. More and more are being abused and exploited whilst local authorities and the government turn a blind eye because it costs too bloody much." He had raised his voice despite all of his preparation. He needed to stay calm. He then explained how in the previous year, more than three thousand unaccompanied minors had landed in the UK. Some were trafficked, some were left here with so-called relatives. Others were delivered in the country by mothers with no official immigration status either. Tens of thousands, possibly more, children lived in the country and had no formal immigration status. That meant no formal rights to education, healthcare, a job, anything. At eighteen, they would most likely be ejected from the country.

"How many did we help to get the right to stay last year?" asked Caro.

"Around five hundred, and we educated more than a thousand. Demand is growing and it's getting more difficult and more expensive." James explained how government budget cuts had robbed many children of the right to legal aid. Without legal assistance, the children had scant chance of building a case to remain. LifeChance filled the gap, paying legal fees and arranging law firms to perform pro bono work. All migrant refugee children, both accompanied and not, could attend LifeChance's education centres, and grasp the opportunity to enrich their lives and contribute to society.

"So, you need to raise more income." Caro sighed. "I've already given you a couple of million for this year."

"I know. Thank you. I'm not asking you for more money right now. But you know, immigration is a difficult sell to most people. Politically, it's a toxic issue."

Caro nodded, visibly weary. She'd sat through this sermon so often. "So, what do you need from me this time?"

"I want your support for my plan to fund a major expansion of the learning centre network. I want to use the City to raise money for our charity."

Caro frowned. It was getting late, and this was not a five-minute conversation. "I've introduced you to most of my City contacts already."

"Not that. This time the City won't know it's helping us. Let's call it, a kind of a sting operation," said James with a mischievous smile.

Caro's mouth fell open and her eyes widened. He could still surprise her, or was it more concern he now saw etched across her face? Speechless. Frozen. He stared at her, waiting for a response.

They heard the timid cry of a child, and their eyes turned towards the door. Olly had padded into the kitchen, naked. He'd wet the bed. His bottom lip trembled, and he began to sob when he met his mother's eyes. Caro gathered him up and hushed him with kisses. She turned to James with fatigue etched across her brow, bleary-eyed with fleshy pouches. The faint smell of urine drifted across the table.

"Let's continue this another time. I need to get this little chap washed, changed and tucked up."

"Sure. You're a lucky boy," said James brushing Olly's blonde hair back across his pale, smooth forehead. James envied his innocence and pitied him that he would lose it

28

before he understood how infinitely rich he had once been. With a poignant ache, James dragged himself away from mother and child.

A couple of minutes later, having thanked Bruce for supper, he sat in a pine scented Prius, chatting to its 'Uber' driver. Nasim who was contemplating changing his name to Trevor, had been born in Iraq and made it to London in his early twenties, having spent several years in Frankfurt living with his sister's family. He now had his own family, two girls. His wife worked in a nursery. He loved his job. He could take the kids to school, pick them up, play with them and then work whatever hours he wanted. He worked hard. He usually worked evenings including weekends. He went back to see his family in Baghdad most years, but he would never leave Britain now. He regarded himself and his family as British. He spoke Arabic, German and English. James had heard similar stories before, the story of immigrants, talented, hard-working, polite and tax-paying.

The traffic flowed as the rain drizzled and the driver spilled his life story. Within twenty minutes he was back in his swish Southbank apartment, a cool two million-pound acquisition following his emigration from Chelsea. James ran through his nightly routine: turned on the TV for latest news, checked the laptop for new emails, rifled through the post, and showered whilst he audited his tumultuous day. He flopped into bed and uttered several silent prayers. He had to make tomorrow better than today.

His eyes flickered over the first few pages of the novel Caro had bought him. Within minutes, words were blurring, and he reread the same paragraph several times. He finally admitted defeat and plopped the paperback on to his tower of bedside books. He switched off the lamp and fell to sleep quickly, unbothered by the traffic in the streets far below, and oblivious to the distant hum of the FCA's computer network in Stratford. A monster munching on data. Artificial intelligence software programs whirring away in the dark night, processing millions, billions of transactional data, seeking out correlations and causal relationships, in a relentless hunt for illicit trading activity. All whilst London, the City and James slept.

Chapter Three   Mark

Mark Phillips had come late to marathon running. He had turned forty and wanted to mark the occasion with a memorable feat. Against his better judgement honed from two decades of practising law, he overlooked an arthritic knee, and decided to join his closest friend Thomas in running the London marathon. He reasoned that there would be many older and less fit participants and he would make sure that he would be well prepared. If he was going to do it, like everything else in his life, he was going to do it with rigorous preparation.

Mark and Thomas had become close friends at university, flat-shared and then settled with their families in the same leafy neighbourhood of south-west London. They had also shared two decades of trail running on commons, through woodlands, and along tow paths in pursuit of changing scenes, challenging surfaces and escapism from family life. Tens of thousands of running miles mapped across every terrain and in all weathers had forged an unbreakable friendship. Thousands of hours had spawned millions of words, conversations often mundane, frequently bawdy and irreverent, occasionally arcane squeezed out as lungs burned.

Their runs, although nearly always social at the outset, were competitive by the finish. Chat became sporadic as shoulder to shoulder, stride for stride, the pace picked up in an unspoken battle for supremacy. Supremacy in the form of not being beaten rather than winning, of not showing weakness rather than strength and simply always trying one's best so as not to let the other down by slowing the tempo. They were hewn from the same middle-aged rock of stubborn resilience with the knowledge that improvement is fractional, painful and slow. Neither were natural runners but they were good in an average sort of way, breathlessly disavowing bodily decline, defying Father Time.

On race day morning, Mark was already awake when his watch-alarm beeped at six thirty, a full three-and-a half hours ahead of the start. Beside him, Cath his wife slumbered on, ear-plugs in place. Naked, he padded over to their open bedroom window and peered through a gap in the curtain. He took a deep breath in, then slowly out. Then another. He'd expected to be nervous. He had read so much on the subject. He had followed meticulously the pre-race preparation programme from his running magazine. He hadn't endured a year of arduous and painful training just to ruin it now with poor last-minute execution.

The climbing wisteria's sweet smell embraced him as he spied a fox slinking its way through Cath's red rhododendron bushes, beyond the lawn at the far end of the garden. He turned back to the bed where she lay, still and barely breathing, oblivious to the regime he had rehearsed. The kids would wake her soon enough. Sleeping on her back gave her the beginnings of a double chin, the shape of things to come perhaps.

He picked up his mobile from the bedside table and checked the BBC's weather forecast, then the Met Office, followed by Accuweather. They all predicted the same, virtually word for word as if they had copied the bright boy sitting bespectacled at the front of the classroom. It was official; the race would be run on a cool, cloudy day interspersed with the occasional shower, and low humidity. Almost perfect conditions for running.

He showered swiftly in the en-suite, then dressed quickly. Kitted out in his running gear, he tip-toed from the bedroom. He crept past Ralph's door, then Miranda's, and paused for a moment to glance into the twins' room. They slept motionless, unfolded and adrift of quilts in their bunk beds. He held his breath momentarily, listening for theirs. Husky exhalations caused him to smile involuntarily as he reflected that the next time he would see Emma and Benjamin, they would be in their usual state of loud hysteria, cheering on their father. Halfway down the curved oak stairwell, polished to perfection by the Czech maid he had never met, Mark forgot to straddle the creaky section. He froze as the crack echoed around the capacious hallway and up into the landing. Cath had still not sorted it with the Polish builder. He'd have to remind her again. He listened but heard no movement. He unglued the offending foot from the stair and gingerly descended.

As he pushed the kitchen door ajar, another creak echoed throughout the hall. Another job not done. He winced and held his breath. He could hear only the tip-tapping of paws on the marble terrazzo tiles as Judge leapt from his basket. The Border Collie wagged his tail furiously but nothing more, evidence of Mark's fastidious training. Patting him gently, Mark saw that everything was prepared, just as he remembered before dropping in to bed at ten o'clock; a pot of overnight soaked porridge sat on the stove, two ripening bananas lay on the side next to several slices of wholemeal bread wrapped in cellophane. A pot of orange marmalade, a porcelain butter dish and a cafetiere, ready to go, completed the line-up.

He filled the kettle and flicked it on. He slid open one of the glass sliding-doors overlooking the patio and squinted. Cath's garden bloomed with bright colours, like one of Emma's paintings. Above, the sun sparkled amidst a blue cloudless sky and burnished the stainless-steel, six-burner barbeque, Mark's latest toy. Judge jumped out to forage among the azaleas. Mark inhaled deeply, imbibing the fragrant air, already warm. It seemed that overnight, spring had sprung and gone while summer had stolen into their neighbourhood. Could the weather forecasters have erred? A hot day could demolish his plan to run under three hours.

Mark had never meant to just run the London marathon to be able to say he had done it. There didn't seem much point to merely walk the course or to take it at all easy. He had to run it as fast as he could possibly bear. His time-consuming investment in self-punishment - hill reps, sprint sessions, interval training, timed track laps, tempo runs and endless miles of endurance training - was aimed at achieving his three-hour goal. A fear of failure drove him on.

It disappointed him that the weather was something he could not control. If it was going to be hot, he had to be particularly well hydrated, as well as fuelled-up with carbohydrates. He grabbed a pint glass from the dishwasher and filled it to the brim with cool water from the dispenser before draining it in several gulps. He refilled the glass, set it on the counter-top and lit the hob.

His mobile pinged at twenty past seven, five minutes late Mark noted. He headed to the front door with his fully laden race bag slung over his shoulder. Judge followed, hoping to be let loose on the common to chase rabbits.

"Not today old boy" said Mark, which appeared to have the opposite effect on the dog, whose excited barks he could hear after he closed the door firmly but quietly shut.

"Fine day for a saunter in the park." Thomas was outside, stretching against Mark's gate-post, as a mini-cab idled nearby.

"Yes, but not twenty-six miles on steaming tarmac surrounded by forty thousand runners," Mark retorted with a grin.

"Ah well, look on the bright side, it will all be over by lunchtime...late lunch perhaps, haha."

The taxi ride across uninspiring parts of south-east London did nothing to settle their growing nervousness. As anticipated, the roads in the vicinity of the start were blocked off. Thomas paid the cabbie and they swapped the air-conditioned capsule for the warming rays of the sun. They were sweating lightly by the time they reached the vast green acres of Greenwich Park. They approached the cordoned-off runners' enclosure and were relieved to see rows of green portable toilets, neatly lined up. Runners in short queues waited their turn. Another vital step in their pre-race preparation plan could be ticked off. Then, with a quick handshake, without ceremony, they wished each other "good luck", and went off to find their starting areas. Thomas had a blue running number pinned to his vest, and Mark's was red, which meant a further walk for him.

The riot of colour and the sheer volume of people surprised Mark even though he had seen many photographs of the event. The park was packed, yet everyone seemed to occupy a solitary space. Mark joined in with the thousands of aspirants stretching, jogging, meditating and embrocating. The air stank of liniment. He was eager to absorb any lessons, anything he could put into practice to shave off a few seconds from his target. As he moved around, feeling invisible to the other participants, the realisation that he was a complete novice began to gnaw at him. The months of training, reading, dietary regimes and general preparation suddenly seemed to count for very little. He wondered whether there were any other runners feeling the same.

A voice boomed from a loudspeaker and snapped him out of his ruminations.

"Runners, you have just one hour three minutes and twenty-three seconds before the start of the race," someone announced in serious monotone without hint of irony.

"Thank goodness for those twenty-three seconds," Mark said quietly to himself. He heard a giggle and twisted around. A young woman, slim, blonde, and muscle toned, wearing a crimson crop-top sports bra and tight, black hipster shorts stood laughing.

"Apparently it's the last twenty-three seconds which hurt the most." She beamed at him.

She had an irresistible smile, Mark thought. "Is this your first time?" he blustered and then immediately regretted how lame that must have sounded. He felt his face redden. He was unused to chatting with younger women, other than junior executives and secretaries in his office which he didn't count. This girl was stunning.

"Yes. Another item on the bucket list to be ticked."

"Long list is it?"

"Almost endless. I'll try almost anything once." She winked. "Life is short."

"This marathon will be long though. For me at least," said Mark, attempting to regain his composure with some false modesty.

"I'm Eva," she said outstretching a hand." Eva Gilman. I'm nervous. That's why I'm prattling on, sorry."

"Don't worry. Me too."

They shook hands, silky smooth from the liniment. Mark absorbed the beauty of the unlined, un-made-up, face grinning at his grin.

Fellow first-time marathon runners, they fell into an easy conversation about the grimness of their training regimes, their injury worries, the race tips they had hoovered up from veterans, and the drink and diet regimes they had tried out. They shared their anxieties about the last ten kilometres, about finishing the race, about hitting their target times. He had found a friend, a rather gorgeous one, someone to share his concerns and hopes for the day. And as he relaxed the minutes evaporated.

He could have sat there for many more hours, idling on the grass, the pair of them chatting animatedly as if on a first date. But they had a race to run as the announcer had reminded them yet again, but this time with a final warning. Eva tapped his number into her mobile, returned it to her armband, and pecked him on the cheek.

"I'll let you know how I get on."

"Good luck." He watched her jog towards her starting block till she disappeared into a converging mass. He felt good. The conversation had taken his mind off the challenge ahead. His pre-race preparation had not been followed to precision, but it no longer mattered. He was ready.

The final few pre-race minutes seemed to stretch for an eternity. All the runners were in place and the TV cameras were rolling whilst an ageing, over-weight celebrity cajoled the crowd to smile and cheer. A miasma of body odours mixed with embrocation and sun-tan lotion enveloped the tightly packed starters. He'd managed to squirm nearer the front, just behind the elite runners. The line-up fell out of the shade of trees and they appeared to be the sole interest of the sun.

He felt hot already and he had yet to run a single metre of the forty-two thousand ahead of him. There would be water stations at each mile and Thomas had reminded him to drink early and often. He drained the last drops from his water bottle before slinging it over the crowd to the pavement, narrowly missing a startled policeman, red-faced and sweating in a dayglo vest over his uniform. The weather forecasters had got it wrong.

Suddenly he heard the bang of the starting gun followed by a massive cheer. This was it; the job needed doing, whatever the damn weather. He activated his stop-watch as he crossed the starting line.

The early miles seemed to pass with surprising ease. He was feeling confident, pleased that his mile laps were just within his targeted schedule. He knew he had a natural tendency to burst out of the blocks a little too enthusiastically, only to pay the price later. Thomas, a marathon veteran and planner extraordinaire, had advised him that he should approach the marathon as a very long warm up for a 10k. Mark was not looking forward to those last ten kilometres. He had found the final half-hour of their twenty-four-mile training runs tough but bearable.

The first ten kilometres ended with a thickening in the crowds as the runners approached *Cutty Sark* and ran through the heart of Greenwich. The noise booming from the crowd was deafening, with shrill shouts of encouragement and waves of applause. Mark heard the increasing roll call of names barked from the enthusiastic on-lookers, and he regretted not having scrawled his name on his running vest. Other runners waved back at groups of spectators and some even stopped for a shared grinning photo. He rejected the idea as ridiculous, a waste of time, energy and focus. He checked his GPS watch to gauge the minutes before the next mile marker and water station. He was already dripping with sweat and his mouth felt dry.

Into his second ten kilometres, he felt comfortable with the rhythm of his running, clocking six minute forty, mile after mile. He began to relax, taking in the passing scenes and allowing his thoughts to wonder. He wanted to remember how it felt, what he would tell his children at the end of the race. He started counting the pubs along the route. Many boasted enthusiastic bands belting out hits of the sixties or brash DJ's with booming microphones and geezer vernacular, their racket competing with the crowd's clamour. He passed several where the air was thick with smoke from sizzling sausages and barbequed burgers. His stomach groaned as he cruised past a fat, balding block of a man, scoffing a bacon sandwich. For a couple of hours, it would be starved of everything other than sweet and sticky *Lucozade Sport* and gulps of bottled water, swallowed on the move.

Mark's gaze lifted to take in the lines of tatty shops on either side of the road. He was loping along a high street quite different to those where he lived or worked. Rejected by retail chains, the area possessed an eclectic charm. *Bludi Carpet* store hove into view sandwiched between *Halil's Grocery* and *Joe's Cafe*. On the other side, *Lily's Launderette's* bright pink, neon fascia outshone dowdy *Doreen's Hair & Now* and the dusty grey, shuttered *Jacobson & Sons – Undertakers*. In a rare gap in the crowd, he glimpsed himself in the reflective darkened glass of Chinese restaurant, *Woo Sun*.

The sight shocked him. Where he had imagined a striding, composed, athletic Olympian, he saw instead the stark reality of a crouched, shuffling figure, with a gaping mouth, and knitted brow. The intensity of his effort was etched across his face. What a contrast with the lightness and joviality of the cheering masses. He watched kids of five or six years old with arms outstretched proffering sweets to the passing torrent pouring past them. The sheer delight when other runners whipped away the morsel from their tender hands lifted his spirits as he approached the turn for Tower Bridge, one of the steepest inclines on the route.

Mark checked his watch yet again. His pace had dropped a little. He wondered whether he had lost concentration, accidentally taking it too easy. Or whether sub-consciously he was avoiding pain, settling for a sub-optimal finishing time. Then he turned the corner and the tumult lifted him. With chest out and arms pumping, he cut through a swathe of runners as the throng, seven or eight deep on either side of the bridge roared their encouragement. He started to search the crowd, first to the left and then to the right, and back again. He had arranged for his family to stand on the bridge to catch their first sight of him. Suddenly, quite inexplicably he felt a tear running down his right cheek. His eyes were welling-up and he realised before he could do anything about it, that he was crying.

Mark couldn't recall the last time he had shed a tear. He kept his emotions under control and particularly in front of other people. But here he was, before thousands of people, with still over half the marathon to go, crying. He was puzzled. It had something to do with the gruelling months of training, the punishment his body had endured and the sacrifices he had made. And that momentarily felt overwhelming because his family would be there to cheer him on. He felt immensely proud of them. It struck him strong, like the force of the ebbing Thames beneath him, that they would be proud of him. Him being a hard-working lawyer meant nothing to them. Running the marathon would mean everything. He allowed himself the transitory thought of Ralph, his oldest son, bragging to his pals in the school yard about his dad's marathon, showing off his medal. Then he had pulled himself together, wiped away errant tears and planted a serene look on his face. He wanted to show them the face of a conquering hero, not a face wracked with tears.

He reached the end of the bridge, trying not to feel despondent, when suddenly he heard his name, chorused in quick repetition at different tenors. He narrowed his gaze to a group of wildly baying, animated figures he didn't recognise. Then he lowered his eyes and spotted in front of them, his children bouncing like balls, squealing with excitement. Cath was grinning over the painted placard she held, "Go Daddy!!!" He waved frantically and grinned manically. Part of him wanted to stop for a chat but the bigger part urged him to press on, to minimise those precious seconds.

In a flash, they were gone, out of sight but not out of mind. He pictured them all together, screeching at him, imploring him on. He strained to stretch out the memory of that fleeting moment, first as a slow-motion video and then into stills like flicking through an old photographic album. The sight of the half marathon marker brought him abruptly back to the present. Time to take check physically how you feel, Thomas had said, to calibrate how the second half should be approached. He considered every part of his body. The knee-support bandage was doing its job. He had the usual slight tightness in his right ham-string and he could feel heat on the side of his big left toe, an impending blister. Thankfully, the right ankle that had caused problems in training was behaving itself. It was just a shame the sun was misbehaving, He had never run in such heat. This was not normal. And then he realised, with all the excitement at Tower Bridge, he had missed a drinks station. Inside his mouth felt parched. He would have to tough it out for another mile.

Not far into the second half, as he ran through an unusually barren stretch with thin lines of on-lookers, he hit his first bad patch. His legs felt heavier and his breathing laboured. A sensation he had experienced many times while training, he knew there was no option other than to dig deep, grit teeth, blaspheme if it helped, and it usually did, in order to come through it to an easier place. He was disappointed to have reached this point so early but then a friend in the form of a rare half mile downhill section came to his aid. By the time he had reached a level plateau again, his rhythm and breathing had recovered. The crowds had once again amassed under the jagged skyline of Docklands' towering temples to capitalism. A slight breeze coming off the water boosted his mood. And even better, he spotted a drinks-station a few hundred metres ahead.

In a single motion, he snatched a *Lucozade Sport* from a girl standing in a line of red baseball-cap-wearing volunteers dangling bottles at arms' length. Behind them, trestle tables heaved under stacks of isotonic drinks and mineral water. He tore off the cap with his teeth before taking his first draft. Although he had practised with the same isotonic solution, he had never quite got used to its sickly, sweet taste. And it had the paradoxical effect of making him thirsty. Reaching the end of the line of helpers, he seized a bottle of mineral water from a startled youth in a soaking white London Marathon T-shirt.

The drinks gave him a temporary lift, but their effect receded as the sun's rays intensified. His head was being cooked. He was the casserole in the oven, left too long, liquid running dry. He ran through a corridor of on-course showers and felt good again for a couple of minutes. But then the burning returned, the back of his neck, a flaming red. He checked his watch. The last couple of miles had been slower, averaging just under seven minutes, outside targeted pace. His left Achilles throbbed and both quadriceps ached from the relentless pounding on tarmac. He looked at the runners around him - glazed expressions, facial lines locked in pain. He was relieved to see the nineteen-mile marker and its water station in sight.

Only a mile to go before the dreaded wall of twenty miles and the graveyard of hope for many runners as limbs mutinied, dashing all prospects of hallowed finishing times, rigorously planned, mentally and physically prepared, over the better part of a year. Mark was not ready to accept defeat yet but he noticed an increasing slew of runners who had, as he ground past them in the twentieth mile. Many appeared much younger than him and adorned in the vests of running clubs, the sign of truly serious or addicted runners. Many appeared to be fading fast. He found solace in his relative progress even as his watch said something different. He didn't feel fine. He hurt and he knew he would hurt more if he was to beat three hours.

He passed the twenty-mile marker where he grabbed a bottle. He devoured the water in a single draw. The coolness felt magnificent as it gushed down inside of him but the aftermath of sloshing water in his stomach was an unwelcome guest. So was the start of his final ten kilometres. Within a few hundred metres he had a stitch, forcing him to slow his pace. Even worse, the sun which had pursued him for two hours and nineteen minutes, was burning not just his neck and shoulders, but his arms and calves. He chided himself for his oversight. The sun cream had been in his kit-bag. It had been a long-standing item in his pre-race list. It was the girl of course or rather the conversation with her, which had diverted him. He wondered fleetingly where Eva would be at this point and imagined, given her more limited aspirations, that she would be several miles behind.

The next three miles were everything that Thomas had promised and more. He felt that he was running on empty, that every painful jarring step was sending a tremor through his body and that his lungs just couldn't seem to get enough air. He was suffering along with his chance of hitting his finishing time. Would he resign himself to missing it, to being a nearly man? Thomas had promised that he would reach a key decision point somewhere along the route: to let the dream time go and focus on keeping going, not stopping but hanging on grimly; or to make one last frontal assault on the beast of pain, deny it step by step and run through the scorching torment because it would be over soon enough. But Thomas had indicated that this stage would be reached with less than a couple of miles to go. He had just over three to go, and just over twenty-two minutes to hit his target. Still a chance. His lungs were competing with his legs for his brain's attention.

Just after twenty-three miles, the sun pounding him on his head, smothered in pain to his blazing feet, Mark caught the sound of a familiar voice. He lifted his gaze from the baking tarmac and swivelled his head to see Eva's smiling face. Astonished at her presence, he automatically looked at his watch to check his time.

"I'm having the run of my life" she breezed. "How are you feeling?"

"Been better" grunted Mark and then between breaths, "You look great."

"Thanks. Must be this new isotonic drink. My friend said it would make all the difference late on. Here, try some, if you want." She stretched out her arm.

Mark hesitated, recalling the words of wisdom from every article on marathon nutrition that he had ever read advising against untried solutions during a race. Yet he felt absolutely appalling. Just keeping up with Eva, who appeared to be upping her pace now, was a hellish struggle. He grabbed the bottle and swallowed a couple of mouthfuls before offering it back.

"Keep it!" said Eva "I've got another bottle. See you at the finish, hopefully," and she lengthened her stride carving a swathe through swarms of precarious, plodding runners.

Her pace, strength and fluency weighed heavily on him. He felt pathetic, weak and dejected. He began cursing aloud at the sun bearing down on him. Nobody took any notice; their glazed eyes fixed on the tarmac or locked on to some distant point ahead, praying for the torture to end soon. He tried to focus on Eva and followed her progress as far as he could until she glided around a bend. When he finally reached the bend, a matter of only a hundred metres, he could no longer spot her crimson vest in the collage of bobbing, crouching staggering mass. By now he had emptied Eva's bottle and flung it, limply landing at the feet of the encroaching, clapping, hoards. This simple act of flinging the bottle seemed to drain him of energy.

Yet he staggered on, in the hope that by keeping moving, he would accelerate absorption of Eva's isotonic drink, releasing its magical formula and producing the carbohydrate boost his body craved. The pain was now so unrelenting that every muscle and fibre cried out for him to stop, to give up and simply walk. How tempting it would be, just for a minute or two, to slip into a walk and relish a brief respite. He could just jog for a while, then gradually stretch it out for the final two miles. But somewhere deep down inside of him, he found the will not to cross that thin line. He harangued himself through gritted teeth, "I'm a runner, not a walker." And he repeated this mantra again and again as he lurched waywardly forward. He was losing time he couldn't afford. He passed a water station without stopping to save a few seconds. It seemed to make sense.

The energising release of Eva's solution never arrived. Imperceptibly, Mark's mechanical motion slowed, synchronous with his grip on consciousness. He felt himself slipping away from everything and everyone. He saw strangers gesticulating at him, hands clapping wildly, teeth clenched, eyes burning with encouragement. But it meant nothing to him. He could no longer hear. He had been cut adrift from the sea of runners as well as spectators, lost on an island of semi-consciousness and brutal pain. The scorching sun overhead, the vague outlines of a Batman and Robin duo passing by, and the blur of Big Ben were his final moments of consciousness.

On the other side of Big Ben, less than half a mile from the finish, Cath and the kids waited impatiently for Mark's glorious arrival. The twins who had been frantic with excitement, now whined that their legs were tired. Miranda and Ralph had started to poke at each other and bicker. Cath's patience was wearing thin. She checked her watch again. According to the schedule Mark had given her, he should have passed them forty-five minutes ago. She was just wondering whether they had missed him when her mobile rang.

"Hi Cath, it's Thomas. I've been trying to get through to you for ages. Where is everyone?" They had pre-arranged to assemble in Horse Guards Parade's 'meet and greet' area, marked with a "P".

"We're on Birdcage Walk. Is Mark with you then?"

"No. I'm here with Kimberly and the kids. No sign of Mark anywhere."

"That's odd." Cath was beginning to fret. She had never wanted Mark to run the marathon, concerned that he might push himself too hard, drop dead and leave her alone with the kids. As usual, he'd over-ridden her concerns, teasing her that his life insurance cover meant that she would be worth more with him dead. She glanced at the kids and automatically smiled. She couldn't show them she was worried. "He should have finished by now, shouldn't he?"

"Yes, a long time ago. Unless he's suffered an injury. He could be limping to the finish. You know how determined he is."

"You don't think anything, you know-"

"Don't worry. If something had happened to him, someone would have called you."

"Unless like you, they couldn't get through."

"I'm sure he's fine. I saw a lot of runners at the finish, dehydrated, being looked after by the St John's Ambulance crew. Rehydration would probably take a while."

Cath bit her lip. What should she do? Stay or go? The kids were getting bored. They needed to move. "Okay. I think we'll come over and meet you now so we're all together when Mark gets through."

"Great. We'll be waiting."

"And are you okay?"

"Fine, fine. Though Kimberly says I look like shit. But I beat three hours, so it's worth it."

"You guys are insane. See you in a few minutes."

Cath pocketed her mobile and told the kids they were going to meet their dad at the finish where there would be ice-cream and their chums - Thomas and Kimberly's kids. She told them all to join hands in a chain and scream if the chain broke. The thought of losing a child in the crowd trumped her concern for Mark. They slithered through the cheering masses, and queued at a crossing point, to gain entrance to the 'meet and greet' area. As she waited, her mobile pinged.

The brevity of the text alarmed Cath. As the named contact of runner 33950, she was requested to attend the medical unit on Horse Guards Parade. Rationally she knew it was just a standard message. Mark had probably just tripped up or strained a calf or an Achilles. But as she waited with the kids, she began to fear the worst. His father had died of a heart attack aged sixty. She had heard of people keeling over dead from running marathons. It would just be her luck if Mark left her alone with four young children to raise. "Bloody idiot," she thought, "I'll kill him if he's still alive."

As they crossed the road, she decided what she had to do. The kids had to come first. She would leave them with Thomas and Kimberly, ask them to take them to their house, suggest pizza and cola for a treat, pick them up later after she'd dealt with Mark. She would go to the medical tent on her own.

By the time she saw the hospital tent's red cross, beads of sweat were pouring down her face and her peach, cotton blouse was stuck to her back. Damp patches spread out from under the arms.

A young man in a luminous St John Ambulance jacket greeted her at the entrance. He needed Mark's runner's number which was in the text message - the one she must have accidentally deleted in a panic.

"I wouldn't have made it up, would I?" she pleaded. The nice young man explained that health and safety issues required him to verify her details and those of her husband. It would only take a few minutes to check on his system and all she had to do was to answer some security questions. She was about to burst out in protest but realised there was no point arguing. And then it struck her that if Mark was in a serious or worse state, she would be rushed through. Security questions, which seemed to amount to perfunctory name and address check, done, Cath was let through.

An aroma of vomit and disinfectant hit her, followed by the thunder of haggard runners retching into buckets. She guessed there were about thirty patients and plenty of room for many more. The marquee was littered with flaccid bodies, beached on beds or shriveled up on chairs. Figures hunched over red buckets or reclined with ice packs on their foreheads. Green uniformed members of the medical-response team strode around ferrying drinks, snacks, blankets, and bandages. A tall man in a green uniform approached her.

"Who are you looking for?" he enquired as if working for an introductory dating agency.

"My husband, Mark Phillips. I can't see him anywhere," said Cath, in a shrill voice. The nurse consulted the list on his clipboard.

"He is at the back, behind that curtain. That's where we put patients who need a saline drip. I think the doctor may be with him now."

"Doctor? Saline drip? Is he okay?" Cath said, feeling her heart thudding against her ribcage.

"Why don't you go on through. I'm sure the doctor can fill you in better than me."

She slipped through the curtain and saw Mark's crumpled figure, propped up on a bed and plugged into a drip. His skin was grey and his face creased. He looked like his father just before he died, Cath reflected. Like a life force had left his body. A thermometer drooped from cracked lips, put there by a figure in a white coat. Her blonde hair and unblemished baby-face swiveled towards Cath.

"He'll live," said the woman whose badge read Dr. Ruth McGee. Her vitality jarred with Mark's torpor. He opened his eyes and grunted. It was a pathetic grunt, insipid and weak. "We'll keep an eye on him for a couple of hours, but he should be fine to go home later."

"What happened? Why is he on a drip?" said Cath peering at the catheter on Mark's wrist.

"He dehydrated. His body overheated. It's a very hot day for this time of year. He probably didn't take on enough fluid. He fainted, fell unconscious for a while. We were a bit concerned to start with, so we thought a saline solution would be best, to replace his electrolytes.

"But he'll be okay, won't he?"

"He'll feel sick for a while longer yet." The doctor withdrew the thermometer and peered at it. "Good. His temperature is normalising."

"So, no long-term damage?"

"Shouldn't think so. We've taken a blood sample, just to be sure." The doctor smiled and this more than anything finally reassured Cath.

"Thank you so much." Cath felt like hugging the young doctor. She didn't look much older than Ralph.

"I'll check back in a while." Doctor McGee swept through the curtain into the main section.

"Are you all right, love?" said Cath sidling on to the bed.

"Bucket" Mark burbled, pointing to the floor.

Cath leapt up and grasped hold of the bucket just in time for Mark to be sick. They had shared a lot in their fifteen years together, but she had never seen him like this, so out of control. He held his drink well and he was rarely ill. A wave of empathy washed over her. He had worked so hard to achieve something important to him and now it had ended like this.

For the next thirty minutes, all she could do to comfort him was to mop his brow with a wet sponge and be ready with the bucket. In between, heaving, retching, shivering and the frequent checks of energetic nurses, Mark had been incapable of uttering a coherent sentence.

"I'm so sorry," he said finally, not looking at her.

"Sorry? What for?" Confusion flitted across her frowning forehead.

"Messing up. I've let everyone down. You, the kids, friends who've supported me, the charity." Mark had collected over thirty thousand pounds from sponsors for the Rwandan charity supported by his firm.

"Oh Mark" she said clasping his hand in hers, "Don't be silly. The kids and I are really proud of you. You almost made it." She regretted using the 'almost' word immediately.

"Almost!" he spat out. "Almost is no damn good. All those hours of training and I didn't even bloody finish."

51

She had rarely seen him so despondent. He usually just strode through life, relishing challenges, and overcoming hurdles. He was used to getting his own way.

"What happened? You were so well prepared." Cath gave his clammy hand a squeeze.

"I don't know. I really haven't a clue. I drank a lot throughout the race but..." Mark's head dropped to his chest.

"When did it get really bad?" Cath asked.

Mark sighed heavily. "I guess after about twenty miles I was feeling really tired. But I expected that and I was coping. Then after about twenty-three miles it seemed to go downhill really quickly."

"So how far did you get?"

"Not sure. I think I remember seeing Big Ben."

"We were just around the corner from there, waiting to see you. The kids were so excited when they saw you at Tower Bridge."

Mark smiled fleetingly. "Where are they?"

"They're with Thomas and Kimberly. I met them just before I came in here."

"How did Thomas get on? Did he break three hours?" Mark grimaced.

"Not sure. He looked tired of course and concerned about you. We all were."

Mark nodded several times and then for a few moments, his mouth gaped open. "I've just remembered. Just before everything went blank, I swear a couple of blokes in capes passed me."

Cath laughed. "We saw them. They were flying, well not literally."

"Great. Overtaken by bloody Batman and Boy Robin. What a joke."

"Well, look on the bright side. They are superhuman, not mere mortals. At least it wasn't the camel we saw later."

Mark gave out an involuntary snicker. "You realise of course, this means I will have to try again next year."

Finally, Cath thought. Her husband was back. Now was not the time to try to dissuade him. So, she just smiled but shook her head.

Chapter Four   Megan

The grey clouds were shedding their load, darkening James's office. He and Megan sat at his glass-topped table, poring over pages of revised financial projections. The dregs from two tea cups and desiccated biscuit crumbs on a plate lingered with them. Megan got up to switch on the light.

"Is that any better?" said Megan.

"Makes the numbers look even worse." He wore a wry smile. "Cutting our investment income by half looks overdone."

"Worst case, I hope. Anyway, we agreed your research team's activities should be wound up, and these forecasts merely reflect that."

James had reluctantly concluded that his private investigative team which he funded personally was not worth the risk they were running. He couldn't blame Akhtar. He was loyal and had done a thorough job. But the results were fickle. James would feed him with leads he had picked up in the market at private members' clubs, not much better than gossip. Usually it turned out to be rubbish. When Akhtar's research corroborated the initial intelligence, they would formulate plans to 'encourage' an individual to trade reliable information, valuable market data, in exchange for withholding secrets they had unearthed. They had reached such a deal with Brad Jensen at WMS. But a non-controllable event had upset the outcome. Often, James's team found nothing harmful or the prospective 'clients' refused to cooperate. Then, they accepted their bluff had been called and closed the case rather than publish anything defamatory.

James leant back in his chair, folded his arms and stared at the ceiling. He opened his mouth, closed it, and sighed. He looked across the table at Megan. "Then we'll have to rely on Eva feeding us more deal information." Eva, his god-daughter, was a junior executive at Gladwyn Morson, a position she had won following internships arranged by James.

Megan raised both eyebrows, glared at him but said nothing. They stared at each other for seconds. The comma in their conversation had become a semi-colon and was proceeding to a full stop.

"We have no choice," continued James.

"We could cut back on the scale of our plans."

"No. That's not a solution, that's a surrender."

"We're asking too much of her. Doesn't she deserve a break after your London Marathon operation."

"She enjoyed doing it. There was no risk. Look, she's an adult. She can always say no."

"She never says no when you're asking."

It sounded to James like an allegation. The pair of them were close, always had been since Eva was a toddler, since when, as Uncle James, he had acted as a surrogate father figure. Now she was twenty-four, and according to her passport, was born in London, and Megan Gilman or James Tait should be contacted in the event of an accident.

Megan had agonised over what to tell Eva about her father, and so had waited until her sixteenth birthday. Finally, she presented Eva with her original birth certificate. A folded-up scrap of paper, faded and yellowing, revealed her father's name - Boris Kovac, and her original double-barrelled surname. Megan told Eva that she was half Slovakian and that her father had died from a burst aneurysm induced by his heavy smoking. She said she'd removed Kovac from Eva's name by deed poll simply for simplicity, freeing her from a lifetime of needless explanations. Even then, she could not utter the truth of what happened when Eva was a baby.

Megan expected the torrent of questions from Eva but like a miser opening her purse, relinquished just a few tarnished coins: Boris's background, his character and a scant sketch of their relationship. Whenever Eva persisted in finding out more, Megan would go quiet and withdraw. Or occasionally, the seething anger, asleep but not dead, would disrupt her habitual calmness. It was only the subject that tore them apart. So much was left unsaid, though she and Eva were best friends. Finally, Megan had got Eva to accept that sometimes secrets had to be kept, to protect those you loved the most.

Megan had always been at the centre of just about everything through her teen years. Raised in a liberal, middle-class family in a large house in the wooded outskirts of Guildford, she jetted through life, unthinking, busy and gregarious. At her high-achieving independent girls' school, she excelled academically, sang in chamber choir, starred in the lacrosse team, and swirled around an adoring group of friends. If asked, her parents, Dennis and Pamela would have remarked that everything seemed to be going to plan. They were pleased, slightly smug, over their choice of school.

Megan loved the place, spending most evenings and part of each weekend attending one or other club, music or sporting event. Her pastoral care and development were provided by a clutch of enthusiastic teachers. The school was doing a rather fine job of bringing her up, whilst Dennis and Pamela threw themselves into the local sports club social scene. That and the endless stream of corporate entertaining.

Then after Dennis's promotion to head up the UK subsidiary of a global insurance group, he and Pamela had to host weekly dinners, attend industry cocktail parties, and pitch up at weekend sponsored sporting occasions. Sometimes, the events were held abroad in cultural cities or in sunny beachside locations. Invariably the trips' expenses were borne by the host company and justified as vital for marketing purposes. Though sceptical of the genuine corporate benefits, he and Pamela saw it as their duty. One that maintained Dennis's high rung on the corporate ladder, sustained their luxury lifestyle and paid Megan's school fees. Whilst they danced to the demands of a hectic social whirl, they reasoned that for Megan's sake, she should become a boarder at her school. They'd still see her. Just not that much. And Megan plunged ever deeper into a separate life, swimming with an elite social circle, in a life of her own. Increasingly, she spent weekends and half-terms staying away in grand holiday houses of her classmates.

Everything changed shortly after Megan's sixteenth birthday. The insurance industry, renowned for its pendulum of boom and bust, swung into deep recession. Dennis's subsidiary was downsized by head office, and he was tipped onto the growing, redundancy heap of over-leveraged, high-living, middle-aged insurance executives. At first, Megan barely noticed; she spent such little time with her parents and in any event, she expected her father would simply get another job. All her friends' fathers had jobs, big houses and holiday

57

homes. Her experience informed her, that's what fathers did for their families.

But Dennis didn't find another job. The downturn in the industry became deeper. Even when the broader economy was faring well, he was unable to scramble to the top of the heap to find employment in the only industry he knew, doing the only job he knew - insurance underwriting, charging a premium for taking on an evaluated risk. Ironically Dennis hated risk in his personal life. Unable to find re-employment in the City, he finally took a mundane job in a local furniture store. He announced they would be moving to a smaller house, and Megan would have to cease boarding. The sale of their large family home would eradicate borrowings, pay for the rest of Megan's education and provide a pot of cash, which cautiously managed would keep them afloat.

Megan listened attentively to him, damp-eyed as they sat on the deck overlooking a pristine lawn bordered by a collage of summer flowers. The more he tried to explain, the more he sounded like the twittering birds in the garden, and the less she understood. Surely, she reasoned, as her father explained in inordinate detail the manifestations of the insurance industry, a cycle keeps turning and one day would return to its previous position.

"Why can't you just get another proper job then? All my friends' dads do!" she finally screamed at him. It was the first and last time that her father hit her. It wasn't a hard slap. But it changed everything. Her mother flew out of the patio doors at the sound of her siren wail and her stream of shrill abuse. Her father was already sobbing and staring at his injurious hand.

"What on earth?" was as far as her mother could manage, struck dumb by the sight of her husband crying.

Megan dashed into the house and upstairs to her bedroom where she barricaded herself for the rest of the day. She was furious at him, at the apparent injustice. Her anger at him grew fiercer the next day, when they drove across town to their future home: a small semi-detached house on the edge of a 1950's council estate, miles away from Megan's friends and school.

"How can you do this to me?" was all she could muster as they took a couple of minutes to look around the property.

Megan was enraged and embarrassed. Acutely aware of her dramatically changed status, she refused to return to her old school for the sixth form and completely withdrew from her old friends. Her parents tried cajoling her, then attempted bribery and finally resorted to threats about her future position and career in life. They were horrified that she intended to study for A levels at the local sixth form college. They failed to persuade her and were mystified by their failure. Previously she had gone along the invisible course they had set out for her. There had never been the need for rules as she always appeared to innately do the right thing. But they had missed her growing up, becoming independent, stopped being parents, whilst they gallivanted about in their corporate bubble.

Megan felt let down and angry. Her shift in mood was both quick and marked. For the first time in her life she had a cause against which to rebel. It consisted of trying to do everything to dismay and disappoint her parents. Their struggle to avoid confrontation and rule-based discipline merely led to Megan doubling her efforts to gain their full attention. Her behaviour spiralled downwards as the battle of wills extended throughout her sixth form.

A tumble of boyfriends came and went, as did passions for a multitude of cocktails, alcoholic and drug infused. Always compulsive and competitive in her behaviour, her former excellence in academic study and extra-curricular activities were consigned to the bin. Instead, she concentrated on the twin objectives of immediate pleasure at almost any cost and displeasing her parents to the maximum extent possible. Extra-curricular activities ceased to resemble anything her former teachers may have imagined. But she would not spare her parents the luxury of ignorance or anonymity. They were hauled out, often in the small hours, to the local police station. Eventually they sat at the back of a forlorn magistrates' court, forced to listen to a judge pass sentence on their daughter for possessing an illegal substance. She was lucky, just a fine and a conditional discharge. But it had just a fractional effect on her behaviour.

Then just eighteen, having flunked her A levels, she left home, saying she had a job and a flat-share up town. She was tired of life in the suburbs. She promised to stay in touch, to send a forwarding address. As the months passed, her calls home petered out, and she never returned calls. After more than a year, her frantic parents contacted the police.

They could do nothing to help; Megan was nineteen, an adult; there was no hint of foul play and the previously over-indulged, vulgar-tongued, and drunken young woman was no longer on their patch. Not their problem.

Out of the blue, she phoned. She had a partner, Boris, and a new baby, Eva. Boris was always angry and his bouts of verbal abuse, fuelled by booze had escalated. The day before, he had hit her, and threatened to throttle her and the baby if she ever left him. She became incoherent with sobbing. Then the line went dead.

In desperation, Dennis decided the only solution was to employ the services of a private detective agency. He cashed in an endowment policy he had been saving for the day he expected to escort his daughter down the aisle. He then set about the task of finding an agency.

He first tried his local services directory, the classified advertisements of the town's newspaper and generally asking around. They were all exceedingly expensive and could not guarantee success. The next day, walking his poodle to escape the stress and tension of home, and the constant reminders of his inadequacies, he scanned a patchwork of cards crudely taped onto a newsagent's shop window. There, amongst the cards for rooms to rent, bikes and cookers to sell, and pleasurable massages to enjoy, he spotted it. In bold, red, capital letters on a brilliantly white card, he read "Missing & Lost Persons – specialist private detective agency", followed in more modest, blue, felt-tip manuscript by "Success guaranteed. Reasonable rates."

James sat freezing in his beaten-up Ford Fiesta opposite 10 Willow Way, a wide tree-lined avenue in Wimbledon. He sighed as he switched off the radio, too much *Take That* already for one morning. Cars had begun to crawl out of driveways and make tracks in the glistening snow. He wiped condensation from the window, then lowered it anyway. He peered again, through snow-laden branches of a giant sycamore tree at the red door which had remained shut since he started his shift at six. He regretted not wearing more clothes, he could barely feel his toes. Beneath his dark winter coat, he wore a policeman's uniform, bought from a fancy-dress store. He thought it worth the investment of buying rather than hiring, if he was going to make a go at his new occupation, private detective.

Fresh out of university and ideas as to what to do next, he had lolled about for a couple of months watching too much TV and wondering if he should have joined his friends on their gap year travels. Either that or follow the herd into the City. He had opted instead for the sofa. He had been vaguely watching a late night private-eye episode when a thought struck him. Earlier that year, he had received an anonymous gift of twenty-one thousand pounds, via a law firm. His repeated enquiries were rebuffed, and the mystery nagged away at him. If he joined a private detective agency, he could pick up the tricks of the trade that might solve the puzzle. And a gap year spent snooping was unusual and would hopefully intrigue prospective employers more than time-worn travel to south-east Asia.

He learnt quickly that a first from Oxford University counted against him. No one took him seriously or believed his avowed motivation to train as an investigator. He finally clinched a temporary position, covering someone's maternity leave, but only because he was willing to work for free. He would get expenses, the equipment he needed and training. He figured his bank balance could support him for a year.

At seven fifteen, the thundering of a diesel engine breached the silence of the suburban street. He noted in his pristine notepad the registration number of the black cab which stopped outside the house. Grey smoke belched from its exhaust whilst the cabbie poured something steaming into a cup. James wound up his window and picked up his new *Nikon Zoom 700* from the passenger seat. After ten minutes and thinking about the meter ticking away, he had to resist the urge to knock on the front door. Finally, the reason for his presence revealed itself when the rangy frame of Boris Kovac hurried down his driveway. He wore a Crombie coat with a red paisley silk scarf and carried a black leather briefcase. James snapped a few shots before his floppy-haired target slipped into the back of the cab. The taxi rumbled away slowly, leaving James to reflect on the man his client had described as a violent bully, a drunk and a gambler.

James reckoned he stood around six feet, and the fit of his coat suggested a slender build. His quarry bore a florid and babyish face for a man in his mid-thirties; thick, blonde hair, steel blue eyes, aquiline nose and plump pink lips. He was not what James expected or feared: a rugged brute of enormous physical prowess, muscled and mean looking. Nor did he fit James's mental picture of a timid, plain-faced, spectacles-wearing accountant, which Boris Kovac happened to be, when at work. The bastard was lean and handsome.

Mid-morning, bored of his own company, scanning radio stations and waiting for something to happen, and blue with the cold, he sneaked out of the car. He donned his beanie, stuffed both hands in his pockets, and set off, slipping and sliding in his leather-soled shoes. He edged along the avenue to the Village, enjoying the imprints he created in the snow and marveling at the size and grandeur of the Victorian family houses with their towering chimney stacks. He warmed himself with two cappuccini and a pain au chocolat in an Italian café whilst contemplating what he should do. Sitting in a car, doing nothing, just waiting, did not suit him. That's why he had bought the police uniform despite his boss telling him his task was strictly surveillance.

"Good morning ma'am," said James, removing his police helmet and looking down at the wan face stifling a yawn. "I'm

63

from the local constabulary and we are warning people in the neighbourhood about a recent spate of burglaries." James held his notebook, poised in a prominent pose. Megan swept her blonde pixie-cut from her eyes and blinked, trying to absorb his words. She had been cat-napping having finally gotten the baby off to sleep.

"Sorry officer, burglaries did you say?" It was the word 'neighbourhood' which had lodged in her mind, reminding her that despite moving in almost a year ago, she knew no-one locally. The detached houses, broadly spread, added to her sense of isolation which had grown since Eva's premature birth, and Boris's increased absences. She felt incarcerated, rattling around the house, reticent about exposing her baby to the cold weather.

"Yes, nasty business," said James. With his mild cockney accent, it sounded to her like someone from a police series she'd watched as a child, "Do you have a burglar alarm ma'am?"

"Yes, I think we do but, to be honest officer, we don't use it, we don't know how to, we're new here you see." It sounded like an apology. Her face blushed as she realised how stupid she must appear to the policeman. She felt so tired and could barely think of anything other than meeting the incessant demands of her four-month old.

"Not to worry. So many people say the same. I can take a look around if you like, check your doors and window locks, make sure there are no easy access points." He had a kind face, thought Megan. It was almost a week since she last spoke to another grown-up, other than Boris who grunted more than he spoke nowadays.

Boris had captivated her when they first met at the nightclub where she worked as a cocktail waitress. Unlike the others, his tips came without touching or louche comments. He was good-looking, sophisticated and generous. Though he was older, she fell for him. She liked his wealth and thought he was fun. Just a few months into their relationship, she discovered she was pregnant. She was scared and thought about an abortion. It was Boris who encouraged her to keep the baby, promised to take care of her, insisted that she move in with him. He admitted to a small lie: he was thirty-four, not twenty-eight. By then she was smitten and didn't stop to wonder how many other lies he might have told her.

Now, he was getting in late most nights, stumbling about in the dark, slumping into bed, alcohol on his hot breath. She would pretend to be asleep, to avoid the groping as much as the arguments. She knew where he had been. Client-entertaining he had explained during their first row. She had found a card when she searched through his suit pockets, gold and black, embossed with the name of the establishment in lurid red letters, 'Lothario's'. A call to the club inquiring about job opportunities confirmed her suspicions that it was a hostess club for 'gentlemen'.

"I'm going to brew some coffee. Would you like a cup, officer?" Megan decided she could do with the caffeine as well as the company. She looked at him with pleading eyes. She thought he looked about her age. An earnest face, idealist perhaps, pleasant rather than handsome. I bet he doesn't beat up his girlfriend though, she thought. She was already rueing her reckless one-way adventure into adulthood.

"Thank you. It's freezing out there. White no sugar please. I'll just have a look around the back first, if that is okay. Is the side gate open?" Megan confirmed that they never locked it and went off to the kitchen.

James wandered around to the back garden, frowning, scribbling in his pad, and checking for unlatched windows and unlocked doors. He supposed he was 'casing the joint' which sounded a good deal more exciting than it appeared to him at that moment.

He then roamed around the house, huge, lavishly decorated, hot and messy. He made a note of its layout, unlocked the patio door and unlatched a window. The drift of brewing coffee led him back to a bright kitchen where Megan was feeding baby-bottles into a white plastic pod. As she bent forward, James noticed two mottled patches, purple and yellow, on the back of her neck. She had a long thin neck, in tune with the rest of her body. In faded jeans and a cotton peach T-shirt, her fragile frame struck James as belonging to a pubescent teenager. She turned, holding two steaming mugs of coffee which she set on a grey melamine table.

"Please, take a seat," she said. "I think we have some biscuits somewhere." He watched as she rummaged through half-bare cupboards. She sighed as she ended her fruitless search. "I really must get to the shops."

"Don't worry. I've got to watch my weight, not like you," he said and immediately regretted it. "Sorry, I didn't mean..."

"Don't worry. I know I need to eat more but right now, with the baby, I never seem to have the time. And when I do, I'm tired and can't be bothered." She had dark rings circling her sunken eyes, glazed and dark sable. Cheek bones protruded from a thin, pretty face. She had yet to smile. How different from her photograph secreted in his jacket pocket; a joyous, exuberant face, raspberry-red cheeks, grinning whilst cuddling a poodle on her lap.

"It must be hard," ventured James, clueless about babies. "Does your husband help out much?" Megan sniggered like a school-girl.

"Husband? We're not married and no, he definitively does not help out much. He works long hours. So, we can live in this house, he says. At least it must keep the burglars happy I suppose," she said, finishing with a grim smile.

"Well I've checked everything over. I think you're pretty secure. Just keep an eye out. I'll just take some contact details for the record." He noted down names and telephone numbers. As he finished, he heard a baby's cry from upstairs. "You go. I'll let myself out." He picked up his helmet, put his pad in his top-pocket and smiled as reassuringly as he could.

Back in his car, James slipped the photograph of Megan out of his pocket. How things must have changed in three years, from triumphant to defeated, independence to dependence, brightness to gloom. How odd that the house felt unlike a home: not a single photograph, or painting on a wall, no souvenirs or mementoes, just the clutter of cardboard boxes, clothes and dirty laundry, as if they were lodging there temporarily, living like refugees. He could see why Dennis and Pamela were so concerned. He had already decided he had to do something, something more than just surveillance. But what?

James jolted forward as the slam of a car door arrested his doze. He rubbed his eyes, wiped the window with his sleeve and peered across to the snow encrusted hedgerows. The nearest streetlamp flickered only intermittently and he strained to get a clear view through the snow splattered glass. He saw the yellow light flick on as the cab pulled away. The swaying figure of the soberly dressed man he had seen getting into a cab that morning was ferreting in his briefcase.

Boris Kovac found his door keys and tottered towards his front door. Finally, thought James, as he glanced down at his watch. Ten o'clock. He had been waiting for four hours. At least he was warm now, having added a couple of layers of clothing. He lowered his window to get a better view of the figure slipping and sliding up the drive. Boris fumbled about at the front door, then dropped his keys in the snow. He bent down and toppled over onto the step. Clinging to the side of the brickwork porch, he slowly and precariously managed to haul himself up. Then he started banging the door with fury. James could hear the muted sound of his cussing and the muffled thumping of his fists against the wood. Eventually, light slid out from the open door, and he caught a glimpse of Megan in her dressing gown. Boris tumbled in, and the door was slammed shut.

James counted off a minute and then levered himself from his seat, out into the freezing, dark night. He stretched, then wrapped his scarf around his neck and zipped up his black thermal jacket. He looked up and down the street. No-one. Nothing moved in the silence of the street. The downstairs lights of 10 Willow Way glowed behind drawn curtains and a pall of grey smoke drifted from a chimney.

He trudged across the road and around the back of the house, his new walking boots scuffing a path through chaste snow. As he neared the patio doors, the faint sound of voices grew louder. He caught 'Bitch' and 'Bastard', then heard a high-pitched scream. Without thinking, James turned the patio door's handle and burst into the lounge, where Boris was shoving Megan towards an open fire.

"Stop" James screamed. The man froze and swiveled his head.

"Who the fuck are you? Get out of my fuckin' house," yelled Boris, slurring his speech.

"No way," screamed James, his heart thundering and voice quavering. It had been years since he had fought anyone, and he was afraid.

"Then I'll fuckin' make you, you cunt," raged Boris, releasing his grip from Megan and grabbing a coal shovel from the grate. James seized the nearest sizeable object, a slate clock from the sideboard, and turned just in time to dodge Boris's swing as he lurched at him. As he recovered his balance, James swung the clock, using both hands and struck the side of Boris's head. He fell, hitting his head on a corner of a coffee table and dropping the coal shovel. For a couple of seconds, James froze and Boris lay motionless. Then Boris, breathing heavily, lifted his head and pushed himself up onto his hands and knees. A slurry of filth escaped from his mouth as he eyed the pair of them.

"Bastard, bastard, bastard," screeched Megan and clattered Boris on the head, with three strikes of the coal shovel before James could restrain her. Boris slumped back on to the carpet and lay still. Open mouthed and breathless, they gaped at the inert lump, then at each other. Tears rolled down Megan's face. They both stood shaking, a mixture of relief and fear. The faint cry of a baby pierced the silence.

"Eva needs feeding." Megan bolted out of the door and James heard her footsteps thumping up the stairs. He peered down at the body and saw blood seeping from a gash on the side of Boris's head on to the rug. A white leaf imprint turned red.

Practical questions bombarded him. "What happens when he regains consciousness? Do I hit him again? If I don't, will he hit me, hit Megan? The guy's a lunatic. Will he go to the police? Who will they believe?" He needed time to think. He stepped over to the window and found what he was looking for, curtain tiebacks. He unfastened both chords and retreated to the prone body. He bound Boris's hands together behind his back in multiple knots, clumsy but tight. The memory of a childish prank leapt into his head and he tied Boris's shoelaces together. Then he went into the kitchen and found a couple of tea cloths to soak up the spilt blood. He turned Boris's body over on its back. Blood had congealed on the side of his head and was no longer dripping. He rubbed hard on the carpet for a couple of minutes, then went over to the open patio door and sobered up on the chill air. He stood watching the snow falling, slow and extravagant. Senses heightened and alert, he swore he could hear snowflakes land, like popping corn. He took a series of deep breaths and contemplated what to do next. After a few minutes, he closed and double-locked the door.

Megan drifted into the room with her baby cutched-up against her shoulder. She stroked Eva's back in small circular movements. James smelt warm milk as Megan drew near with her cosseted bundle. Her eyes darted to the heap on the floor.

"He hasn't moved," said James. "I've tied him up, just in case."

Megan's gaze fell on the bloodied rags on the carpet, then to shovel on the floor. "Will the ambulance be here soon?"

James hesitated. He hadn't considered the possibility of Boris being badly hurt and, in any event, he was surprised by Megan's apparent concern. "Erm, I've not called them yet," he mumbled. "I thought we should talk first."

"Please don't take my baby away from me. It was self-defence, you saw that. He really meant to do it this time." Megan perched on an armchair and wept as she rocked slowly back and fro. James knelt on the floor in front of the vulnerable pair. It was time to lead, time to explain.

"Don't worry. We'll sort this out. First, you should know I'm not a policeman." Megan lifted her head and stopped rocking. James explained how he had been hired by Megan's parents and urged her to return home to them and to their care.

"I can't do that. I can't bring them into this. He said he'd kill me if I ever leave, them as well, if I went back home." Megan confessed her part in the misadventure with Boris.

She was young, Boris was much older and so it seemed natural to her at first that he should be in control. But gradually the control exerted itself into every aspect of her life. Nothing she did was ever good enough for him. He earned all the money, worked hard, provided her with everything, he said. All she had to do was look after the baby. The shouting which he'd always done, like his boozing and his betting, had begun to escalate during her pregnancy. She couldn't be certain when he had started being physically violent with her, but it was after Eva had been born. He had got into a routine of coming in late most nights, stinking of booze. He'd always say that it was work-related, but she discovered he had been visiting tarts' bars. He had never admitted it outright until tonight. He swaggered in, demanding dinner and she told him to get one of his tarts to cook it for him. It had been like lighting a fuse. He started screaming, revealing what he had done with this tart, other tarts and that he was going to fuck her the same way whether she liked it or not.

"I slapped him. For the first time, I fought back. That's when you came in," said Megan. "A few seconds later, and I'd have been in that fire. She wiped her nose on the back of her hand and sniffed.

"Has he ever done anything like this before?"

"Not this bad. He almost throttled me last week. Of course, in the morning, he's always sorry, says it's the booze and it won't happen again." Megan started to weep. "He'll kill me one day. I know it. He's mad. He'll kill Eva too." She looked up, red watery eyes appealing to the man who still felt like a boy. This was his test, time to become a man, to become an adult. He had lost his innocence as a three-year old, and it was time to stop treading water.

"I won't let that happen," said James." Go and pack some stuff. You can't stay here. I'll think of something." He spoke with a boldness created by compassion, rather than experience. His head sounded confident and his stomach churned clueless.

They both got up and Megan crept out of the room with her precious bundle. James picked up the shovel and looked down at the prone body. He froze for a moment, wondering whether he dared to finish the job he'd started. He bent down and grabbed a boney wrist. Under clammy skin, a pulse fluttered. He stepped over Boris to the fireplace, shoveled coal into the fire, and jiggled the poker to make the flames leap. He slumped into an armchair and glared into the angry hearth. What would his mother have done? He prayed for inspiration, some divine intervention, a sign. None had arrived by the time Megan returned. But he needed to say something, and the sight of a slumbering Boris made him feel uneasy. He needed more time to think.

"I noticed your garden shed - does it have a lock?"

"No idea. I've never used it. I think it's full of rubbish. Why?"

"He can sleep off his excess in there."

"It will be freezing in there."

"Perhaps," agreed James, "but not as cold as the doorstep where he'd still be lying if you hadn't let him in."

Megan agreed without much persuasion but on condition that they both stayed in the house overnight and confronted him together in the morning. She would leave him then, rather than skulking away in the middle of the night. They bound his legs together with curtain chords and gagged him with a pair of her tights. Together, watched by a slip of the moon, they struggled to cart the coated heap to the snow-capped, wooden shed at the foot of the garden. Aside from a muzzled grunt as they let go of the body onto the wooden boards, Boris made no sound. James switched on his mobile's flashlight and scanned the surrounding junk. He tugged an old blanket, out of a cob-webbed cardboard box. It stank of mildew. He tossed it over Boris and turned off his light. He ushered Megan out, closed the door, and turned the rusted key. They looked at each other for a second, then in silence, retraced their footprints back to the house.

Megan and James barely slept that night. Eva slept well but Boris slept the best. James snuck out to the shed before dawn. He found the body, pale, frozen and stiff. James checked for a pulse, both wrists, his neck, his head. Nothing. His initial shock gradually mutated into relief. It saved him an otherwise hideous task. Plan A had been to terrify Boris, by cracking a few bones and threatening much worse if he dared to contact Megan. Plan B, to go to the police and use the law courts was a less favoured option, necessary in case he hadn't the stomach for Plan A. Plan C was now in progress because God or fate or freezing temperatures had intervened. Justice had prevailed. James felt guiltless. But he needed a new plan: how to dispose of the body.

The following evening around eleven, Boris's BMW, black with tinted windows, snaked through the traffic, turned off Shaftsbury Avenue and slinked towards Golden Square, in Soho. Despite the atrocious weather, Saturday night revelers were packed in the orange glow of pubs and trudging to clubs, acclaimed by fairy lights and beefy bouncers. Groups huddled together, cackling as they slid along slushy pavements. The BMW's sleek, leather steering-wheel slithered through James's gloved hands as he turned the car into the dimly lit square. The car crept around to the west side and halted, close to two traffic cones. James was relieved to see them still in the same place. He had spent much of the morning, wrapped up in a hooded black anorak, trudging around the snow-covered Soho streets and alleys falling within a few minutes' walk of Lothario's.

He leapt out of the idling vehicle, glanced around and seeing no-one walking on the street, moved the cones aside. He jumped back in and maneuvered Boris's prized possession into a tight slot between parked two cars. He checked his wing mirrors, saw nothing but wispy grey exhaust fumes and then killed the ignition and lights. He took a deep breath, then listened and scanned the square.

The west side still retained its terrace of Georgian buildings, seven stories high and built for the gentry. The residents had long ago sold out to commerce. All the office building windows were dark. MTech Media Enterprises's office lay in the shadows adjacent to Boris's parked car. Only the scattered streetlamps cast small oases of light. James heard muffled voices and a group sloped into view in his wing mirror.

He allowed a few minutes to pass before he pulled his black balaclava over his head. It itched but it covered most of his face and was fit for the freezing night air. He got out of the car and stood by the passenger back door. He glanced to his left, to check the distance to the galvanised steel steps leading down to MTech's basement entrance. He could feel his heart thudding and the clamminess gathering under his balaclava. He heard the growl of a black cab. He saw its amber light appear on the east side of the square and ducked down until it had disappeared on its way to Piccadilly. He surveyed the square one more time, and then with swiftness and strength that surprised him, he opened the door, hauled the black body-bag out on to the passageway and hurled it down the steep steps. He slammed the door, locked it and looked around. Then he slipped gingerly down the steps, shoved the dead weight to the foot of the steps and then dragged it behind two black bins. He stood up, arching his back and took a few deep breaths, now out of view from the pavement above.

He tore off the black bin liners, then sneaked Boris's bulky key-ring, and Lothario's membership card into his jacket-pocket. He dumped his cashless wallet by his body. He felt his heart lurch with the first sound of a siren overhead. He pinned himself against the wall. He was damp with sweat. He heard shouts, and swearing, then laughing as the siren's wail receded. The slurry of footsteps squelched into his hearing, then like the siren dissolved. He was almost certain no-one had seen him.

James gathered up the bin liners into a tight ball and stuffed them into his coat pocket. He crept up the steps, straining his ears to detect the sound of people or cars. Back on the pavement, he picked up the cones and crossed the road, peering all around. He slung the cones into the darkness and heard a dull thud as they landed somewhere on the snow-covered gravel, out of sight. After a final look around, head down, he tramped away from the square to the shadows of Beak Street. He withdrew Boris's *Nokia* from his pocket and extracted its SIM card which he threw into a drain.

He picked up speed, heading east towards Tottenham Court Road tube station. He looked over his shoulder along the narrow winding street. No-one. He tossed the bin liners and the *Nokia* into a road-side rubbish skip, then tore off his balaclava. He lifted his face to the purifying snowflakes, teeming down from the heavens. It was done. He felt elated.

They towed away his car before his body. By Monday lunchtime, the ticketed car with a suitcase of Boris's clothes in the boot, had been hoisted away to a car pound on the outskirts of the city. The weekend snowfall had done a fine job and the grim discovery of a cadaver by a bin-man, delayed until Tuesday. Megan was sipping tea and chatting with her parents when her mobile phone rang. She had made numerous unanswered calls to Boris's mobile, but this was the first call she had received since she had arrived in her old family home on Saturday morning.

She was poised and prepared, receiving the sensitive police-woman's grisly news with an appropriate measure of faux grief. She tripped out the same story to the police that she had reported to Dennis and Pamela a few days earlier. Boris had said he was going away for a work conference for a few days. She had tried to reach him but his phone didn't appear to be working. They had tracked her down having detected a mobile number on the back of a demure photograph of her, inserted in his wallet. She had put it there on Saturday.

Megan's majestic performance conned the police, her parents and the sprinkling of old friends who had distanced themselves over the past year. The freezing weather conned forensic investigators and the pathologist. The autopsy concluded that the cause of death was uncertain; either a ruptured aneurysm triggered by a blow to the head or hypothermia, perhaps a combination. The police were sure that Boris had been mugged, thrown down the steps, banging his head as he fell. His wallet had been emptied and his mobile phone was missing. Having interviewed staff at Lothario's, the police concluded that Boris was attacked on his way to the club where he'd been a regular client. They suspected he must have been having an affair and used the work conference as an excuse to dupe his wife. Their interrogation of his laptop's disk drive revealed massive gambling debts and several work colleagues mentioned that he liked his drink.

Two of them came to the funeral, alongside Megan and her parents in a functional crematorium on a cold grey day in the concrete sprawl of south London suburbia. The non-religious service was brief, no tears were shed, and no-one bothered to collect the ashes afterwards.

The next evening, Megan and James dined at an Indian family restaurant in a quiet road off Wimbledon's High Street whilst Dennis and Pamela doted over their grand-daughter at home.

"Cheers," said Megan to the sound of chinking glasses of *Cobra* beer. James poked the pile of poppadoms and the cacophonous crack splintered fragments across the table which made her giggle. It was a long time since she had felt such relief.

"To a bright future," added James.

"Thank you for everything you've done," Megan said, spooning onion chutney onto a slither of poppadom. She felt barely a scintilla of guilt. Boris had brought it on himself. It was him or her. The world was a better place without him. She now had a chance to start over again. "This meal is on me."

"No no, your parents have paid my bill. I want to celebrate the closure of my last case." James explained that private detective work ill-suited him; not the deceit, he could handle that, but the endless hours spent hanging around, waiting for something to happen.

"We'll go fifty-fifty then," said Megan.

"Okay. To partnership," said James, raising his glass again.

She liked the sound of that. A partnership bound by a secret, stronger than blood ties. "In crime?" laughed Megan.

"That and much more hopefully."

"One condition though," said Megan, "we never mention the B word ever again.

Chapter Five   Scam

"That's one of your maddest proposals," Caro said before forking a headless prawn. James's previous grand scheme for LifeChance had been a people's lottery for refugees. "It'll never work."

"Lots of charities have trading subsidiaries."

"Yes. Ones making profits without resorting to creative accounting, and nothing to do with gambling," hissed Caro.

James had just outlined his latest big idea. He had been introduced to a young American, ex-MIT, nerd turned tech-entrepreneur. He claimed to have developed a unique algorithm, AI software based upon a mountain of sports data. It enabled betting companies to set odds with more precision. Greater precision meant risks could be assessed more accurately, allowing more attractive odds to be offered to customers whilst enlarging the win percentage for the company. The entrepreneur had attracted venture capital funding but all that money had been spent, and bankruptcy now loomed. The venture capitalists had lost patience with repeated failures to meet forecasts and after one too many rescue-rights issues, were now prepared to hand over their shares to avoid the public embarrassment of being connected with a liquidation.

James smiled, keeping his poise. He had to remain calm. Paulo, their Italian waiter from Puglia, pale-skinned and camp, refilled their glasses with sparkling water. His fastidious uniform, buttoned-up white shirt, black tie and waistcoat over a brilliant white apron, matched the urbane lunch-time crowd of city suits: overfed men with thinning hair and thickening girths or tanned gym bunnies with slicked-back gelled hair sipping slim-line tonics. A sprinkling of smart women in silk blouses, tailored jackets and hints of jewellery, befitted the room's elegance.

James adored this former Georgian banking hall with its soaring corniced ceiling, ornate chandeliers, central glass cupola and huge windows. Its airy capaciousness and neo-classical architecture served to remind its clientele of its two hundred years of tradition and of the grand mercantile era of the empire. It also conveyed the buzz of the City, being at the heart of unseen financial forces, huge and inexorable, unfathomable to outsiders but understood by its privileged diners. James sensed that there was a deal being negotiated at every table. The urgent din was perfect cover for a confidential conversation.

"It doesn't matter if it doesn't work as long as it takes a long time not to work," said James catching a whiff of sausage and mash being carried past their table. "Look, remember the dotcom bubble, loads of hi-tech companies valued in the millions, billions even, and they never made a penny. Most don't exist any longer but plenty of investors, those who got in early, made fortunes by selling out to punters who had bought the story later. This would be just another of those stories."

"But that was then. The market has moved on. Governance standards are much higher now." Caro waved at an entering diner, a hedge fund competitor. So many of them gathered here for a quick, expensive bite. Just around the corner from the Bank of England, it was an easy dash at lunchtime. And in the evenings, under dimmer lights, its circular bar served cocktails and fizz, to partying punters, celebrating deals before pouring into the subterranean network below, to transit to harsher realities outside the City bubble.

"Well what about Karhoo or Fling then? Their stories raised tens, hundreds of millions before they disappeared into administration?"

"Yes, indecently quickly. The venture capitalists lost their shirts, but I don't recall any of the original investors taking money out."

"How about Skype or Instagram, both loss-making companies sold for billions."

"You know as well as I do, they were bought by global companies for strategic reasons."

"Yes, on the back of unproven but compelling stories. Our story will be compelling and credible, with explosive growth underpinned by a bit of judicious accounting," said James before bolting down a mouthful of quinoa salad. He regretted that his recent medical was still fresh in his mind.

"And when the auditors find out you've been cooking the books, you'll go to jail, and believe me, it's not fun," said Carol as she plucked a petal from the white hydrangea adorning the centre of their table. She inhaled its floral scent and popped it into her mouth.

"They'd never find out, and anyway even if suspicions were raised, we'd have sold our shares long before. Time will have faded memories, records will have been obliterated, people will have died even. No-one will be able to prove anything, certainly not sufficient to meet the demands of a court."

81

He had explained his plan to inject funds into the company, bring in old friends as CEO and financial director, draw up a compelling business plan and attract further millions from new venture capitalists. They would focus the nerd solely on developing the software and databank. He had worked it all out. They would present an ambitious set of long-term forecasts, strong sales growth but with projected losses, big ones, over the first few years. LifeChance would inject several million to show commitment and raise twenty million pounds from a venture capital firm. A year later, they would take the company public and sell some of their shares. The key was convincing the market of the huge potential to win in a global market. They would plough funds into software development and marketing their on-line site. If needed, they could book fictitious sales to create an appearance of scale. This would be offset by exaggerating costs, so that funds could be channelled covertly back to the charity returning its initial investment. So, the shares would have cost LifeChance nothing and could turn out to be hugely valuable.

"The new investors will want to visit, kick the tyres. They'll expect to see a big operation," Caro persisted, before sniffing the sea as she tipped a dripping oyster into her gaping mouth. She always insisted upon a side silver-platter of Colchester Oysters. She adored their explosion of brine and butter as she bit into the living flesh, the fizz of the lemon juice at the back of her throat as it slipped down. The memory of her first boss treating her to a first taste of oysters over a celebratory lunch, remained fresh. Eating oysters for Caro equated with success, confirmation that she had made it.

"And we'll give it to them. We'll rent space, some terminals, desks and so on, populate it with part-time actors we'll have rehearsed. The extras will be told we are making a

TV series. The operation will look and feel like the call centre of a betting company, a bit like a dealing room. None of the investors will be any the wiser. We'll only need to do it a few times each year. And anyway, the whizz-kid might be right. This could work, in which case there'll be no need to pretend. Our shares would be worth a fortune."

Caro glared at James with her sceptical face; raised eyebrows and pinched lips. He had gone too far. He had overreached, to the point of using an argument he didn't truly believe in.

"James, you know, and I know, that the vast majority of early-stage ventures fail, and clearly, this one already has. You also know that there will be a ton of due diligence done. You'd be crawled over by lawyers, accountants, consultants, investment bankers and so forth. They are bound to find you out."

Her voice momentarily rose above the din of the room, enough to attract glimpses from a couple of nearby tables. She returned their snide glances with a stare, just as she had done when she entered the restaurant like a rampaging Boudicca. Their slanted looks, confirming that she was still gossip-worthy, disintegrated before her.

James sliced into his mushroom and chestnut quiche and Caro attacked another prawn. This is not going according to plan, thought James, as he sat munching in silence, head bowed over his insipid plate.

"Caro, investors lose money all the time. In fact, investors have lost money on more than seventy per cent of companies ever listed on AIM." He sighed, feeling he was getting nowhere. "Look, I have really thought this through. I have worked up a detailed plan, I have the people lined-up, I even

83

have a draft business prospectus." He leant forward to grasp her hand, beseeching her with appealing eyes, to trust him.

"But is it worth the risk? If it goes wrong, and you get found out, it would destroy you and LifeChance."

"It won't happen, and the potential prize could be huge. Think of the difference we could make." He clicked his fingers like a magician creating a card trick. "I know, remember *Lastminute.com*. What a great story. It listed on the stock market with sales of a few hundred thousand and was valued at three quarters of a billion pounds at one point. Later, its shares crashed when it failed to meet the market's expectations. It was bought five years later, still loss-making for a fraction of its peak value. It still exists. No-one went to jail. Lots of people made a lot of money."

"From people who lost a lot of money."

"So what, they were mainly institutions who could easily afford it. That's all the market is. You know that better than anyone. A pendulum continuously in motion, swinging between fear and greed."

"But you're overlooking the fact that no-one at *Lastminute* broke the law."

"You don't know that. Neither do I."

"Really?" Caro's mobile vibrated on the table. She was shaking her head as she picked it up. "Hi Marta," said Caro. "What's up?"

James peered around the bustling room, absorbing the animation around him. His gaze fixed on a blonde-haired woman, pale skinned, high cheek bones with pouting lips. She sat still, serene and cool, above the clamour. He saw other men casting sly glances, sharing a morsel of her beauty. Opposite her sat an older man, short and balding, wearing dark glasses. He was frowning at a menu which he gripped in his stubby hands, his fat fingers bearing chunky gold rings. Russian, rich and non-resident for tax purposes. Stereotypes existed for a reason, he thought.

"Sorry James, but I have to go," said Caro.

"Emergency?"

"No not all. Our largest Saudi investor has just popped in for a coffee whilst he is in town on other business. Just wants a catch-up with me."

The clatter of crockery broke upon them, as a passing waiter slipped on the limestone-tiled floor. James looked down - pear and chocolate tart and a crème brulée lay splattered. What a terrible waste. His stomach groaned in sympathy. Several staff rushed to clear up the mess, and the hubbub resumed.

"Couldn't he join us here for lunch?"

Caro snorted.

He realised it was a preposterous idea. She would never risk James meeting one her largest backers, no doubt worth several billion dollars to the firm. She was always letting him know he was too impulsive, that he would scare most of her investors with his risk-taking. How ironic he thought, given the risks hedge funds like hers routinely took.

"He doesn't do lunch. He doesn't drink either, or smoke, or sleep around," said Caro, clutching her burgundy Chanel flap-bag.

"Sounds ghastly. What does he do then?"

Caro rose with a broad grin. "Prays to Allah several times a day, tells wicked jokes, works hard and makes vast amounts of money for his family conglomerate."

"Sounds like his prayers are answered."

"He has been a loyal friend. Like you, James. And I trust his judgement."

James waited for her to add 'like yours, James' but she clamped her mouth shut, and they exchanged stares. "Well, will you at least think about my idea? Otherwise I'll have to appeal to a higher authority, like your friend."

Caro smiled. "Maybe. But if I do, in exchange, I'd like you to think about another test for the Weasel? I so enjoyed the last one."

"Course." James beamed. He was reluctant but realised he had no choice. Not unless he abandoned his plan, which he refused to countenance.

"Excellent. Must dash. Lunch is on my account, so just sign the bill and they'll send it on. We'll chat in a couple of days."

"Thanks Caro." He watched her swivel and followed her swift exit as the sound of her clicking heels merged with the hurly-burly clammer of deal-making. He needed her support, both financially and to gain the backing of LifeChance's board. Without her, his ambitious growth plans would be as dead as the 'Dubs' child refugee scheme: the government had shabbily scrapped its pledge to take in three thousand unaccompanied child refugees. Evidently, the shocking images of a Syrian boy washed up on a beach had faded from the front pages, and the political-media merry-go-round now waltzed to a different tune.

He caught the eye of a passing waiter, ordered an espresso and asked for the bill. The coffee arrived within seconds, delivered by a pretty, doe-eyed waitress, he had not seen before. Marissa turned out to be from Sicily where she couldn't find a job, and life was boring. It was her first month in London and first week at the restaurant. But too soon, Paulo from Puglia barged in with the bill and Marissa evaporated into the throng. Bill settled, a simpering Paulo, gratified by James's gratuity, scampered ahead to the exit, where he topped off his performance with a 'curtain call' bow. Paulo grasped hold of the burnished brassware handle, and with practised panache, swept open the heavy mahogany door.

Humidity and pollution assaulted James as he stepped down marble steps and out from the climate-controlled, filtered-air of the restaurant to the traffic smog at the heart of the City. The convivial buzz of the restaurant had been replaced by the blaring horns of vehicles, jostling for space with cyclists whilst pedestrians criss-crossed jammed streets. James opted for a stroll back to the office rather than suffer the frustrations of sitting in the back of a stationary cab, or the stifling heat of the underground. Walking on familiar ground granted his mind licence to roam. He sauntered along Cheapside, dodging groups of map-reading tourists and iron-jawed executives marching to meetings. He hurried past a building site where the rat-a-tat of pneumatic drills vibrated in his head, and white dust mushroomed in the windless air. Ahead, he could see several other gantry cranes looming over competing skyscrapers under construction. He had chosen a liminal location on the south side of the river for his office: on the edge, out of the financial fray, on the border of the City. He hoped a degree of detachment would contribute to creativity. Distance delivering him, ever closer to fulfilling his vision for LifeChance.

He ambled westward, still thinking about his big idea, how he could convince Caro, and what else he needed to put in place. He was walking towards Blackfriars Bridge, the same path he'd trodden hundreds of times. Then at the junction where he would normally turn left toward the bridge, struck by the thing Caro had not said as much as what she had, he headed straight on, through the bustle of Fleet Street.

Turning off the street, he sauntered along an alley, under the shadow of the St. Bride's Church's spire. He approached the weathered stone north wall and shouldered open the heavy oak door to one of his favourite refuges. He had stumbled across the ancient relic in his mid-twenties, when he was at a loss, in need of inspiration, seeking something divine to direct his thoughts. Sometimes, he would wander down to the crypt and study the Roman mosaic pavement. Or stand in front of the Journalists' Altar, contemplating reporters' lives lost in war zones where they covered conflicts that spawned human tragedies and prompted refugees to flee. The journalists had paid the ultimate price for simply doing the jobs, for pursuing their passion, to publicise truth and bring justice. By contrast, what he risked at LifeChance was pathetic.

Often, he would flop onto a wooden pew and pray for a few minutes, hoping for some presence and settle for the absence of a presence. And then he would allow his mind to wonder. He would contrast his challenges of running an unloved, unfashionable charity with the immense obstacles that Celtic monks of the sixth century had overcome in establishing the church and proselytising the English. They were guided by Bride, the daughter of an Irish prince. She gave away so many of her father's possessions, that he allowed her to enter religious life.

Over the centuries, St. Bride's Church had faced adversity and been destroyed many times, but always rebuilt. After the building's destruction in the Great Fire of London, Sir Christopher Wren had redesigned it. Even the bomb damage of the second world war could not extinguish that. It rose again from ashes, forged by ordinary people determined on doing something extraordinary with their lives. James had set the course of his new life on the same path.

Inside, the clocks had stopped, the traffic hushed, and the air infused with incense. He exchanged a welcoming nod with an elderly woman staffing the shop by the west wall. He made his way up the nave, to his usual spot on an oak pew, where he crouched and faced the eastern wall. Candles flickered on the main altar stationed below an oil painting of the Crucifixion. Above, an oval stained-glass panel of Christ in glory dazzled in the light seeping through vast leaded windows on the south wall. Other than the woman staffing the shop, he had the place to himself and God. He would come here for a peaceful chat whenever he felt things were getting on top of him, when he craved for a tranquil space away from the frenzy. Away from disturbances, demands and distractions of daily life. He now felt he may have come to another cross-road.

He had built the charity steadily, though it had been much more difficult and frustrating than he had envisaged. He had underestimated the strength of antagonism aimed at refugees. Raising funds just to maintain the status quo was challenging enough in the face of so many causes more appealing to people. He ploughed on, raising ever more funds, to enlarge his mission. But he could never raise enough. Much of society wasn't listening and many rejected his overtures. So, he had been forced to rely on Caro, and bend some rules. It was a struggle, always. Some days, like today, he questioned himself, whether he had the stomach for it. He felt like Sisyphus. Life had been so much easier in investment banking. People patted him on the back all the time, fawned all over him endlessly, and threw money at him.

"What's the bloody point?" he muttered, peering up at the barrel-vaulted ceiling. Invariably, this was how he would start his conversations with the Almighty. It was how, as a disaffected teenager, he had begun the conversation with Father Tait. James had met him having gone through a series of foster homes and schools, unable to cope with his tantrums. Educational psychologists diagnosed him as suffering from Oppositional Defiant Disorder, and ADHD, caused they decided by devastating events in his early childhood. His various foster parents described him as a difficult, and sometimes impossible child and many of his teachers concurred. He'd had enough of professionals trying to cure him by talking.

"What do you think the point is, of your life?" said Father Tait as he munched on a chocolate biscuit. James had been dragged along to church for several weeks by his latest foster parent, Mrs. Murphy. He went to escape Mr. Murphy and his thick-headed Sunday morning bouts of ranting and bullying. He'd clouted James once when he had been a bit too clever for his own good. Mr. Murphy didn't bother him most of the time. And Mrs. Murphy gave as good as she got, whip-lashing her husband with her tongue, and belting him over the head with her rolled-up 'Sunday People'. She baked amazing apple pies and cakes and believed that the Lord would light James's path. She had asked Father Tait to have a chat with him.

"Dunno. You're supposed to be the expert," was James's surly retort as he plucked a biscuit from the priest's plate. James gazed around the cramped study. Books lined the walls, or were stacked on table-tops and chairs, or piled precariously in corners on the floor. They sat in two rickety wooden chairs on a threadbare red and grey rug, facing each other, sipping from mugs of tea. A faint smell of incense drifted in from the adjoining church.

Father Tait laughed, licked a couple of plump fingers and then rose up on tiptoe to jerk a book from a shelf. "Well you may find an answer in there. Then again you might not. But until you read it, you won't know."

James frowned as he peered at the cover of the book held in front of him - 'My Man Jeeves' by P.G. Wodehouse.

"Now why don't you have a look in there whilst I have a wee chat with Mrs Murphy, outside."

James waited until Father Tait had left the room before opening the cracked cover of the book. He had expected a lecture from the old man, or a biblical tale, or perhaps a prayer book thrust at him. The pages had yellowed and their texture felt rough. He had nothing else to do, so started to read. And as he read, he began to laugh.

It had been the start of something. The more he read, the more he laughed. He found he couldn't be angry when he laughed, when he was in another place, away from rules. Away from the torments that interrupted his thoughts and invaded his dreams. Afterwards he would be a regular visitor to Father Tait's library, borrowing books, chatting over mugs of tea, and laughing together. Father Tait, fat, flushed and funny, never judged, only questioned, and never answered his own questions no matter what trouble James had caused at home, school, or elsewhere. It became James's refuge and because of it, to please Father Tait, he continued going to church, got baptised, took his first holy communion and became confirmed all on the same day.

Despite the initial embarrassment, James adored the theatre of celebrants: a packed congregation, the candles ablaze with the lights down low, the bulbous arrays of white lilies, the bushy green and red poinsettias, and the orange dahlias, adorning the church. Father Tait beamed throughout the ceremony and afterwards presented to him a small wooden crucifix, a black-beaded rosary and a massive tin of assorted chocolate biscuits. His teachers at the comprehensive remarked on a shift in his attitude, and he started to excel as he buried himself in books of all kinds. The other kids still left him alone, unsure what to make of the mad, angry, un-sporty boy transformed like magic into a nerd. But it was no magic, other than the influence of Father Tait, and James's realisation that he had the ability to choose his path, and not allow the path to choose him. And he had learnt that he could make himself happy.

Several years later, he called in to see Father Tait on return from his first term at Oxford. He had brought with him a gift wrapped present to augment his surprise visit. He had unearthed a battered first edition of 'Right Ho, Jeeves' in a back-street second-hand book store. He had lugged his suitcase from the station and had stood on the *Priests' House* doorstep, listening to the choir's carol practice drifting from the church. Fairy lights adorned the church porch and spotlights illuminated a stable and crib scene under a makeshift shelter. He could see Christmas cards through the windows of the lit house. He was looking forward to sharing stories over mugs of tea and a plate of biscuits he'd bought, in the study. But instead of Father Tait, a young smiling priest greeted him at the door. The old man had suffered a heart attack and died a month before. It had happened during the night and he was found dead in his bed by the housekeeper. The funeral had taken place a week later and a memorial service just the previous day. The newly installed priest invited him in. He declined but left the biscuits. Another door on the corridor of his young life closed forever.

Mrs. Murphy said she had not told him for fear of upsetting his studies. After that, he stayed in Oxford.

He retrieved a tapestry cushion and sank to his knees. He closed his eyes, genuflected and clasped his hands together in supplication. He breathed in deeply, inhaling the fusty aroma. He found it easier to meditate in this position and to block out the intrusions of other visitors. Sometimes, he would even nod off in this position and wake himself with his snoring. He recounted his options, running through the pros and cons in his mind. After about twenty minutes, he thought he had given God enough to think about for now. He didn't expect an answer immediately. From experience, he understood that would come later, often when he least expected it and from unexpected sources.

He rose stiffly, his left knee joint clicking as he did so and felt guilty that he had not done his morning stretches. As he turned down the aisle, he saw the source of the whispering that had interrupted his contemplation. A small group of tourists, Asian and camera-clad were leafing through guide-leaflets by the door. He diverted his path to the candle-stand and as usual, lit two Tea-light votive candles, one for his mother and the other for Father Tait. He slotted a folded ten-pound note into a metallic slot, and stood for a while, watching the flickering flames, lighting a corner of dimness. Then he quietly slipped out, easing past the tourists and out into the anarchy of Fleet Street.

Chapter Six   Examinations

Wimbledon Common Clinic was the sort of place that greeted patients with flowers, newspapers, digital screens and sparkling smiles. Mark sat in a lamp-lit corner, sipping an expresso and eyeing the evening's breaking news - another premier league manager sacked for dismal performance. A five million pounds termination payment, no wonder the bloke's grinning face filled half the back page. He'd find another job, sign another lucrative multi-year contract and date another young model.

Mark thought about how hard he had to work for his paltry millions. His millions were never enough. Now Cath kept banging on about the property in Majorca, her friend had recommended. They had bought one, a five-bedroom house overlooking the coast, for a mere two million pounds and Cath thought it would be fun to join them, spend summers there so the kids would have playmates. He sighed into the cleavage of Ms Cruz, as the smiling receptionist bent down and whispered to him that Doctor Gibson was ready to see him. He rather wished Ms Cruz was ready to see him instead. He followed her hips as she sashayed along a white corridor lined with pictures that meant nothing to him. Modern art.

"Interesting artwork," he said, whilst imagining her peeling off her panties.

"You can buy them if you like. We have a catalogue at a reception. I painted this one," she turned, beamed at him and tapped on the door of Doctor Thomas Gibson.

"Great," he said, forcing a smile, "maybe later."

"Please go in."

Thomas sat behind his desk tapping on an Apple laptop. A mellow jazz soundtrack played in the background blending with the occasional blare of traffic. Framed poster-sized photographs of sporting icons packed the walls, alongside one of him in his golfing attire next to Jack Nicklaus. Thomas spent Friday afternoons at Royal Wimbledon Golf Club.

"John McEnroe - are you serious?" said Mark eyeing one of the pictures as he plopped himself down in a chair facing Thomas.

"Legend," said Thomas and looked up. "So, do you like the new clinic?"

"Feels just like the city - all glass and metal. What happened to wood?"

"We're running out. Where have you been? Ah yes, I remember - lying about on tarmac."

"I would've broken three hours you know." It rankled him still that not only did he fail to finish but that Thomas had clocked under three hours.

"Hmm...well, let's check your blood pressure first. Then maybe we can move on to your deluded mental state."

Mark chattered on about his marathon time splits and how fresh he felt at twenty-two miles whilst Thomas wrapped the cuff around his arm. The cuff whirred into life, its inflation gripping Mark's left bicep. Mark felt his pulse beating, and reverberating in his head.

"Breathe normally and stop speaking for a few seconds," said Thomas peering at a monitor on his I-phone. Mark's gaze landed on a digital photo-frame on the desk; happy faces of Thomas's wife, Kimberly and their three children rotated every few seconds.

"How was St. Lucia?"

"Good. Now stop talking." Thomas took his pulse and then checked the rhythm of his heart. They had been silent for almost a minute and Mark was beginning to worry. Thomas's tanned face looked like an over-baked potato, one huge frown.

"So how long have I got Doc?" But the joke fell flat.

"That depends...on you really, at least I think so." Thomas returned to his desk and flipped his laptop screen towards Mark. "These are the results of the medical tests taken at the emergency unit on the day of your marathon."

"Took their bloody time to get here." Mark peered at a screen of red and green numbers and medical terms that meant nothing to him.

"See this," said Thomas pointing at the screen, "that was your blood pressure, 85 over 50. That compares with the reading I've just taken of 120 over 80, which is regarded as normal. So, both your systolic and diastolic measures were incredibly low."

Mark looked at him blankly. "What does that mean?"

"It means your blood pressure was so low, not enough blood was reaching your brain and so you fainted. Your body is two-thirds water and if you're dehydrated, there's not enough of it to keep your body functioning. Your heart is working incredibly hard but it can't cope without adequate hydration."

"But I drank a lot, water as well as *Lucozade* Sport."

Thomas stared at him for a moment. "Mark, if that's the case, how do we explain why your sodium, potassium and magnesium levels were so dangerously low?" Thomas pointed at several numbers on the screen. "You see, isotonic drinks are supposed to maintain fluids and electrolytes in your blood stream."

"Well how should I know. You're the doctor," said Mark, his voice rising in mild irritation.

"The blood test results also revealed traces of Hydrochlorothiazide. Are we ringing any bells yet?"

Mark stared at him. "Thomas, what are you talking about. I have no idea what hydro whatever is."

"Okay. I take it you've heard of diuretics."

"Of course. I'm not stupid. They make you pee."

"Indeed. And diuretics are used by some elite athletes to improve their performance by excreting fluid for rapid weight loss allowing them to mask the presence of other banned substances, such as DMAA."

Mark frowned, trying to grasp where this conversation was heading. He leant back in his chair and sighed. "You've lost me now."

"Thiazide diuretics are prescribed by doctors to lower a patient's blood pressure. They contain Hydrochlorothiazide."

Mark finally got it. He slapped his hands on his thighs and laughed. "You're accusing me of being an elite athlete. Recognition at last."

"Mark, this is serious. You could have suffered a cardiac arrest. You were unconscious for several minutes. You could have died."

"But I didn't take anything, no banned substance, no diuretic, just water and *Lucozade*. I told you. I wouldn't be that stupid."

"You were determined to break three hours. I've known you long enough to know that when you focus on something, you'll go to extreme lengths to get what you want. You become fixated."

"Yes, but not that. I'm no cheat. You know that. It would be a pointless, hollow victory."

An awkward silence settled in the space between them. Finally, Thomas slapped his laptop shut. "Well, something here doesn't make sense. I'll check to see whether there's been a mix-up with your test results."

"Thanks. Now how about a recovery run on the Common on Saturday morning - usual time?"

"Sure. Provided you take it easy, keep it under an hour."

"I don't do jogging, and neither do you," said Mark as he rose to shake Thomas by the hand.

"Meet at the Windmill at seven-thirty then. And bring some water with you. You need to keep hydrated," Thomas said as he opened the door.

"Of course, Doc. Don't work too late." Mark smiled and headed for reception to look at a painting catalogue and Ms Cruz.

He was waylaid by a message left on his mobile by James Tait asking him to call back as soon as possible. He had a problem.

On the thirty-third floor of the pyramidal Shard overlooking the dirt brown, languid Thames, James stood before one of the reception desks at the prestigious law firm, Bone, Cumberbatch and Smith. It felt to him like an airport check-in area, except here, all the white-bloused receptionists were perfumed, polished and pretty. A young woman, pale faced, as indiscernible as a Noh actor, looked up from her booking screen and said she'd let Mr Phillips' assistant know he'd arrived. She invited him, in a soft Irish brogue to take a seat for a minute. She gestured to the collusion of low backed leather sofas arranged around smoked glass coffee tables. A digital theatre of competing screens screamed urgency from each wall.

James selected an FT from the rack, sat down and peered over the top of his newspaper. A group of blue-suited Japanese executives had settled opposite him, all turned out in crisp creased trousers, white shirts and identical red patterned ties. He listened to the staccato of their chatter and pondered on a corporate culture dominated by such collaboration. He sat alone, pensive, no longer trying to read or listen. He had not shared the burden of the FCA's investigation into his trading activities with anyone other than Mark. Caro had originally introduced him to the lawyer at a LifeChance charity gala evening. She had been gushing about him and about his firm then. How times had changed.

A soothing voice interrupted James's reverie, and asked him to follow her to 'Euripides'. Bone, Cumberbatch and Smith possessed an affectation for classical Greek, its ancient writers and philosophers. Unlike many of the pre-eminent international law firms with which it sought to compete, it was youthful, having been established in the late nineteen seventies by a small group of junior partners spinning out from the blue- blooded firm of Simpkin More. At the time, the impeccably cultured Simpkin More, with its deeply embedded public school foundations and extensive government client base, saw the move as regrettable but mostly tiresome and somewhat irritating. It certainly did not expect the start-up to feature as a genuine competitor. Both firms had fared well since, beneficiaries of the explosion in financial services in London servicing a global client base.

Bone, Cumberbatch and Smith was founded by a cohort of ex-Grammar school meritocrats. They resolved to change the world of legal practice through the drive and aggression of a team with much to prove. Paradoxically, as the firm became successful, and egged on by a scramble of marketing and brand consultants, it had come to ape aspects of Simpkin & More, itself now a member of the 'magic circle' club. The firm now hired almost exclusively from Oxbridge, boasted average earnings of well over a million pounds per equity partner, and provided full-service offerings embracing a panoply of niche specialisms.

BCS, as they were becoming increasingly labelled in the acronymic world of the money-rich time-poor City of London, worked harder than any of their peers. From partner down to the most junior associate, the culture oozed an excess of collective sweat and toil with the singular ambition to be the best, most admired law firm around. It was also about money, making ever increasing piles of it in order to top published income league tables and deliver the mountainous bonuses upon which London's ever monstrous real estate market relied to defy gravity. But for all the material trappings or corporate marketing spin, nothing could alter the reality that the firm lacked a distinguished history. It lacked ancient, opaque connections and a corporate brand that oozed with an assuredness of being the best. It was still regarded as an up-start in the conservative circles of the legal profession.

So BCS found itself inundated with applications from fiendishly clever mavericks with deep reserves of arrogance and energy. Properly channelled, such qualities could propel the firm towards the top and the prize of elite peer approval and recognition. The same characteristics could also lead to a completely different path; one where the intensity and appetite for risk precipitates misjudgement and misadventure, leading to implosion and bankruptcy. The aggressive culture of winning at almost any cost, within the framework of legality, the twenty-four seven work ethic and aspiration to be regarded by clients among the elite, set the firm clearly apart from the crowd. To the outsider, BCS appeared to be something of a cult; loved by a few but loathed by many more who feared having to beat the same path.

James entered 'Euripides' in which a classical marble bust of the ancient tragedian playwright stared out dull-eyed from a softly lit recess. For the moment, he could observe nothing else remotely classical. His eyes scanned the room and he was struck by the images portraying the firm's philanthropy. The walls were adorned with chic natural wooden-framed black and white photographs of grinning African school children playing games. They were distantly familiar to him. He read the etched inscription below the largest digital print; 'St Patrick's School, Gisenyi, Rwanda - children at play'. He stared at the exuberant faces and remembered, before tearing away his gaze towards the far end of the room where a gigantic plasma screen dominated the wall. Below it, on top of broad maple sideboard, he spotted what he needed most at that moment.

He lifted the bulbous jet-black flask from its pristine silver tray and started to pour. He breathed deeply as the coffee's hot vapours escaped into the chilled air-conditioned room. He took a sip as he surveyed the rest of the room; an elliptical board table, maple naturally; tubular leather-backed chairs in varying soft hues of brown, beige and grey, probably of Italian design; and at the far end, sheltering in a corner, perched precariously open-paged on top of a tall glass rectangular plinth, an ancient looking and dog-eared copy of the *Bacchae*

101

paid homage to the minimalist classical pretensions of the firm. James approved of the room. It made sense to him; a nod to an ancient period but with the balance tilted firmly in favour of modernity and the future. The room's cool design and technology married to the most visible theme of helping the less fortunate, somehow exuded lavishness, restraint and generosity in equal measure. James reflected that it must have cost a small fortune simply to design and furnish this single room and wondered how many more lined the corridor. But then, he knew the firm and its partners were prospering.

He checked his watch and fiddled with his mobile, catching up on market movements and news alerts. A breathless Mark thundered through the door like an amateur thespian in a village hall farce. His melodramatic entrance clearly intended to communicate his senior status, and that his expensive time was at a premium. James proffered a firm handshake and a warm greeting, instead of an instinctive guttural laugh.

"Mark. Good to see you again."

"James. Welcome to our humble abode."

"You must be doing well."

"We're busy, frantic in fact. Always hiring but it's not easy to get the right staff."

"Well it's good of you to see me, at short notice."

"Well any friend of Caro's is a friend of ours. Terrible, what happened to her. Monumental injustice." Mark sighed dramatically. "But one is always exposed to the randomness of the legal system, no matter how well prepared. All it took was one rogue judge."

"Indeed. She doesn't know I'm here, by the way."

"Of course. Everything we discuss is confidential." Mark smiled reassuringly.

"Beautiful pictures." James gesticulated with a broad sweep of his hand. "Such joy on the faces; you must be very proud of what you've achieved."

"Yes, they are rather good. We've supported the school for about five years now. Witnessed vast improvements. We encourage our staff to raise funds by getting sponsored for a whole range of crazy ventures and then the firm provides a matching contribution. In fact, I ran the London marathon recently and raised about fifty thousand."

"Impressive. I bet you ran it in a decent time as well," said James swallowing a smile.

"Not too shabby. It was worth every aching muscle."

James noted how easily Mark had become myth-maker, bolstering his self-image. In his experience, such men convinced themselves that small lies didn't really matter, and oblivious to the habit, small lies grew into big lies. He was a master himself.

Mark continued as he poured himself a coffee. "I visited last year. It was one of the most humbling experiences of my life. These kids have so little and are so grateful for what we give to them; an education means a passport to a better life."

The runner had found his natural rhythm now, James thought. He was tempted to ask Mark what percentage of the firm's profits were committed to the project but guessed it would be a tiny fraction. Otherwise the figure would have been emblazoned across the firm's website. Then he scolded himself for being churlish. It was a lot better than doing nothing at all.

"That's what we believe at LifeChance too. Thank you again for your support at the gala dinner. Most generous." Mark had bid in the auction and written a hefty cheque.

103

"Don't mention it." Mark peeked at his watch and clapped his hands together. "Now the letter from the FCA you sent me. It's a standard opener from them. We must not at this stage reveal anything we might live to regret later."

"So, no need to worry?" James grimaced as he rhythmically tapped the table.

"Certainly not yet. We need to find out what they've got. They could just be fishing."

"You haven't asked me whether I'm innocent." James managed to maintain eye-contact without blinking.

"And I won't. It's not my job to prove your innocence. It's the FCA's job to prove your guilt. I want you to answer the questions I choose to put to you honestly and directly. But no more."

James started to feel he was in the hands of an accomplished expert, even if Caro now thought otherwise. "I see. May I help myself to another coffee?"

"Of course. One of my colleagues will be joining us shortly. His job will be to prepare you for the FCA's interview. It's pretty standard, so not worth your paying for my time. So, if it's okay, I'll dip out, and come back at the end to see how you've got on. We'll run through it all again just before the meeting next week."

Late afternoon, the Financial Conduct Authority's dazzling lobby was buzzing with human traffic. Sombre faces strode up to the reception desk, before picking up speed again, accelerating to an allocated meeting room. Lawyer, Stefanie Zuegel, a director within the FCA's Enforcement division was one of them. Her black heels added three inches to her leggy five-feet-nine figure. Below, a junior assistant scurried alongside, eager to be involved in her first forensic investigation, an 'Insider Dealing' case involving illicit share trading on the London Stock Exchange. Stefanie knew immediately she burst in to meeting room 14, interrupting the whispering, who bore the guilty face.

A pleasant faced man in his forties, stared up at her over the brim of his teetering coffee cup. His lawyer spoke first. Mark Phillips, pin-striped, pristine and passing for late thirties, introduced himself, his position and firm. Next, he presented his two younger colleagues and last, a blushing James Tait. The lawyers each fitted their on-line profiles: elite public school, Oxbridge and oozing entitlement from their privileged pores. She suspected smirking, as the junior lawyers, whispering, turned their backs and replenished coffee cups at the gloss-grey credenza. Despite her senior status, relative to them, she was poorly paid and a public servant. The youngest one gallantly offered to pour her a coffee. He overlooked her assistant entirely. She declined, politely. She anticipated they would under-estimate her: a woman, from a small town in Germany with a degree from a university they would not recognise. She intended to prove them wrong.

"Thank you for coming in today. As you know, Mr Tait," she started, " you are being interviewed under caution in connection with Part V of the Criminal Justices Act 1993, which deals with Insider Dealing and Market Abuse. You have received certain information from us already. "

"We have advised our client he should remain largely silent at his stage" Phillips interjected. She had expected that. They wanted to find out what evidence she had before committing themselves. Refusing to respond just underpinned guilt and if it came to trial, Tait would pay for it. The jury would question why an innocent man would not answer questions if he had nothing to hide. Stefanie nodded, and paused for a few seconds, whilst her assistant scribbled notes. She smiled grimly and then addressed Tait.

"The questions I ask now will be repeated in court. The jury may well question why a man claiming to be not guilty, chose not to answer them now."

"You need evidence before anything can come to trial."

She ignored Phillips and his patronizing smile, and held her gaze on Tait, whose glistening face reflected the recessed ceiling lights. "How well do you know Richard Ross, head of Mergers and Acquisitions at Goldwyn Morson?"

Phillips nodded to his client.

"He's an old colleague. We worked together for over a decade."

"You both lived in Chelsea. Do you socialise much together?"

Phillips nodded again. They had rehearsed this question too.

"Occasionally. A handful of times a year perhaps."

"Do you talk about the deals he is working on?"

"Never by name."

Phillips coughed eliciting an involuntary "sorry" from his client who should not have responded in that way.

" So, you do talk about deals?"

Phillips leant forward and raised his hand to stop Tait speaking. "My client and Mr. Ross have business in common. They talk in general terms, not about specifics."

Stefanie kept her gaze on Tait and thrust a sheet of paper across the table. "Please take a look." Stefanie had listed details of five takeovers of large public companies over the past year, in which Goldwyn Morson had been lead adviser. She knew that in each case, Tait had bought shares through LifeChance, several weeks before official announcements that

106

the companies were being acquired at substantial premia to the prices he had paid. Profits of almost £2.5m had been generated as a result.

Tait swallowed and looked to Phillips who nodded.

"I know of them, but not in any detail. They are well known corporate names. Anyone in investment banking would know them."

Stefanie emitted a dismissive grunt. These early interviews were always like *Strictly Come Dancing* without the celebrities, over-rehearsed dance routines that fell flat." And I presume you would know that Mr. Ross and his colleagues acted as advisers in each case, and as such possessed price-sensitive and privileged information?"

"Ms ...um, Stefanie. My client is managing director of a highly reputable charity. Likewise, Goldwyn Morson is a pre-eminent organisation, with rigorous compliance standards and strict policies preventing information leakage. I presume some of your colleagues carry out regular reviews of Goldwyn Morson's systems and are happy with them." Phillips ended with a smug smile.

Stefanie ploughed on, her eyes boring into Tait's. He had a boyish face, and a soft silky voice. He was leaning away from his lawyer, and she sensed he wanted to disown Phillips's latest riposte.

"Our statisticians have calculated that based solely on publicly available information, there is less than one chance in a million, that those share trades would have been made together."

Phillips sighed. "All most interesting but do you have any evidence at all that Mr Ross passed privileged information to my client, as a result of which, he bought those shares?"

Stefanie shifted her gaze to the pink silk handkerchief fanning out from Phillips' breast-pocket. She had an urge to blow her nose on it. "I was just coming to that."

She thrust several photocopied sheets on the table and drilled Tait with an inscrutable stare. He had a nice face. Blue eyes, straight-edged nose, perfectly symmetrical, and cupid-bow lips. "Perhaps, you can explain these."

Several copies of his credit card statements and four restaurant bills: each from *The Lofthouse*, a five-star modern British restaurant in Belgravia, and each for more than a thousand pounds. Tait blinked and looked to Phillips whose eyes barrelled down on the documentary evidence, his mouth grimly locked. She could tell, they had not expected this.

"Well okay, we must have met four times I guess over the past year. Richard is a bit of a foodie and loves his clarets." Stefanie had discovered from scrutinising Ross's digital diary, that he had met with James for dinner at regular intervals.

"You always pay." Stefanie pointed to the circled figures on the credit card statements.

"Could I have a moment with my client, please." For the first time, Phillips appeared bewildered, whilst his client appeared to grow in confidence, ignoring him.

"I do because he is a great supporter of LifeChance. Not only does he donate personally but he has assembled a giving circle of donors at Goldwyn Morson. We owe him a great deal."

Stefanie blinked. She had to admit that the explanation was credible, and she was sure it had not been rehearsed. Nevertheless, the pattern of share trades, spewed out by the FCA's artificial intelligence software, was too coincidental.

One side of the table stared across at the other, before Phillips broke the silence. "Unless there is anything else, I suggest we adjourn."

"I need a list of all the people in the giving circle, a list of all the people you know at Goldwyn Morson, with their contact numbers, a list of all the share dealings you have transacted, for yourself and LifeChance, over the past year, and all your diary entries for that period. "

"Naturally. Anything else you'd like?" Phillips's mouth twisted into a smile again. He slapped the table with his palms and stood up. She could tell he wanted the meeting over before his client went 'off piste' again.

"Almost certainly, after we have reviewed the information I have requested." Stefanie rose, picked up the papers and smiled at James. "We shall meet again soon."

They trailed in silence to the lobby. The frostiness at the end of the meeting had not thawed. They parted with curt farewells and cursory handshakes. Except for James. Had she imagined that he had lingered over their handshake? Had he not gripped her hand a little too long? He had smiled at her, only her, when they parted. Slow and generous, not the usual fleeting smile at a slant. And he had glanced back towards her as he reached the exit.

Chapter Seven   Beginnings

With the evening light fading, the revolving doors to the FCA's offices continued to whirl. James had been waiting for over an hour, watching the ebb and flow of visitors and employees, wondering what lay behind their frowns, and wishing he could take a peek as each checked their mobiles for messages. He spotted her upright, willowy figure marching across the concourse, clutching a small leather briefcase, and shouldering a black kit-bag. He leapt up from the bench, eyes fixed on the black bun as it bobbed up and down above the heads of the hordes pouring from the illuminated glass cathedrals of globalisation. He weaved through the crowd, scurrying until he had a clear view of her long legs. He moved up alongside her, matching her stride. She looked at him, turned away, and accelerated. By now he was almost running to the clatter of her heels on the pavement.

"Do you always walk this fast?"

"Do you always stalk women?"

"Only the ones I find attractive." He instantly wanted to disown his words. He was utterly useless at this game. He had misread the signals again. Yet he detected a slight softening in the rigid form of her lips, not quite a smile. She looked at him.

"Does your lawyer know you're here?"

"Mark? Of course not."

"What is your purpose?" He liked the sound of her Germanic diction, admired her precision and directness.

"How about a glass of wine?"

She stopped abruptly and turned to consider him, almost causing a pile-up as pedestrians fanned past them, staring sullenly. She seemed to be weighing up something.

"Fraternising with you would be regarded as a personal conflict of interest by our compliance department."

"I promise not to talk about the case." He sensed an unlikely chink of light as he matched her gaze. She pursed her lips and a small furrow appeared between her eyes.

"I have an aerobics class booked."

"Afterwards then."

She peered at her watch for a few seconds. Her mouth curved into a hint of a smile. "I prefer beer to wine."

"Great. I love beer too. There are plenty of bars around here." They had stopped just outside one and could hear the roar of workers casting off the tensions and frustrations of the day.

"No, not here. I will message you a venue. I will be there at nine." And she was gone, leaving James open-mouthed and wondering whether she meant it. Presumably she had his mobile number. He wondered what else she already knew about him.

Just before nine, James stood in front of a scruffy brick building with a torn awning, constructed beneath a railway arch near Waterloo station. Overhead trains rumbled past. He pushed through a battered door, and discovered a bevy of pot-bellied, middle-aged men and the odd broad-beamed woman, all sinking pints of ale. Their chatter and larking about competed well enough with the squealing wheels above. He looked at the perplexing run of beer taps along the bar. As the barman approached, he felt a tap on his shoulder and swivelled to find Stefanie standing there with a broad grin and an empty pint glass. Her long black hair hung loose, softening her angular face.

"I'd recommend the 'Old Boxer' - 4.3 ABV. I will have another please, barman." She handed over her glass.

"Right, same for me then." He felt flustered, out of his typical zone of upmarket bars or private members' clubs he frequented to pick up his market intelligence. He was clueless when it came to beer.

"I'm sitting there." Stefanie pointed to a table in the far corner. "Please bring my beer. If you are hungry, the food is passable. They have my card behind the bar."

"Okay," he smiled. James stared after her, then around the room, eyeing the pub paraphernalia, mirrors and chalk boards, hung on flaking painted plank walls. He spotted a few flashing games machines crammed along the edges and peered down at the worn beer-stained wood floor. He shuddered to think about the state of the lavatories and the kitchen. He'd pass on the food. He wondered whether the place was a theme pub or just plain grotty but decided not to risk asking the bearded behemoth behind the bar.

Stefanie was tucking into a mound of fish and chips. The first pint had gone to her head, and she felt emboldened. She didn't expect much from the evening but was intrigued. She had been surprised by James's approach, and despite knowing that professionally she was treading a dangerous line, had been tempted by his clumsy charm. The last time any man had shown real interest in her had ended badly. It usually did. Thirty-six, single, professionally successful, and lonely. It had been months, since she had updated her on-line dating profile, and over a year since she had bothered with a date. She had convinced herself she was too busy, too busy for games.

"Help yourself to a chip," she said as Mark slid the two pints across the stained wooden table. He wondered why they bothered with beer mats. A salt cellar and vinegar bottle swam in a slop of beer in the middle of the table.

"I shouldn't." He patted his stomach as he lowered himself onto a dark wooden chair covered in greasy red leatherette. The food smelt delicious.

"My mother would call you well covered." Stefanie chuckled and took a swig from her glass. "What would your mother call me?"

James flinched. He never talked about his mother to anyone. Not even Megan nowadays. Yet the nightmares still recurred. "In need of nourishment I imagine."

Stefanie snorted, with a mouthful of fish.

"Maybe just one," said James, stealing a chip.

"So, tell me - why did you give up investment banking?" She had clearly done her homework on him before the meeting.

James smiled a sigh. It was a question he had been asked many times after his 'Road to Damascus' moment. It was a long story, but with practice he had refined it to just a few words.

"The money was good but the price was too high." It was a line he stole from a Graham Nash song, or something like that. It usually did the trick.

"Go on." She speared another chip.

"It's a long story."

"Good. I have a full plate. I can listen. You can talk."

This was not how James had intended the evening to go. Usually he found the women he dated, began by talking about themselves, followed, after a few glasses, by a litany of failed relationships, and finished with an apology that they'd talked too much. It was only later, when being a good listener was not enough, when they tried to dig below his charming facade, that things fell apart. Megan was always urging him to share his feelings directly, rather than scuttling sideways like a crab evading its predator.

But was Stefanie merely trying to find out about him to help her win the case? Subconsciously was he trying to do the same in reverse? He either had to jump in or leave. Nothing else made sense. James fiddled with a beer mat as he plunged into a pool of memories he now referred to as his 'gap year'.

James couldn't identify the moment he first felt that his life had been hollowed out by spending it on stuff he no longer valued. Perhaps it was as he clicked into the second half of his thirties and started to look ahead to being forty, proper middle age. His few friends thought he was fine, and the married ones claimed they envied him - still young, successful in his career, wealthy, no strings. He had endured their label of 'eligible bachelor' and dutifully turned up at dinner parties to be matched with one of their friends. A string of dates had resulted, but after a couple of months, either he got bored or was dumped, usually because they said he would not open up, let them in, share his vulnerabilities. He had never let a single one of them stay overnight at his home.

He had excelled at Gladwyn Morson and they were shocked when he said he wanted to resign. He was at the top of his game, one of their key deal makers, earning him and the bank a fortune. They could not understand his reasons, understandably because neither could he. They rejected his resignation and put him on a year's sabbatical, hoping he would come to his senses after his travels. He had no clue where he was going but knew he had to escape somewhere, anywhere away from his present situation.

One day he turned up at Heathrow, looked up at the departures board, spotted a flight to Berlin and bought a one-way ticket. He moved around capitals of Europe visiting museums, architectural relics and art galleries, and lost interest. He flew to the USA, travelled around and got bored. He spent time in South America before escaping to Asia. By then, he was moving almost every day, never settling, always searching. He sampled the Middle East, but trouble flared up just as he arrived in Syria. So, he hopped on a plane to Africa and landed in Ethiopia. Clueless, he joined a group of seasoned independent travellers in a minibus tour to Kenya via South Sudan and Uganda. They assured him it would be safe, that all the fighting was over, that he would have fun.

The bus broke down near a village in Pibor County, a rural community in South Sudan where there had long been tribal tensions. Stranded there for several days, he was horrified by the poverty; people living in mud-floored thatched huts without running water or electricity, the sour stench of sewage lying around, and emaciated cattle with staring eyes idling nearby. Violence visited the town on his second day there.

At first, he didn't recognise the rattle of automatic weapons. But then, he heard the screams, saw the hundreds fleeing towards him, and spotted the machetes being wielded. He turned to run but tripped and found himself buffeted and trampled by the shrieking mob. He could smell smoke and to his horror, recognized the stench of burning meat, human flesh. For a while he lay still, remembering as a child how to play dead and started to count; and kept counting until he was sure that the bandana-wearing, machete-waving, high-on-hooch gang had passed on. Bruised and bleeding, unable to walk, he crawled to what felt like a grassy verge. He wiped grit from his eye and used his shirt to smear dirt from his face. He heard a child's voice, screaming, terrified, getting louder. Suddenly out of a cloud of dust, a pin-stick girl with white glaring eyes, shot towards him, buffeting him as the puny urchin threw herself into his lap. He heard the slap of footsteps, and a throaty laugh. Seconds later he was peering up into the broad smiling face of a child, no more than fourteen or fifteen, a magazine slung over his shoulder, carrying a machine gun in one hand and toying with a machete in the other.

"I'm in the wrong place at the wrong time, I've got no quarrel with you, any of you, and neither has she" he heard himself say, as put his arms around the cowering child in his lap. Sweat poured from him. He was unable to move and so had only words to defend himself. Words that this machete-wielding murderous boy could probably not understand.

"Me, English, British." He fumbled for his passport in his deep pocket and held it up. "English, British, Great Britain," he repeated. He threw a bundle of crumpled dollars at the boy who gathered them up. He was terrified, all over again. The boy stood there, grinning down at him, fingering his blade. Then he heard a man's shout and the boy turned his head and said something he did not understand. The boy raised the machete where it lingered. James found himself crying out to God, beseeching him to be spared and promising to be in the right place at the right time doing the right things for the rest of his life. He wrapped his arms around the child and squinted up to peer into the boy's face.

"Wayne Rooney," he said with a beaming smile and then he skipped away towards the sound of the calling voice.

James felt tears on his cheeks. He had been unaware of them till that moment. Tears of terror now mingled with tears of relief. He had been saved, not because he was a man, but because he was a white British-passport-carrying man, and that still counted for something, everything, even here in the darkness of a tribal civil war. The wonderful terribleness of this insight struck him almost immediately as the child unfurled her tiny body, glanced at him with her big eyes and scampered off. No-one had seen the most heroic act James had ever performed in his life. He felt terrible and exhilarated. He knew that he could stop travelling now, that he could do something useful, that his life could serve a purpose.

He didn't know what. Nor did the other terrified tour members when they regathered in shock. Witnesses to horror, their personal stories seeped from the stunned silence. They told and retold their tales of bloody carnage. By sunrise, by a smoldering camp-fire, talk got around to transforming their ordeal, their shared nightmare, into something positive. Over the next couple of days together, bumping along dirt roads, their plans took shape. A commitment was agreed upon to set up a charity for refugees back in the UK. Back home, within a couple of months of returning, personal commitments lost their contours. One by one, the tourists returned to their civilized lives of routine and security and consigned their experience in Sudan to the shadows. Only James remained true to the commitment. He had made a promise.

"Did you ever see her again?" asked Stefanie when he had finished speaking. She was leaning forward with her elbows on the table, next to her empty glass. Opposite a tidy mound

117

of cardboard squares torn from the beer-mat lay by James's half empty glass.

"Yes. Later that day, after the massacre had ended and people started to return to the village, she appeared with a woman, her mother I supposed. She smiled at me, they both did, magnificent, radiant smiles amongst all that carnage - dead bodies in the dust everywhere, and so many flies. The smell was awful."

"She had come to thank you, for saving her child?"

"She took the necklace from around her neck, yellow and purple, plastic beads, and gave them to me - probably her second most prized possession in the world. I never saw either of them again."

"You left?"

"The next day. The spare part for the bus arrived with the government's army. No point us staying. What use is an investment banker in that situation?"

"Or any situation," she said without a hint of irony. She studied his serious face for a second and burst out laughing.

James smiled and picked up her glass. "One for the road?"

"Thank-you but no. It has been fun, but I must be in the office early tomorrow." She sounded like her mother when as a child she had become too spirited and still had homework to get done. She had inherited her mother's habit of delayed gratification until all the work was done. The problem was that there was always more work to be done. She rose, gathered her coat from the back of her chair and picked up her kit-bag and briefcase.

"Okay. Me too, when I think about it. Breakfast with an investment banker who has some wonderful insider tips for me."

Stefanie froze for a moment. then saw the grin on his face and laughed. "Okay, I deserved that."

"Actually, I have a difficult board meeting I need to prepare for. Wish me luck."

They parted outside on the pavement with an awkward handshake and a glancing kiss on each cheek, like players who'd forgotten the rules of a game once played. She insisted that he should not contact her, but that she would be in touch. Should she stick or twist? Had she not earned the rare gratification of being desired by this warm, handsome man?

But to take it any further would be to risk her entire career. If discovered, she would be fired. How much did she care? She had toiled excessively to succeed at work. It had cost her so much. She had almost become her job. Nothing else seemed to identify her anymore. She had loved her job and believed she was doing something meaningful for the good of society. Yet, she was growing more frustrated and irritated at work with her new boss. He was barely older than her, had benefited from an unexpected promotion when his predecessor, her mentor, dropped dead from a heart attack. So now she answered to someone she regarded as a peer. Someone who thought his instincts made him a genius. Earlier that day, he had over-ruled her recommendation to pursue a case against a major investment bank. She had spent months assiduously compiling evidence and was convinced that the firm was guilty of breaching regulatory obligations. He waived away her arguments and chided her for being too blinkered and not seeing the big picture. What she could see was a man frightened of taking on a global organization with the deepest of pockets to hire a bevy of the brightest and best lawyers. He feared failure.

Perhaps it was time to find another job, and to invest in a cheap pre-pay phone. Even though a relationship was unlikely to develop with James, it would be better to play safe. Maybe, he wasn't being genuine, like others in the past. She would not allow her own mobile phone records to be used against her. If James's case ever reached court, she could imagine a defence barrister's twisted insinuations appealing to a jury. She would be disgraced.

The next morning, members of LifeChance's board were gathered in its large corner meeting-room. Floor to ceiling windows presented the distraction of a panoramic view during the duller moments. The city evaporated northwards into haze, and the Shard and Cheesegrater buildings disappeared into grey clouds. Despite the whisper of the air-conditioning, the humid overcast day seemed to be infecting the mood within the room. The meetings always made James jittery because he was no longer in control. As Chief Executive, he was legally accountable to the board, though he felt their oversight was a burden of dubious worth.

The final item on the agenda had led to animated and extended debate. James could tell from the frowning face opposite, that the chairman had severe doubts about investing the charity's funds in a gambling venture. Shahid Khan was a silver fox in his mid-sixties, physically attractive and immensely wealthy. He had sold his ingredients business to an international conglomerate and had now become part of the establishment, fully occupied with burnishing his reputation. With an MBE already pocketed, he had an eye on the upper house. It was rumoured that he had cut a few corners in his younger business-building days, but now his focus was on preservation, of his looks, physique and reputation. He threw money at them all. He ran his wife of forty years close on the number of tucks, and a personal trainer at an elite gym on Park Lane kept him trim. He was proud of his various philanthropic activities, all of which were accurately detailed in his Wikipedia entry and repeated ad infinitum in glossy magazine profiles. James had no doubt that his generous annual gifts to LifeChance would cease the moment he stepped down as non-executive chairman of the charity. His view mattered, particularly as he could sway the two younger non-executive members of the board, Ramesh and Roger.

"It's one hell of a risk and I have to question whether such a step is truly appropriate for a charity such as ours," said Shahid in his urbane manner. Following years of elocution lessons, his accent was languid and refined. When he arrived in the UK as a young man, he spoke Butler English badly.

"I think the risks are greatly mitigated by the quality of the management team we have put together. And the projected returns are game-changing for our organisation," said James, broadening his gaze to appeal to Ramesh and Roger.

"But early stage ventures are so challenging, so intense, so tough to succeed in such a competitive market." Shahid was holding court with his arms outstretched, feasting upon the room's attention. It seemed to James that Shahid was savouring the sounds of his own words. Maybe he had been practising the use of repetition, in preparation for use in the upper house one day.

"You always say, when the going gets tough, the tough get going," said James thumping the table synchronically and clamping his lips together to stifle a smile. James had won an office sweep-stake at their last annual staff dinner. Shahid had mentioned this, his favourite aphorism, five times during his motivational end of year speech.

"Perhaps we should take a brief comfort break," suggested Megan. The meeting had been going for a couple of hours, the air was hot and stale, and the coffee pots needed replenishing. General assent was accompanied by a squeal of chair-legs on the lacquered wood floor. James hung back whilst the other men headed for the toilets.

"You need to speak to him, one to one," said Megan. "He's wily. I bet he suspects you're not telling him something."

"You're right. But if I tell him too much, he won't go for it either," James removed his glasses and rubbed his eyes. "Necessary evils, these board meetings," He stood up, stifling a yawn. James set off in search of Shahid, whom he found loitering in the corridor checking messages on his mobile.

"Shahid..."

"This makes no sense. It's too risky. You're not telling me something," interjected the chairman.

"You're right." James hesitated, knowing he was walking a tightrope and could easily lose his balance. "I don't want to bury you in detail. I respect your position as a non-executive. I'm not sure you'd want to know absolutely everything."

Shahid blinked and the two men stared at each other. Shahid knew the game. He had pulled a few tricks in his career and he would have guessed that James had done his homework on him.

"I cannot be chairman of an entity where I know or have reasonable suspicions about anything improper going on." Shahid spoke slowly, picking his words like step-stones over a racing river.

"Of course not, and as chief executive, I will take full responsibility, should the board approve my plans."

"The board takes decisions based solely upon the information presented to it, and on the responses to its questioning. If something is omitted, it cannot be held responsible."

"Quite so," agreed James.

"It's a large investment. You know what I could achieve with five million pounds into my Mumbai slum projects." James had read about Shahid's largesse in a recent Sunday Times business article. He remembered the grinning faces of the small boys and girls, ragamuffin faced, as they crowded around Shahid's pristine white suit. His community projects, improving sanitation, housing and education had made him a hero in the Mumbai Muslim community whose slums were the bottom of the pile, often literally founded on municipal rubbish dumps.

"Caro has promised to chip in at least a couple of million to help," said James. She hadn't, nor had she yet agreed to support his plans. But there was no point worrying about that until and unless the board gave its approval.

Shahid lent in closely and whispered, "It's your neck if this goes wrong." He then turned away and drawn by the scent of fresh coffee, headed back to join the others.

As soon as Shahid started summing up the pros and cons of James's proposal, he knew his corridor chat had done enough. Like a skilled judge leading a jury, Shahid orchestrated the discussion to grant the necessary approval but without taking personal responsibility for the decision.

"Megan, you go first," said Shahid, confident that she would be a strong supporter. In fact, Megan had severe reservations which she had debated in private with James and was not in favour. But her loyalty to him, trumped that.

"It's a big risk, so are the potential rewards. I'm in," was her pithy response.

"Ramesh?" The twenty-one-year old was a poster boy for the charity. A refugee from Kashmir, trekked four thousand miles before landing at Dover aged sixteen, frightened and alone in the back of a tropical fruit truck. LifeChance fought for him to stay, paid for English lessons, and used its professional network to provide internships and assist with university applications. He was just about to graduate from Warwick University with a first in International Business and had a job lined up for a global accountancy firm. As a LifeChance alumnus, he'd contribute five per cent of his salary to the charity. He was in awe of James, who had been his personal sponsor since his arrival.

"I agree. It is very exciting and can make a huge contribution to our causes. We all have to take risks if we want to get somewhere," said Ramesh.

Shahid nodded to Roger, the final member of the board. James knew he could be tricky. He was fiercely bright, independently minded and unpredictable. Roger Feinstein was the son of a Jewish émigré, who like James's mother, had arrived in Britain from Berlin on Kindertransport in 1939. Roger headed his own currency trading operation and managed funds for some of Caro's clients. His wiry frame twitched non-stop as he sat at the board table, fiddling with a pen and drinking endless cups of coffee.

"I'd like to know what you think," Roger said rocking back in his chair and spearing Shahid with a stare. Shahid smiled condescendingly and straightened his Reform Club tie.

"Chairman's privilege to speak last," said Shahid. "I would not wish to sway the jury."

Roger scowled. "You won't sway me, but no matter." Roger swallowed a mouthful of coffee, his prominent Adam's apple rising above his open neck shirt. James waited

124

nervously. Under their articles of association, he needed four members to vote in favour on any matter associated with gambling. He thought it ironic that the charity's share dealing activities were considered otherwise, not requiring board approval.

"If we invest five million and we believe your forecasts, we make twenty-five times our money. I put the chances at less than five per cent, so maybe that is a fair equation. However, if we're forced to put in further money, which everyone knows is normal, then our multiple will fall. I am not in favour of that." Roger took a sip from his cup and eyed James over the rim

"You appear to be sitting on the fence," Shahid interjected with a thin smile.

"Not at all," said the currency trader used to taking positions of extreme risk with billions of dollar value each day. "I would approve the five million pounds on condition that we inject no further. All the rest of the funding must come from other investors, as indeed you project. If you fail to do that, then we walk away, lose our five million, cap our downside." James felt a small victory fusing inside of him. He could live with that qualification, at least today. Maybe he would have to fight it again on another day.

"That said," continued Roger, " I do not believe the board should proceed with such a non-strategic investment if the chairman is opposed to it. He is the public face of LifeChance and may be called upon to justify its actions." He was not allowing Shahid a free ride. James's stomach tightened a notch as he turned his gaze to appeal to Shahid.

"Thank you," said Shahid and without faltering proceeded to hold forth for several minutes with a speech that James was convinced had been prepared and rehearsed. "So, in a nutshell, based solely upon the information presented to the board, I do not find myself in a position to give a green light but neither am I saying it's a red light," he finished.

"You appear to be sitting on the fence," said Roger with a smirk.

"Not at all, young man," Shahid bit back in a patronising tone. "I am merely not ready to jump off the fence until we have more due diligence and research done."

James's face reddened. He had told them that a firm go-no go decision had to be taken at the meeting or else the small gambling company proposed as the platform would be sold to another bidder. He was stuck in the middle of a spat between generations and a Jew versus a Muslim. "Look, we need to take this decision today, or else the deal is off," insisted James.

"And I am happy that you have the requisite board majority to proceed. I am not against it. I am merely abstaining from the vote at this stage."

"But are you happy to defend it in public if called upon?" said Roger.

"A chairman is called upon to do many things and must always act in the best interests of the institution, putting aside personal opinions as necessary. "

What a slippery fish, thought James, now admiring the performance. "I need to make a call in the next half an hour or we lose the deal," said James, sensing the momentum was back with him.

Roger nodded curtly and Shahid announced that the deal could proceed.

With no further business, the meeting broke up almost immediately. James walked a sulking Roger to the lift and thanked him for his support. He had to remember that despite the frustrations they caused him, the non-executive directors were all unpaid and gave their time, and indeed money, because they believed in the charity. He now needed to call Caro before the chairman got to her.

Chapter Eight   Playtime

Mark heaved his tired body out of his Porsche, parked by the windmill on Wimbledon Common. His mood matched the pencil drawn sky, mostly clouded, muted and monochrome. It had felt like a long week, not helped by the two-hour conference call with their New York affiliate firm, which had achieved nothing other than delaying the start of his weekend. The kids were already tucked up in bed by the time he had got home the previous evening. He had cracked open one of his Gran Reserva Riojas and finished the bottle. Cath had gone to bed early after supper to read, so he'd uncorked another bottle. Cath was snoring by the time he had lurched into their bedroom and flopped into bed sometime after midnight.

"Morning!" shouted a one-footed Thomas stretching a quad on a grassy verge. "Fancied a lie-in, did you?" Mark peered at his *Garmin* watch. It was 7.35 on a Saturday morning. Only bleary-eyed dog walkers, insomniacs and middle-aged runners bothered the Common's flora and fauna at this time.

"Thought you could do with the extra stretching time, you being so much older than me," said Mark, leaning against the car-park barrier to stretch his calves. His joints were tight, and his muscles ached. He had ignored Thomas's advice to rest or at least slow down after his disastrous marathon. His failure to complete still burned.

Thomas grinned. "Well I'm up for the hour loop. Think you can manage that?"

Mark wished he hadn't made the quip. He knew Thomas would punish him later in the run, urging him on up the rises. He was already envisioning the final ascent up the rutted mud-track by the graveyard. His lungs would be screaming, and his ears would refuse to listen. "Just about. The legs are a bit tired still, and maybe I shouldn't have drunk the entire bottle last night, and I'm a bit worried about my left achilles."

Thomas smiled. They both understood the rules of the game. Get your excuses in early so you're never shamed. "Recovery run then. Nice and gentle."

Mark returned the smile. This was code for starting a bit slower, ratcheting up the pace in the middle, and finishing with a mile at ferocious pace. It was going to hurt. And later he would tell Cath what great fun it had been, and she would shake her head, non-plussed.

Thomas peered up into the sky and laughed. "Don't you just love running in the rain. So refreshing." It had started to drizzle warm rain.

Mark scowled and set his watch. They headed off through a woodland of oak, silver birch and beech trees, down a steep hill to Queensmere pond. The canopy of giant mature trees shielded them till they reached the pond's edge. Drizzle had turned to steady rain, and the pitter-patter of the deluge on leaves mingled with their chatter. Mark sucked in the pungent aroma of the wet earth under-foot. He was beginning to feel a bit better.

"How's work?" said Thomas, as they trudged along.

Mark ran through his usual frustrations with the firm's irritating bureaucracy, his annoying clients and politicking colleagues. He finished by boasting in a small way about his involvement in the firm's pro-bono work for charities. He told Thomas about meeting with James Tait and his charity, LifeChance.

"Do you realise that thousands of kids get trafficked into the country every year? It's a scandal. And the government don't want to find them, because then they'll have to take care of them. It costs about fifty thousand a year to keep a child in foster care."

"Sounds awful," agreed Thomas. "Our kids are so lucky." The conversation drifted onto their respective families as they burst out onto open heath-land, carpeted in purple moor grass and mustard-yellow gorse. A large, brown-speckled bird floated above them.

"Look at that buzzard," said Thomas pointing.

"Yes" Mark panted, finding the pick-up in pace a challenge and not caring one way or the other what bird was above them. He was counting down the minutes of their running hour, steadfastly hanging-on, but trying not to show it. He'd let Thomas do the talking for a while.

"Did you know they mate for life?" Thomas continued. "No infidelities, totally loyal. Bit rough if the pair don't get-on I suppose. Like being a Catholic, no divorce allowed. I wonder if that makes buzzards Catholic? Maybe they have a pope too."

Mark grunted. He was so intent on matching Thomas's loping strides, that he was barely listening. His face was twisted in a grimace, and his eyes stared straight ahead. He was blowing hard and sweat dripped from his chin. They still had half an hour of their loop to go. He was paying the price for the times when their roles had been reversed, when Thomas had clung on to Mark's punishing pace as if his life depended upon it. It was his turn. He would simply have to endure the aching lungs and the pounding in his chest.

Slowly, Mark's agony eased. Either the endorphins had rushed to save him, or Thomas had imperceptibly eased the pace. By the time they were skirting Rushmere pond, on the edge of Wimbledon village, Mark could squeeze out short sentences rather than grunt single words between his panting breaths. They had reached the safe harbour of football chatter and harmonic moaning about the lamentable management and performance of Fulham. The rain had stopped, and they were alone, apart from the dragon-flies hovering over the water and the swifts swooping down for breakfast.

"You know, they have Koi carp in this pond, somewhere under all those rushes."

"Really? How'd they get there?" said Mark. He had always secretly admired his friend's treasure-chest of curious facts. Facts that weren't of any practical use, and so slipped like quicksilver from Mark's mind.

"Who knows. A bit like your blood test."

Mark cast him an oblique glance and kept running without breaking stride.

"I checked up. The results were yours, no mix-up. A bit of a puzzle."

Mark reckoned that Thomas probably thought he had taken steroids, to cheat his way to a better performance. When they had spoken about it at the clinic, he too had been mystified. Days later, driving home, the recollection of Eva handing him her sports-drink bottle struck him like a dart between the eyes. He lost concentration, before screeching to a stop at a pedestrian crossing, drawing glares from two mothers crossing with their toddlers. Since then, his mind had re-examined the possibility over and over. It still made no sense, but he could think of no other explanation.

"I've been thinking about that." Mark told him about the woman who had shared her drink with him during the race, when he was feeling in dire need of a boost. He explained he had got chatting to her during the build-up, that she had run alongside him, and ultimately had surged ahead of him. He did not say that she was an attractive woman in her twenties, that he fancied her and that he had given her his mobile number.

"Well, she was taking a huge risk. Given the mineral deficiency in your blood, if she was drinking that stuff the whole way through, I wonder how she didn't keel over as well." Mark had been brooding on that all week too.

"I didn't actually see her drink from the bottle she gave me. She had another one." Even running side by side along the rutted path beneath the avenue of London plane trees, he could sense that Thomas was wearing his incredulity face with the protruding bottom lip and flared nostrils. "I know. I don't understand it either. Why would anyone?"

The twittering of birds and drone from traffic along Parkside filled the awkward silence between them. They turned into the heart of the common, picking their way through the low growing shrubs of the grassland. They accelerated as they headed for the final ascent past the cemetery, up Stag Ride to Curling Pond with its croaking frogs. With heaving lungs and legs laden with lactic acid, they turned with relief onto the flat, dirt-track back to the windmill.

"If I was you, I'd want to find out for sure what happened with that woman," said Thomas. "Can you track her down?"

Mark swiveled his head towards Thomas. His friend still wore his quizzical face, its furrowed brow struggling to rationalise what Mark had told him.

"Maybe," was as much as Mark wanted to concede at this point. "I remember her first name, and there is a list of finishers on the marathon website. I can start there."

That same May morning, over the river and across town, in Hyde Park, children were running and shrieking, whilst bleary-eyed parents yawned and read snatches from voluminous newspapers. Caro and James sat in rain-coats on a park bench, sipping from cardboard cups. Olly and Rosie, wrapped up in padded parkas, dashed in and out of the pirate ship in the Diana Memorial Playground. Six-year-old Rosie sprinted to a slide, frantically trailed by Olly. Just like he had pursued Caro almost forty years ago, James thought. In so many ways, he was pursuing her still.

"This stuff is barely drinkable," said Caro wincing at the bitterness of the coffee."

"I'll have yours if you don't want it."

"Bugger off - I need something to wake me up ... Rosie, let him go up first and stand behind him," Caro shouted. "She's such a good girl - always does what I say."

"Don't we all," said James, before taking a gulp from his cup. "Listen, I've been mulling over your request - another ruse to test our special friend."

"The Weasel. Good."

"We know he's an ambitious sod. Sees himself as a future leader of his firm. A tainted reputation would ruin his chances."

"Sounds interesting. Go on."

133

"Well you mentioned a while back that you were still niggling over his legal bill."

"That's right. He asked for just over a million - which is bloody criminal. Said they had more than that on the clock."

"So, you've not agreed it then?"

"Almost. Got them down to seven-fifty. A lawyer friend said that was a reasonable deal. So I thought, do I really want to go through the whole drawn out process of arbitration and audit. Dealing with the e-mail exchange has been tedious enough already, let alone having to speak with the obsequious toad."

"Do you have that deal in writing?"

"Just waiting for their confirmatory letter and a revised invoice now."

"But you've not formally accepted it, or put anything in writing?"

"No but for the sake of moving on, I did indicate to the Weasel that I was minded to agree. Course, he thinks we're still best friends. Idiot."

"Excellent," said James, gleeful. "So, you've not actually paid it yet then?"

"Erm, some of it. I think I've paid about five hundred or so on account ...Olly, be nice," Caro hollered, watching her son jostle with another boy in the line for the slide.

"It's dog eat dog out there," laughed James.

"He'll learn soon enough when one of them clumps him."

"Well, back in our fantasy world, I have a rather devilish plan. When you get the confirmatory letter from his law firm, ignore it. Ignore any reminders, which are bound to come from their accounts department. Keep ignoring them and be unavailable if the Weasel calls, and do not respond to emails, until they start threatening to take legal action."

"That's just childish-"

"Wait, I haven't finished yet. Whilst ignoring their reminders, you pay the quarter of a million or whatever you still owe into the Weasel's personal bank account. Dribble it in over a couple of months in three or four instalments."

"What just to cause him hassle?" said Caro with a frown.

"Hopefully if my plan works, a very great deal of hassle. You see there's a decent chance he won't even notice your payments into his account. Big city law firm partners share out millions amongst their partners at this time of year and most lawyers I know are hopeless at managing their own financial affairs."

"I still don't get it."

"At the point they threaten to sue for the debt, you send an indignant response to their accounts department, pointing out that you have already settled their bill and providing details of the payments including the Weasel's bank account and sort code numbers."

"But won't they simply get him to transfer the funds over to them?"

"Not without asking some interesting questions within the firm first. For example, why had he given you his personal account details? Why hadn't he redirected the money to the firm already? They might even begin to wonder whether he had agreed to a reduction in the fees charged in exchange for other payments into his personal account. They are bound to insist on a thorough investigation."

"Surely they'll just assume I made a mistake."

"Not if you refuse to talk to them or communicate with them on the matter. Why should you? After all, by then they would have treated you shabbily with their regular reminders and threats."

"Hmm, doesn't sound very...Olly, will you leave that poor boy alone!"

"Look, worst case for you is that he notices you have paid funds into his personal account at which point you simply say your accounts department has made an error. Best case is the firm starts questioning the Weasel's integrity or at least his organisational abilities. Hardly the sort of person you would want leading your firm one day."

"Your plan, which I doubt will work anyway, suffers from a fundamental flaw. I don't have the Weasel's bank account details."

"But I do. At our charity ball last year when you introduced me to him, he took a table. He also wrote a cheque to LifeChance that evening, ten thousand pounds for one of the auction prizes, a week in a Tuscan villa. We keep copies of all the cheques we receive."

Caro nodded and half smiled. "I still don't think it'll work."

"But worth a try?"

Caro sighed. "I suppose so...Oh now what? Here he comes, bawling his eyes out. I knew it. Boys. You never learn."

Chapter Nine　　　Stefanie

James stifled a yawn as he peered over Megan's shoulder and lingered on a view of St Paul's Cathedral in the distance. He was looking forward to the choral concert there that evening with Stefanie, in support of the Lord Mayor's charity appeal. When he had suggested Bach, she had quipped that she preferred Iron Maiden, but if there was dinner afterwards, she would endure the torture of St John's Passion.

"James, why are you smiling? What's so funny?" Megan sat across the small circular table in his office, her finger stabbing a corner of a spreadsheet of numbers. She had recast the year's forecast showing a deficit of two million pounds by the year end. Her second spreadsheet showed a breakeven position but required a cessation of the new centre opening program and some headcount reductions in the office. She had just presented her cost reduction plan in detail.

James blinked back to the moment and straightened his face. "Sorry but there just has to be another way." He tapped the spreadsheet in front of him and ran his index finger along the bottom row of bracketed numbers. They didn't change. He remembered as a child the magic colouring books where the pictures would appear in different shades as he dabbed a wet finger across the page. He needed to create some magic.

"I've looked at everything. Unattractive maybe, but this is our best option right now."

"What about the money Caro is providing for WinBet? Couldn't we divert some of that?" Caro had agreed to stump up five million pounds to fund the betting operation deal approved by the board. But only as a bridge loan until James managed to lure the twenty million pounds from venture capitalists he had promised the non-executives that he would deliver.

"Doesn't help. With WinBet's current cash burn rate, that will last six months. It won't even get us to the year end."

"What if we raise the money earlier?"

"What if we don't?"

James leant back in his chair and pinioned his hands to the back of his head. He breathed deeply catching a trace of Megan's floral scent. They stared at each other for a few seconds. The rumble of a jet overhead mingled with the clunk of his printer which had sprung into motion. He had no clue how either worked. But he understood how deals worked.

"I can't ask Caro again."

Megan shrugged. "So what do you suggest?"

"I think Acorn TechVen has to come up with the cash. Hand over WinBet with a cash cushion. We could channel that into LifeChance." Acorn TechVen, the owners of WinBet, was a global venture capital firm with offices in Silicon Valley and London. They had agreed to hand over the shares of the loss-making company for a pound and to fund it until the month's end. Otherwise, they had maintained that they would place the company in receivership and walk away without any further financial obligations.

"They won't do it. They have been clear throughout our negotiations that they are unwilling to commit more funds to the company. They've written off twenty-five million already." Megan's voice had risen an octave. She had been the one doing the negotiations whilst James remained in the background.

"I think they will. They have a three-billion-dollar fund. An injection of three million would be invisible to their investors. And this way, they avoid all the bad publicity of one of their investments going bust. And they avoid endless, embarrassing conversations with their investors about what went wrong."

"Three million?"

"Well ask for four or five even, then settle at two, no less. That way they feel they've won something."

"And what reason do I give for us renegotiating? We've done all our due diligence and told them there are no material issues."

"Anything. Tell them our assessment of the market has changed, that we will have to sink more into marketing before we reach cash break-even."

"And when they say no to us, are you happy to walk away?" For the first time during their session, James detected the faintest relaxation of Megan's mouth, an innuendo of a smile. She had been clear from the outset that she thought the WinBet acquisition was foolhardy, that James was risking too much, and endangering all they had achieved. But as ever, she remained loyal.

"We walk away first and tell them we will only do a deal if they inject cash into the business." James anticipated that they would bluster for a few days but would revert with some form of counter-offer. He recalled an old colleague at Goldwyn Morson whose mantra had been that you had a to walk away from a deal three times before you got a good deal. Times had changed, but not that much.

"But if they refuse, we still have a two million hole to fill."

"Indeed. Then we'll have to find a different solution."

"Okay." Megan sniffed and made a show of gathering the papers from the table. She had been assiduous in working out the detail of her cash saving plan yet James had barely considered it. He was intent on pursuing his growth path no matter what. "I'll put these back in the drawer till then." Her fleeting smile belied the scowl on her face. She thrust back her chair and leapt up.

"Just a minute. There's one other thing. I haven't mentioned this to Caro, not yet, but I will, if I have to, at the right time." James paused, waiting for Megan to sit down. "I was called in by the FCA last week. They wanted to question me about some of our share trading."

"Oh no. You promised not to bring Eva into any of this."

"And I won't. I promise. They have no evidence. I've hired Mark Phillips. He says they have no case."

"Well how comforting. The Weasel who always gets it right says it'll be fine." James realised Megan's shrill sarcasm shrouded the trepidation that her daughter could be implicated in a criminal act.

"I promise-"

"You can't. You can't possibly control everything James. Can't you see the risks you're running. You're endangering others and putting LifeChance itself in jeopardy."

James bowed his head and sighed. He concluded now would not be a good time to tell her that he was dating the prosecuting lawyer.

James sat sipping coffee, flicking the pages of Bone, Cumberbatch and Smith's glossy brochure replete with go-getting images of model lawyers in mid-flow - perfect teeth, perfected frowns, perfectly tailored suits. All perfectly plausible until you met the real thing. He glanced at his watch

140

again. Lawyers and doctors, he reflected as he waited, valued their time highly and everyone else's barely at all. He'd finally made it to the 'Sophocles' meeting room, after his previous visits to 'Euripides' and 'Aesychlus'. 'The Three Giants' of Greek Tragedy and here he was in the middle of one of his own creation.

He scanned the room again. It was like all the others, same colour combinations and furniture, a classical marble bust, and more framed photographs of school children in Rwanda. His gaze fixed on a picture by the door - black children, beaming and robust looking, surrounding an incongruous limp white adult, a representative of the firm no doubt. He looked nothing like the images in the brochure.

The door burst open with Mark pouring out apologies for his tardiness, and his pallid assistant following with a bundle of papers in his arms. "Don't get up. Water please Justin. Never enough hours in a day."

"Well as long as they're all chargeable" James grinned. They had discussed fees at their last meeting when Mark had explained they had used up all the year's pro bono hours allocated to LifeChance. James had committed to pay the fees personally.

"Ha ha. I'll be able to provide you with an estimate once we know whether the FCA decides to pursue the case through the courts."

"Have you spoken to the FCA again?"

"Several times. They have started to interview the people on the list you provided. Well done. I've never seen such a long list. That will keep them busy for a while." James had compiled a list of more than fifty names and had buried Eva's name in the middle. He had been correct in guessing that Mark would leave it to his assistant to review the list in detail, name by name.

"What we need to do now is to cross refer the names with your diary entries for the past two years." James peered at the thick paper pile on the conference table. "It's always better to work off hard copy. You miss things with digital."

"How long will this take?" James frowned and glanced at his watch. He was meeting Stefanie in two hours.

"Depends on what we find, but you'll need at least a day with Justin." The young man blinked but otherwise retained an inscrutable look.

"You won't find anything," James said shaking his head, "so what's the point?"

"We have to be thorough. It will be worth putting in the time now." My time not yours, my money not yours, James thought.

"And what about the share trades? Are they at least happy with the data I sent?" James's doodling spiraled around the pad on which he had not written a single note.

"They want more. Probably a good sign that they didn't find what they wanted. They want to go back three years."

"Three years! That will take us ages to review." It had taken a full day with Justin to go through the last twelve months' trading. Two more days and in Justin's case, nights as well, when he summarised his notes. Long hours, loads of money, no life. No wonder the poor chap looked ill. James recognised the path he too had trudged.

"We have no choice if we're to fight this case."

"So you think they have a case?"

"They have no hard evidence linking you to trading in shares based on inside information."

"That's not what I asked."

142

"They appear to have strong circumstantial information but in my view that is insufficient to secure a conviction."

"So if, or rather when they find nothing, they are unlikely to take the case to court?"

"That's a hard question," said Mark with a wince. "In the past, I would have been confident that they would drop the case. But ever since Caro's trial, they seem to have become much more aggressive. There was a leadership change at the FCA. And the government wants to be seen to be tough. It buys votes. Joe Public thinks the rich are all tax dodgers and scammers who've been getting off scot-free. No-one's allowed to love the City now. It's toxic."

James knew all this but didn't want to hear it. He knew Mark had been caught out by the sudden shift in the political environment. They had discussed Caro's case and Mark had been surprised by the decision of the jury. And he had been astonished by the judge's summing up and sentencing. And subsequently shocked that the judiciary, a bastion of objectivity, rationality and stability, appeared to bend to the will of their political masters. Lawyers' cocktail parties buzzed with chatter about the new paradigm. James could see that the new environment was keeping Mark busy. Not surprising given his reputation as one of the top white-collar crime lawyers, despite losing Caro's highly public case. The result proved the old adage - 'there's no such thing as bad publicity.

"So, we're in for the long haul I suppose."

"Unless you want to plead guilty. Not that I would recommend that. Three investment bankers were recently sent down for five years." Mark gulped down the last mouthful of water, whilst Justin rediscovered his knuckles.

James wondered if this was the standard test, the point in proceedings with the clients when they were off guard, defences down and as transparent as the *Evian* bottle in his hand. Pointless. He shaped a slow wry smile and waited for Mark to put down his glass. "How can I plead guilty when I'm not?"

Mark grabbed the arms of his chair and sprang up. "Good. Then I'll leave you in Justin's capable hands. No point you paying for my time as well."

"That, we can agree on," said James, certain now that his hoped-for trickle of fees would become a torrent, flowing into the great pool of profits for the partners of Bone, Cumberbatch and Smith.

Stefanie stood lofty on the top step outside St Paul's peering down and scanning the chattering mass. A smartly dressed crowd, feisty from the City or fresh from the suburbs thronged over the approach and streamed into the cathedral's cool, cavernous body. The sun's lengthening rays shone on the remaining step dwellers, as they waited patiently for the security lines to die down, and she waited for James to arrive. Stefanie peered over the top of her new *'Ray-Bans'* but she still couldn't spot him. She had been on time, precisely. And he was late, imprecisely so. She once again opened her *Givenchy* handbag to retrieve her mobile to message James. With just a few minutes to go before the official start of the charity concert, she had decided it was okay, and not too 'Germanic'. She didn't want to admit it, but she was nervous.

Then she saw him, fifty metres away, half running half walking, his briefcase banging against his thigh and his left arm pumping the air. As he drew closer, she could see his strained face, shiny from sweat, and his head moving from side to side as he searched for her. She laughed to herself. He was nervous too. Finally, he caught sight of her waving and scampered up the steps.

"Sorry I'm late. Bloody lawyers," he panted. "Not you of course."

She laughed. "I think you need to sit down. Let's go in." They joined the diminishing bag-check line and entered the nave, gloriously cool and dimly candle-lit.

Stefanie gawped at the cavernous baroque interior and the vast statue of Wellington as they hurried to their seats under the dome. Always men, often on horses, leading other men in war to glory, to their death or wherever, thought Stefanie. As she shimmied along the row to her seat, she gazed wide-eyed up into the ornately painted dome, and then the vaulted ceiling of the eastern apse, decorated with mosaics, high above the quire and altar. She had been to St Paul's as part of her school's foreign exchange program and had always meant to return. But somehow, now suddenly inexplicable to her, she had never found the time. Now it had found her, in a most unexpected form.

The Dean's welcome, opening-up of the cathedral for hosting charitable events was unlike her memories of the Lutheran church she attended as a child. But the opening prayers took her back to that old feeling she had not dwelled upon since teenage years. She still felt conflicted, part of her feeling stupid for aping those around her, as the congregation stood with closed eyes seeming to pray. And part of her still wanted to belong, to believe there was a god, something more than she was yet capable of sensing. Out of the corner of an eye, she saw that James was deep in closed-eye contemplation. Then suddenly she heard 'Amen' followed by the clamour of people sinking onto their chairs.

145

She had a spectacular view of the robed choristers now standing in their ancient carved stalls. Accompanied by a small chamber orchestra, the performance began in a flurry with a baton-waving grey-haired man. His entire body jerked with passion and energy that challenged the living to embrace his fervor, and the dead to rise from the crypt below.

It was her first visit to a choral concert just as it was the first time, she had dated someone she was supposed to be prosecuting. She shifted on her hard seat. She had not lost her childlike inability to sit still for long. She feared she could be facing a couple of uncomfortable hours. Her eyes roved up and around her. She marveled at the huge organ, the abundant artwork and gilded niches that shone in the dim light. Gradually, the music and the choir voices seeped into her. The harmonies becalmed her as she found herself immersed in the movement's rhythms and waves. To her surprise, she discovered the sound of the voices in German were beguiling.

"You fell asleep," whispered James as they shuffled towards the great west gate exit, trailing hundreds of bobbing heads.

Stefanie's gaze lingered on the columns, cornices and candelabras flanking the nave. "Was I snoring?" she asked in a tone that led several people to turn their heads towards her. "I'm a very capable snorer."

"More snuffle than snore. Off-beat syncopation mainly. Surprised Bach hadn't already thought of it."

"I hope the audience appreciated my efforts." Stefanie turned to him and smiled.

"Well they certainly clapped loudly at the end." It was James's turn to smile.

Outside, her hand felt his, as he threaded a path down the steps, where groups had gathered. His hand felt dry and warm and comforting. She could get used to hands like that, she thought. For a fleeting moment she imagined his hands caressing her, her face, her breast and down to her thighs. Then just as quickly she stopped, reminding herself of her three-date rule before she slept with a man. But had it really achieved anything, she wondered? Here she was, accelerating into late thirties with a sex life as arid as a communion wafer. And this attractive man appeared to like her. He had been persistent in arranging the date. Why? Maybe he just wanted to undermine her, to steer her away from prosecuting? Then when the case was dropped, drop her.

"I hope you're hungry," said James as they reached the street. The traffic idled, facing west down Ludgate Hill, against a sapphire blue sky. Tail lights blinked red.

"Ravenous." It had been a fine day and they could feel the heat rising from the road as they crossed St Paul's Churchyard and headed to Peter's Hill. "Where are we going?" This was a part of the city with ancient narrow streets that she had rarely trod.

"I've booked the *Oxo Tower* over the river. We've got a table on the terrace. Great view of the cathedral."

"Great beer too I hope." She chided herself for not saying, "that sounds wonderful." She was trying too hard to be entertaining company. Just be nice.

James laughed. "I believe the bar serves an array of alcoholic beverages."

They skipped down the steps onto the pedestrian walkway. Directly ahead, in the distance over the river, she could see the lit-up Tate Modern, the old power station's brick tower reaching for the sky. She had always loved the building and its modern art collections. She had spent many otherwise lonely wet Sundays, sauntering around its giant interior, seeking solace in surrogate company of fellow visitors.

The river opened out the moment they reached Millenium Footbridge. She had fallen for the bridge after learning about its 'wobbly' epithet. She decided to see for herself and remembered bouncing over it, like a free fairground attraction. Even now after visiting the Tate, she liked to skip over it, feeling the vibrations resonate up and down her limbs as she pounded the aluminium walkway. She found it quaintly British that engineers had fixed it, and yet the wobble persisted. German engineers would have fixed the wobble and ended the fun.

"Come on. Race you to the middle," Stefanie shouted, and clattered onto the bridge, narrowly avoiding an alarmed pedestrian. She had forgotten she was wearing studded heels rather than her weekend trainers, and her progress ended abruptly in a heap of flailing limbs. The fall gave her bruises but what hurt more was the sight of James grinning back at her from mid-point after she had picked herself up.

"Thanks for being such a gentleman," she said with a risible sneer as she approached him. "I would have beaten you in my trainers."

"Don't be a sore loser."

"I didn't lose. I opted out."

"You can't opt out."

"My game my rules."

"Your rules gave you a five metre head start. Hardly fair."

"Life isn't fair. Didn't your mother teach you that?" She could tell by the way his face froze that she had said something wrong. James grunted something inaudible, leant against the metallic railing and stared upriver. She joined him, hands

148

sliding along the smooth tubular handrail, close to his. Quiet, apart from the distant thrum of the city. A pair of trains seemed to merge entering the station on Blackfriars rail bridge.

James turned around, and looked downriver towards the dazzling Shard skyscraper, soaring heavenwards like a futuristic spire. Beyond, cars and buses hummed across London Bridge. Further downstream, the bascules of the illuminated Tower Bridge were closing as the dark shadow of a ship faded away. The castle's high walls lurked in the dying dusk. A police boat, its blue light flashing, chundered white wakes towards them. A light breeze brushed their cheeks, a balm after the heat of the day.

"Don't worry - you won't end up in the Tower," quipped Stefanie, filling the silence between them.

"With you on my case, how can I not be worried?"

"Good point, but I thought we agreed -" Stefanie began.

"Sorry. I promise not to mention the case again. James took a deep breath and pointed to a ferry leaving Bankside Pier. "What a wonderful way to commute to work."

"I love seeing all these bridges. I grew up in a small town in Northern Germany, and we had two: one for trains and one for cars. I used to spend hours watching the trains crossing or just what was happening on the river - the Weser."

"The river Weser deep and wind, washes the wall on the southern side."

Stefanie looked quizzically at him.

"Robert Browning's poem – 'The Pied Piper of Hamelin' drummed into us at school to scare us to death."

"Of course, the folktale of Goethe. If the piper had come to Hoja, my little town, I would have followed him out of there. It was so dull. Going to the bridge was the only thing to do."

149

"I like bridges too. You always feel you are going somewhere, there's a purpose, things are moving forward when you cross them."

"Like a momentum you mean."

"Yes, and a connection."

"Possibilities of something new."

"The excitement of a journey, not standing still."

"I'm not good at standing still, or even being still. I prefer to be doing something. Make something happen. Unlike my parents. They were forced to move to Hoja as children, refugees from Poland after the war. They resolved never to move again."

"What a contrast. Half the world seems to be on the move these days. And now it's our turn," said James peering at his watch. "Just a short walk along the river till you can sink your first beer."

"That is very good news." Stefanie smiled and held out her hand. "Please. Show me the way."

They walked the few minutes to the restaurant hand in hand, sauntering along the towpath under soft lighting, gazing at the inky, ebbing river. Stefanie felt comfortable, amazed that she did not feel the need to fill the silence, to gabble away as she usually would on early dates. This felt dangerously different.

Chapter Ten   Eva

It was usual for James to signal the start his weekend, by cooking supper at home for Megan and Eva, who would regularly call last minute to say she was bringing someone. That someone was always male, typically a handsome City banker, lusting for her, and thus fawning over Megan, and gushing about James's Thai cuisine. The ones Eva liked sometimes got a second showing. But mostly she jettisoned them by the end of the weekend. They would arrive laden with wine, too much, which they would finish off after the curry whilst they all dissected the debacle of James's latest on-line dating episode or more often the absence of any off-line activity. He had yet to unveil Stefanie as an agenda item. He could escape for another week, as this evening, he, Caro and Bruce had their own special date in Notting Hill.

As James and Caro lounged in her sumptuous basement cinema, comfort-cooled and low-lit, Bruce tripped in carrying a tray of salmon and soft cheese canapés. James had never been a massive fan of the sparkling stuff, but Caro had insisted on *Moet* champagne to celebrate. As a build up to the main event, they were catching up on the day's play at Lords. It was Caro who had taught James how to play cricket. She always insisted on batting. James had developed into a passable fast bowler during his school days and when he wasn't suspended, opened the bowling with his great loping stride and left arm over the wicket. It was rare for him to sit still for any length of time. Cricket was about the only thing that did the trick for him.

With Bruce now settled on the other side of Caro on the sleek L-shaped sofa, and glasses refilled to brimming, James clicked the remote to start the show. The jerky image of marathon runners filled the screen.

"It does get better. Some of Akhtar's team are not natural camera men." James had explained that they had been tracking Mark's progress from the runner microchip on his shoe and had picked him up just after the 30k point. "Here he comes. There, the guy in the white vest and blue shorts. And in a second you'll see Eva tracking him."

"Oh dear, he doesn't look very happy," said Bruce. "Eva looks marvelous. Such a brilliant performer."

"She is. She'd only just joined the race at this point." He was proud of Eva, regarded her almost as a daughter. He'd given the headstrong girl what guidance he could. He recalled advising her on A levels choices to prepare for life; yesterday is history, today is art, tomorrow is politics, and economics makes the world go around. She'd heeded his advice. She still listened to him but she made up her own mind whatever anyone else thought. She lived her life as a continual performance, each act a tour de force. After sixth form success, she performed as an academic at Oxford, and now performed as an investment banker at Goldwyn Morson. She loved the excitement and riskiness of deal-doing. And her extra-curricular acts for LifeChance gave her the thrill she continually craved.

"In a moment you'll see Eva pulling up alongside him." James continued the commentary as the video cut to further scenes of the pair running.

152

"There she is," said Caro bouncing about like a toddler, pointing at the screen and slopping her champagne. "She's handing over a bottle." She sniggered. "He looks dreadful."

"Just wait. From here he slows down, so the team could track him almost continuously." The film showed Eva leaving Mark behind. Increasingly the edited video intermingled close-up images of Mark's grimacing face with medium and long shots of a tottering figure.

"He looks grey," said Bruce just before Mark stumbled and fell. The camera zoomed in on the fallen figure. He tried to get back up but fell again. Onlookers screamed at him, encouraging him to get up, telling him he was almost there. Finally, a woman in a St John's Ambulance uniform entered the picture, and a man followed with a wheelchair. The plan had exceeded James's expectation which had been to leave the Weasel incapable of running rather than collapsing into unconsciousness.

"In a minute, you'll see him in the medical tent. We even managed to get some footage of him talking to his wife." They lingered on the increasingly pathetic figure as he lay on his bed, a drip stuck into his arm. They saw the scenes of him throwing up into a bucket. And they saw his paltry tears as his wife tried to console him.

"Poor woman," said Caro. "How does she put up with such an arrogant, cheating arse."

"We don't know for sure that he cheats. There are rumours, but we have no firm evidence."

"Well, we should get some then," snapped Caro whilst Bruce refilled her glass. "We should bloody well nail him."

Inside, James groaned. He had hoped that the marathon ruse and the fee-billing plot to discredit his reputation within his firm would satiate Caro's thirst for vengeance.

"What do you mean?" James reached forward and helped himself to another canapé. Bruce topped up James's champagne.

"Simple. We should set him up with someone. Film it. Send it to his wife." Caro wafted a hand in the air as her head whipped backwards, and champagne gushed down her throat. The bubbles were working too well.

James put down his glass and stared at Caro. An operation like the one she was suggesting was anything but simple, not to mention illegal. "Caro, he has four children. Do you really want to be responsible for breaking up his marriage?"

"Wouldn't be me. It would be him. I'd be doing her a favour. Letting her know the person she actually married rather than the one she thought she married."

"I don't know if that's such a good idea Caro." His eyes appealed to Bruce for fraternal support. "Bruce, what do you think?"

"Me?" Bruce shifted backwards on the sofa but there was no escape from Caro's stare. "This is really between you two."

"Bruce, you can't have forgotten already what it was like when I was incarcerated. If not for you, then for me and the children," said Caro with a hard edge of bitterness in her voice.

Bruce sighed, and peered into his glass as if looking for an answer, the right answer for Caro. "Of course, I haven't forgotten. It was hard, horrible. More than you can imagine, James." Bruce reached across to take Caro's hand. "I would never cheat on you."

"I would cut your balls off if you did," said Caro, as her lips curled into a smile, "So you see, James, by comparison, I'm being lenient on our Weasel friend."

James could barely manage a sardonic grunt. Leniency had never been one of Caro's traits, least of all concerning herself.

154

And he recognised only too well, the implacable smirk set like stone on her face.

In his corner office, James and Megan hunched around a table, oblivious to the rumble of overhead jets. They pored over revised financial models, surrounded by the detritus of a sandwich lunch. The room smelt of tuna and crayfish. Avocado and spring onions blended with the ripeness of mango and strawberries. An empty water jug and glasses were wedged between the scatter of Megan's spreadsheets.

He had been right. Over the weekend Acorn Techven had caved in and accepted that they would inject a further two and a half million pounds into WinBet, subject to two conditions. Firstly, LifeChance also had to inject two and half million pounds of permanent equity into the business, as they wanted assurance that WinBet would not become insolvent so quickly that creditors sought recourse from them. Secondly, the deal had to be completed by the weekend.

"We can do it." He could sense the buoyancy in Megan and hear the excitement in her voice at the prospect of closing her first corporate acquisition. She felt like a winner. "I've lined everyone up and cleared diaries. There'll be a few overnighters, but we'll get there. He remembered that feeling of adrenalin close to the finishing line of a deal, when it could have gone either way, and the counter-party, reluctant and morose, recognises and finally accepts the best option is to cave in rather than walk away.

James leant back in his chair, eyes closed and thumbs rubbing his temples. He heaved a sigh.

"What's the matter? I thought you'd be pleased. We'll be in a better cash position. We can keep going with the learning centre expansion. And we can close the WinBet deal." Megan counted off each objective achieved with her fingers and held them up in front of James.

He opened his eyes and sat up straight. "Caro. Caro is the matter. Caro and her cash."

"I thought you'd squared that off with her."

"I had, have. But I didn't think she would need to conjure up half of the five million pounds we asked her for by the weekend."

"She can do that. She's loaded."

"She is. But her cash comes with a condition." James had been hoping to play for time, hoping that Caro's appetite for revenge would dissipate, that she would become more reasonable. But now he had no time. He was cornered.

"Go on."

James groaned. "The Weasel. She's not finished with him."

"What's that got to do with LifeChance?"

"Everything apparently. I don't really agree with her. I think she should stop now."

"Are you saying she won't fund LifeChance unless you agree to play another trick on the Weasel?"

James nodded several times. "She didn't actually say that explicitly. She didn't need to. I know Caro. Trust me, she'll have a hundred good reasons why the money can't be there in time, if I don't go along with her scheme."

"What does she want you to do now?"

"She wants me to set up a sting, to lure him into an affair, which we then expose to his wife."

Megan shrugged. "Well if he's a cheat, why shouldn't he be exposed?"

"That's what Caro said."

"So, what's the problem?"

"Megan, he has a family, four young children. Think of the fall-out, the damage to his wife and innocent kids. I don't want to be responsible for breaking a family apart."

"But you wouldn't be. He would, unless of course he's not a cheat."

"He's not an evil man, Megan."

"No, he's an egotistical narcissist. Your words, not mine."

"He erred professionally, made a mistake, a poor judgement call. We all do that sometimes. I've checked him out. Most say he couldn't have predicted that jury decision. On the last day of the trial, the newspapers were full of screaming headlines of hedge funders and bankers paying no tax. The judge was under enormous public scrutiny to be seen to be harsh."

"All that may well be true. But so is our five million-pound hole."

"I know. And I know what Caro has suffered. And so, yes, I know I have no choice." James sighed again. "I'll put my conscience back to bed."

"So how are we going to do this?"

"Not sure yet. First, we need to find the right woman. Someone we can trust absolutely. Someone who is charming and smart. And someone who is so alluring, he will be unable to resist."

"And we need to do it quickly. Not easy," said Megan, fixing a frown on her forehead.

The door burst open, and Eva barged into the room, with a carry-out tray of coffee cups. "Surprise! Had a meeting next door, so I thought I'd treat you fossils to a little pick-you-up. Stop you napping."

"Darling, so thoughtful," said Megan, rising to kiss her daughter.

"Lovely to see you, and the coffee, said James." He cleared a space on the table for the tray, then hugged his god-daughter.

"We could do with some inspiration." Megan shared with her the conundrum they'd been discussing; Caro's demand and James's moral conflict."

By the time Megan had finished, Eva sat with a crooked smile. "Well, the solution's simple. I agree with you mum, there is no real moral issue. The Weasel hangs himself if he chooses to. LifeChance needs the money urgently, therefore Caro's command has to be carried out urgently."

"Thank you," said Megan, pointing her face at James.

"I'll do it," said Eva. "It'll be fun."

Megan's face froze. "No. Don't be ridiculous."

James winced. "We'll find someone else."

"Who?" said Eva.

"We'll use a prostitute," said Megan.

"I think you mean sex worker, mum. They get paid for providing a service. You don't use them."

"Don't lecture me."

"Well then don't use pejorative words."

"You're not a sex worker."

"Of course not. But I have lots of sex with whomever I choose, for lots of reasons. I would be doing this because I care about LifeChance."

"You're not doing it."

"You can't stop me."

"James, tell her, she can't do this."

"Eva, you've done enough already. This is asking too much, it's too risky," said James.

Eva laughed. "No it's not. Risking jail by giving you insider tips is risky, but shagging a highly rated lawyer?"

"It could still be dangerous.," said Megan.

"Mum, he's a bit of a prick maybe but he's not dangerous. He's not a wife beater or anything. I'll be the one in control, not him."

"We'll find somebody else."

"You won't be able to, not in the time you've got. I already know him. He won't be suspicious. Besides, who else can you trust, totally?"

The question floated in the air, filling a few seconds whilst James and Megan exchanged glances. He looked guiltily away because though he hated the thought, he knew Eva was right.

"Mum, LifeChance needs the money."

"I know that better than anyone," said Megan pointing to the array of spreadsheets littering the table. "But there has to be another way."

James walked over to the window and stared out on a grey sky, a single cloud canopy. The river was a slate of grey. Nothing moved. He tapped the window, with the wand of his finger, as if by magic he could change the scene, and conjure up sunshine and blue skies. Instead, he decided to change the subject. "Eva, no more insider tips. It's too risky."

"I know that. Compliance are all over us like the plague. So that makes Caro's money even more vital doesn't it."

"We're working on another plan, which given time, could be very big."

"Time you don't have though."

Megan crossed her arms and looked with a stern face at her daughter. "We'll find a way. We always have."

Eva smiled. "Okay. Well if you change your mind, I'd love to play the femme fatale role for LifeChance. I've always wanted to star in a movie." She picked up her coffee and walked to the door. "I have a work dinner tonight, so I'll be late."

159

Mark checked the message string again whilst grunting feigned acknowledgements to the rambling cabbie.

"hi! how did you get on? Eva xx." The text had pinged on his mobile during a dull partners' meeting at the firm. He'd idly checked the message as a preferable alternative to listening to some accountant droning on about new expense claim procedures. He'd sat bolt upright and stared at the screen. He didn't know any other Eva, so it must be her, he'd reasoned. He'd felt a shiver run through his body as he'd tapped out a reply.

"Not well - bit of a story. You?" His heart had beat heavily against his rib cage. He was more than intrigued by what she had to say, why her name did not appear in the list of marathon finishers.

"hmmm...we should swap stories some time xx," had come the immediate response. Mark was hooked. He'd begun to wonder what the two x's meant. Was it just standard texting, or something more. She wanted to see him. He'd felt elated. Mark had shot back a response.

"Drink after work?" He hated doing lunches. They got in the way of his hectic schedule and he could never relax.

"prefer dinner...next week?" Eva had shot back. His mind was still reeling. Perhaps she really does like me. Mark had checked his diary app. Cath never expected him home till late most evenings and then he recalled that she had her monthly outing with old university chums on Thursday evening, so she would be late.

"Thursday is good for me."

"it's a date... i'll book somewhere for 8."

"Great. Looking forward to catching up!" Mark never used exclamation marks. He thought them the preserve of the over-excited young and the unthinking. He felt something stir, a frisson he had not felt for an age.

The following week, a black cab rumbled to a halt outside a brasserie in Aldwych. It was a new venue to Mark who'd never have thought to book a central European restaurant. He could feel relaxed there. He could be anonymous in a vast, dimly lit, humming restaurant, miles apart from the usual City crowd.

The noise accosted him as soon as the liveried doorman had pushed the swing door open for him. As he checked in at the front of house desk, he spotted Eva's slim profile. She was sitting at the bar, sipping something long and pink, and chatting to the pony-tailed barman. Her golden hair was brushed back and fell loose down to the middle of her back. She wore a sleeveless, fitted black dress revealing her long neck and just enough of her cleavage. Suddenly she turned her head and spotted him. She flashed a smile, brilliant white teeth and rouge-red lips. He waved back, a bit too enthusiastically, like a cheerleader. She was stunning.

She greeted him with a kiss on each cheek and an affectionate squeeze on both biceps. As she leant in close, an aroma of zesty lime intoxicated him. She beckoned him to sit on a stool-bar opposite her and introduced the cocktail she had pre-ordered for him, a something sizzler with vodka, limoncello, lime and other ingredients he instantly forgot. Mark didn't usually drink cocktails, but he didn't want to appear boring. And he was drunk with desire for her, and at that moment would agree to do most things if it led to kissing those lips, that neck, her breasts.

"You look so different in a suit," said Eva, raising her glass and flashing a grin that revealed pristine molars. Years of visiting orthodontists and wearing braces had led to Mark always paying close attention to teeth. His had been levered into their precise places, filled and de-rooted. Regularly and expensively maintained, and immaculately whitened, his teeth led to his nickname of 'Ultrabright' in the office. This nomenclature had become annoyingly fitting to his rivals within the firm, as Mark ascended the ladder on the rungs of high-profile case wins and ever greater fee generation.

"You look exactly the same, except for the heels. Not *Nike* I assume," said Mark glancing down at Eva's pointed red stilettos. She laughed as Mark peered over the rim of his cocktail glass. Eva licked the glacé-cherry on the end of a cocktail stick and then sucked it whole into her mouth, smiling and fixing him with a glint of her blue eyes.

"So, have you fully recovered now?" she asked, startling Mark. How could she have found out about his collapse?

"How did you know?"

"Sorry?" Her brown eye-brows almost knitted together and the faintest of frown lines surfaced.

"About the marathon."

"I don't – that's why I'm asking. It took me a couple of weeks to get over it," said Eva.

"Ah – I see, yes, me too. In fact, a bit longer because of what happened."

"What do you mean?" Her voice resonated with a mixture of concern, interest and sincerity to Mark. He told her about the events which had unfolded shortly after losing sight of her diminishing figure amongst a sea of runners ahead of him.

"What do you think caused it?" she asked when he had become silent and momentarily glum at recalling the experience.

162

A maitre d' appeared, to let them know their table was ready for them and he led the way through a throbbing throng to a small candle-lit table in a corner. Mark glanced around the crowded, bustling room as they sat down. Groups of boisterous, engaged diners, mid-thirties and over, and crucially no-one he recognised. He felt his shoulders easing as the wave of relief washed over him. He was glad they were in the West End, away from the City. He had an alibi prepared in case he bumped into someone familiar, but he preferred not to use it, not to lie unless forced into it. He had been careful in telling Cath that he had a dinner with a potential new client and he predicted correctly that she would not bother asking whom. He had avoided an outright lie and convinced himself that the possibility of truth remained.

Mark suggested they should get the ordering out of the way before chewing over their marathon tales so they would not be interrupted. He selected the only wine he vaguely recognised from the wine list, without consulting Eva, and instructed the waiter that they would require a bottle of sparkling water for the table. He gazed at Eva.

"What do you recommend?" Mark paid scant attention when he and Cath pondered over menus: they sat in silence and munched bread until their ordering routine had been accomplished. But now, he was alert and interested. He watched intently as Eva ran through her personal favourites. The way she pursed her lips in contemplation over the stilton soufflé or the tuna tartare, the movement she made with her tongue when she chose the Lemon Sole, and the flicking of her eye-lids at the young waiter when she ordered, seemed to him like sexual foreplay. Beneath the table, he felt palpitations in his groin. When it came to his turn to order, he was a little breathless and impatient to be rid of the waiter. He craved all

163

her attention as he dispensed with the wine tasting and insisted on filling their glasses himself.

"So, did you break three hours?" Mark had searched the results for finishers' names with Eva and found no-one close to three hours.

"Not even close," Eva said gulping down a mouthful of chilled wine.

Mark imagined its cool stream fizzing through her body. Now in his work role of interrogator, he felt energized, confident and in complete control. "But you looked so good. You loped past me like a fox."

Eva laughed. "Well about a mile later, I felt dreadful, a bit dizzy. I thought, I can't do this. I almost stopped. But I didn't."

"So, what was your time?" asked Mark as casually as he could. He held his glass in mid-air and held his breath.

"I finally managed to crawl over the line in three hours twelve."

Mark blinked. He was certain that no-one named Eva had finished in under three and a half hours. He took a gulp of wine. What reason would she have to lie? "I must have missed your name amongst the finishers. I was really curious to see how you'd done," said Mark, blinking and looking down at the table. He hoped the dim light would mask any blushing.

"You won't find that anywhere. I used my friend Abby's entry. She pulled out when her ITB flared up."

He smiled inwardly, relieved that the explanation had been so simple. But a part of him, the lawyer part of him, wanted more, the evidence. But to ask the name of the friend would sound as if he distrusted her.

"Is she okay now?"

Eva giggled. "She's ecstatic. She says she's never run such a fast marathon. There it is, on record, three hours, twelve minutes and ten seconds."

Mark made a mental note to check. "That's a great time."

"Would have been even better but for hitting the wall – never happened before. I guess I pushed it too much too early."

"Maybe it wasn't that," said Mark tentatively. "Maybe it was the drink." Even in the dimness of the candle light, Mark detected the reappearance of the furrowed brow and caterpillar eye-brows.

"I hadn't touched a drop for a week before," said Eva in mock outrage. "How dare you."

"I meant the isotonic drink you had. You gave me a bottle, don't you remember?"

"Er, vaguely. Abby's magic mixture. She swears by it. She plays around with the formula whenever a new craze hits the headlines in the running mags." Eva explained how her friend's concoction involving various supplements, all legal, had made such a positive difference to her running times. Abby had supplied the bottles which she had handed to her at pre-arranged places on the marathon course; near the *Cutty Sark* at Greenwich, just past Tower Bridge at the half-way marker, and then at Canary Wharf approaching twenty miles.

Of course, thought Mark. It made sense. Particularly if her friend had experimented further with the final batch. But why would she? He served up the details of his blood test results and Thomas's thoughts on the matter.

Eva appeared dumbstruck, her mouth and eyes wide open. "I'm so sorry if it was the drink."

"Maybe she simply made a mistake," Mark concluded.

"She can get overly enthusiastic about trying out new substances," admitted Eva, "but she would normally tell me. I'll ask her?"

"No need, "I just thought you should know, for your own good."

"Thank you. That is so kind." Eva beamed and lent forward to squeeze his hand.

The waiter arrived with a steaming waft of stilton as two plates of soufflé were laid before them. The waiter insisted on refilling their glasses with an airy flourish. A waft of pear and apricot floated between them.

"Another bottle of the Riesling please," Mark signaled to the waiter as he replenished their water glasses. He noticed that Eva was keeping pace with his own drinking.

"To faster marathons," said Eva raising her glass.

"And to us. Bon Appetit," said Mark, suddenly feeling ravenous and grabbing a spoon to deflate the soufflé.

Their chit-chat floated away from their shared marathon to how they fitted training regimes into busy schedules and drifted into their professional and personal lives. Mark didn't realize how much he was drinking, nor how much of the conversation was about him. He talked about Cath, as if she were a perpetual project, to be managed and progressed. He enlarged on the characteristics that irritated him, magnified her annoying frailties, and exaggerated his frustrations with her inept management of the household. Unlike Eva, he pointed out, she had never had a proper career. He shied away from talk about his children, deflecting questions with platitudes.

"Don't you have to get home soon? I mean, won't you be missed?" said Eva interrupting his ramble about how much time Cath spent in coffee shops with her chums. Mark peered

166

at his *Rolex*, a Christmas present from Cath, and winced at the time – 10.45. If he left now and grabbed a cab he would still make it home before her.

"Blimey, you're right. I have an early start tomorrow." He signaled to a passing waiter for the bill. The restaurant still buzzed with noise as the post theatre crowd settled themselves in for a long evening for the staff.

"I'll handle the bill," said Eva. "It was my idea." But Mark insisted on paying. They hadn't talked business but as Eva worked for Goldwyn Morson, he could would justify the evening as a legitimate business expense.

Outside the warm summer air greeted them as they stood on a corner swapping business cards. The street hummed with activity: chains of people walking and bobbing about, a sea of humanity, while the throaty roar of red buses and black cabs flew nearby.

"We should do this again – soon" said Mark, feeling more than a bit tipsy.

"Very soon," echoed Eva as she leant into kiss Mark goodnight. Mark moved his head for the expected brush of kisses on cheeks and was startled to feel Eva's lips planted on his. Gently at first. And then he felt her tongue searching for his. She made precise, gentle movements and the taste of their fresh strawberry dessert oozed in Mark's mouth. It was delicious, and different to kissing Cath. Then suddenly it was all over and the weight of her taut body against his, released.

"Call me," She smiled and turned, mingling with the hordes as they weaved their ways into the start of their nights out.

The throbbing in Mark's groin lingered in the cab as he relived the scene of their parting to the vague soundtrack of the driver's wittering. As the car tore over Waterloo Bridge, he gazed east to the illuminated citadels of the city and then west to the dim-lit gothic hulk of parliament. He loved this city and he loved his life. He worked hard. He deserved a bit of harmless fun, he reasoned. Eva knew the score and Cath didn't need to know. He didn't want to upset her. He resolved to make love to her when he got home. She was usually a bit tipsy after a night out with her mates, and so even though it wasn't the weekend, she wouldn't be reluctant. The bulge in his trousers hardened just as the cab's horn blasted a pair of pedestrians dashing across their path.

"Some people," growled the cabbie, "got a bloody death wish. I mean…" Mark grunted and returned to his reflections on Eva, while the driver's tirade droned on above the engine's purr.

Chapter Eleven   Trap

Mark sat fidgeting and rereading the first page of his *Legal Review* in the soft-lit cocktail lounge of the five-star Clift Hotel overlooking Hyde Park. To the side of the bar, a crooner in bow-tie and DJ, tinkled a mini-grand piano and in smooth silky tones, serenaded the early evening cocktail crowd with Frank Sinatra and Tony Bennett favourites. At the winking of an eye or the faintest wave of a hand, uniformed bar staff floated over discreetly, to take cocktail orders and lay out bowls of assorted nuts. The lounge effortlessly combined intimacy, service and informality. Yet Mark was anything but relaxed.

He imagined that the young girl at the check-in desk knew precisely what he was up to; the way she had remarked – 'just the one night, sir?' Mark had reserved using his corporate credit card but he planned to settle everything with a bundle of cash so nothing was traceable. Mark's heart fluttered as he considered the possibility that his wife might discover his affair. How could she? He knew he had taken a risk but he was used to taking risks all the time at work, always weighed and calculated. He had been careful. His mobile access was secured by a private password. He would make it home before she had returned from her late evening out. But he was already dreading the check-out.

He peered at his watch again. Eva should have arrived half an hour ago. It had been her idea to book the room. He lifted his index finger to a waiter and signaled he would like another gin and tonic. As he did so, he caught the eye of a work colleague, Gordan Cumberbatch, who waved at him. Mark's heart skipped a beat as he chided himself for asking Sandra, the PA he and Gordon shared, to recommend a mellow hotel cocktail bar. Gordon leapt up and flounced over from a be-suited group of middle aged, fozy gentlemen.

"Hello Mark. I didn't know you used this bar too."

"My first time. Sandra suggested it."

"My older clients like it very much, I find. Good for relationship building." Gordon looked around. "Would you care to join us?"

"Thank you but I'm expecting a client, a potential client any minute," said Mark with a rictus grin. He was dreading Eva appearing now.

"Can be a tad noisy, on some occasions."

"Right."

"I once saw President Clinton in here, and Tom Jones. Not the same evening, you understand."

"Well, my guest is not a celebrity," said Mark trying to draw the conversation to a close. Then over Gordon's shoulder, he spotted her striding through the bar pulling an overnight case.

"Actually, I think she has just arrived," mumbled Mark as he stood up and gazed at the lithe, blonde figure in a midnight-blue silk suit approaching them.

"Good evening Ms. Gilman," he barked and extended a hand to shake whilst Eva was several metres away. It seemed to do the trick. Eva blinked but did not break stride.

170

"May I introduce a partner of mine, Gordon Cumberbatch," said Mark. Gordon's mouth had momentarily dropped open and his eyes flicked from Eva's face to her suitcase and then to Mark. Mark groaned inwardly, knowing that Gordon rarely missed a trick.

"Eva Gilman," she announced, taking a firm grip of Gordon's hand and looking directly at him.

"Eva works for Gladwyn Morson in their Investment Banking department. They are seeking some preliminary advice on an internal conflicts issue." Mark realised he was blabbering and instantly regretted opening his mouth. Gordon would know that you did not meet a potential client in a cocktail bar. It was not an appropriate setting for a first meeting involving discreet legal affairs.

"Enchanted to meet you," said the Wykehamist with a crooked smile and a nod towards the suitcase. "Are you coming or going?"

"Both," retorted Eva without further elucidation. An awkward silence settled upon them.

"Right. Well here's my card in case you get tired of my colleague," Gordon said with an expansive smile. "Do you have a card?"

"Every investment banker in the world carries cards." Eva produced a business card from a black leather wallet. "You never know where the next new client might pop up."

"Ha ha. Too right." Gordon scanned the card and put it in his pocket.

"I'll see you in the morning then," said Mark.

"Indeed, bright and early as usual," continued Gordon with a faint smirk. "Nice to meet you, Ms. Gilman." With a final glance at Eva, he swiveled on his heels and slithered back to his group of jowly businessmen tucking into their nuts and gulping champagne.

"Sorry I'm late," breezed Eva. "Chaos on the Tube – some bomb alert. I feel sticky and disgusting."

"You look divine," said Mark, relieved that she had arrived at last.

"Do you have the room key? I'd like to freshen up and dump this case." Mark dug into his jacket pocket, cast a glance at Gordon who seemed engaged in deep conversation, and with a furtive handshake, slid the key into Eva's silken grasp.

"Room 501. What would you like a drink?"

"Something long and cool and refreshing…an English Bulldog please." Noticing Mark's perplexed look, she added, "the waiter will know."

"Okay. Don't be long. We have a lot to get through," he said with a sheepish grin.

"I do hope so," said Eva with a voluptuous curl of her lips. He lingered for a few moments, watching her as she glided past the pianist, drawing a cheery smile. Mark felt as smitten as he could recall. He could feel his body throbbing, on fire with lust, and impatient to touch her.

Upstairs on the fifth floor, Eva began surveying the room as the heavy wooden door clunked shut. Above the TV on the light-grey wall facing the bed, a slate bowl with shiny green apples sat on a shelf. Just within reach. She shifted the bowl six inches; perfect for her plan. The massive bed's upholstered linen headboard dominated the facing wall and looked down on a mountain of scatter cushions and pillows on a plumped-up white quilt. Billowing mink drapes curtained elongated windows with views over Hyde Park. Matching penciled prints of iconic London buildings hung on the adjoining walls.

172

Cherry wood furniture adorned with buttermilk cotton fabrics stood upon light hardwood flooring, partly covered by a plush beige and brown rug. A predominance of neutral colours lent the room an airy, spacious ambience, luxurious and contemporary, as the hotel's web-site had promised. She was impressed. Mark had done well. Now she would make it better. She hastily set about preparing the set for the consummation.

She was enjoying playing the role of femme fatale and determined to present an Oscar-winning performance. Mark was lean, well preserved, probably good looking in his twenties. She'd slept with worse. She would have sex with him once. Her mother had acquiesced but would not view the production, captured on video and in print. Eva would reel him in quickly, then reel him out again, slowly. It would serve him right. His loss would be LifeChance's gain.

When she returned to the lounge-bar, the crooner had turned up the volume a notch so that his rendition of 'Fly Me To The Moon' rose above the bustle as the sway of cocktail hour surged into evening. Staff whizzed about ferrying silver trays of drinks and canapés. A small platter was laid out in front of Mark. He rose to greet her, still careful not to physically embrace her. He could tell that Gordon was casting oblique glances in his direction.

"I got us something to nibble on, with our drinks." He was hoping she would not suggest dinner first, as time was marching on and he had to be home before eleven, just in case Cath came back early. He absent-mindedly checked his watch again, a typical lawyer, totting up the chargeable minutes.

"Cheers," said Eva raising her glass to his, before taking a deep draught of her cocktail.

"Taste good?"

"Bliss. It's tangy - vermouth with gin and lime. Try it."

Mark leant forward, clasped the glass and took a tiny sip. "Not bad, but I think I'll stick with my wine."

"Don't be boring. Two more bulldogs please," hollered Eva at a passing waiter. "Don't worry I'll drink them both if you don't like it."

Mark was less worried by the challenge of swallowing a cocktail he didn't fancy than by the smirk on Gordon Cumberbatch's face. How was he going to get Eva to the room with him sitting there watching them?

"Do you like the room?"

"It's lovely. I adore the small things – the sun flower in the stone vase, the scented rosewood candles, the Swiss chocolates on the pillows. A great view over the park as well." Eva took another deep draught of her 'Bulldog' and then sat back and sighed.

He was pleased. He had wanted it to be perfect. The evening would cost him a small fortune. But she was worth it. He craved to kiss her lips, her breasts, her thighs, to wrap himself around her, and dive into her. He loved the silkiness of her voice, the vibrant way she animated her words, and her girlish laughter. She seemed to be equally mesmerised by him as well.

"Have you ever seen such a massive bed?" said Mark.

"Is that what you always say to potential clients?" She giggled again and took another gulp.

"Usually only the men, the fat, balding ones mainly." He signaled to a passing waiter for another large glass of sauvignon. He would have to wait until Gordon and his crowd left before they could venture upstairs, and the drink would steady his nerves. He had never had a proper affair before, did not know the rules, and was anxious to perform well.

"I've never been to bed with a fat or a balding man. What's it like?" They laughed loud and drew glances from neighbouring tables.

Gordon peeked over from across the room. Mark coughed and dug into his briefcase for papers to strew upon the table. They were going to make a fist of their client-lawyer meeting. Mark outlined the case before them. He was her defence attorney, providing advice regarding allegations of her stalking a bevy of fat, balding middle-aged men. They indulged in a cocktail fuelled hour of fun and nonsense whilst they marked time till Gordon departed with a wide grin and wave.

Mark left a few minutes' gap before following Eva up to the room. He was suspicious that Gordon might skulk about for a while. As he got out of the lift on the fifth floor, he felt exuberant and a little giddy from the drink. He knocked gently on the door. Eva appeared almost immediately, already changed into a white towelling robe, several sizes too big for her. She hauled him into the lamp-lit room and pinned him against the wall, thrusting her pelvis into his groin whilst her tongue thrashed about in his mouth. He breathed in her scent of vanilla and almond. Then abruptly she released him.

"I've ordered some champagne and now I'm taking a shower." she said. "Come and join me once the bubbly's arrived."

Minutes later he was shuddering in the shower as her delicate fingers smoothed soap suds over his entire body. He groaned as she slid a slippery hand up and down the shaft of his pulsating penis. He clamped a hand over hers just in time to prevent himself climaxing. He tried to draw her up but she slithered away out of the cubicle with a lascivious smile. She returned wrapped in a white towel and beckoned him with a curl of a finger to join her in the bedroom. He turned off the shower and still wet, padded from the steamy bathroom into the bedroom, leaving in his wake foot-sized puddles on the wooden floor. She patted him dry with her discarded towel and pushed him backwards with force onto the bed, now spotted by a sunken overhead light.

"Further up," Eva instructed.

Mark hauled himself backwards to the pile of pillows against the headboard. She had him in her mouth immediately, her wet hair tickling his thighs as her head bobbed up and down. He gripped the top of the padded headboard with both hands. His bulging eyes stared at their shadowy reflections on the facing TV screen. This time, he was incapable of stopping her. Within seconds, his anguished gasps were drowning out the sounds of her slurping. He exploded in a sequence of violent convulsions and primeval shouts. His grunting faded to groaning and her sucking gave way to licking, until he could take no more.

"I'm sorry. I couldn't help it." Mark felt elated but tormented. It had all happened too quickly. What would she think of him? What would the people in the next room think of him? He didn't usually make such a clamour.

"Don't be sorry, just get even," she said with a grin. "Your turn." They swapped positions and Mark set out to redeem his priapic performance with his tongue and knuckle. He sank into the valley of her thighs. Her juices tasted sweet in his mouth as his tongue explored her cavities and searched out her clitoris. She moaned gently, then began instructing him on where to press harder, where to put a cushion, where to put another finger and with each demand her cries grew more intense and her limbs rose and fell. Just when he thought she had climaxed, she would push his head back down. Finally, with a sweaty brow she raised her head and instructed him to sit on the edge of the bed. She conjured up a condom and then clambered on top of him. Mark could make out their silhouettes moving on the facing screen.

"Let's try the *hot seat*," said Eva rocking her pelvis to and fro. Within a couple of minutes, she had turned around and introduced Mark to the *lap dance*. Next, she had shoved him onto his back and rode him in *reverse cowgirl* position. Mark lost count of the positions and their names after that. Eva dictated each activity, the pace of movement and the pressure applied. It felt like he was part of her workout. Like a skilled gym-bunny, she used him as her equipment, skillfully changing devices whenever she sensed he was nearing an orgasm. Finally, astride him, they climaxed together and then drained, lay face up, side by side, staring at the ceiling light.

"Not bad for an old man," quipped Eva, slapping Mark on his thigh as she maneuvered off the bed and headed to the bathroom.

Mark's face flinched. The word 'old' stung him. He felt strange. He had enjoyed it, every second of it, but something was missing, something nagged at him. He was a master in his field of law but she was the mistress in the bedroom. Was it the giving up of control that bothered him? Or perhaps the tacit cold fact that they had used each other simply for physical gratification? But he liked her, and based on her taking the lead, she clearly liked him, thought Mark.

He leant over and snatched a champagne glass from the bed-side table. Mark grimaced as he swallowed a sour mouthful of lukewarm, lifeless liquid. He bounced off the bed and grabbed the champagne bottle from its ice bucket. It was still cool. He took a swig and found it flat and disappointing but at least he could swill out his sticky mouth. He spotted a small bottle of mineral water next to fruit bowl on the shelf above the TV. He reached for it, tore off the cap and started to glug.

He was about to reach for a juicy apple when he felt Eva's feathery kiss on the back of his shoulder. He turned to see her fresh face, pink from the shower. She was naked except for a towel she held rubbing her hair. She smelt of pine. He could feel pulsations reigniting in his groin as his eyes moved from her firm breasts to her tiny strip of hair between her legs.

"You don't want to be late," said Eva turning to gather her clothes draped over the back of a chair. Mark groaned inwardly and checked his watch. He reckoned he could stay for another half hour.

"One for the road?" said Mark, trying to make a joke out of a yearning to have her again. Eva's black sheer lace thong snapped into place.

"I have a 7.30 breakfast meeting and I'm the host." She started to pull a matching basque over her damp hair. She had said it with such finality that Mark knew it was pointless to try to entreat her. Anyway, he hated to beg for anything, hated to even ask for something from somebody, hated to feel he owed, that he might be in someone's debt.

"Of course," he mumbled and sloped off to the shower. He stood there for several minutes, scouring his body with soap, cleansing his pores of the scent of her and the smell of their fornication. He toweled himself dry, brushed his teeth and gargled with the hotel's tiny bottle of mouthwash. He paused for a second in front of the mirror. He didn't look like a different person to the one the day before he had cheated on

178

his wife. And he was unsure whether he felt different. The sex had been different; more energetic, more positions, more mechanical, more noise. But it had been less intimate. Their mouths had not touched once when in bed, and they had not lain together wrapped in one another's arms at all. Perhaps the next time would be different again, he thought.

He set his face with a jolly smile and opened the door expecting to see Eva dressed and waiting to kiss him goodnight. But all that remained of her in the now fully lit room, was a cursory note on the bed – 'thanks message me.' He felt disappointed and deflated. She could have waited a few minutes. The note seemed abrupt, almost clinical. Then again, perhaps her delicate kiss on his shoulder was her intimate way of bringing their evening to a fitting end.

The puzzle lasted all the way home as he sat feeling numb, being thrown about in the back of a taxi driven by a morose cabbie. For a change, he would have welcomed a cheeky chappie driving him. He looked out of the rain splattered window at the cars queuing alongside. He wondered whether any of their inhabitants had spent the evening cavorting illicitly in a hotel room. He heard himself sighing, just as the cabbie uttered a curse at the car in front. It was not just his wallet that had been emptied. Something, somewhere inside him had been vacated.

He peered out of the taxi and saw they were passing the illuminated window displays of Harrods. Mannequins in assorted lacy lingerie stared back eyeless at him. He pictured himself on the bed with Eva again, and gave out an involuntary groan. But the next minute, with alcohol effects wearing off, nagging doubts, regret tinged with guilt, began to invade his thoughts. He sought refuge in checking his mobile for new messages whilst the traffic crawled along in a corridor of exhaust fumes and blaring horns. But that didn't work for long. Locked up in his black cubicle of plastic, glass and metal felt like purgatory. But as usual, once they reached Putney Bridge, the glint from the flowing Thames lightened his mood. He would be home soon.

As he opened his front door, the familiar smells of home greeted him. Natalia, the live-in Hungarian au pair had been baking cookies for the kids. The house was quiet and only the kitchen light seeped into the hall. He wandered in and grabbed a chocolate cookie. He was starving. He took two bites and popped the rest into his mouth. Then he picked up another. He checked his watch - five to eleven, which gave him time to shower again. A note on the table told him that Thomas had called about meeting up for a run early Saturday morning. He sauntered over to the wall calendar and penned an entry. He noted that Cath had arranged dinner for them with friends on Saturday evening but he was relieved to see that tomorrow night was free as usual, family time to kick-start the weekend.

Mark thudded up the stairs slowly, gripping the banister rail to heave himself up to the landing. A shallow light drained from the twins' bedroom. He crept into their room and tip-toed over to the bunk beds. Benjamin slept silently, his thumb hanging from his drooping mouth while down below, Emma, all splayed out like a starfish, breathed faint snores. Mark pulled up the quilt to cover her and stole a sniff of her hair.

He backed out of the room and peered around Miranda's door. She lay on her side, her breath rattling with a cold as it rasped from her mouth. She looked most like her mother and copied her in so many ways. Her quilt was tucked up neatly below her neck and her delicate hands were clasped together like a supplicant. Mark knelt down and touched her hand with a tip of his finger and felt the soothing balm of its warmth and smoothness. She had fallen asleep reading a book. *The Wicked Witch* clung perilously to the edge of her pink *Polly Pocket* quilted bed. He picked up the book and flicked through several pages. He must have read these words at least a dozen times at weekend bedtimes with his daughter, but each time it seemed fresh and new to both of them. He smiled as he put the book by Miranda's bed, at the happy thought of being six and life being so much simpler. He backed out of the room slowly, gazing at the wonder of her perfect form

Then he tiptoed cautiously along the corridor and peeped into Ralph's untidy bedroom, the floor littered with books, toys and scattered unwashed clothes. He always insisted that his door be left wide open and a side light kept burning through the night. He was curled up tight in a ball wearing his prized Fulham Football Club pyjamas. They never missed a home game at 'The Cottage.' When Mark had splashed out on season tickets, his son had shrieked with glee. Mark felt that joy whenever he walked across the bridge to the stadium, the chattering boy beside him, his small hand in his. Ralph's post-match babbling bettered the game itself. Mark sat on the edge of the bed and gently leant over to plant a kiss on Ralph's forehead. After a couple of minutes watching the rhythmic flow of his son's inhalations and exhalations, as delicate as gossamer, Mark reluctantly crept back out.

Out on the landing, Mark caught snatches of mumbling. Natalia was watching television up in her room in the eaves. He supposed he ought to let her know that he was home and would deal with the kids if they woke. He swiveled to go upstairs and then froze. The antidote of seeing his children was already evaporating. He couldn't bear to face speaking to anyone, answering any questions or indulging in small talk.

He suddenly felt drained and deflated and so turned around and headed to his bedroom.

The room smelt of Cath's rose scent, the one she had worn since he had met her, the one he always bought her for birthdays and Christmases. He could tell from the heap of clothes on the armchair that Cath had had a clothing crisis of what to wear to her book club. Always the same he thought, just like his routine of taking off his shoes and socks, right foot first, then his jacket followed by his trousers, next unbuttoning his shirts and finally wiggling free of his underpants. Socks, pants and shirt into the corner laundry basket, navy blue suit hung in the wardrobe and black brogues stuffed onto the shoe rack. He lumbered into their en-suite bathroom, stepped down into an open shower, turned the dial and allowed his face to take the full blast of warm water. He stood there, unmoving, feeling the water cleanse him, inside and out, erasing the scent of the hotel's soap and the remnants of Eva lingering in his nostrils. He could not remove the recollection of the evening. He didn't know whether he wanted to or not, and part of him felt he had dreamt it or been an onlooker, somehow separated from the events in which he played the protagonist.

As he slid into his familiar bed, he heard the click of the front door opening downstairs. Cath would be upstairs in a few minutes, having set the dishwasher going and having checked that all the external doors were locked. She would peep into each of the children's rooms and then weave into their bedroom in a tipsy state and unleash upon him the local gossip from her book club. They seemed to chat about everything but the book, Mark thought. But he was usually happy to hear about it and they often ended up having sex afterwards.

182

Tonight however, he could not face Cath. He heard the creak of her footstep on the loose Edwardian floorboard outside their bedroom, and then her tip-toeing noisily into the darkened room. He lay on his side, dead still and listened to her undressing. He felt a draught of air as she climbed into bed. He felt her arm around him and a wet kiss on his neck as she whispered entreaties in his ear. He feigned heavier breathing and kept his eyes tight shut. Not long after he could hear Cath's snoring. He was wide awake.

Chapter Twelve   Art

For their third date, James took Stefanie to the Summer Exhibition at the Royal Academy. He had received an invitation for himself plus guest from PKE, an international accounting firm sponsoring the event. His name languished on countless corporate databases, a hangover from his investment banking days when his in-box teemed with corporate entertainment events. Stefanie had mentioned to James over their dinner at the Oxo Tower, that she wanted to spruce up her apartment with some fresh artwork. He'd been to the event many times, and guessed she'd be entertained by the glitz and impressed by the cornucopia of more than a thousand exhibits on show.

In the ornate courtyard of Burlington House, a seventeenth century Palladian mansion, dark corporate suits and flowery cocktail dresses were filled with upper-crusters quaffing rosé champagne from Swarovski flutes etched with PKE's unfathomable logo. In competition for the fading evening sun, plastic pink flamingos posed amongst fountains and statues. A few yards away, outside its sculpted arched gateway, twenty-first century buses, taxis, tour buses, trucks and cars of all colours and shapes, choked their way home for the weekend.

James led Stefanie through the throng to the foot of a stone staircase leading up to the exhibition, from which a constant rumble tumbled down. Brightly coloured confetti littered the steps. On either side of the stairwell, elegant made-up men in pink ballet tutus and black 'Doc Martin' boots, held silver trays of fizzing glasses.

"I love your boots almost as much as your lipstick," said Stefanie as she helped herself to champagne. A tall, blonde man giggled his thanks whilst glasses teetered precariously on his tray. James grabbed a glass from a hairy squat guy opposite, who suggested with a wink that he was welcome to take two.

They collected 'List of Works' catalogues from a bronzed, booted, tutu'd brunette with a beard, and crimson sash across the shoulder, emblazoned with yellow lettering, 'Not For Sale'. As they weaved a path to the first exhibition room, James suggested that they play a game whilst eyeing the artworks. He explained that anyone could submit work to be included in the exhibition. In practice only ten per cent were accepted by the judging panel of artists. Work from first time amateur artists would hang alongside established names, with prices varying from a few hundred pounds to hundreds of thousands of pounds.

"What are the rules of your game?" said Stefanie as she swapped her already empty glass for a full one proffered by a passing waiter. She pressed the fresh, cooling glass against her forehead, then cheeks, as the sound of popping bubbles filled her ears. People around the room were using the catalogues as fans.

"Simple. In each room, I pick a painting and you have to guess the selling price. Then we switch over. If you get within ten per cent, you get a point." James emptied his glass as the smell of strawberries surged up his nose, flooding his senses.

"What's the prize for winning?"

185

"Dinner, cooked by the loser."

Stefanie took a considered sip of rosé and smiled. "Then I can't lose, and you can only lose. My mother says I am a terrible cook; always in a rush."

"I'll take that risk. Right, see you back here in five minutes."

They wandered off in different directions, scanning the walls of contemporary art, unified only in its eclecticism. They threaded themselves between chattering, imbibing groups and wayward watchers, individual or in pairs, immersed in a trance of artful watchfulness.

"You're late," said Stefanie when James reappeared. "You've had forty-eight seconds extra, so I get to go first."

James smiled. "Right. This is serious. So, I'll only take four minutes in the next room. Show me what you've got."

Stefanie pulled James gently towards an artwork featuring an oblong red canvas over an oblong blue canvas. Each was framed in a blackened burnt frame. "I'll give you a clue. It's called 'red over blue'."

"Well, now you've given it away." James blew out his cheeks and scratched his chin as he closed in on the piece for a better view.

"Stop stalling."

"Well I'd say that would have to be a few thousand, maybe five, at least five, possibly more."

Stefanie opened a page from the catalogue and with a delighted grin pointed to the featured item. "Totally wrong."

"Twenty thousand! That's....oh, well he's an RA. That explains it."

"RA?"

"Royal Academicians, renowned artists elected by their peers at the Royal Academy." Stefanie wrinkled her nose in utter puzzlement. "Basically, it's a brand, like your *Hermes* handbag," said James pointing at the sleek, black bag dangling from her shoulder."

"I've never heard of this artist."

"Well if you did, you could probably add another zero to the price. The art market is no different to any other. Supply and demand determine price. Forget aesthetics."

"But I could go home and paint that. It would take me five minutes."

"And no-one would buy it, because you're a nobody. I mean-"

"It's true. My mother says my painting is lousy too."

"Remind me not to meet your mother some time."

They both laughed and freshened their glasses before venturing off to find the painting James had selected. They settled in front of a gigantic lump of acrylic sculpture attached to the wall, which looked like some kind of internal body organ. It reminded James of a hunk of grisly meat he had seen on a bloodied butcher's block in South Sudan. Rather like the flies then, this piece was attracting a crowd.

"What's the title?" asked Stefanie.

"Trust me, that won't help you. But I will tell you that the piece is by someone famous in the art world. That's a big clue by the way."

Stefanie looked at the red, grey and white thing, then at the staring horde. She turned to James with a smile. "It has to be a lot. So, I guess fifty thousand pounds."

"Not even close," howled James. "Try six hundred and fifty thousand."

Stefanie's mouth fell open and she stared unblinking at James. "No. Show me," she said, leaning in to James to check the price in his catalogue. "Well I hope the artist is a woman, and a man buys it."

James grimaced. "Let's move on shall we."

Several rooms later, with game points at nil-nil, and glasses of champagne sunk, at about seven or eight all, Stefanie mouthed to him across a giant room under a seething siege of bacchanalians, that she was headed to the toilet.

James flicked the pages of the catalogue in search of the price of a brightly coloured abstract painting in front of him. At nine hundred and fifty pounds, he decided that at least he would have something to go home with. Then his sight was drawn to a massive pink canvas. It contained an upright viola painted in vibrant colours. He liked the look of that too and so checked his catalogue. Two hundred and fifty thousand pounds, and it was missing a bow. He chuckled into the din around him and raised his head over a crowd to see what he could have missed. He felt a tap on his shoulder and swung round.

"Hello James. Bloody good champagne this," gushed Mark, "and free, unlike the stuff on the walls." Mark snorted and stuffed a round fishy looking canapé into his mouth. In his tie-less, unbuttoned and animated state, Mark appeared to James, as if he were celebrating a release from his lawyers' penal colony.

"Mark. Gosh, I didn't expect to see you here." James rearranged his stricken look with the expansive smile of a clown. The thought of having to admit to Mark that he was here with his opponent seemed all too complicated and unwelcome. He didn't fully understand it himself.

"You'll never guess who I've just seen." Mark's shiny face, as pink as his champagne, brimmed with the excitement of a schoolboy with a secret. James, certain of the answer, began to shift his feet so that he could see the entrance. "Only that woman who's after your blood. Stefanie 'bloodhound' Zuegel. Keeps bombarding us with information requests. One after the other. Never ending."

"Only doing her job I suppose." James wanted to believe that so much, yet a part of him, a fraction, still nagged at him that she might be getting close to him, just to help her case. He buried the fleeting thought with a final glug from his glass. "Must get a refill," said James and took a step toward the entrance.

Mark put an arm across his path. "Chap behind you with a full tray coming our way." He waved his glass in the air, attracting the attention of the hovering waiter.

Fresh glass in hand, Mark manoeuvred closer, close enough that James could smell his breath of strawberry and prawns. "Thanks for instructing my colleagues on that new betting thingy. Sounds like a cracking deal." James had hired a partner at BCS to advise on the WinBet deal, as he could gain more negotiating leverage that way, keep control of fees.

"I hope so," said James with one eye on the entrance. He could feel the base of his shirt against his moist back.

"So, are you looking to buy something?"

"I have an eye on one piece. I suppose I ought to go to the desk and buy it before someone else does."

"My wife most likely. She's bouncing around somewhere. No doubt she'll blow a hole in our bank account again this evening. Last year, it wasn't so much a hole as a crater. You single chaps don't know how lucky you are."

James barked out a laugh and glanced at the entrance again. He could sense the sweat gathering at the foot of his nose, and a drip teetering from a side of his temple. He had to get away.

He wiped his brow with the back of his hand. "It's like a furnace in this room."

"Yes. Bloody rammed. Looks like half the City's come."

"Too hot for me, I'm afraid. I need to find some water." And with a cursory tap on Mark's arm as a farewell, James sliced through a wave of people cascading through the entrance. He didn't look back until he had waylaid Stefanie just outside.

"Game abandoned," James shouted above the clamour. He pointed down the stairs, "Got to go."

Stefanie looked startled. "But I was just getting into my stride."

"I'll explain outside." James grabbed her hand and concentrated on not falling over as they lurched down the steps and out through the courtyard. Striding along Piccadilly, he told her about Mark. The traffic had thinned, and the dry, cooling air felt like a celebration after escaping the intense heat of the Academy. James suggested they walk towards the river and find somewhere casual to eat in one of the Southbank's eateries.

"I think you should cook me a meal. You owe me. You abandoned the game after all." Stefanie's mocking voice was accompanied by a squeeze of James's hand.

"Tonight? Now?"

"Unless you've had a better offer?" She smiled and held his gaze.

"No, great. I can rustle up something. Thai or Italian or -?" His heart thumped. He had not expected Stefanie to have made the first move. He always dreaded that moment of indecision, when and how to metamorphose the purely tactile to raw sex. More than a few of his ex-girlfriends had derided him post event for being too gentlemanly. But he preferred that than to risk rejection.

"Italian sounds great."

They sauntered off, arm in arm, passing stragglers dashing into West End theatres, hearty drinkers crowded on pavements outside pubs, and young families gazing into closed shop windows. They passed through Trafalgar Square, a cauldron of European youthfulness being entertained by myriad street performers. A few teens had slipped into the fountains' waters, and James wished he could have joined them. They headed instead past Nelson's Column to the Embankment where the street lights flickered into life just as they reached Golden Jubilee Bridges. They stopped mid-way across to marvel at the glow of Parliament, golden as a low sun crept further west on the horizon. Big Ben peeled its sombre warnings on cue. Once they reached Southbank, Stefanie insisted on taking a 'Selfie' of themselves, with a purple illumination of the National Theatre behind them. Only a few hundred yards to his apartment building, and his heart thudded away like a teen on a first date.

From the moment they were greeted by the smiling service manager behind a marble topped reception counter, Stefanie felt like she'd entered a five-star hotel rather than James's apartment building. As the perfumed lift swished up to the seventeenth floor, Stefanie logged further clues inscribed into polished stainless steel - B1: spa and wellness gym, and L35: rooftop bar and restaurant.

James slid a card into a slot and his apartment door clicked open. "Lights. Level C," he announced and ushered Stefanie into a room with soft sunken lights fading-in as she stepped across the threshold.

"It's huge." And she thought, modern and unlived in. No clutter. Sleek low-level sofas, tables and chrome legged chairs. Large abstract artworks hung on high ceiling walls. Pastel colours matched with vibrant silk padded cushions, perfectly positioned. An enormous glass vase of white lilies stood on an amber, art deco cocktail cabinet in front of the windows. She was having a job reconciling the style of the room with the cultured man in front of her. After jabbering on about a couple of the paintings, he was suggesting they should open a crisp bottle of Greco Bianco, explaining that it was originally grown in Greece but now mostly in southern Italy.

Stefanie followed James into the kitchen which lit up on entry. Just like the lounge, the kitchen was several times the size of her own. It was spotless, brilliant white and everything fitted into straight lines. A massive oblong island, unscratched and gleaming ran along the middle. Two opposing walls were lined with identical work surfaces and units from floor to ceiling. As James approached one of the units, he shouted "Chiller. Open", to reveal a wine chilling-cabinet.

"I'm afraid that won't work with me. Well, not until you have cooked me dinner." Stefanie roared with laughter.

James turned with a bottle in hand, and they came together, tongue twisting with tongue, and pelvis grinding with pelvis. Stefanie felt her entire body glowing. "I prefer sex on a full stomach," she whispered in James's ear as they finally drew breath. She saw on his face, the look of unexpected joy and bemusement as if he'd just won a court case he expected to lose.

"I'd better get cooking then." He grabbed two glasses from a cabinet which had opened automatically to his touch. "Why don't you relax in the lounge with some of this, whilst I get on." James unscrewed the bottle and started to pour.

"Clearly you are a serious chef. You don't want me to steal your secret recipe."

"Something like that," smiled James as he handed her a large glass of wine. "There's a TV remote on the coffee table. Just press the red button and a screen will descend with instructions."

"Can't I just give it a command? TV. On."

"It only has one master, and that's me."

Stefanie's mouth curled into a crooked smile. "That makes life simple." She kissed his lips and sashayed into the lounge. She was intrigued by this mysterious man. She looked around the room for anything remotely personal - a photograph, letter, address book or even business papers, but discovered nothing. She took off her shoes and tip-toed across the plush cream carpet to a door she had not noticed when she had come in. She opened it gently and entered a hallway with several doors on each side.

The first bedroom reminded her of a plush hotel in Hong Kong that she'd stayed in whilst attending a law conference on international fraud. A king-sized bed adorned with a gold-silver patterned cover and half a dozen cushions dominated the space. Its wood-panel headboard covered most of the end wall and incorporated bedside tables inlaid with buttoned panels for lighting. She opened a drawer to find a red bible. For a moment, she wondered whether she was nosing around a short-stay serviced apartment.

A side door led into an en-suite bathroom with slate tiled floor, walls and surfaces. A mirror stretched over the breadth of the facing wall above a pair of white vanity hand basins. A white bidet toilet with a digital touch-pad and a walk-in shower with several water-jets completed the bathroom suite. A chrome stacker was stuffed with pristine white towels. Next to the left-hand basin, *Molton Brown* shampoo and conditioner bottles lined up neatly alongside a ceramic bowl containing scented soaps. On the far side of the right-hand basin, Stefanie spotted a tumbler containing a toothbrush and a partly used tube of toothpaste. Adjacent to it, lay a razor on a white flannel. A half empty tube of ocean-blue shave gel lay next to it. These were the first personal and imperfect things she had seen in the apartment. As she reached for the toothbrush and paste, she became aware of something in the mirror. James was at the door wearing a quizzical look.

"I have a new toothbrush in the cupboard if you like."

She stared back at him. "You're supposed to be in the kitchen." She knew she had been caught snooping, and as usual her first line of defence was attack. She slurped a mouthful of wine and grinned. "I needed the toilet."

James shook his head but smiled. "You'll find everything you need in the cupboard beneath the basins. Now, do you like prawns?"

"I adore them." Stefanie closed in for another protracted kiss, pinning James against the wall. They tasted green apple and zesty lemon.

"Gamberi alla busara coming up," said James with a flourish. "It won't take long. Have a snoop around the apartment if you want."

"I shall. And later I intend to do some extensive undercover work in there," said a Stefanie with a nod to the bedroom.

James laughed. "I promise to reveal everything, your honour."

"Are you okay?" Stefanie must have heard him crying out. She had turned on a bed-side lamp, and now peered down at him, her hand caressing his bare chest.

His toddler's nightmare had stayed with him all his life, fitfully reappearing, unpredictable and real. The cast of women with horrified faces changed but the plot never altered. They smothered him, passed him along, tried soothing words, anything but let him be with the lady lying in the road with a fixed stare and arms outstretched. Moments before, he had her to himself, his tiny hand secure in her leather-gloved hand, her smile returning his as they played 'I Spy' on her way to work. She would drop him off at an old lady's house close by, so she could visit him in her lunch-hour, and then pick him up, after work when it was dark, and they could play 'Simon Says' as they skipped along to the bus stop.

That morning, they were late or the bus was early. They heard its thundering diesel-engine just before the squeal of its brakes as it pulled up at the stop on the other side of the road. "Quick," was her last word to him, as they stepped off the pavement. Another screech of breaks and the force of his mother's hand on his back, as he was hurtled into the middle of the road. A loud smack behind him, as he was flying through the air. A thwack as his hands thumped the tarmac, before the thud of his head. Hurt, bloodied and dazed, he cried out for his mum. He smelt the diesel fumes, heard the idling of a car engine, and saw grown-ups freeze, staring in his direction. He was frightened and twisted his head and called out to his mother again. But she wouldn't answer him, wouldn't get up, just stared at him open mouthed.

He got up and tried to reach her but a woman was tugging him back. Then another woman, crying, bent down and clasped him to her, pushing his forehead into her shoulder. The shouting had already started, and as he kicked to get away, people were everywhere. He squirmed around but could no longer see his mum, only a group of men and a big black

195

car. He screamed for his mum, but she still wouldn't come. He was passed to another woman who wore a hat and said she was a nurse and promised him a sweet, if he was good. His screams became sobs as he was passed from one woman to another, before one of them in a blue uniform carted him off and sat by him in a white car with a blue flashing light on top. He was scared as the car drove away, taking him away from his mum. The woman gave him a red lollipop and promised him that his mother would be coming to see him soon, after the doctors made her better. But afterwards, every time a door opened, and he expected her to walk into a room, she was never there. It was just another woman. Tonight, Stefanie was one of them.

"I'm fine. I just need some water." He didn't want to lie to her about this, but neither was he ready to tell her the truth. He got up and padded off in the dim light to the bathroom. He closed the door, locked it silently, fumbled for the dimmer switch. He turned on the tap and splashed his face. He felt his heart pounding; it usually quietened down after a couple of minutes. He turned off the tap and then sat on the toilet and waited. It was probably too much to hope that Stefanie would have switched off the lamp and gone back to sleep. He knew it had been a risk, letting her stay overnight. He flushed the toilet, switched off the light and in a single movement, slid the bolt and opened the door.

"You were screaming." She was lying, frowning faced with her head angled upwards, supported by two pillows.

I'm sorry I woke you." He slipped quickly under the quilt. Despite a couple of hours of sensuous lovemaking, he was not yet comfortable standing naked in front of her.

"Nothing ever wakes me up." She yawned.

"Just a nightmare. I get them sometimes. Probably the alcohol."

"Or a guilty conscience?" She smiled faintly.

"Let's leave the interrogation to the court room." He rolled over and lay on his side, facing her, and closed his eyes.

"What was it about?"

"The usual stuff." He faked a yawn.

"What's that?"

"Oh, too boring for the middle of the night." Stefanie grunted and twisted over to switch off the lamp.

"Night." He snuggled up to her, his chest brushing the warm skin of her back, and kissed her neck. There was so much she didn't know. How was he going to tell her?

"You can trust me," she said into the darkness.

Chapter Thirteen   Interrogation

Mark despised meetings at the FCA. Commuting out to Stratford in a crushed rush hour tube was not his idea of fun but the alternative crawl in a cab was worse. He envied their ultra-modern offices, superior even to BCS's glass edifice, and hated the thought that taxpayers like himself were funding it. The time-consuming process of getting through security always irritated him. Whilst the meeting rooms were cool and functional, the coffee was bitter. He slyly checked his watch again whilst the woman drilled another routine question at his client.

They were well into the second hour and had worked their way down about a quarter of the list of Goldwyn Morson names which James had produced. Mark looked blankly at the notes his assistant had compiled from his session with James. It was all so tedious. How did he know the person? How long had he known the person? Describe the nature of the relationship. How often did they meet? How often did they speak? What did they talk about? Endless. He knew they would be comparing James's answers with the people selected to be interviewed at the bank. Goldwyn Morson were cooperating fully with the FCA, conducting their own investigations and making their findings, including recording of interviews, available to the regulator.

"What about Eva Gilman?" said Stefanie. For a split second, Mark thought the question was aimed at him, and sat bolt upright, surprise etched all over his face. He scanned the record of names on the paper in front of him. He couldn't see her listed anywhere.

"Eva?" said James.

"Excuse me," said Mark interrupting. "I thought we were going down the list of his old contacts at the bank?" He was sure James must have left the bank before Eva joined as a graduate recruit.

"And the newer ones too. If you turn over the page, you will see her name."

Mark flipped over the paper and saw Eva's name listed in the middle. He glared at his assistant who on cue handed him the brief note he had taken from his conversation with James.

"May I respond to the question now? " said James, before taking a sip from his water glass. Mark nodded curtly.

James parroted the notes that Mark was now reading. He explained that Eva was a relatively junior executive in the acquisitions and mergers department, whom he understood was highly rated for her energy and insights. She had joined several years ago on the bank's graduate scheme having read PPE at Oxford. He had no reason whatsoever to discuss share trades with her.

Stefanie leaned forward, pouting her lips and nodding in silence for what seemed an age. "We know that she joined after you left. So how do you know her?"

It was Mark's turn to stare at his client. He was beginning to wonder if the girl had a fascination for older men, that he had something unexpected in common with James. His client wore a wry smile.

"I helped get her a summer internship when she was a student. She did well. They invited her back again the next year, then again and finally hired her."

"And why would you help someone like Eva Gilman? asked Stefanie. Mark thought he knew the answer. She was gorgeous and made you feel desirable all over again. His mind momentarily switched to an image of her naked, astride him on the bed. The horror that she might still be seeing James struck him. What did this make her? What did this make him?

"Because," said James leaning across the table to mirror Stefanie, "as I'm sure you must already know from your interviews at the bank, she's my god daughter."

James's response was both an anodyne to Mark's emotional torment as well as a professional irritation. His opponent knew this fact before him. He would need to have some firm words with his client, whilst he surreptitiously discovered more about the girl he could not stop thinking about. They had exchanged flirtatious texts since their tryst but nothing more. Eva had either been working abroad on a project or had a full social diary. But now finally they had agreed a date, a forever fortnight away.

Mark had convinced himself that the affair was good for his marriage. The weekend after the date, Cath had commented on his joviality and liveliness. They had got tipsy together and made love on Saturday night. It had been good, the best sex they had had in a long time. He had tried out a position Eva had insisted upon. Cath seemed to have enjoyed it, not that he bothered to ask her and she did not volunteer her feelings. So as usual, he took silence to mean concurrence with his view of the world.

"That's most interesting." His opponent switched her gaze to him for a purposeless point-scoring moment. Then she scrutinised his client's face, and with a sneer, continued with her jabbing. "Your god daughter must be privy to lots of confidential deal information."

"In her role, she is bound to be."

"Do you discuss her work with her?"

"I take an interest in her career."

"Do you ever discuss specific deals?"

"Both Eva and I are too professional to do that. We both know the rules."

"How frequently do you speak to her?"

"Quite a lot."

"Meaning what?"

"Every few weeks, I guess."

"And how often do you meet with her?"

"Perhaps a handful of times a year."

"And yet you never ever talk about deals."

"Correct."

Mark had sat unusually still and silent, watching the unflinching exchange which reminded him of a pre-fight stare-down between boxers. Their heads, held fixed, were barely eighteen inches apart. Finally, Stefanie blinked and shunted backwards in her chair. Mark was satisfied that James had listened to their practice drills. He answered the questions directly, and no more. He showed no overt emotions and remained unflustered.

"Well, we'll see what she has to say when we interview her," said Stefanie in a sullen tone.

The meeting was adjourned after three hours, when Stefanie had to dash to another appointment. They'd covered about half the list of names, and Mark considered the meeting had gone well. They gathered together outside on the plaza, enjoying the breeze as it funneled through the tall buildings. Office workers trailed across the square like ants, the returning ones carrying paper take-out bags.

"Well done in there. Thought you handled madam very well," said Mark.

"Thanks. I quite enjoyed it."

"I'm glad because you'll have to get used to it. She's thorough. Very thorough. We can't afford to slip up."

"I know."

"So, we also need to be thorough."

"Of course."

"You should have told us about your god daughter."

"I didn't think it was relevant."

Mark paused a moment and narrowed his eyes, wondering whether James knew about him and Eva. "They're bound to focus on her. She should be prepared for an intense interrogation."

"Eva can handle it. She's bright and tough."

"They will scrutinise recordings of her office phone calls. And the firm will have a log of her mobile calls and perhaps even her movements via GPS. Is there anything we should be concerned about?" asked Mark, beginning to worry that his mobile number could feature in the call log. His mind spun into overdrive, conjuring up several plausible explanations, he could use if required.

"Absolutely nothing. We don't talk business."

"So, what do you talk about?" Mark felt his left cheek twitching.

"Usual stuff. Work, holidays, friends, running. She's a mad keen runner. Ran the London marathon this year."

If he does know anything, he's a damn good actor, thought Mark. "And how did you become her god father?"

"Her mother and I are old friends. I got Eva a summer internship at the bank. She did the rest."

"That doesn't look good," groaned Mark. It could complicate matters. Let's hope they don't focus on her too much.

"Just to be clear, I alone am responsible for investment decisions at LifeChance. I do my own research. No one else is involved."

"That's not the point. The point is what it would look like to a jury. Assuming they fail to come up with compelling proof, any hard facts, they'll base their case on circumstantial evidence. Anything that supports their statistical claim that your dealings were based on inside information."

"So, what should we do? "

"Let me give it some thought. That's what you're paying me for," said Mark, slapping James on the back. "That reminds me, I've been told I have to send you an interim bill. Accounts are on my back again."

Gordon slithered through Mark's half-open door, and discreetly closed it. Mark sat with his elbows planted on the desk and his chin cupped in both hands. He stared straight ahead, and the stark gloom inscribed on his face matched the darkening clouds hovering outside his window.

"Are you okay, old man?"

Mark sighed deeply. "Just been ticked off by SP over some client accounting issue."

"Yes, I heard."

Mark blinked and looked up sharply. "You know?"

"SP called me in, just now, after he'd seen you. He wants me to do the investigation. Sorry."

The sound of the word 'investigation' resonated in Mark's mind, threatening something far more ominous than the cursory review the firm's Senior Partner, known as SP, had mentioned to him. Was there a conspiracy to remove him, and was Gordon part of that?

"It was just a silly administrative cock-up. I don't know why Boyle even bothered SP with it. He should have come to see me," said Mark in a disgruntled voice. Boyle had been in post as the new financial director for the past year and had set about on a mission to modernise the firm's ragged accounting systems with a zeal that had upset most of the partners. Chief amongst their criticisms was that Boyle issued regular demands for partners to collect outstanding fees more expeditiously. Previously, such bills meandered their way through the system, with junior accounts clerks sending polite reminders every so often. It suited the Senior Partner to hide behind the new zealot.

"I'm sure it was but you know Boyle. I think SP is a bit scared of him."

"He's a bull in a china shop. As a non-lawyer, he has no idea how to treat our clients."

"Well I've got to meet with the charging bull later this afternoon for a briefing. So, when would you like to get together?"

Mark huffed again as he consulted his on-screen diary. "I have a free slot between eleven thirty and lunch tomorrow."

"That should do it. I'll check my schedule and revert," said Gordon with a reassuring smile.

"Okay. Leave the door open, please."

Within a few minutes Mark had received Gordon's confirmatory email. It also referred to Boyle's request for sight of Mark's personal bank statements for the previous two years, when Caroline Noble had become his client. Mark thumped the desk and rose up with the intent of finding Boyle. The bean-counter needed to be put in his place. But then he stalled, realised the futility of lashing out and the even more damaging impact it would have on his carefully constructed reputation, and hence career prospects within the firm he was determined to lead one day. He would not allow a single stupid administrative oversight to derail his ambition.

So instead, he reached for his personal mobile and tapped out Eva's number. As usual, the number went to voicemail. He needed to see her. The occasional text was not enough. She had been forced to cancel their planned rendezvous because at the last minute she was required to work late on a deal. They still hadn't managed to arrange another date. Maybe, he should track her down, pretend to bump into her in the city. He googled Goldwyn Morson, jotted down the address and folded the scrap of notepad into his trouser pocket.

The next day, Mark was in a foul mood. He had just reviewed a draft compromise agreement prepared by a legal assistant and lost his temper. He had spotted a couple of minor errors rather than general sloppy drafting and had lashed out. The junior staff outside in the open plan area froze in unison as Mark's exasperated yelp stung their ears. The previous evening, he had got to bed late having waited up for the police to arrive to take his statement and record details of the mugging. He had been walking home from the station on auto-pilot, his thoughts bouncing like a rubber ball between the firm's internal investigation and Eva. He had been unaware of the scooter's roar until it was level with him on the pavement and his briefcase had been snatched by the helmeted pillion passenger. Startled, he cried out, initially thinking it must be a practical joke. The muggers had rounded the corner and disappeared before he realised he had been mugged for the first time in his life.

It had taken numerous calls to enable him to cancel his debit and credit cards, a task made more difficult because his personal records were in such a poor state at home, and some of them were at work. Cath had been no help at all, especially after his ranting had woken the twins. And now he was in trouble with the IT department for not calling them immediately so that they could locate signals from his mobile and laptop before the tracking devices could be disabled.

He had got in early in order to print off two years of bank statements, only to discover that the bank had put a block on his on-line access to their accounts. He had to wait another five working days before a new PIN and cards would arrive. So, when Gordon walked into his office, he had to start with an apology and an explanation.

"We can do this another time if you prefer," said Gordon, reacting to the irritation and stress in Mark's tone. He was drumming his fingers on the desk and fidgeting with a desk-toy, an executive sand-timer gifted him by client.

"No, let's make a start. The rest of the day, in fact my entire week is back to back with meetings."

"Okay, if you're sure, old chap," said Gordon tapping his pen and his note pad. "I'm really sorry about having to do this. SP didn't really give me a choice."

"Let's get this done. No doubt Boyle has bored you with the accounting detail already. This is what actually happened. I'll start with some background."

Mark outlined how Caro had first been introduced to him by a mutual contact and how her case had evolved and grown into a beautiful monster, and with it the time commitment and hence fee levels. The billed hours ended up topping a million pounds but they had only collected half of that by the time of the trial and judgement. He admitted he could have been quicker in requiring payment, but that it would have been a difficult discussion to have had at a sensitive time with the client. After the judgement, a short-term penal sentence, which everyone knew had been a risk, he felt it would nevertheless be difficult to ask for the full amount. So as a goodwill gesture, and with sign-off from SP, they had agreed to reduce the fee to nine hundred thousand. A revised bill was sent, an original having gone out in error for the full million. This had clearly riled the client. Over several months, they'd had protracted, sometimes robust but always civilised communications on the size of the bill. Eventually a reduced fee of seven hundred and fifty thousand had been agreed, and the final bill sent out.

"That was the last I heard about it. I presumed Accounts had handled everything. In the old days, someone would have nudged me to ask whether I would mind sending a reminder email or something. I had no idea until yesterday there was an issue. I certainly would've stopped a standard letter threatening litigation going out. I can completely understand why the client appears so livid."

Gordon had listened without interruption, scribbling notes furiously as Mark presented his version of events. He paused before looking up again. "Did SP sign-off on the seven-fifty figure?"

"Yes. I remember having the conversation with him. He must have done."

"Right," said Gordon slowly. "It's just that I couldn't find anything on file and Accounts say they don't have any documented evidence for it."

Mark swallowed hard and his face reddened. "Gordon, you know this is ridiculous. The form probably got lost somewhere in the system. Check with SP. I'm sure he'll remember."

"I'm sure he will. It's just a shame that we can't find any piece of paper with his signature, that's all. And he's such a busy chap-"

"Just speak to him," interrupted Mark. "He will remember."

"Of course, of course. Let's move on. So what puzzles me a little, is how two hundred and fifty thousand ended up in your personal account."

Mark sighed with frustration. "Me too. Until yesterday, I had no idea the money was there. Of course, I've already transferred it to the firm."

"Forgive me, but a quarter of a million is rather a lot to overlook, is it not?"

"I suppose it is," admitted Mark. "But it appears to have come in three installments over a couple of months. Look, I don't take much notice of the financial stuff. Cath deals with most of the bills and as long as the balance hovers around a million or so, I stay well clear of it."

"A million? You should be investing that old chap, not leaving it lying around."

"Afraid not. Cath has an eye on a property in Majorca and says we may need to move fast to get the right one."

"So that's why you kept such an amount in the account."

"Maybe. Yes, I suppose it is. But there's always something. Last year, it was the boat."

"I see, yes," said Gordon scribbling once more. "But returning to the fundamental point, why do you think the money was sent to your account and not the firm's account, where of course the first half million went?"

"I have no idea. I tried to call the client yesterday and left a message. Maybe their accounts department made a mistake. It's not unknown," said Mark with a wry smirk.

Gordon scratched his chin in contemplation. "How does one go about finding out people's bank account details?"

"I have no idea, and before you ask, I also have no idea how the client got my details. That's what I hope to clarify when I speak with Caroline Noble."

"Yes, without knowing that, it is difficult to comprehend much more at this stage. We know the facts but not the motivations that generated those facts. So objectively speaking, one cannot interpret the facts as yet."

"You're beginning to sound like a judge rather than my friend now." said Mark.

"Sorry old chap. But I have to present my findings to the Standards and Ethics Committee."

Mark groaned. He had hoped the matter could be dealt with informally, quickly and in confidence. The committee involved five or six of his peers and tended to sit once a month.

"Don't worry, Boyle's not on it. Everything will be fine. Let me know when you've spoken to the client. And let me have those bank statements some time."

Chapter Fourteen   Revelation

From James's balcony, Stefanie looked across to the lantern-lit path of the Embankment and traced the line of the river to the hulking shadow by Westminster Bridge. She breathed hungrily, inhaling a fresh breeze blowing in from the west. Even at this hour, she could see helmeted cyclists down below, heading home. She took a sip from her chilled glass, a German Riesling James had selected to accompany the Pad Thai he had cooked. Her mouth still tingled from the chilli, and her breath stank of garlic. She was on her third glass, and finally she was feeling her muscles unfurl. She felt the tickle of his kiss on her nape, where James had nuzzled beneath her still damp hair.

"Suits you," said James as he resurfaced and put an arm around her. She was wearing a white toweling robe from James's bathroom.

She sighed with relief. "This view is perfect. It must have cost a fortune."

"I was lucky. I'd owned a house in Chelsea for a long time. The property market did the hard work, not me."

"Why did you move?" She thought that British people were irrationally in love with houses, that apartments were considered somehow second best.

"Felt like a change. I was surrounded by families, and there I was, rattling around in a five-bedroom house."

"How long did you say you had been here?" She still felt like the place was a hotel, that everything felt temporary.

"I didn't. But about four years now."

"I don't see any of you in here. No photographs, no mementos, no clutter."

"I got rid of it all when I moved. Everything went to auction. It felt like a huge relief."

You should see my place. Full of stuff."

"I'd like to see your place."

Stefanie snorted. "You wouldn't if you saw it. I have no view and all the noise from trains at the back. I swear it shakes when a fast train shoots by."

"Handy for the tennis." James smiled.

"Handier for the train station for work." Stefanie had been attracted by the idea of living in leafy Wimbledon, with its bijou restaurants, bars and eclectic shops in the village. But even six years ago, all she could afford was a pinched two bed apartment in a modern block in an unfashionable area with a fashionable SW19 postcode. "I've never ever been to see the tennis."

Work had dominated her life. Work defined who she had become and also how people responded to her. Until now perhaps. This enigmatic, generous, warm man by her side treated her differently. Yet the shadow of her FCA investigation lurked and materialised spasmodically. She doubted his innocence but not his principles. She hoped he would be found not guilty. Better still, if the trial never came to court.

"James, you know I have to do my job-"

"I know."

"And I have to be seen to be doing my job as well."

"I realise that."

"If sometimes, I come across as aggressive, like I don't really care about you, you understand why-"

"Of course-"

"That I do care."

James pulled her close and kissed her. "Come inside. I want to show you something."

She followed him into the lounge where smooth jazz played softly from unseen ceiling speakers. He uncovered a small safe, hidden behind a picture. He withdrew something and gestured for Stefanie to take a seat.

"I owe you an explanation." James said as he sidled along the sofa. "About the nightmare I had when you were here last. I get it, the same one, from time to time."

Stefanie looked at him prizing open a tarnished tin box. It looked like a museum piece, something from the second world war era perhaps.

"This old tobacco tin belonged to my mother. She was run over by a car when I was young." Previously James had told her that he'd been fostered from a very young age, that he had no family. He'd closed down the conversation, saying he preferred not to think too much about his childhood. She had taken the hint and not pressed him. In the past, she would probably have bludgeoned on, insisted on knowing the facts. But the pained look on his face had been enough. She didn't want to ruin this chance of a relationship, like the others. Was she finally learning to heed her mother's homespun wisdom, 'Everything comes to those who wait.' She'd always ignored her, been in too much of a hurry, to escape and forge her own path.

James began telling Stefanie his memory of the day his mother died. As he did so, he carefully removed each of the artifacts in the tin and laid them gently on the coffee table: a smoker's pipe, a brass thimble, an embroidered lace handkerchief with the initials 'E J', a rubber banded collection of early 1970s Kellogg's cereal football cards, a folded piece of paper, an envelope addressed to 'Esther', and a faded Polaroid photograph.

"This is me with my mother," said James picking up the photograph. A tall, slim pale-faced woman in a gold, white and red, flowery pinafore dress. She was standing, holding a small child. Both faces frozen in mid laugh.

"She was very pretty. How old were you?"

"About two. Probably taken not long before the accident."

"By your father?"

"No. I very much doubt that." James picked up a fragile piece of paper, unfolded it and handed it to Stefanie. "Take a look."

Stefanie cradled the ancient script and scanned an original signed birth certificate. Where and when born: 2 May 1974, St George's Hospital, Tooting. Name: Alon Jäger. Stefanie frowned and then slowly lifted her head. "Is Alon Jäger you?"

"Was." James nodded. "Read on."

Sex: Boy. Mother: Esther Jäger, 17 Gilbey Road, SW17. Father: -. Stefanie pointed to the blank space where the father's name was supposed to be. "You don't know who your father is?"

"I didn't. Not until a few years ago. But I know now."

"So, do you see him?"

"No. He's dead. You need a refill. I know I do."

James got up and headed to the kitchen to fetch a fresh bottle. Stefanie leant forward and picked up the thimble of her boyfriend's dead mother. It fitted snugly on her index finger. She flicked through playing cards of long-haired footballers whose faces and names she did not recognise. She supposed they were real and not made up. Just like all of this before her. Just like this room, this situation she found herself in. She picked up the battered envelope as James re-entered with a bounce in his step, an uncorked bottle in one hand and two glasses in the other.

"Thought we'd migrate to something a bit special. A 2005 Côte de Beaune if that's okay."

"What's in here?" asked Stefanie as James poured out two full glasses. She could smell the red berry fruit already.

"That," said James glancing momentarily at the envelope in Stefanie's hand, "is a letter from my father to my mother. Read it."

Stefanie withdrew a folded piece of paper from its matching cream envelope. It unfolded stiffly and the thickness of the paper made it feel as if it had been woven. The writing in black ink was neat and easy to read. No crossings out or markings out of place, as if it must have been copied from a draft prepared in advance.

My darling Esther,

I am so very, very sorry. I have agonised over this. I cannot leave Miranda and the children. The pain and damage that would cause would be unbearable and I don't think I could carry on living with the guilt. I know this is terribly hard for you. Should you decide to have the baby, I will do my best to provide some financial help. But we must keep it a secret. If Miranda's father were to be made aware, then I'm sure I'd be out of the firm without a penny the same day. That would be terrible for both of us.

Please forgive me.

John

P.S. I shall always love you.

No address or date, Stefanie reflected as she ran a finger-tip under the last line, feeling its roughness. She looked at him, expecting an explanation, but his eyes were fixed on the ceiling. "So, your mother had an affair with a married man?"

"Yes. And I was the consequence."

James came to sit down beside her and handed her a glass. "I'll give you the short version." He took a deep breath.

On James's twenty first birthday, he received a letter from a London law firm requesting him to get in touch as they had been instructed by a client to bequeath twenty-one thousand pounds to him. Thinking it was a hoax, he threw out the letter. A second one arrived two weeks later. When a third one landed on the doormat of his dingy student house-share, he finally picked up the phone. The letter was genuine, and he was given the choice of being sent a cheque or having the money wired to his bank account. The lawyer refused to give any other details, other than stressing that the donor insisted on remaining anonymous. A cheque arrived two days later attached to a one-line letter repeating the assertion that no details would be forthcoming on the identity of the benefactor. James called the lawyer again but elicited nothing other than a hint that the benefactor was still alive.

James puzzled over it throughout his final year at university and shared his thoughts with Caro. She agreed the money could only have come from one person, his anonymous father. So, he decided, instead of joining his peers on their gap year travels around the cheap party hotspots of the globe, he would agree to work unpaid for a private investigations firm based in Chiswick. He thought the skills he would pick up, could be the key to finding out about his father. But half the year done, he had got no further, and resigned himself to never finding out.

Six years ago, late on a damp October evening, he answered a loud knock on his front door in Chelsea and came face to face with a grey-faced old man, with a mop of greasy unkempt hair. He had reached into his pocket for something to give the bedraggled figure. The head leaned into the room, and with foul breath and bloodshot eyes, accused James of being Alon Jäger. The decrepit soul was his father who proved his identity by quoting word-perfect the letter he had written to Esther. He had sent the money and had lived with remorseful guilt all his life.

James listened as John Taylor tumbled out his story and polished off a bottle of single malt whisky James had been saving. John had been a lawyer at the firm where Esther had worked as a secretary. The firm was owned by his wife Miranda's father. The affair started when his three children were very young. It had lasted only a few months but was intense. He loved her he said. He got scared and decided to end it. Then Esther discovered she was pregnant. She left the firm shortly afterwards and he never saw or heard from her again. He heard about her death a few days after the accident and went to her funeral along with a few others from the firm. It was a small affair in a crematorium in Streatham, south London.

He discovered drink as a way of forgetting for a while. Over the years his drinking crept up, but he could still function. His children grew up, left home and left him and his wife rattling around the ancestral home left by her father. He

216

no longer had to work as they could live off her inheritance. So, he drank instead. As he drank more, they argued more, until finally Miranda threw him out. He couldn't remember quite when, but at some point, she had stopped sending money. Now he lived in a bedsit in Camden and had run out of money. He had spent the last of his savings on paying a firm to find James. Now there he was, asking whether James could lend him some money, whether they could get to know one another, whether he could move in with him, and whether James could forgive him.

James was livid. He raged like a forlorn child that his father had rejected him on three occasions: when he was born, when his mother was killed, and when he was twenty-one. He ranted about the series of foster homes he had run away from. And he boiled over with the recollections of crying himself to sleep in lonely rooms after his mother died. He had started with nothing and built a successful life for himself and didn't need his father now. His father had done the reverse with his life.

As he opened the door to the hunched progenitor, he wavered. He grabbed a business card and stuffed it into the pocket of his teary father's jacket. He withdrew some notes from his wallet, stuffed them into the old man's shaking hands, then shut the door. A few seconds later, he opened the door and shouted out to his father, telling him to phone the next day.

When James got to Sloane Square early next morning, he discovered the tube line was down. A person had fallen under a train. He thought nothing of it other than being a bit of a nuisance and hopped on a bus to work. Later that morning he received a call. The police had found James's card together with a few coins, in the pocket of someone who had fallen onto the tracks near Sloane Square. Subsequently, he had to identify his father's inebriated body. Then he left. If there was a funeral, he was not invited. Rejected in death as well as in life. To his father's family, to his half-siblings, he would be a stranger, an unwelcome guest, and a blot on the memory of their childhoods.

Stefanie had both hands covering her mouth and was staring with watery eyes as James picked up his wine glass and the room fell silent. The whine of a plane passing overhead leached through the open balcony doors.

"I'm so sorry," she said, with anguished hoarseness.

"Me too." James drained his glass. "I rejected my father just as he had me. I failed to forgive him. And I threw away the chance to get to know him, and myself. Instead, I quit my job and got on a plane. Finally faced up to the fact that my life meant nothing very much to me. Pointless. Something, maybe everything had to change."

Chapter Fifteen   Pictures

Mark sighed with relief as he opened his front door, just before nine as usual. It had been an exhausting day with back to back meetings. And the firm's investigation of the Caroline Noble billing cock-up was dragging on. The damn woman had not returned any of his calls, and his emails had not elicited any response. To make matters worse, SP had only a vague recollection of their conversation about reducing the bill, and certainly could not recall the figure he was supposed to have approved.

He was relishing the thought of a shower, followed by dinner washed down with a couple of glasses of chilled wine, and catching-up on the day's tittle-tattle with Cath. He threw down his briefcase by the coat-stand and noticed a large black suitcase stationed there. He must have forgotten that one of Cath's clan was staying again – there were so many that he could never remember all the names of cousins and other distant relatives, who treated their home like an inn, checking in and out at freewill. He stifled a groan. The looming prospect of playing convivial host depressed him. He was so looking forward to unwinding, and not having to make any effort.

He dawdled towards the kitchen where Cath would be cooking and singing along to one of her Spotify 'nineties' playlists. It struck him as odd that he could not smell the usual spicy aromas nor feel the warm air drifting from the kitchen.

The house was strangely quiet and still. Cath normally cried out, 'how was your day?' when she heard him in the hall.

As he entered the brightly lit kitchen, Cath sat at the kitchen table, still sporting a light tan from the fortnight at their house in Salcombe. He'd only managed to snatch a couple of days with them. No wonder he felt so drained. He needed a break. Cath was topping up her glass from one of his vintage bottles of Burgundy he kept for special occasions.

"Shut the door," said Cath.

That sounded and looked to him as if the hurricane of his mother-in-law must have landed with her suitcase of unfettered opinions. "Someone important staying I see," said Mark, making sure Cath knew she had opened one of his Grand Crus.

"No. Just me and the kids." Cath stared at him and took a sip.

"So," said Mark gesturing behind him, "whose is the suitcase in the hall?"

"Yours." She wore an impassive expression.

"Mine?" squawked Mark, his vocal cords reacting fractionally ahead of his brain which raced past misdemeanours to what he feared the most. As the surprise settled on his face, Cath tossed a large brown envelope on to the table.

"This came for me in the post. Take a look."

Mark froze. The fear in his brain had reached his stomach. He gulped open-mouthed but no words escaped.

"Let me show you then." She said it with a thin smile in the passive-aggressive tone she used to admonish the children when they were being naughty. She said it kept her calm when she felt like indulging in physical assault. With slow deliberate movements, Cath laid out six A4-sized colour photographs. She had saved the worst to last, his face a fist of mouth-gaping, eye-popping ecstasy, and Eva's head thrown backwards, as she sat astride him.

"I think that one's the best."

"I...I..." began Mark, slouching down on a seat, elbows resting on the table, and holding his head in both hands. "Shit, shit, shit."

"At least we can agree on that," said Cath from the other end of the table.

"I can explain."

"The floor is yours."

"It's not what you think."

"And what is that? You have no idea what..." said Cath, suddenly stopping. She stilled herself, smiled briefly and waited.

"It only happened once," said Mark to Cath's snort of incredulity, "honestly."

"Who is she?" demanded Cath, displaying a split second of anger.

"Her name is Eva," began Mark, sighing heavily, and then presented a factual account of how they had met at the marathon, how she had pursued him, their dinner together and their tryst at the hotel. "That's it, that's all there is to tell." He sighed again, too heavily, overplaying the stock character he had become.

"You expect me to believe that?"

"It's the truth." Cath eyed him for a few seconds. He could tell she wasn't convinced. "I swear."

"She is very pretty... and young. Is that how you like your tarts? How old is she?"

Mark grimaced. "I'm not sure. I never asked."

"Was the sex good? Was it better?" said Cath in a composed and clinical tone. Mark looked away, shaking his head, wishing he could be anywhere but here.

"What did she taste like?"

"Please, stop." Mark stood up and gathered the photographs back into the envelope. He was always careful not to eradicate evidence.

"Me stop? I'm the one who hasn't started anything. I'm just the loyal idiot staying at home, looking after your children, managing the home and dealing with every last bloody thing, so you can swan around being patted on the back for doing what you love."

"So I can support my family," said Mark in a rising voice. "That was the deal."

"And you just broke it. Do you love each other?" persisted Cath.

"Don't be ridiculous," erupted Mark. "It was just a fling."

"Oh well that's okay then," said Cath and glugged at her wine. "No supper, straight to bed, and we start afresh tomorrow."

How he hated her patronising tone. "It's not all my fault."

"Ha…I wondered how long it would take you to get that out. You know, the funny thing is, you've not even said you're sorry."

"Of course I'm sorry.

"Sorry you got caught or sorry you did it?"

"Cath, I'm sorry, okay. It was stupid."

Cath sat back, arms folded, and glowered at him for an uncomfortable forever. "Why?"

"Why what?"

"Why did you do it?"

222

Mark's mouth fell open, hanging there, grappling with an acceptable response. "I don't know. I honestly don't know," mumbled Mark glancing down to avert Cath's piercing stare.

"Then you need to think…and think very carefully if you want to stand any chance of saving our marriage."

"You can't be serious." Mark's voice rose with unfolding panic, realising she was serious. She had never before been this serious.

"I've booked you in to the Cromwell House hotel. I've packed your suitcase for you."

"Cath, please." He wasn't used to pleading, so even this cry sounded like he thought she was being utterly unreasonable.

"I need some time on my own, to think."

"How long?"

Cath said nothing but speared him with a look of contempt.

"You can't make me go. This is my home too."

Cath poured herself some more wine, took a sip and sat back in her chair, as if measuring out her thoughts. "I cannot forcibly remove you. I cannot legally remove you. But if you don't go, I will show these pictures to the children over breakfast, starting with Olly."

"That's terrible. That's immoral," said Mark making a grab for the envelope.

"Don't you dare lecture me on morals," said Cath, her voice shaking with ferocity. "And do you really think I would be stupid enough not to have copies, you prick?"

"You wouldn't do it."

"I would," said Cath with a cold calmness. The steel in her voice convinced Mark that her threat was real.

"Just for tonight," said Mark, rising to the sound of his chair skittering back over the tiled floor. He swivelled to go and then stopped and glared at her. "You hired someone to follow me, to take those photos, didn't you?"

Cath glared back at him. "No, of course not. I presumed it was your tart getting her own back on you." He could tell from the perplexed look he had seen over so many years of marriage when he had tried to explain the intricacies of a case to her, that she was being sincere.

"Why would she do that? We've never argued."

"I thought you said it only happened once?"

"It did, the physical thing." He couldn't bring himself to utter the actual word, sex. The euphemism provided him with some protection against guilt, against the seedy truth.

"You will end it, or...." Cath's voiced trailed off.

"Yes. Yes, I will end it," said Mark unable to hide the moroseness in his voice. Eva had just committed to a date the following week, had sworn she would not need to change it yet again, had already taken the initiative and booked the hotel. With a heavy sigh, his drooping figure slumped out of the brightness of the kitchen into the sombre-lit hall. He halted at the foot of the stairs and was about to sneak up.

"They won't miss you till the weekend," said Cath from the kitchen doorway. Mark picked up his briefcase, grabbed the suitcase handle, and opened the front door. Without glancing back, he sloped off into the humid still air of a moonless late evening, disturbed by his trundling suitcase on the cobbled drive and the clunk of the door as it closed behind him.

Mark stood before a table topped with tourist pamphlets, that doubled up as a check-in and concierge desk. A pallid faced clerk bearing the plastic name-badge 'Inga' sat behind it.

"We have you booked in for three nights sir," said Inga, with a thick central European, and a stern face at Mark.

His forlorn figure sank onto a chair, and nodded affirmation with a grunt.

"Credit card and sign here, please," she instructed as she began the drawn-out rigmarole of guest registration and extolling the virtues of the aspirant three-star hotel. "Would you like to join our loyalty program?"

Mark politely declined and set off along a weaving corridor, painted white, carpeted lime-green, in search of his room. Like him, the room had seen better days but at least it was clean and lacked a smoker's stench. The shower dribbled lukewarm water over him and the stiff towel abraded his skin. He switched off the light and crashed into bed to a chorus of squeaking springs.

He slept fitfully, tormented by his self-inflicted predicament and the nagging question of who had taken the damaging pictures. At some point, he must have drifted off, as he was awoken by the shrill siren of the bedside phone. He fumbled for the receiver and groaned as a chirpy voice informed him that it was his six-thirty alarm call. He couldn't remember ordering one the night before.

By seven, he found himself in a functional dining room, surrounded by foreign families with small children, eking out the dying days of their summer breaks. He felt deflated not having seen his own kids the previous night and distraught at the thought that Cath could divorce him and take custody of them. He kept telling himself, she couldn't be serious, that she just wanted to teach him a lesson. He'd be home by the weekend, surely.

He finished the last mouthful of croissant and swallowed the remnants of his tepid mug of tea. Neither had tasted of anything. He picked up his briefcase and strode in his City suit towards the exit, parading past gawking kids. A harried waitress scurried after him to remind him to sign the chit on his table. With a loud sigh, he made the return journey, scribbled something illegible and then marched out into the fumes and furore of rush-hour.

Packed platforms and carriages greeted him at every point of his journey into the office, and everything seemed to be delayed. The walk from the underground to his office seemed longer and hotter. The wait at his favourite Italian deli for coffee stretched for minutes; their card reader was playing-up, and no-one seemed to be carrying cash other than him. He finally gave up, cursing under his breath at the stupidity of technology and other people.

He arrived at his desk with his shirt stuck to his back and a sheen of sweat across his forehead. He tore off his jacket, loosened his tie, and headed to the toilets where he drowned his face in a basin and slaked his thirst direct from the tap. He peered into the mirror, red and baggy eyed, resolving to bury himself in work until ten-thirty, when he thought Cath would be back from school drop-offs and coffee with her clan. He put on his cheery face and went to find Sandra to ask her to nip out to *Cafe Nero* for him – he needed the extra shot of caffeine this morning. Gordon was with her, sorting out some travel arrangements for a conference in New York.

"Coffees all round?" bawled Mark, smiling and clapping his hands. "My shout," and he handed a twenty-pound note to Sandra.

"Why not?" said Gordon.

"The usual?" said Sandra. "Double-shot macchiato, and a normal latté for you Gordon?"

"You're a marvel, Sandra," said Gordon. "Do you have a moment, Mark? It won't take a minute."

"Sure." Mark followed Gordon past a phalanx of desks housing the junior staff, and into his glass partitioned office. Gordon closed the door.

"Take a seat," said Gordon, going to his desk and unlocking a drawer. "I regret this is rather embarrassing...for both of us." He withdrew a large brown envelope and set it squarely on the desk between them.

The envelope, its colour and size, its white label and type font, was identical to the one Cath had confronted him with the previous evening. "Oh god," groaned Mark, his face reddening and his shoulders sagging. "Photographs, I presume."

"Indeed. Rather lurid pictures of you and your new client in flagrante delicto."

Mark sighed and ran his fingers through his hair. He thought he could detect the feint of sincerity betrayed by a miniscule curl of Gordon's lips.

"Okay, I'll be straight with you. She is not my client."

"I had gathered that the other night. Rather, I wondered if you were her client."

"No, nothing like that. She is just a friend." Gordon's raised eyebrows and involuntary smirk invited Mark to expound. "Well, more than that clearly but..."

"No need to explain old boy. What you do in your private life is up to you," said Gordon pushing the envelope towards Mark, "as long as SP doesn't find out. You know how he hates any thought of impropriety that might besmirch the firm's reputation." The thought that SP, the firm's Senior Partner, Mark's boss, might have received an envelope filled him with horror. His career at the firm would be finished.

Mark's mouth fell open. "You don't think he was sent the photos do you?"

"No idea. No idea why I was sent them either. There's no accompanying message. No clue as to the sender."

"What a mess," groaned Mark, cracking his fingers to release some of the tension he was feeling. For a brief moment, he considered telling Gordon about his wife receiving the photos. But too much of his private life had already been exposed in the office. It could be used against him, when it suited someone.

"Is someone trying to blackmail you?"

Mark exhaled heavily and slapped the desk with both hands. "No one has been in contact, there has been no note, phone call, text, nothing," said Mark, shaking his head. He could really do with that coffee arriving. He noticed his fingers were quivering. They looked like they belonged to someone else, someone peering over the edge of a dark abyss.

"Well then, you must have upset someone, rather badly it would appear."

"Can't imagine who," murmured Mark. His mind was already racing back through historic cases, dim recollections of uncivil arguments with opposing solicitors. But he could not recall anything remotely hostile that would explain this intrusion into his hitherto closely guarded private life.

"Another woman perhaps?"

"No," cried Mark, "I've never been involved with any other woman. That," he said picking up the envelope, "was the one and only occasion. Honestly." Even though, that was not strictly true, Mark allowed himself to believe it. He considered a frantic shag with a junior colleague at a drunken Christmas party to be part of carnival, separate from everyday life, and without taint of sin.

"Hmm...evidently someone is attempting to defile you."

"Why? I haven't done anything," said Mark with a half shrug.

"You've done your job, and very well. You are bound to have upset some lawyer or other."

"But that's the job, it's what we do, that's what we're paid to do."

"Someone might find it too hard to lose if he, or she, has invested a great deal in a case."

"Perhaps, but surely not to go as far as hiring someone to break into a hotel room and plant a camera. It would be foolhardy. They would be risking their entire career, go to prison even, if they were discovered."

"I presume you've discounted going to the police."

Mark stopped chewing his finger-nail abruptly. "Absolutely not. I've got to keep this quiet. If they know, they'll start asking questions of everyone around here. I might as well resign now." Mark froze as the opening bars of Chopin's Funeral March rang out.

"Sorry. Better get that if you don't mind," said Gordon reaching for the handset. As Gordon took the call, Mark gazed at the black and white photographs hanging on the walls, glossy, framed in thin black wood edged with gold-leaf. He had been in Gordon's offices so many times before but had never studied them. Now he realised they were all shots of Rudolf Nureyev.

"That one's him with Margot Fonteyn at Covent Garden, 1962, Giselle. Wish I'd seen them but born too late sadly," said Gordon, replacing the receiver. "Sorry, I must dash. A client has arrived, and she who pays the piper calls the tune."

"Of course," said Mark stumbling to his feet, "and Gordon..."

"Your secret is safe with me old chap." Gordon put a finger to his lips.

"Thanks." Mark held the door open and then followed Gordon out past the junior staff burrowing away in their desktop cells.

He returned to his office, closed the door, and behind his desk, withdrew the photographs from the envelope. It was the first time, he had been able to study them. Despite nauseous gyrations in his stomach, he couldn't help but feel aroused. Eva was ravishing, and her enraptured face revealed that he must have satisfied something in her. He glowed with the thought of seeing her again and wondered whether he really had to end it. He would have to be more careful, take precautions, and he would have to find out who held such a grudge against him. He knew he ought to tell Eva about the photographs. Mark slid the pictures back into the envelope, which he buried amidst papers in his briefcase. He'd admire them again when he got back to his hotel room. He'd decide then whether he should meet Eva the following week, and tell her about the pictures, face to face, perhaps.

He forced himself to concentrate on his work for the rest of the day, though he struggled repeatedly with the invasion of images of himself with Eva. Thoughts about the identity of the perpetrator nagged away at him like toothache. He wandered into Gordon's room and chatted about their chance meeting in the Clift Hotel's cocktail lounge. Gordon had been curious to know more about Mark's new client. Gordon could rival Mark for the top job of Senior Partner one distant day. But he had never shown much interest in office politics, and during the decade they had worked together, he had always been transparent and fair-minded.

He toiled through to eight o'clock before slinking out of the office, deep in thought. The call with Cath when she had finally picked up the phone, had been terse and tense. She had been implacable, refusing to be drawn on when he could return home. The kids were fine. He wasn't missed.

He dragged himself to the hot stale air of Bank's underground, to the aptly named 'Drain' or 'Misery Line'. A train rattled into the station and he edged forwards to make sure he got a seat. The doors rumbled open and he darted in. He picked up a copy of *The Metro* from a seat and plopped down. The dance for seats ended and then they waited in silence. He looked around at the faces of other haggard commuters, longing to escape to the distant allure of homes. Lucky them, he brooded.

A thought struck him as finally the doors slid shut and the train jolted forwards with a bang. Maybe he had been followed. Perhaps someone was following him now. His eyes skittered around the carriage: the young bloke opposite with his McDonalds stinking out the place, or the prim looking woman next to him glaring at a Kindle, or the suited executive opposite, much like him, gazing idly at his disposable newspaper? The clanking of the wheels on the track rolled on and the train squealed around a corner. No one looked up or moved a muscle. He was being ridiculous. He would not find the answer by searching for facial clues in a packed train carriage. He went back to *The Metro*. He'd be done with it in the few minutes to Waterloo. He'd pick up some food there, before getting on the train to Putney. He couldn't face the hotel restaurant tonight.

Chapter Sixteen   Devotion

Mark had his feet up on his desk as the sun sank red on the horizon. He was reading through a draft submission to the FCA his team had prepared for a wealthy investment banking executive who had been accused of being party to interest rate collusion. Mark had met him once, briefly. He was pretty sure the man was guilty but thought the evidence against him had weaknesses that could be attacked. He was confident he could create reasonable doubt in the minds of the jury. He would win.

Today, he was still finding it difficult to concentrate and had to keep re-reading entire pages. His mind floated back repeatedly to Eva and their upcoming date. In his mind, he had concocted a reel of their lively antics on the hotel bed, which he luxuriated in replaying. He had been surprised how assertive Eva had been, how she had instructed him; where to touch her and the sundry sexual positions she had led him through. He had been counting down the days to their next assignation. He had not felt the same excitement since being a child on the eve of Christmas.

Mark's mobile vibrated on the desk. He glimpsed at the caller number and seeing it was Eva, his heart lurched. It felt like someone was playing drums inside his chest. They had agreed only to message each other. For a horrible moment, he thought she could be calling to cancel.

"Well, hello there," Mark boomed into the phone, forcing a grin.

"Mark, what the hell are you playing at?" screamed Eva. "If you're going to take photos, you should discuss it with me first. I'm not a bloody prude but you've no right to -."

"It wasn't me," interjected Mark. "Shit."

"Come on Mark. Stop playing games. What's going on?"

"Eva, honestly I have no clue who took those photos."

"So how come you know what I'm talking about then?"

"Because," Mark sighed, "my wife was sent a set, and so was my colleague, Gordon, the one you met in the hotel bar."

Silence reigned for a few seconds. Are you still there?" asked Mark.

"You are kidding."

"Wish I was. Let me guess, six A4-sized photographs, no note, in a brown envelope."

"Of us fucking together. Jesus Mark, it was posted to my office. At least it had a private and confidential label, otherwise the whole bloody department would know." Her voice had quietened to an urgent whisper.

"Okay, calm down," said Mark feeling like he was drowning, his head swimming with snapshots, none of which made sense. "Let's think. Who, no, where was the camera?"

"That's what I'm asking you."

"Eva, for god's sake, I have no idea. I can't imagine who or why anyone would do this, or how." He was sweating now and found himself pacing his room. He soothed his pulsating temple with a thumb and finger.

"Mark, come on. At least admit it."

"It wasn't me," Mark screamed as he gazed out of the window at the lit tower blocks illuminating the dusk. "My wife has kicked me out."

"You're scaring me now."

"I'm scaring myself. I didn't tell anyone about our date. It wasn't in my diary."

"What about your wife?"

"What about her?"

"Maybe she hired someone to follow you."

"She had no reason to."

"You've been disloyal. You've cheated on her. Maybe she was suspicious. Have you done this before?"

"No!" shouted Mark with indignation. "I've never done anything like this before.

"Really?" said Eva, followed by what sounded to Mark like an incredulous snort.

"Really, insisted Mark. "Look I need to see the photos. Check whether they're the same ones, or different ones from a different angle."

"What does it matter. What would that tell us?"

"I don't know, but, but there might be a clue hidden somewhere." He knew it sounded dubious, but he was desperate to see her. "Can we meet, tonight?"

He heard Eva exhale loudly. "Mark, I don't want to get messed up in your marital affairs."

She already was, thought Mark, but to say as much would not help his case. "You won't be. I'll be back home in a few days, once she calms down."

"But what if you're being followed and someone photographs us meeting?"

"I'm not. I'm sure I'm not. I keep checking."

"You can't know that."

"I do. Look, if we get together, I'm sure we can fathom this out."

He heard Eva sigh again. "I don't know, Mark. I-"

"You just don't want to see me again, do you?" His desperation sounded like an explosion. He no longer cared. He ached for her, he could not stop thinking about her, he had to see her.

"Mark, you're being ridiculous."

"Please." He held his breath and waited an eternity, hoping she would light up his gloom.

"Okay, okay. But I can't tonight.

"Tomorrow, then."

"I can't. I've an important client dinner."

"Friday. Surely you can make Friday. No-one has business dinners on Friday."

"I thought you had family Fridays."

"I do but this is more important. The kids won't miss one Friday."

Another sigh, louder. "Okay. I'll cancel my plans."

Mark punched the air. "Shall we meet at my hotel?"

"No, not there. Somewhere more public, a bar where it would be normal for us to be having a drink together." Mark heard the snap of his pen as it cracked in his fist.

"Maybe we could go somewhere afterwards," Mark said tentatively.

"We'll see. I'll text you a place and time."

"Great."

"And Mark, make sure you're not being followed."

Eva hung up, leaving Mark's pulse racing as he pondered the possibilities of another night with her. It wouldn't solve the fundamental question, who wanted to damage him and why. But it felt like a just reward for the crap being heaped upon him at work and at home.

The aroma of fish still hung in the air as Bruce hovered about clearing up plates and bowls from dinner. The cod with feta, wild garlic and pine nuts, had been as pleasing to James's palette as his update on the Weasel had been to Caro's ears.

"So he's clearly had his fun, now I'm having mine," said Caro prodding glossy photos of Mark and Eva, naked on the bed. James had not brought the video he'd reluctantly skimmed through to select the stills. The god-parent part of him, that kept striving and failing, divined that showing the video would be a further act of sacrilege.

"I don't think he's having much fun by now. I sent copies to both his wife and a work colleague. "Eva said he was freaking out when she called him earlier."

"She's done a great job. I must thank her somehow."

"Not asking her to repeat the experience would be enough. I promised it would be just the once."

"Well let's hope his wife gets rid of him straight away then."

"She has already. He's living in a hotel."

"Good. His family will be better off without him."

James winced. The video was a tragi-comedy. Mark trying hard and failing to follow Eva's commands, whilst succeeding in ruining his marriage. "Eva's meeting him on Friday, just to finish it properly. She'll also try to find out about any fall-out within his firm."

Caro laughed like a vent disgorging raw sewage. "He has tried to get through to me at least a dozen times already this week. Your invoice ploy seems to have him rattled."

"I think it may well put a break on his career aspirations."

"I don't want a break. I want to end them."

"Caro. It's nine o'clock. You promised to tuck the kids in," said Bruce, as he clattered plates into the dishwasher.

"I did. Doesn't time fly when you're having fun," said Caro, rising from the table. "Don't go James, we need to think of something else for our Weasel friend."

James's spirit wilted momentarily. He had thought this was it, the final twist of the knife in the Mark's back. He wanted to move on. After all, Mark was his lawyer, fighting his case, and he could do without him being distracted any further. He waited until the sound of Caro's footsteps on the stairs had disappeared. He picked up a dish, still half full of asparagus with tofu, and carried it to the counter next to where Bruce stood, swilling a saucepan with suddy water.

"Thanks for dinner, Bruce."

"My pleasure. I wasn't that sure about the tofu."

"It was all excellent."

"Thank you. I'm thinking about culinary school next year."

"Sounds fun. Go for it."

James picked up a tea-towel and attacked a casserole dish draining on the side whilst Bruce scraped away at a saucepan with a steel sponge scourer. "Bruce, don't you think the Weasel has suffered enough? That we should all move on?"

Bruce didn't look up and the sound of scouring increased. "James, I have no idea just how much that man has suffered. But I do know how much Caro has had to endure. I saw close-up how it affected the kids. Olly still wets the bed. Rosie sticks to her like a limpet-"

"I know-"

"And it's even worse for Jess and Jack. They're old enough to misunderstand. People, parents, children all gossip. The school were good but they still got teased a lot. You can never escape bullies, I know that. But I'm scared they'll be frightened to take risks in case they make a mistake like their mum."

"They're robust kids. They'll be fine. They've got you and Caro as parents." said James stuffing the tea-towel into the middle of an oven dish.

Bruce sighed and met James's gaze. "I hope you're right."

The two men re-sought the safety of their menial tasks. And James contemplated for a moment what it must have been like for Bruce. He had always appeared so stable, a permanent fixture of dependability and constancy. "And how did you cope, Bruce?"

"Ha." Bruce went to work on a large frying pan with intense interest. "I just did. I had no choice. But thanks for asking. No one else ever has."

"Probably because you always seem so unflappable, in control of everything. The power behind the throne. Caro could never have achieved so much without you."

"I know," said Bruce rinsing his final pan under the tap. "And I'll always support her. Like she's always supported you."

James understood the earnest look Bruce now directed at him, a confirmation of loyalty. It meant he could forget about getting Bruce on his side to convince Caro to ease up on Mark. "And I'll never let her down either," said James locking eyes with Bruce.

By the time Caro returned, tabletops had been wiped clean, pots and pans washed, dried and put away, and both dishwashers whirred and whooshed away. James refilled their wine glasses as Caro entered.

"What a pair of domestic gods I have."

"My mother taught me to be a cook in the kitchen, a gentleman in the living room, and a stud in the bedroom," said Bruce with a lascivious smile.

"I guess two out of three's not bad," said Caro as Bruce picked up his glass.

"Careful or you'll find me sleeping in my study. I'll leave you two to talk business. I have a year three Tudor project to research." Bruce sauntered out of the room crooning his favourite Abba tune - 'Gimme! Gimme! Gimme! A Man After Midnight'.

"Your husband has an undying penchant for cheesy anthems."

"He can be as camp as a row of tents you mean. At least he always pitches up." James groaned, as Caro inspected his face.

"Okay, okay. What do you want me to do with our mutual friend?"

"I want the Weasel to know what it feels like to be without his children."

"I think we may have already achieved that."

"No. I mean the fear of permanently losing them. When I was in prison, I coped with everything but separation from the kids was the hardest thing. What sustained me was knowing I would be with them again in a few months. But if someone had taken that away, for good, then.... " Caro tailed off.

"I'm not sure what you're asking me to do," said James with a look of concern and confusion across his forehead.

"I want him to experience the fear of losing a child forever."

James froze in horror. "I am not harming any child."

"I'm not asking you to. I just want him to think he has lost one of them."

He was dumbstruck for a moment. "Caro, what...how on earth am I supposed to do that?"

"I don't know. You're the creative one. You'll find a way."

James shook his head in exasperation. "And then what? What next? When does this end?"

Caro shifted in her seat. "When he's ruined."

James sighed deeply. "Caro. I can't do this anymore."

Caro sniffed, folded her arms, and sat upright. "James. I've always supported you.

"I know that."

"And LifeChance would not exist without me. Think of all those kids."

"I do. Every day. And you know we're working hard to generate other income streams we can rely on."

"You're still a long way from not needing my support."

She was right, of course. The underlying threat of her withdrawing her funding would remain, unless and until the WinBet deal paid off spectacularly. So, he figured he might as well tell her. He had hoped that he could avoid this moment. That the FCA would drop the case.

James took a deep breath, looked away for a second, and then speared her with a look that begged for forgiveness. "Look, there's something you've got to know."

"What?" said Caro, blinking. He could still surprise her.

"I've hired Mark to act as my defence lawyer."

"You idiot. I told you that gambling company idea would end in tears."

"No, not that. I've been accused of insider dealing in shares. For LifeChance, not me. I've been meaning to tell you."

Caro glared at him but remained silent.

James outlined to Caro the details of the FCA's case against him. He explained that he had checked various contacts for legal recommendations, and the responses pointed to Mark as one of the best in his game of white-collar defence. He ran through Mark's present view of the strength of his case.

"So, when does this come to court?" asked Caro, as soon as James had finished.

"Don't know yet. Don't know if it ever will. But I don't want to distract him any further right now."

"Right," said Caro, ignoring James's voice of gloom, "so after the case comes to court or is dropped, you have no objection to my suggestion." It sounded like a statement of fact rather than a question. "Actually, it might be even better waiting till then. He may have gotten his life back on an even keel, and then we destroy him all over again."

Sometimes, James reflected, Caro could make herself very difficult to like. Driven by vengeance, she was blinkered in her pursuit of Mark. She had given scant attention to the painful consequences he himself would suffer, if he lost the case. For someone who had herself been incarcerated, loved her own family so much, her lack of sensitivity was staggering. Equally, her single-mindedness explained her success in business-life.

"Okay," said James feeling anything but. He recognised more than ever, that the WinBet deal had to work for LifeChance in order to extricate himself from Caro's inordinate demands. But he needed to make it work sooner rather than later. The tap of Caro's revenge which he himself had turned on, now forebode a flood of retribution.

"It's a new day for me. And I'm feeling good," sang a sultry voice as James pushed opened the swing door to the Royal Festival Hall's Foyer Bar. A jazz four-piece was parked on the edge of the bar area, being ignored by packed tables of post-work employees and friends, catching up. The long bar buzzed with mixologists fixing cocktails, and staff pulling pints and pouring wine, as customers waving plastic competed for their

241

attention. He spotted Megan and Eva perched on a small round table at the far end. Even from this distance, he could tell they were laughing out loud. They looked like older and younger sisters together.

"James. You made it," shrieked Eva, standing up and leaning in to kiss him. "Sorry I'm late," said James. "Bloody lawyers again."

"You look tired," said Megan moving her bag from the seat they had saved for him. "Let me get you a drink."

"A cool beer would be great, large," said James as he put his jacket on the back of his seat and flopped down. "Thanks."

"Same again for me, mum," said Eva.

"I'll get us another bottle," said Megan and went off to do battle at the bar.

"Busy day?" said Eva.

"The usual." Twelve-hour workdays were still the norm for James. They'd been that and more for as long as he could remember. "Just ending it in a turgid legal meeting is frustrating, that's all."

"I was interviewed again today at the bank. This time some bloke from the FCA attended."

"How did it go?" James asked.

"Good. I enjoyed myself. Same old probing questions."

"You need to be careful."

"Don't worry. I know what I'm doing," said Eva with vague smile.

James reached across the table and squeezed her hand. Her fingers were cool from her wine glass. "I know you do. And I'm sorry again for putting you through this."

"Chill. They've got nothing as far as I can tell."

"I hope not. But they might have," said James with a grimace.

Eva raised an eyebrow. "You're not going to ruin our Thirsty-Thursday sesh are you?"

"My lawyer just told me that the FCA has a reliable witness to testify against me. Apparently, our idiot ex-broker told the FCA that he thought I had inside information. That I implied it on several occasions before instructing him to sell stock."

"Why would he ever say that?" said Eva.

"Because I fired him."

"That wasn't very smart."

"He was never available. We weren't a big enough client to get his attention. After lunch, he was hopeless, utterly unreliable."

"Still, you could have just wound it down slowly."

James looked at Eva and forced a resigned smile. She was the antithesis of his broker. She was downright dependable and nothing other than professional at work. "You're right, as ever. That was a mistake."

"So it'll be his word against yours then?"

"I guess."

"So you have to destroy his character. Undermine his credibility."

"That's precisely what Mark said."

"I'm meeting him tomorrow night," said Eva with a broad grin.

"Last time," boomed Megan returning with a frosted glass of lager and a bottle of Frascati. She set them on the table with a crack, slopping some of the beer. "You've done more than your fair share of the dirty work."

"Mum. It's for LifeChance. It's fine. It's no big deal."

"It's a big deal if you get caught."

"I won't. Stop worrying. I know what I'm doing."

"You do. But your mother's right. They'll be watching you like a hawk at work."

"They always do. Our phones are tapped, all calls are logged, and they insist on having access to our social media accounts. I'm used to it."

"I know. But as agreed, all the share dealing stuff is over. And you'll finish it with Caro's Weasel tomorrow."

"I will. I've rehearsed it all. I'm planning a few tears, a cocktail of sorrow and melancholia, but no regrets, no blame."

"Poor bloke," said James. "Doesn't stand a chance."

"Never did. That was the point," said Megan raising her glass. "Let's have a toast. "To Eva and a horrible job well done."

They drank.

"It wasn't that bad, mum. I mean he's not half as good as-"

"I don't want to hear it. You wouldn't want to hear what Alicia and I get up to, would you?"

"That's disgusting. I'm your daughter."

"So, let's move on."

"Okay, so let's hear about whatshername instead," said Eva. "She who must not be named."

"Ha ha. Stefanie is fine-" said James peering into his beer. He had finally come clean on his relationship.

"And I bet the sex is so good, she's going to throw the case so she can spend the rest of her life with you," said Eva, starting to giggle.

"She must feel terribly conflicted," said Megan.

"We never talk about the case. The elephant in the room is always asleep." James wished it was. But as the probability of a trial seemed to increase, so his thoughts turned to the nightmare of having to face Stefanie in court. The elephant was wide awake, just mute for now.

"So, nothing to report?" said Eva with a leer.

"Nothing," said James, with a half-smile.

"How did the BBC interview go this afternoon?" asked Megan changing the topic.

"Fine, I think. I managed to get LifeChance in a few times, but we'll have to see how much gets through the editing process." James had been interviewed for a TV documentary about immigration. He was there to put the case for immigrants. Explain the facts, the history of a mongrel nation, and appeal to traditional values of tolerance and humanity. "We just keep having to repeat the same things and hope more and more people listen. Once we get the venture capital funding into WinBet, we'll be able to afford a proper marketing campaign."

"Sure, but we still need to be careful how we channel funds into LifeChance," said Megan.

"We can trust them Megan, don't worry," said James. Them were the new CEO and financial director, whom James had recruited through his contacts at one of his clubs. The CEO was 58, with a career in start-up companies and broken marriages. He had recently remarried for the fourth time. He was a credible figurehead for the venture capitalists to accept. But most of all, the man was desperate for a job that brought a lucrative income and the chance to build wealth through share options. The financial director had been involved in string of start-ups, mostly successful. But a very public failure two years ago, meant that he had failed to find a position since. Mid-forties, he had a young family attending fee-paying schools. He was peering over a financial cliff-edge when James approached him. Despite his reputation for financial probity which would satisfy the venture capitalists, James found his principles pleasingly elastic when LifeChance was explained to him.

"How long till you get the deal done?" asked Eva.

"A couple of months. We're pushing ahead as fast as we can," said Megan.

"Hopefully sooner. We have three venture capital firms competing for it, so good healthy tension. We may only have to give up about thirty per cent of the equity for twenty million," said James.

"Well that's probably too ambitious, but we'll almost certainly retain a majority," said Megan.

"That's vital," said Eva. "You need to control the board composition and key shareholder votes."

"Correct. Otherwise we could be exposed," said James.

"We still need Caro to come through with some funds," said Megan crossing her arms. "She still owes us two and a half million."

"She owes us nothing," said James, "but she'll come through with it."

"She promised."

"She did. And she'll deliver if we do." James glowered at Megan, allowing her to feel his frustration for a few seconds. It didn't always feel like they were on the same side. Stuck between his two 'adopted' sisters, who demanded different things from him. He wondered if that's what happened in normal families, not that he was ever likely to find out.

Chapter Seventeen   Drink

Queen Elizabeth Hall Roof Garden overlooked the relentless flowing Thames, close by Waterloo station, so a popular place for snatched early-evening assignations. With summer reluctant to slither into autumn, the place was packed. All the benches appeared occupied and the lawn was strewn with a hip-looking bunch sporting shades, the women in floral summer dresses and the men in cut-off cotton shirts and light-coloured chinos. Mark felt conspicuous in his navy-blue suit and mustard and blue-dotted silk tie, as he scanned the bar for Eva. Though it was unlikely anyone there would recognise him, Mark wished he had remembered his sunglasses. He had spent the trip over from the City, peering over his shoulder intermittently to check if he was being followed. He heard her voice calling his name and his eyes darted to the far corner of the lawn where Eva's waving hand flailed in the air above the carousing mob.

He edged around a mass of bodies to find Eva sitting on the grass with her long, pale legs stretched out in front of her. She donned a pair of pink tortoiseshell cat-eye sunglasses and wore a peach floral jacquard dress. Her cream jacket and calfskin leather briefcase lay on the patch of grass she had reserved for Mark, next to an ice-bucket containing a bottle of Rosé Champagne.

"I started without you. It is such a lovely evening," she said, beaming at him.

Whatever frostiness he had detected on the phone had dissolved. How he wished he could take her, there and then. "Yes, the weather's wonderful."

"Bubbly?" She filled a flute with bubbling pink liquid and handed it to him as he crouched down to sit on the grass opposite her. The champagne matched the glow of her cheeks.

"Nice place," said Mark scanning the scene and feeling much older than the assembled crowd. Sun tan lotion mingled with the aroma of their sweating cheese and Proscuttio di Parma platters.

"Take your jacket off, get rid of the tie, and unbutton that shirt. Relax."

"Sorry."

"And don't apologise. I should be the one to say sorry. I wasn't very nice on the phone. I was thrown off balance, that's all. I'm fine now. Cheers," said Eva raising her glass.

"Cheers," said Mark before inhaling a whiff of red berries and spice as he tipped the fizzing elixir into his mouth. He felt the warmth of the sun on his face as it drifted west towards Whitehall. Eva reached into her briefcase.

"Actually, these photos are quite sexy. I keep having to take a peek at them." She handed him the brown envelope which he set on the grass between them, while savouring a mouthful of champagne. "Go on, take a sneaky look." Eva handed him the envelope.

Mark looked around. Everyone else appeared oblivious to his presence. He edged out the photos, furtively holding them close to his chest.

"They're the same as the other ones," said Mark before sliding the photos back into the envelope.

248

"Who showed them to you first?"

"My wife. Mark looked away and blew out hard. "A bit of a shock."

"And you don't think she hired someone-"

"No, or at least I don't think so." Mark peered at her furrowed brow and the cute dimple that appeared whenever she seemed perplexed. "Then Gordan Cumberbatch, my colleague you met at the hotel bar, showed them to me-"

"I thought he was your friend-"

"He is, or at least I think so.

"I'm confused."

"So am I." Mark explained how Cath and Gordon had received the same photos in identical envelopes and without any clue of the sender. Trying hard not to sound as if he felt sorry for himself, he skated over the minutiae of the conversations he had had with each of them. He summarised Gordon's vendetta theory and Cath's threat to tell the children.

"So, I've been slung out of my home, and there must be a risk I'll get slung out of my job next. Not the best week of my life." Mark drained his glass and topped up their glasses. "At least we got to drink the champagne this time," he said with a thin smile.

"Mark. I'm so sorry. I didn't mean to-"

"Not your fault. It's mine. All mine." He'd just endured a tortuous telephone conversation with Cath. She had left open the possibility of him returning to stay at the house over the weekend, but only if he gave his word, that the affair was over. He had given his word.

"Your wife will calm down. She's angry. I would be too."

"No she's not. I could cope better with that. She is calm and thoughtful."

249

Eva reached across and patted his knee. "She will realise that your kids need you back."

"I hope so. I really hope so, mainly because I can't bear to be in that crummy hotel much longer," quipped Mark.

"I could find a place for you, but perhaps your wife wouldn't take kindly to that."

Mark leant forward and with a delicate peck, kissed her cheek. "I think my wife would definitely hire someone then, probably to kill me. But thanks."

"So is that it for us then, all over?" said Eva with a hint of a trembling lip.

Mark averted her gaze, squinting up at chalk-lines in blue sky, as jets trailed into the distance. He could see them, but he couldn't hear, touch, taste or smell them. They seemed unreal or at least not part of his domain. Maybe that was how it would have to be with Eva. Mark looked sideways to check that no-one was listening.

"Cath says it has to end, otherwise there is no future for us, no family."

Eva slugged from her glass and sniffed. Rheumy eyed, she said, "I understand. Family comes first."

"I'd love to keep seeing you, but...but if she found out.... God, if I knew who was behind those photos..." He trailed off as Eva wiped her eyes with the back of her hand.

"Such a shame we have to end it. We were just getting going. But you're right." She sniffed. "Let's finish this damn bottle."

Mark could not keep his eyes open. He was slumped in his seat with his legs spilling into the aisle, and his hands gripping his laptop-briefcase. Diagonally opposite, a fellow commuter with his tie slung over his shoulder battled with a disintegrating takeaway. Mark was vaguely aware of people clambering over his feet and the stopping and starting at stations. By the time, 'This is Putney' hailed from a platform loudspeaker, he was snoring. The train trundled on. He woke up to the beeping of train doors opening and cursed as he saw the sign for Richmond station. He leapt out of his seat and squeezed through the carriage doors as they closed. He swore again and crossed the platform to wait for the next train back to Putney. He was about to venture to a kiosk at the far end of the platform to buy a bottle of water when his train pulled in.

The stench from the day's detritus lying about the carriage hit him as clambered on board. He was alone. He picked up a dog-eared copy of the *Evening Standard* from the floor, more to stay awake than out of interest. Within a few minutes the train slid into Putney. He half stumbled onto the platform and weaved his way to the station steps. He hauled himself up using the handrail, with his bag banging against his leg, unaware of the oblique glances of the people who sped past him at a safe distance.

The aroma of baked pastries lured him into the station's pasty shop. He left without his change, then leant against the wall, munching a Cornish pasty and draining a bottle of water. A vagrant wandered by just as he was finishing and started on a story about needing money to get back to Exeter to live with his dad. Mark was about to tell him to fuck off, but the man was big, so he dug in his pocket and handed over a few coins. It was enough to send the man shuffling off to another late-night commuter.

He felt weak and angry and victimised. He was about to head off to his hotel, when a voice roared inside him that Cath had been utterly unreasonable on the phone earlier, refusing to countenance him visiting the house except for weekends. It pissed him off even more when she said that he had to arrive early the next morning so that she could spend the entire day out with a friend. He would show her. He spun around and headed off to the back-roads of parked cars, London plane-trees and dim lighting. Elegant Edwardian houses intermingled with modern apartment blocks built after the war and set well back from the roads. Mature fruit trees draped their branches over ancient garden brick walls. He had trodden this path for too many years of his commuting life. As he plodded, his head began to clear a little. If he turned up unannounced, Cath would leap off the deep end. And he didn't want to wake up the kids, just see them. So, he pulled his mobile from his pocket and dialled home, fixing his glassy eyes on his feet in a conscious effort to walk in a straight line.

The phone went to voicemail. She was still shielding his calls.

"Cath, this is Mark. Call me back. I'm on my way home."

The return call came within seconds. "Mark. We agreed. You are coming at eight tomorrow morning." The tone was brusque, aggressive even.

She could get like that after a few glasses of wine, Mark thought. "You agreed you mean. Have you been drinking?"

"Mark. Listen. I'm bolting the door."

"That won't stop me."

"I'll call the police."

That set him off. How dare she threaten him. She had no right to bar him from his own home. In that moment of ranting, he unleashed all the frustrations of the months since the marathon. He screamed into his mobile, spitting out words, unaware of anything around him. When Cath cut the line, he cursed out loud, a fraction before he was hurled against a brick wall, head first.

Someone was pushing his forehead against the mortar and something sharp into the base of his spine. His attacker had pinned him against a wall shrouded by an over-hanging tree. Other hands were rifling through his jacket pockets. He could feel hot breath on his skin. His nose hurt but he could smell fruit. He couldn't open his mouth to speak. His heart was thundering against his ribs. And then a knee in his back and he crumpled onto the pavement. In the gloom of a moonless dark blue sky, he caught the outlines of two figures running, just before they dissolved into the night.

He looked around and checked himself. He tasted blood. He wiped his chin, smearing more blood on the back of his hand. He ran a finger over his grazed forehead, damp and sticky. His pockets were empty. They had taken his wallet and his ring of keys. But worse, he suddenly realised they had stolen his laptop-bag which also included some confidential documents he had brought home, meaning to read over the weekend. He felt sick, knowing that was the last thing he needed at work. His career was on the line, like most aspects of his life, he thought.

He slowly jerked himself upright. Nothing appeared to be broken and the ache in his back had become a mere dull throb. Something was under his foot. He bent down delicately with one hand supporting his back. It was his mobile, still seemingly functioning despite its shattered screen. He took a moment to think what he should do. He had never been assaulted before and he was shocked that it could happen so close to his home. After a couple of minutes, he called his bank's lost card number, then his firm's IT emergency number, and finally the police.

Two young police officers were waiting for him in the foyer of the hotel where the receptionist gave him the same oblique look that passers-by had done on his way home. They dutifully wrote everything down that he told them. They tried their best to be sympathetic, and not bored by the bruised and bloodied object before them. The best hope was a tracking device installed by his IT department on the laptop. But the younger police officer added that most muggers were tech savvy enough to disable that. The best they could offer was a crime number for insurance purposes. They left him with a leaflet proffering advice on street awareness, a part of their campaign to reduce low level crime statistics.

As he crossed the hotel courtyard to the annex with its corridor of rooms, he shook his head with a rueful smile. On the one hand, he felt like a fool. On the other, he had achieved a great deal over the past hour. He had walked the best part of a mile, he had rowed with his wife, he had been expertly mugged and relieved of his personal and professional possessions, he had wrapped up an entire police investigation, his nose had stopped bleeding, and he had sobered up.

He put his over-sized key in the lock, pushed open his room door and made straight for the fridge which he had stocked with beer. He kicked shut the door, removed his jacket, and sat on the edge of the bed till he had drunk the entire can. He stripped off and headed into the shower. He closed his eyes and lifted his face to the shower-head. The tepid water ran pink as it streamed from his forehead, down his body and through the plug-hole. A shame, he thought that it could not wash his cares away too. His world seemed to be disintegrating. Someone unknown was threatening him, perhaps with bribery to come. He was being persecuted at work for a stupid administrative oversight. His wife was screwing him in all kinds of ways, not least in making him end his relationship with Eva. And now he had become a victim of crime with the bruises and abrasions to prove it.

As the water cleansed his body, stinging his cuts, it also refreshed his mind, purging negative thoughts. Life was unfair. He did not deserve what had happened to him. He had to fight back, even harder. He shut off the shower and reached for a towel which he put around his waist. He went to the fridge and got himself another beer, then stood in front of the mirror, holding in his stomach and flexing various muscles. For someone of his age, he looked good. Why else would a beautiful young woman like Eva be attracted to him. He took a swig of beer. He was starving. For food and also company. He deserved both. And if he couldn't have Eva, or Cath, he'd have to make do elsewhere. His back ached and he could do with a massage.

He crossed the room to the bureau and took a red Gideon bible out of a drawer. He opened the back cover and withdrew his emergency stash, a crisp pile of twenty-pound notes. He counted three hundred pounds, more than enough. He sat on his bed and started tapping on his mobile. He ordered in an extra-large Sicilian pizza, followed by Sapphire, a leggy, busty, blonde Czech escort from SW15Babes.com. He cracked open another cold beer, flicked on the TV, and waited to spend his cash.

Chapter Eighteen   Autumn

Stefanie peered over the top of the *The Times Weekend* review. She was failing to read an article on 'Top Twenty Walks for the Autumn', walks she knew she would never go on. It was typical piece of escapism for a languid Saturday morning. The kind of escapism which had lured her into what was supposed to be a short illicit fling with the man opposite her. Something had gone wrong, or maybe right. A creeping want, had spread like a virus, into need. She even liked the way he was making a mess with the hot croissants she had got up early to buy, fresh from Pascale's Boulangerie. As a special treat on her return, she had licked him awake for sex. She recalled the salty taste of him on her tongue.

She could smell James now, damp haired and lime fresh from the shower, with its growing collection of male toiletries. His skin, scraped clean, still glowed from their week together in Tuscany. And his stubble shone golden under the rays of a mid-morning sun. His right hand was groping for his coffee mug, whilst his left dangled a croissant, dropping flakes onto the newspaper spread out on the small table, squashed into her kitchen.

Since his first visit, she had had to clear up more than the obligatory once a week so that her Brazilian cleaner could do her job. Leticia needed to get in and out in under three hours, so that she could get to her second job in Fulham, before finishing at her third in Putney. So, Stefanie's clutter was piled up in corners, shifted but never thrown out, precarious towers constantly re-erected. Being in James's spacious apartment so much had made her compact two bed flat seem tiny. Perhaps she should move. But then she'd miss her shared patch of brick-walled garden with its litter of plant pots and tiny shrubs. And to move home would cost. She'd have to move area and she'd be at a loss without Pascale's, Mimi's Brasserie and the other eclectic stores up the hill in the village. She would have to move jobs, switch to a higher paid position in the lucrative private sector; defending white collar-crime rather than prosecuting. Like James's foul lawyer. No, she was still not prepared to do that.

The FCA's decision to proceed to trial with James's case had been taken by her boss against her recommendation. She had strived to remain objective, and not allow her secret life to taint her professional judgement. She felt the evidence whilst technically strong, lacked sufficient corroboration. Her boss felt the tide of public opinion against rich City bankers would sway the jury sufficiently. He was also under pressure to show value for money, and with the department's budget under threat, he needed convictions fast. He had at least agreed with her recommendation that the charity itself, LifeChance, should be spared prosecution. He didn't want the jury's empathy for a charitable cause to dilute their disdain for a fraudulent criminal. His words.

The process had formally begun. The summons had been issued and they had both appeared at the Magistrates Court for the initial hearing. It was all procedural. She had heard James say his name and address and utter his 'not guilty' plea. The case was duly referred upwards to Southwark Crown Court, where serious sentences could be handed out. Throughout the brief hearing, they had not looked at one another once.

As she now sat gazing at James, she could feel her heartbeat throb. This decent man worked tirelessly and passionately for a laudable cause. He had probably broken laws with just intent. But if he had, justice demanded he pay a penalty. If he was found guilty, then what? Prison undoubtedly, but for how long? Maybe he could be out in a couple of years. She could wait for him. It might not be too late. A train clattered by on the tracks behind the garden wall.

James looked up and caught her looking at him. "What?"

"Who are you James Tait? Why James? Why Tait? What was wrong with Alon Jäger?"

James put down his paper. "Almost everything. The name change was a chance to reinvent myself at university. Leave the name and all the bad stuff behind." James then told her about how he had discovered that his mother had escaped Germany on one of the last Kindertransport trains, seemingly alone as a toddler. He couldn't recall ever being Jewish, just human and hopeless.

"But why, 'James'?"

James laughed. "I think I'd been studying the Stuarts in history at the time. And I thought James I sounded like the luckiest bugger alive, inheriting two kingdoms just because of who his mother had been. Felt ironic to an eighteen-year-old. And I thought the name sounded cool.

"And Tait?"

James sighed. "He was the father I never had. Someone who never judged me, always loved me. Simple really." James spent half an hour telling Stefanie about Father Tait, and his happiest childhood memories munching biscuits with the priest in his lawless library.

Stefanie leant over and kissed him on the lips, still sweet from strawberry jam. She had doubted this man at the start. She'd struggled with the conflict between her private and professional lives. She'd taken a massive risk and it could still pay off.

"I know I said we shouldn't, but I think we should talk about the trial," said Stefanie.

James stared back at her with his mouth half open. She owed him an explanation. She sat back and crossed her long slender legs. She'd always thought her ankles were her best feature. Behind him on the counter top, purple freesias and white roses erupted out of a tall glass tumbler. The week before, it had been pink stargazer lilies. She had still not got used to being bought flowers.

"I want you to know that I hope we lose, even though I have to do my best to win." Stefanie could feel her face burning. She was smart but struggled with intimacy.

James folded his arms and swallowed. "I realise that, and I don't expect-"

"Listen," Stefanie interjected, "if it goes the wrong way, I still want us to be together. As long as we remain a secret, we can. Do you understand?" She nodded several times as if willing him to give the right answer, like a teacher encouraging her pupil.

"I want that too." He shrugged with a smile. "Worst case, you can keep my apartment warm for me." James grinned.

Stefanie lent across and kissed him again. "In that case, I have every incentive to win." She giggled at her own joke. "You might as well give me the keys to your castle now."

Chapter Nineteen   Weekend

As James approached the dirty-beige brick fortress of Southwark Crown Court, he felt sorry for its architect. He must have been under austere early 1980's budget pressures to propose something so lumpen, ugly and unimaginative. It seemed a crime to house the brilliant minds of eminent judges and leading barristers in such a building. He was hoping the interior would compensate for the exterior. He was meeting Mark in the coffee pod. His lawyer wanted him to experience the courts in which his case was to be heard, to hear witnesses being cross examined, and to watch barristers showing off before juries. Mark had been relentless in reminding him that his performance in the witness box would be critical to the outcome of his trial. He was to expect mock court grillings from Mark before the real thing.

James edged past a gaggle of press photographers, loitering behind a metal fence strapped with blue and white tape, fluttering in the wind. He was clearly not the celebrity they were waiting for. He entered through the main doors and straight into a short line for the security area. He could see Mark through the scanner sitting on a low chair, staring at his laptop. He was yawning and rubbing his forehead.

James slapped him on the back, not too hard. "Morning Mark. Sorry I'm a few minutes late. I joined the tourists and took the scenic route along the river. Fresh breeze this morning."

Mark glanced at his watch. "Don't worry. I've been here an hour trying to catch up." He had black shadows under his baggy blue-green eyes. James thought he looked awful.

"Can I get you another coffee? Something else to eat?" The evidence of Mark's breakfast-on-the-go lay on the floor in front of him; a paper plate dotted with croissant fragments, and black coffee dregs in a cardboard cup.

"The coffee is barely drinkable, but it's better than nothing. Thanks," said Mark, returning to study his screen.

"Okay, won't be a second." James walked over to the counter and ordered two black americanos. The server's chirpiness contrasted starkly with Mark's gloom. He was glad that Caro's vengeful appetite had been stalled till the conclusion of the courtcase. Mark's gentle mugging that James had orchestrated was enough to satiate her for now. He needed his lawyer to be in good form for his trial. Since the news that his ex-broker would testify against him, James had become more concerned about the outcome.

"So," said James, trying to sound as uplifting as possible, "I guess if you're busy, that's good. More money for the partners."

Mark grunted as he packed away his papers and laptop into his new briefcase. "Tell me. Caroline Noble who introduced us originally, do you see much of her?"

"Occasionally. She's always so busy," said James without missing a beat, "running her business and a dealing with a big family."

Mark sighed. "Damn hard woman to get hold of."

"E-mail is probably best." Caro had forwarded to James, Mark's increasingly imploring e-mails.

"Tried that. A few times now." Mark grunted. "Never mind. Let's pick one of the courts, shall we?"

They waited five minutes for a lift to take them up two floors. They stepped out onto a fraying orange carpet, saturated with stains. People lingered along the dim corridor outside courtrooms. Smart suits mingled with jeans and t-shirts, and gowned barristers. Mark led James to a ripped cocoa-brown leatherette sofa. Above them, an ancient air-con unit clicked and whooshed.

"We'll go in court two when we've finished our coffee. It's a credit card fraud case. Nothing too complex." Between bitter mouthfuls, Mark explained that the centre contained fifteen courts dealing with criminal offences. Foremost at Southwark, were cases dealing with fraud. He could only stay for half an hour, but suggested James should spend more time wandering around the courtrooms, to get a feel for the place. Half of the courtrooms contained jury trials whilst in the others, judges sat alone deciding upon issues just as bail pleas, and pre-trial challenges. He urged James to focus his attention on the judges and juries.

"Don't forget James. This is all about the twelve men and women of the jury. If they like you, and it's important they do, they will find it harder to find you guilty, even if technically they believe you've broken the law. So, watch how they react to the defendant in the dock, and also the witnesses when they give evidence."

They slipped into the public gallery of Court Two, the room dressed in wood like every court drama he'd seen on screen, but now festooned with computer screens and laptops, instead of pile-high paper. A frowning judge peered over his spectacles at a barrister who was standing and addressing a man in the witness box. A sprinkling of other bewigged barristers, and be-suited men and women, sat alongside and behind him. A couple of clerks tapped away on keyboards near the front. To his left, James saw a young man, the accused, in a locked glass cell with a uniformed guard. Diagonally opposite sat the jury. They could all have been drawn from the carriage of an underground train, such was the mix of age and ethnicity. But something was different, no mobiles and no distractions. Each jury member had their eyes fixed on the witness and listened intently, like a rapt theatre audience. Other than the speaking barrister, there was complete hush.

Except for Mark whose incessant whispering in James's ear, trying to explain matters, had the opposite effect. James lost track of the line of questioning. He was glad when Mark tapped him on the arm and signaled they should creep out. Back in the corridor, Mark suggested a couple of other courtrooms James should visit, one involving the laundering of proceeds from criminal property, and another concerning the possession of indecent images of children. Then he checked his watch, said he was late already and had to dash.

"Have a good weekend," said James as Mark turned to go.

"Slim chance of that." And without elucidating further, Mark left.

James ignored the lift and opted for the stairs. They were deserted and like the rest of the building had not been touched for decades. Cobwebs dangled from strip lighting fastened to polystyrene ceiling tiles. The stair carpets were even more stained than the corridors, and the entire staircase, encased by dirt-smudged walls, stank of old plastic and dust. He was relieved to get back into a courtroom. It looked similar to the first one other than the actors and the tragedy being played out. Improper images had been found on the accused's computer following a police raid interrupting a drug-infused party. As far as James could make out, the defence was based upon the accused maintaining that his flat-mates also had access to the same computer and that he was not responsible for downloading the child pornography. The jury would have to decide whether to believe him.

The defendant, an architect in his forties was being questioned gently by his own barrister. He was sobbing intermittently, claiming he had suffered depression since being diagnosed with HIV. He had resorted to drug-taking and drink to alleviate his symptoms. He had recently lost his job because of his illness. It was either a brilliant acting performance or just another sad tale of a life turned upside-down. James couldn't tell and wondered how the jury could decide. After all the legal arguments put by the prosecution and defence, what would move them the most, rationality or emotion, prejudice or impartiality? And what about all the other witnesses? How might their testimonies be assessed, their characters appraised, and their credibility weighed?

James left the court at lunchtime and took a stroll by the river to ponder. He lent on a railing and gazed northside, to mesmerising space-age buildings of the City. They looked faintly Cubist from this angle and distance. Nearby, a guitar-playing busker sang Dylan's 'Like A Rolling Stone'. He stopped to listen. He was worried. He didn't feel in control of his destiny. Mark, conductor of the orchestra would be leading him, first violinist, through endless rehearsals. He was fearful that Mark had become distracted by the incidents, which he had set up to destroy his lawyer's ordered life. How ironic if he were to be the architect of his own downfall. Though they hadn't discussed the trial, he knew Stefanie well enough by now. The prosecution case would be thorough, well organised

264

and corroborated by leading experts. His defence needed to be better. Maybe he should have listened to Caro. But it was too late to change legal advisor now. He had to take a more active role in the case, instead of being a reluctant participant. Until the trial, his legal case had to take precedence over LifeChance. He would speak to Megan about stepping up. He could rely on her. The busker finished his song to a ripple of applause. James chucked a few quid into his tin and wished him all the best.

As soon as they heard his key in the lock, squeals erupted from the kitchen and they stampeded to the front door. All four of them wrapped themselves around him. Mark felt a huge wave a relief to be back home. After two combative phone calls, Cath had relented to allow him to return, but only for weekends and on condition that he slept in the spare room in the eaves, next to Natalia's room.

He limped into the kitchen with Benjamin riding his leg like it was a Bucking Bronco. Emma and Miranda hung on each arm and Ralph clung on his back, half strangling him. Cath was ferrying tea plates and juice beakers to the dishwasher.

"I'm home," Mark announced with a cheesy grin, "and it's Friday, which means..."

"Swimming," yelled the kids in unison.

"And pizza for a treat," said Mark eyeing Cath, "if you're good. Is that okay mum?"

Cath cocked her head. "Go and get your swimming trunks kids, and don't forget your pyjamas for afterwards." The kids bolted off and scampered upstairs, their pounding echoing throughout the house. It felt so good to be home again thought

Mark, imbibing the household smells and noises like a soldier returning from the front.

"I thought pizza would be good, save you cooking," said Mark.

"It's fine," said Cath, turning to swill a glass in the sink, "but I won't be here when you get back. I'm going out."

Mark froze. He was dumbstruck. Friday nights were hallowed in the Phillips' household, reserved for family, heralding the start of the weekend, the kids allowed to stay up an extra couple of hours, then an order-in from the local Indian, lazing in front of the TV with some beers and more often than not some soothing sex before drifting off to a well-earned sleep.

"I've packed the swim-bag with everything you need; towels, goggles, floats, shampoo, and some stuff for you. It's at the foot of the stairs," said Cath turning around to face him.

"Right," said Mark struggling to come to grips with this unwelcome and unexpected news. Despite his unease, he manufactured a fake smile. "Going somewhere nice?"

"Just out for a drink, then a meal probably," said Cath flatly.

Mark was dying to ask her who with, where, what time she would be back, but he was determined not to give her the satisfaction of confirming that he was bothered. "Shall I tell the kids you'll tuck them in when you get back."

"Best not. I'm not sure what time I'll be back. Don't wait up for me." Cath folded her arms across her chest and half-smiled momentarily.

Mark blinked. He was certain she was playing with him now, but he was damned if he would acknowledge it. "Right," he said, shaking his head but smiling.

"Natalia is away for the weekend, so you won't be disturbed upstairs. Here's the pizza menu," she said, extracting a leaflet from a drawer stuffed with take-away menus. "Don't forget, no fizzy drinks - they won't sleep." Cath was using her patronising voice again, and he wanted to scream at her that he was not a child. But then, he knew she would tell him to stop behaving like one, grow up and take responsibility for his actions.

"I know," said Mark holding up his hands, as the thundering of feet reached the bottom of the stairs. Cath followed them to the door, giving each of the children a hug and a kiss, telling them to be good, and promising them pancakes and maple syrup as usual for breakfast on Saturday.

They crashed out of the door and into the BMW MPV. They hurtled to their private sports club and spent a hurly-burly hour in the pool. Then shower, pyjamas and pizza in front of *Cartoon Network*. By the time, he had read bedtime stories, tucked the children in bed and finally got them settled enough to stay put, he was exhausted. He couldn't be bothered with cooking or ordering-in just for himself. He grabbed a beer from the refrigerator and slung a couple of slices of the kids' left-over pizza into the microwave. Then he flopped onto the couch in the kitchen's snug area and flicked on the television. He held the bottle to his cheek for a second, then flipped off the cap. A hiss later, he drew the neck to his lips and put his head back, the ale's malty bitter taste bursting inside him. That is so good, thought Mark, sighing with satisfaction. He sensed his body uncoiling. It was so good to be back in his house, with his family, surrounded by his paraphernalia, the comforts of home.

The chaotic familiarity of home provided a safe relaxing space, physical and mental, to contemplate what had upset his previously well-ordered life. As he watched an entertainingly daft chat show, his thoughts kept drifting back to the photographs and a reluctant deduction. No-one had bothered to bribe him. The pictures had been sent to Gordon Cumberbatch. The firm's investigation of the Caroline Noble billing must have been triggered by someone at the firm. Who other than Gordon at the firm knew he was at the hotel that evening with Eva? Who had been put in charge of the firm's investigation of his billing? Who at the firm knew his wife and where he lived? Who stood to have a clear path to be the next senior partner in his own absence? In short, who had everything to gain? Gordon. That was the only rational explanation. But his instincts resisted such rationality. It was too neat. And anyway, Mark rated his own assessment of character. Over many years he had known Gordon, though never a close friend, the man had been a reliable and supportive colleague.

He gave up thinking, picked up the TV remote and flicked through the channels, finally returning to where he had begun. A young singer, attractive, strong voice and with a thrusting pelvis, gyrated on stage. A vision of Eva on the bed, instructing him what to do flashed into his head. He took a swig of his beer and started flicking through the channels again. He finally settled on a film he had seen at the movies more than a decade earlier. Soon, his eyes began to flicker and after a brief struggle, he surrendered to slumber on the couch. He woke with a start just after midnight, needing to pee. He thought he heard the latch on the front door but was mistaken. Cath still wasn't home. He sighed heavily. What a mess he had made. He took his thoughts and tired limbs to bed, alone, up in the eaves.

When he left the house early at eight the following morning for a run with Thomas, the kids were already in the 'Snug', glued in front of the TV. Cath had not shown her face, which was no surprise to Mark. He had lain awake listening out for her return and finally heard her key in the front door. His mind somersaulted with speculation; where had she been, with whom, and what had they got up to till two in the morning. It was another hour before he nodded off. He was tired and as prepared for a long run as a condemned man for his hanging.

"Beautiful morning for an amble," said Thomas pushing against a post to stretch his calves. The car park at Roehampton Gate was already filling up with weekend dog-walkers, and the cafe was spilling over with fluorescent lycra-clad cyclists.

"Let's head across country, get away from the crowds," said Mark who had a particular disdain for joggers who used the perimeter path of Richmond Park. What a waste of thousands of acres of glorious woodlands, grasslands and hills, he thought.

"How long do you want to run for?"

"Can we just run. I'll lead," said Mark, intent on keeping the pace down.

"That'll be interesting. You'll be lost within five minutes."

This was true. Mark had a dysfunctional sense of direction, but this morning he wanted to get lost. He didn't want to know where he was going, or how long it would take, or their average speed. He wanted to lose himself in the fauna and flora of the park, to escape.

"If I did have a plan, that would be it," he said, easing into his stride across the open fields towards White Lodge, the resplendent stone-built Georgian house, now home to the Royal Ballet School. He could see the rise through the woods ahead and headed towards the obscurity of its cool shadows. Thomas ran alongside and gave Mark a quizzical look. Usually he led the way and chose the route, so Mark understood his bemusement.

"How was your week?" said Thomas, as Mark suddenly veered off along an undulating dirt path towards the nearest copse.

"Had better. Yours?" said Mark hoping to divert the conversation to Thomas's world. His trick worked. Thomas launched into a tale about an octogenarian patient who had entertained him throughout his medical assessment with wisecracks about his ex-wives. He was now on his sixth who, nearing thirty, craved to have a child with him. He wanted to know if his vasectomy could be reversed.

They arrived in Spankers Hill Woods and intruded upon a children's party of hide and seek. Mark found himself gawking at the wooden dens made from fallen branches and wishing he could have the carefree life of a child once more. They noticed a grown-up, a parent most likely, eyeing them. They exchanged pleasantries, as they bounded over the mulch of past winters' fallen leaves and headed deeper beneath the canopy of ancient oaks beginning to turn copper.

"You do know we're now heading towards Pen Ponds," said Thomas.

Mark managed a grin and immediately swung left towards light and the edge of the woods. "We're not now."

Within two minutes they were trudging along a red-brown horse-riding trail, soft under-foot and heavy-going with a steady incline. Mark was beginning to regret his abrupt change of direction. He gritted his teeth, focused on the summit and lumbered up the hill to the hope of level ground.

"How's the family?" he gasped, trying once more to get Thomas to do the talking.

Thomas chattered away about his kids in turn, and then about Kimberly joining some poetry evening class. Mark was barely listening, instead concentrating on his breathing, keeping up and avoiding hills. A descent of a few hundred metres down a grassy path softened the slog. They were now in a flat area of a long grass which lashed against their legs as Mark forged fresh tracks. The soft tufted surface and hidden rivulets would slow Thomas down.

Out of the long grasses, they stumbled across Isabella Plantation. Thomas opened the gate into the ornamental woodland garden whilst Mark snatched a breather. Aside from the sound of the latch, they could hear only the trickling of water along the narrow streams and ponds, lined by evergreen Azaleas. A few months back they had been a blooming red inferno of sweet fragrance. They meandered at half pace, so that Thomas could take in the changes since their last visit.

When they reached the gate to leave, Thomas shot him a concerned look. "You've barely said a word this morning? Are you okay?"

"Sorry. Just a bit tired that's all."

"How about a coffee at Pembroke Lodge? That will perk you up a bit."

Thomas led the way, and Mark counted down the minutes as they heaved themselves up the final hill to their temporary resting place. They stopped off at Henry's Mound first, to take in the view of St Paul's Cathedral through a sightline in the trees. Then Thomas went to order the coffees. Mark sank into a shaded seat, listened to the twittering overhead, and watched a small bird on the next table feasting on cake crumbs.

271

"Great tit," said Thomas returning with two filter coffees, some water and a pain au chocolate to share. "This will give you some energy."

"Didn't get much sleep." His head was pounding, he felt physically drained, and a queasy feeling squatted in his gut.

"Kids keep you up?"

"No, Cath. Didn't get home till two." He was not used to confiding in anyone, but he felt like he was about to explode.

"On the lash with the girls, was she?"

Mark closed his eyes and screwed up his face to stem the tears on the verge of breaking out. He looked up to the sky, opened his eyes and blew out hard.

"What's the matter?" said Thomas.

"Okay. I'm going to tell you something." Mark figured that as a doctor, patients, even strangers confided in Thomas all the time. He was his oldest friend. Surely, he could trust him. "But this absolutely must stay between us. You can't even tell Kimberly."

Thomas blinked and stared back at him. "All right. I promise."

"I've been an utter pillock, a complete idiot," said Mark. And then a full account of his infidelity, his feelings for Eva, the stand-off with Cath, and his longing to be back with his family, gushed out in a torrent.

Thomas sat listening without interruption until the flow had run dry. "Blimey Mark. A bit of a mess."

"More than a bit. I think Cath wants a divorce."

Thomas groaned. "I hope not. Everyone loses then. One of my partners at the surgery, three young kids, is stuck in the middle of a custody battle. Utter nightmare."

"Did he have an affair?"

"No. His wife did, and improved her back-hand at the same time," Thomas quipped.

"Ha. What a cliché."

"A bit like an older man falling for a younger woman." Thomas winked.

"Ouch," said Mark with a reluctant smile.

"You know, this Eva woman of yours seems to bring you bad luck. First the marathon mystery and now this riddle of the secret surveillance."

"What are you suggesting?" said Mark.

"I'm not sure. Maybe somehow she is involved in a conspiracy against you."

"No that's ridiculous." Mark had never been much of a believer in conspiracy theories. Coincidences happened all the time in life. "She's…she's just gorgeous. Everything about her. I wish I could completely forget her."

"Well, that would make life a lot simpler again."

Mark nodded several times slowly, unsure if simpler necessarily meant happier. "Thanks for listening. I knew I could rely on you for a healthy dose of bleak humour."

"Anytime. And of course, I won't breathe a word. Come on," said Thomas levering himself up from the table, "if we go via Pen Ponds, we'll be back in twenty minutes."

With stiffness now settled in their joints, they set off at a leisurely pace, skirting Queen Elizabeth's Plantation to shield from the sun's glare. A herd of red deer regarded them with nonchalance as they shuttled along a path, still muddied from the previous day's rain. As they crunched along the pebble path dissecting the ponds, they ratcheted up the tempo without speaking, aware that they had an audience of families feeding Mallards and Canada Geese, and stick-throwing dog-walkers.

"Look at the heron. It's just caught something," said Thomas pointing over a silver specked pond as the bird of prey soared up into the cloudless sky. Mark was glad they were back on familiar terrain but also relieved that he had shared his predicament with his closest friend.

The rest of the weekend surprised Mark. Like a badly written play performed by seasoned actors, he and Cath had made a passable job of delivering routine lines of a plot going nowhere. They were pleasant enough to each other, cordial even. They managed to play happy family with the kids and kept the show going at a party with a gossipy gang of other school parents. There was no drama when each went to separate bedrooms. No-one could have guessed that Mark would be heading back to the Cromwell House Hotel come Sunday night. Least of all the children who had been told that daddy had to be away for work a lot.

He had hoped for a last-minute reprieve, but Cath was insistent that they stuck to the deal agreed on the phone. When she had started off again about lack of trust, loss of respect and broken promises, Mark retreated immediately. He could see that she needed more time, that she needed him to suffer more, and she needed to discover the cause of his infidelity. He was tempted to say, because I could, but he knew that was both inflammatory and wrong. Cath was right to force him to interrogate his feelings as she was interrogating her own. And that is what really concerned him. The thought of losing all that he had got. He wished he could simply dismiss all thoughts of Eva.

Chapter Twenty   Trial

James sat in the dock stewing, as his ex-broker, Christopher Chivers, lied on the witness stand. After the prosecution had outlined its case, Chivers had been brought on as a star witness. An overweight, thin haired, jowly faced man, squeezed into a grey pin-stripe suit, breathed heavily as he lent against the front of the witness box. The act of speaking seemed a physical challenge as he wheezed out his responses. He was being primed and pumped up by the prosecuting barrister, and presented as a paragon of professionalism, experience and trustworthiness. It was bullshit.

The wheezing figure was led safely through the detail of the ten share deals James had done involving Gladwyn Morson as advisor. He confirmed that James's actions, confounded him and frequently went against his advice. James would remind him constantly of the importance of close friendships at Goldwyn Morson. In his view, it inferred that James had been supplied with privileged information. Because of his suspicions, he had resigned as his broker. The prosecuting barrister's rhythmic flow of questions was met by the ebb of the sweating hulk's embellishments, omissions and occasional outright lie. James, tight lipped and shaking his head, glared at Chivers who never returned his gaze. The jury appeared to be enthralled, scribbling on their pads, until the fat man's testimony ended in time for lunch.

James felt frustrated. He'd been forewarned by Mark about Chiver's testimony, but a cloud of gloom had nonetheless descended upon him. Mark was waiting for him as he was released from his secure dock. "I've got us a table at a pub just around the corner. The fish is excellent." Mark wore an easy smile. "Cheer up. By the time Andrew has finished with him, I guarantee you'll have a smile on your face."

Andrew Smith, James's barrister with a disappointing name had been polite and polished on the couple of occasions the three of them had met together, to prepare for the trial. James had been surprised by how little he had said but noted how every single word carried weight. He was small and thin, and anything but suave in physical appearance. In fact, the opposite of how he'd seen barristers portrayed on screen. He recalled Mark's wry smile and counsel that a lot of people had under-estimated Andrew Smith to their great cost.

After lunch, Christopher Chivers appeared with a flushed face, and swallowed nervously as Andrew Smith rose with a pleasant smile, first to the jury and then to him.

"Mr Chivers, may we get you a chair."

"Er, no I'm fine, thanks."

"Excellent. So. Is it not true that my client fired you because of your drink problem which led to you to being unreliable?" James had finally sacked him after his unavailability in carrying out a share trade, had cost LifeChance a few hundred thousand pounds. James had appointed him originally on the recommendation of the charity's previous chairman, who had turned out to be equally useless.

Chivers gulped and recoiled momentarily. "No, of course not," said Chivers sounding outraged.

"Which? You don't have a drink problem, or you weren't fired?"

"Neither."

James's advocate sighed volubly, scratched his chin, and paused for several seconds. "So, how often would you say, do you spend your lunchtimes drinking in a pub?"

Chivers swallowed again. A sheen of sweat glistened under the ceiling's strip lighting. "It varies, depending on the week."

"From what to what?"

"Some weeks, I have to entertain clients most days, other weeks none at all?"

"So, what would you say is a typical week?"

Chivers blew out his cheeks and frowned as if trying to give the matter serious thought. "Once or twice perhaps."

"I see. So, let's take last week for example. Still fresh in your mind no doubt."

Chivers blinked and shot a glance at the prosecution counsel. "Erm, let me think, erm, erm," he mumbled as he counted off the days with his fingers.

Andrew Smith put his hands together and shared a beneficent toothless smile with the jury. The courtroom waited.

"Erm, once or twice I think. No maybe it was three."

"Pardon me, but you don't sound very sure."

"Three then," said Chivers gripping the front of the witness box.

"Are you sure?"

"I think so, yes." Chivers face was running with sweat now.

"Hmm. Hmm," said James's advocate, through pouted lips. "Could some kind person give Mr Chivers a tissue please." A clerk of the court sitting nearby rushed over and handed him a tissue.

"Mr Chivers, allow me to jog your memory." A moment of uproar ensued as Andrew Smith announced to the judge that he would like to admit new evidence. Snapshots extracted from the *Cock and Bull's* CCTV footage showing the time Chivers entered and left the pub every lunchtime during the previous week, and a written statement from the outlet's manager. It asserted that Chivers drank there every day, usually on his own, and he would typically drink five or six pints whilst having his lunch. The prosecution and defence barristers approached the bench, and when the whispering huddle finally broke up, Andrew Smith presented copies of the photographs and the statement for the clerk to hand to the jury.

James looked at the array of faces surrounding him. The jury still solemn, scrutinising the pictures. The judge deadpan but possibly some mild amusement in the twinkling eyes. The prosecution counsel, grim and lips firmly closed, staring at his hands. And poor Christopher Chivers, dabbing his forehead, looking at the photos, frantic eyes darting to the prosecution counsel.

"So Mr Chivers," Andrew Smith began, kindly as if speaking to a child, "it seems your memory of last week has failed you." He cocked his head and waited a couple of beats for a reply.

"I must have forgotten," Chivers mumbled.

"Please speak up Mr Chivers. The jury won't be able to hear you."

"I must have forgotten," repeated Chivers avoiding all the courtroom's eyes conspired against him.

"Yes, you did. How unfortunate to forget. You forgot what you did last week and yet you appear to recall, word for word,

278

conversations you say you had with the accused up to two years ago. Don't you think that's odd?"

"I,I, I'm not sure," stammered Chivers, "not necessarily."

Andrew Smith raised both eye-brows and slowly swivelled his head towards the jury, then back to Chivers. A silence filled the courtroom. Finally, the judge asked James's barrister if he had any further questions for the witness.

"No more questions, your Honour."

The shambling figure of Christopher Chivers slunk out of the courtroom with his eyes firmly planted on his feet. James's spirits had risen. His counsel had seemingly destroyed the credibility of the prosecution's key witness, and without even referring to the illicit share dealings of which he was accused.

A flood of optimism flowed through James as Richard Ross, Gladwyn Morson's M&A divisional head, took the oath. He looked impeccable in his navy *Pierre Cardin* suit, cuff-linked *Brooks Brothers* pin-striped shirt and plain yellow *Hermes* tie. He wore his typical wry smile of tolerant amusement as the prosecution counsel went to work on him. He stood upright, with one hand resting lightly on the edge of the witness box and refused to be riled by accusations that expensive dinners routinely paid for by James were in return for favours in the form of privileged deal information. He explained crisply that James had insisted on paying personally for the dinners, in recompense for the income he had been responsible for generating for LifeChance. Ross had set up a generous donor circle for the charity at the bank, which continued to grow.

Whilst Richard Ross retained an even temper and answered every question with plummy-voiced precision, James sensed a shifting mood in the courtroom. As the prosecution counsel read from a series of restaurant bills, which contained five hundred-pound bottles of claret and one bottle of dessert wine costing fifteen hundred, bills for two diners running into several thousand, James noted open-mouthed incredulity on the faces of some jury members. They lived in a world divorced from such over-privileged habits, so divorced as to seem unreal. People simply did not spend that kind of money on that kind of thing. Unless, it was a reward for something.

By the time Richard Ross stood down, James could see him differently, through the eyes of the jury. A man of privilege, confidence bordering on arrogance, a sense of entitlement buttressed by a smile that came too easily. An intellect that justified all his actions, whether good or bad, moral or immoral, fair or unjust. Even the steady clip-clop from his polished black brogues as he walked from the room was a reminder that the man's direction would not be altered by anything, if he had set his mind on it. The prosecution had created a credible caricature of slipperiness merely by allowing Ross to show off his character at ease in the witness box. No hard evidence had been evinced from him but something more damaging and corrosive had been unleashed. The insidious message conveyed to the jury was that this privileged class of tricky men, such as Ross and the defendant had been getting away with it for too long.

When the court adjourned for the day, James was fighting off a fit of despondency. Mark had warned him that the court proceedings would feel like a ride on a roller coaster. He cast a sly glance towards Stefanie who had already gathered her papers and was heading for the exit. They had agreed not to see each other during the course of the trial, a decision he knew was right but at that moment felt wrong. He was free to step down from the dock but wasn't sure of the court etiquette at the day's end. All of a sudden with the judge's exit, the ordered silence broke into a babble of voices as people began wandering in all directions. He caught sight of Mark beckoning him over. He had just finished talking with the Andrew Smith and was wearing his inscrutable face.

"All in all, not a bad day," said Mark. It sounded too equivocal to James.

"What happens tomorrow?" James had no appetite to pick over the bones of the day.

"The prosecution will start with Eva and then bring on their expert witness. They'll be hoping he's more compelling than Mr Chivers." Mark permitted himself a tight grin.

James hated the thought of Eva having to appear. "Eva will be fine." He knew that the prosecution had no hard evidence linking her to anything other than her close personal relationship to him.

"I am sure she will. She appears to be a very confident young lady," said Mark pursing his lips and nodding towards the exit.

James turned and saw Eva waving at them. "How about a quick drink before we disperse for the evening?" James suggested.

Mark blinked and started tidying up his papers. "You go ahead. I have to get back to the office."

Eva wore her most conservative charcoal suit with her haired fixed in a bun, and her face scrubbed free of make-up. If Richard Ross appeared to present the repugnant side of the City's excesses, Eva embodied its antithesis. She charmed the jury with her serious sincere face, a soft contemplative voice, and a humble demeanor. Her assertions of moral rectitude rang out with authenticity. All the prosecution managed to insinuate was that she loved her godfather very much and by so doing could be controlled by him. It was their mistake, as it gave her the opportunity to expound on his virtues and his remarkable achievements at LifeChance.

James sat in the dock, feeling the immense pride of a parent watching his daughter debuting in the lead role of a stage drama. It was a quiet tour de force, of which Megan would have been proud. Megan had refused to attend the hearing, partly because she couldn't bear watching the fiction being played out, but increasingly because LifeChance needed her at its helm. Decisions on new centre construction and staffing issues tumbled out through her mornings, co-ordination and planning for investor meetings at WinBet filled her afternoons, and her normal day job of financial management flowed into late evening.

James studied the jury, seven women and five men. The youngest, tattooed, skinny and purple-haired could have been a teenager. The oldest was a balding, bespectacled gentleman in a tweed jacket. The majority appeared middle-aged and well fed. They all listened and watched with intent. The setting and the day's scenes reminded him of being at a fringe theatre. He was a member of the *Donmar Warehouse* theatre, where routinely he would find himself speculating about the identities of the people squashed in around him, and puzzling over the direction of a plot's twists and turns. Interpreted and performed by actors, a few feet away, like the truth, they were within touching distance, but untouchable. Tantalisingly close but never truly captured. Eva's testimony was a five-star rated performance and had lifted his spirits.

After a brief break, the FCA's expert witness stepped into the box. A tall spindly man with a nose too large for his face ran through his arm-length list of credentials. He then spent the rest of the morning eroding the foundation of James's

282

defence by eliminating chance as a possible explanation for his string of share trading deals. Rationally, logically, patiently, and clearly, he showed the jury how the probability of James transacting the particular deals he did, was one chance in a million or possibly ten million depending upon certain assumptions made in modeling the events. In a nasal voice that grated as the hour mark passed, the expert gave his sombre conclusion. Based on his experience of over twenty years, and many similar cases, there could only be one realistic explanation for the pattern of trades: the defendant must have had access to information which was unavailable to the rest of the market. James sank in his seat in unconscious sympathy with his feelings.

He glimpsed over to the jury box and saw several heads nodding in apparent acquiescence. He managed to retain the passive face which Mark had encouraged to practice in front of a mirror. He watched as the prosecution barrister smirked as he finished up. The man swiveled as he sat down and gave a reassuring nod to Stefanie in the seat behind him. She remained bolt upright, still as a statue as she had been throughout the morning. He could see a slither of the side of her pale cheek. Its shape which he had gotten to know intimately, told him she was not smiling.

James's barrister rose briefly to ask a couple of questions, reminding the jury of the witness's credentials covered at the start of the testimony. He ascertained that the expert had received his mathematics doctorate at University College, London, where he been lecturing ever since, and was recently promoted to professorship. Then, to James's dismay, Andrew Smith sat down, leaving the expert's testimony unchallenged.

After a short debriefing with Mark, James spent the lunch break walking alone, along the river in the rain, towards Tower Bridge. He passed the sprucely painted *HMS Belfast*, the iconic warship involved in D-Day landings, now a museum. He'd always meant to visit. He would, once he'd fought his own personal war around the corner, at a place he'd never intended to visit.

He gulped in a damp easterly breeze, filling his lungs. He tried to imagine how it must have felt to be rowed along the Thames to be incarcerated in the Tower. Would their faces ever again feel the revitalizing droplets of an autumnal shower? He wondered what justice for them meant, whether their lives would have been saved by a jury in place of the whim of one man. He had noticed how the odd jury member had glanced awkwardly towards him at the end of the morning's session. None had held his gaze. Mark had warned him that this would be the worst moment in the trial, the end of the prosecution's evidence. After lunch it was time for the defence to turn the tide. James glanced at his watch, and with the wind at his back, strode damp-haired in the drizzle back to the courthouse.

James's barrister had changed the running order to start with the defence's expert witness. Andrew Smith wanted the jury, fresh from the previous session of the prosecution's expert witness, to discern the sharp contrast with the defence's expert. His opening questions to the cheery mid-fifties woman allowed the Oxford University Professor of Mathematics and Computer Science, to roll out her thirty-year career of distinction. She also revealed to the jury's delight that she was regularly featured on a popular TV science programme, and advised several commercial companies including one on-line

284

betting company. She excelled in both academia and the real world.

"Professor Carey, would you say that the previous expert witness was incorrect to conclude that the defendant must have had access to inside information to have undertaken the share dealings in question?" asked James's barrister.

"Haha," said the professor showing her tobacco stained teeth, "if only life were that straightforward and simple."

"So his calculation of the odds, a million or ten million to one are incorrect?"

"Not incorrect necessarily, but incomplete. You see it all depends upon the assumptions you build into your computer model which generates these probabilities."

"Please explain."

"Well in the UK, to take the other chap's odds, you have a one in ten million chance, of being hit by lightning during any year. However, I guarantee if you spend that year standing under a tree, the odds will shrink considerably." A ripple of chuckles spread through the jury box.

"You have a one in two million chance of dying after falling out of bed in the UK, but actually that's concentrated on the very young and very old. You have a one in eight thousand chance, of being killed in a car accident. But actually, just six per cent of fatalities occur on motorways. So which roads you drive on, what weather conditions you drive in, what time of day you set out etcetera etcetera, will all materially influence each individual event."

"So how does that affect this case?"

"Well," said the Professor grinning at the jury, "the number of possible variables that could have affected what trades were carried out by Mr Tait, are great and so therefore must be the range of probabilities."

"So what probability range would you put on those trades?"

The professor laughed again. "We have modeled literally hundreds of potential scenarios. Indeed, one scenario produced a result of less than one in two hundred. That may sound unlikely still, but it's about the same as being involved in a car accident." The professor sniffed. "I'm afraid to say, I've had more than my fair share. Entirely my fault. You should see my premiums." Laughter rumbled across the courtroom from the jury box. Even the judge smiled momentarily.

Cross-examination from the prosecution counsel failed to dent her enthusiastic and robust defence for her almost infinite range of probabilities. She maintained that it seemed quite reasonable for an investment specialist to focus on dealing in shares of companies he knew from his past experience. The only concession she allowed was that it was for the jury and not any technical expert witness to take a view on the reasonableness of assumptions used in calculating probabilities. She finished with a devastating line to put down an aggressive question from the prosecution barrister.

"Let me remind you young man, there is but a one in fourteen million chance, of winning this country's national lottery. Someone has to win it and when they do, no-one accuses them of breaking the law."

By the end of the afternoon's session, James's mood had swung back to optimism mode. Following the professor, a series of 'good' character witnesses trotted onto the stand, to expound upon James's high ethical standards. Even Shahid, who had been disgruntled in being informed of the case late on, put on a good show. Though the case excluded LifeChance, he would forsee the probable damage to the charity and hence to his reputation, should James be found guilty.

The next day would see the end of witness questioning, with James last to appear. He knew he had to be at his best, and to fake sincerity with utter authenticity. He had chosen to swear an affirmation rather than an oath. He thought Father Tait would understand that and accept if not approve of it.

That evening after catching up on the phone with Megan, James opened one of his Montrachet Grand Cru's he'd been keeping in reserve and cooked himself a seafood linguini. He kept checking his mobile for messages in case Stefanie had at least sent a text. They had agreed not to exchange anything but several times he had to obliterate half written texts. He could smell her scent on the empty pillow as he finally lay down in bed waiting for sleep to carry him off till morning.

James stood in the witness box in a pale-blue, open-necked shirt and navy-blue, herringbone wool trousers. He had taken the only snippet of advice that Stefanie permitted herself to proffer, to eschew City suit and tie, in favour of smartly informal. His advice to himself was to secrete in a pocket, his precious purple and yellow beaded necklace, as a reminder that others faced much worse. In another pocket, rested the wooden crucifix from Father Tait to give him hope.

As he went through his responses to his barrister's questions, he felt calm and serene, almost outside his body watching his own performance. They had rehearsed these lines, and he made sure he answered in a serious and respectful tone. Yes, he had poured in a significant portion of his own wealth to get LifeChance going. No, he didn't take a salary from the charity, nor claim expenses. Yes, he did work over sixty hours a week for the charity. No, he did not deal in shares for personal gain. Yes, all his share dealings were for LifeChance. No, he had not ever used illicitly gained information to trade shares. Yes, he had got lucky on several occasions but he had also lost money on some share deals. No, he would never dream of asking old colleagues to supply him with information. Yes, his reputation was everything to him, and yes, he was proud of what he and his team had achieved in building LifeChance. The session continued, with his barrister extracting select pieces of the 'noble' James puzzle, so the jury could only draw one conclusion - this was a decent man, wrongly and unjustly accused.

The following act, when the prosecuting barrister eased into his stride was altogether more taxing, requiring a great deal of improvisation. He started by filling in the pieces of the puzzle that James wanted to remain in the box. Yes, he had made a good deal of money working in his previous job in investment banking. No, he didn't need to work for money now. Yes, he did have an appetite for fine wines and expensive restaurants. No, he was not married and lived alone. Yes, he was a close friend of Caroline Noble, the disgraced hedge fund owner, guilty of money-laundering regulations who went to prison. Yes, she continued to support the charity with large donations. No, he did not believe it was wrong to help economic migrants to remain in the country and added that LifeChance helped all kinds of child migrants including those fleeing from war, and the children of refugees born here.

With an incredulous tone, and eyes flicking continuously towards the jury, the prosecution barrister then went through the detail of the share trades connected with Gladwyn Morson. He pointed out to the jury the particular occasions when James had dumped shares just before share prices had crashed immediately after public pronouncements of takeover bids aborting. Each time, James stared back at his accuser, unblinking, and in a measured tone provided a variant on the themes of getting lucky, past knowledge of the company, investment judgement honed over many years in the business, and pure gut instinct. He denied each time having done anything illegal. Each time, the barrister paused for a few seconds and looked with raised eyebrows to the jury, challenging them to seriously consider the credibility of the witness.

Finally, as he stepped down from the witness box, he glanced at Stefanie. For a split second, they made eye contact. Then she turned her pale, stern face towards the empty press box. James had been fortunate that none of the media had bothered to show up. A soap star's indecent assault case was taking place in an adjoining courtroom and had soaked up all their attention. Inside, he felt his heart thumping. Outside just the clamminess of his hands betrayed the anxiety he felt, knowing that after lunch and summing up from both sides, the jury would be sent out to consider their decision.

Downstairs from the courtroom, the foyer was filled with the bustle and relief of people escaping for an hour or two. James made a beeline for the toilets and bumped into Stefanie coming out of the Ladies. She extended her arm to shake his hand.

"Well done. You did well in there," she said, with an inscrutable face.

"I hope so." James exhaled deeply. "I'll be glad when it's all over." He stroked the outside of her hand with his thumb.

"You know I never wanted this to come to trial." Her eyes darted behind James in case anyone was watching. "But for obvious reasons I couldn't be the one to be seen to stop it."

James nodded, indicating he understood. "Let's hope it's all over and done with today."

"Assuming it goes the right way, I don't want us to ever talk about the case again."

James cocked his head and opened his mouth. This would be the third secret he would have to take with him to his grave. He stood there soundless for a couple of seconds. "Okay, if that's what you want."

"I do. And I don't want either of us to be in this position again. Rules are rules no matter how noble the justification for breaking them." She stared at him, her cheeks and lips tight.

James blinked, but before he could respond, he heard Mark's voice booming behind him. He immediately let go of Stefanie's hand.

"Too late to extract a confession from my client now, Miss Zuegel." Mark appeared in ebullient mood.

"I believe he said he had nothing to confess," Stefanie shot back with a grim smirk.

"Indeed. Waste of public money. Should never have come to trial."

"You seem supremely confident of the outcome," said Stefanie.

"If I was a betting man, I'd put down a wager."

"I don't bet, Mr Phillips. Life has too many uncertainties already. Let's hope your summing up is as solid as your conviction."

"I'm greatly looking forward to hearing yours first," said Mark with a curl of his lip.

"Sorry. I must get to the toilet," interjected James trying to put an end to the pointless bickering.

"See you in court Mr Tait," said Stefanie as they parted in opposite directions.

More than a day had passed since James had stroked Stefanie's hand. Waiting for the verdict had been the most difficult part of the entire process. The judge had sent the jury home after they failed to reach a unanimous verdict. At eleven the following morning, the judge had called everybody back into court to say that he would accept a ten to two majority decision. It was now three in the afternoon, and finally the endless drinking of coffee, rereading of newspapers, and idle chit-chat was over. James stood in the locked dock, and a stout woman stood in the jury box. She held a slip of paper in her shaking hand.

James felt his heart would explode out of his chest, as the judge asked the foreman whether the jury found the defendant guilty or not guilty. His mouth tasted of dust and a queasiness had settled in his stomach. He gripped hold of the ledge in front of him. The woman coughed. She had a kindly face, rotund with a wide upturned mouth. But none of the jury would look at him. All their eyes were fixed on the judge. The room was still. The woman cleared her throat. A split second of silence.

"Not guilty.

Chapter Twenty-One   Gamble

If James needed reminding that not guilty didn't mean innocent, the disgruntled non-executives of LifeChance's board, Shahid and Roger, were there to remind him. They lambasted him for the reputational damage his appearance in court might have had on the charity. They couldn't risk the possibility of a scandal, by which James was certain, they meant their personal risk of association. With support from Megan and Ramesh, he had survived a heated discussion about whether he should resign. The dissident non-executives reserved their position pending a confidential meeting they demanded with James's lawyer, Mark Phillips, to satisfy themselves. James knew he was safe, that Mark would do a fine job, and that the non-executives could tick their governance box and carry on. In the months leading up to Christmas, he worked hard to ingratiate himself with them all over again.

By December, he felt confident enough to show them around the operations of WinBet and hold their monthly board meeting there. Megan had done a superb job in supporting the new management team, and assisting James in attracting venture capital. Pantech Ventures had injected twenty million pounds for a thirty per cent stake. The business appeared to have scaled-up substantially from the operation they had acquired just a few months ago.

The board members had not looked out of place in their suits as they stood in the ground-floor betting outlet, an air-conditioned emporium of flat-screens and flashing gaming machines. Stylish steel frame and light wood tables matched the chic uniformed employees who wandered around with hand-held terminals taking bets. A cool café served organic food and artisanal coffee. The refurbishment of WinBet's single retail outlet, aimed at showcasing its brand, had gone surprisingly well. It seemed like half of Hammersmith's office workers were gambling on some early Christmas presents. Better still, this part of the operation was entirely genuine.

On the first floor, James and Megan had led the non-executives around the hub of the open-plan operation, where desks were arranged in groups according to the sport, or the functional area, such as marketing and finance. Megan pointed out the largest two groups, football and horse racing, then rattled off a long list of smaller sports they covered. Staff sat at screens, some updating web pages, others scanning odds offered by competitors, and a few with headsets speaking live to customers.

They introduced the board to Buck Kruger, WinBet's founding entrepreneur and the young boffin whose team was still working to improve its football-odds algorithm. His team had been cut in half and resources applied to on-line marketing. James remained skeptical about its efficacy but it sounded convincing enough to the uninitiated. If they were going to list the company on AIM, London Stock Exchange's market for young growing companies, they would have to convince a more cynical audience of brokers, investors and accountants of the credibility of their growth strategy. A successful tour around the company's buzzing headquarters would convey much more than thousands of pages of legal and accounting jargon.

On the second floor, where the group now stood, surveying an expanse of desks populated by young staff staring at screens and speaking into their headsets, Megan had worked her magic. To James, it felt like a subdued trading floor. To his guests, it looked like an operation struggling to cope with a tsunami of incoming calls. A few operators swiveled their chairs momentarily as the group surveyed the talking heads.

"I thought everything was more or less done on-line these days," said Roger with a frown.

"A lot of people prefer the phone," said Megan. "Not everyone, particularly our older clients are tech savvy. And increasingly people are worried about security on the internet."

"This must cost a fortune though, compared with an automated digital operation."

"It does, but we have both. This is our privileged client centre for high rollers. The minimum bet is a hundred pounds so it's still economic."

Roger gave an affirming grunt. The reality however was quite different. James had suggested that they needed to show a growing physical presence and a level of frenetic activity to convey that the business was powering ahead. So, they had hired a bunch of out of work actors, given them scripts of fictional conversations with fictional clients, loaded dummy customer accounts onto the IT system, and created fabricated transactions. The 'extras' were told they were engaged in scene making for a new 'reality' TV series and cameras had been hidden to record their activities. They had to stay in character, particularly when other actors appeared on the floor in the guise of investors or professional advisors. The best performers could audition for bigger roles for the second series. They were called upon usually fortnightly and were paid twice the going rate in cash.

Shahid drifted towards one of the operators and peered at a screen as she chatted into a headset microphone. He was leaning in, with his mouth close to her head, trying to listen to the call.

"It's part of our marketing strategy to go after the wealthier client, give them a personal service," said James edging close to Shahid. He didn't want him asking the woman any difficult questions.

Shahid nodded as he studied the screen, containing the customer's name and other personal details. "What are those figures on the right?" he asked, pointing to a column of figures down the right of the blue screen.

James exchanged a quick look with the woman and cut in before she could respond. "That's the history of all the bets the customer has made. It's highly confidential. All the operatives have to sign non-disclosure agreements. They can't talk about a customer to anyone. And no-one is allowed to listen in on customer conversations. Everything is recorded and stored securely in accordance with new GDPR requirements."

"Of course," said Shahid leading the group across smoke-grey carpet tiles to reach the furthest bank of desks. "These grey desks are a bit grim."

"Melamine. The carpet is polypropylene, and the computers are Chinese," said Megan. "We're hard on costs."

"Are you profitable yet?" asked Roger.

"Close to cash breakeven, if you exclude the capital costs for the shop refurbishment and kitting out this floor."

"So how long before the cash runs out?"

"That all depends on how aggressively we want to grow," said James "We'll need to spend a lot more on marketing if we want to double sales next year. That will mean heavier losses initially."

"But at the moment you are on budget?" said Ramesh, parroting what James had told him earlier during a private conversation.

James smiled at him. "We are indeed. And we've already begun tentative discussions about an AIM listing next year, so-."

"All very good," Roger interjected, "but how long before our cash runs out? Give me a range at least."

"We're running different scenarios, which we can present at the next board meeting," said Megan.

"You mean you don't know," said Roger with a scowl.

"It's at least a year," said James glaring back at him. If you put Roger in a room on his own for five minutes, he'd have an argument, thought James. "I suggest we move back to the boardroom and finish off our meeting."

They ambled back through the hubbub and down the staircase to the first-floor meeting room, a dull featureless quad whose one window gave a view of a red brick block, a few metres away. Sleet was falling and the light fading. Fluorescent lighting flickered above them as they reconvened with coffee from the corridor vending machine.

The tour must have gone well, James surmised, as they rippled through the meeting's agenda with a warm breeze of concurring murmurs. The non-executives nodded approvingly as WinBet's management team concluded their power-point presentation. LifeChance's new centres were all open as planned, and a Head of Fund Raising had been lured from a much larger national charity. Now that James could no longer rely on a flow of funds emanating from Eva's insider tips, LifeChance desperately needed a more effective fund-raising operation to fill the hole. James had never been particularly good at begging for money and he was looking forward to handing over the role to a specialist. Meanwhile he intended to steer WinBet to a profitable flotation for LifeChance.

With best wishes for Christmas exchanged, James parted company with the non-executives, and returned to the small meeting room. Megan was struggling to open a window which had been painted shut. He switched on a pedestal fan, next to a thin gurgling radiator. Half-filled plastic coffee cups littered the stained wood veneer table. Scuffed peach-coloured walls and stained blue carpet tiles completed the nineties decor. It hungered for a lick of paint.

"Unbelievable," said James chuckling, "Shahid is downstairs putting a bet on a horse."

Megan laughed and gave the window a final heave. It wouldn't budge. She turned to face James. "So stuffy in here."

"Well they've gone now. I think the management team presented well. Even Roger seemed pacified for a change."

"I'm not sure he was convinced with our nerd and his algorithm."

"Buck? Neither am I. But we'll find out soon enough."

"I sense Buck's getting suspicious about our 'extras'.

"What has he been saying?"

"He asks why it takes so long to train operators for the telephones. He's noticed that none of them have joined the staff on the first floor yet. And he wonders why the training sessions only happen on days when we have visitors."

"Buck's a smart guy. He was bound to figure something out, sooner or later."

"So what do we do? We can't just get rid of him. He's bound to start flinging mud around."

James sat down, elbows on the table and clasped his hands together, as if praying. He closed his eyes for a while as Megan came to sit opposite him. She was used to sitting in on James's mindful minutes as he liked to term them. The fan whirred noisily obliterating James's deep breathing.

"I think we need to put the pressure back on him. He knows his football algorithm currently works no better than the horse racing odds where we balance the book just like our competitors. So, we give him one more member of staff and three months to prove it finally works."

"And if it doesn't?" said Megan folding her arms.

"Then we offer him a very generous settlement to leave. We give him more share options, we put him on paid garden leave for a year, and a two year non-compete for which we will pay a lump sum at the end, provided he signs up to a stringent confidentiality undertaking. He can't talk to anybody about anything to do with WinBet. But also allow him to use the gardening year to do anything he likes as long as it has nothing to do with the gambling industry."

Megan paused for a beat and stroked her bottom lip with her index finger. "That could work. He's always going on about new business ideas he's bursting to pursue."

"Good." He glanced around the room. "Now that Roger has been here, can we finally upgrade this floor?" said James rising to deposit several cups into a rusting bin. Roger had been consistent in his criticism of their largesse on office decor at LifeChance's headquarters. "We're going to be bringing lots more City folk here next year. We need to impress them."

"Contractors start next week. But we have a tight budget. We spent too much on the ground floor redesign and fit-out."

"Well it's pulling in the punters." James had settled on the redesign having viewed competitor offerings. He had regarded them all as tawdry and uninspiring. Whilst competition on-line was intense, he wondered whether there might be a retail roll-out opportunity by updating an old-fashioned bricks and mortar sector.

"It is, but we still need to be cautious about diverting funds to LifeChance for the next couple of months. If the cash drains away too quickly, Pantech will start asking questions."

"Okay," said James. The after effects of his court experience had chastened him. He had no intention of going back there.

"Well, not okay unless Caro comes through with the cash she promised. I can't believe we're still waiting."

James looked at Megan, saw the challenge in her eye. "When do we need her funds?"

"Yesterday would have been good. I'm already stretching out payments to the builders for the new centres. But they are screaming to be paid by Christmas."

James rubbed his chin ruefully. "Well then, that settles it. We'll have to do what she's been demanding."

"I don't want any part in abducting a child." Megan glared at him.

"What if the child doesn't realise?"

"What do you mean?"

"It's just an idea that came from something Eva mentioned to me. Mark's youngest son has a birthday coming up. I thought maybe we could give him a treat." James outlined his idea to Megan and said he would run it past Caro face to face the next day. He and Stefanie were going over for dinner.

Megan raised both eyebrows. "Wow. You've never done that before."

"No. I just thought it was about time. Can't be put off forever, not if...you know."

"She's for keeps?" Megan smiled.

He was unwilling to say aloud what he hoped, in case he jinxed their relationship. Most people his age would have compromised by now. He never had, nor would. Stefanie was no compromise. "It's important she gets on with you, and Caro. For me."

Megan sighed. "I remember when I introduced her to Alicia. Like meeting your parents for the first time. Caro's very protective of her tribe. She judges quickly."

"So does Stefanie. That's what worries me." His mind drifted back to the first non-date in the pub under the arches. He had been surprised by her forthrightness and indifference to petty social norms. She'd got him to open up. She was a cure for his emotional constipation.

"I like Stefanie. They'll be fine together. But I'd worry about your abduction plan. It's risky."

"It is. And maybe it won't work, but I think it's the least worst option we have. For LifeChance."

"We cannot involve Eva in any of this." She stared at him, pausing in protest. "You promised me."

"And I've kept my promise. She saw Mark off her own back. I think she's feeling a little sorry for him. Rumours about his professional and private life are swirling around the firm. And he's still stuck in a miserable hotel and only allowed home at weekends."

"Lucky to be allowed home at all."

James smiled. He understood better than anyone why Megan was hard on most men. "How is Eva? She hasn't been around for a couple of weeks."

"A new boyfriend on the scene. A Russian. Rich family. Father has a jet. Last weekend they flew to Paris. This weekend, they are off to Venice."

"Do you think she'd benefit from some moral guidance from her godfather?"

Megan cocked her head and contrived a crooked smile. "I think she's had quite enough of that already."

James laughed. "Have you met him?"

Megan grunted. "No but I feel I have. She tells me everything, too much. Then she tells me what I should be doing, with Alicia. How Alicia should be allowed to move in. How we should get married. How we should go on an exotic honeymoon. How we shouldn't keep worrying about her."

"Maybe she's right. You know, Picasso once said, 'it takes a very long time to become young'. I'm still working on it."

Stefanie felt ridiculous. Here she was, a successful professional, well into her thirties, confident and independent, talking too much and giggling at Caro's mildly amusing tales about James as a small child. He had been dragged upstairs by one of Caro's children to read a bedtime story. In the biggest kitchen she had ever sat in, German made and stacked with German devices, she felt far away from home. She drained her wine glass, the second since arriving just a half hour before. Bruce left his chicken breasts sizzling on the griddle and skipped over with a fresh bottle, ice-cold from the giant Bosch fridge-freezer. She thanked him as he unscrewed the cap and refilled her glass whilst she listened to one of Caro's anecdotes of carting a drunk James back to his student lodgings after a summer ball.

"Couldn't hold his drink in those days. I had to train him intensively," said Caro whooping with the pleasure of retelling, and reliving the incident.

"Well I can confirm you have done a thorough job," said Stefanie, aware of her facial muscles as she smiled. She was determined that Caro should like her.

"Ah, here he comes. So Rosie finally released you."

James sank into his seat next to Caro. "One story somehow became three. So," said James pouring himself some wine, "what have I missed?"

"I've been telling Caro how you stalked me outside my office when we first met."

"I told her you've been stalking me since the aged of three," said Caro.

James smiled. "Bruce, help me out here. Would you say we were the stalkers or the entrapped?"

Bruce suspended chopping red peppers. "I think," he said, pausing for effect, "you need to fight your own battles, James." The women whooped again as Bruce looked beyond them to the small figure in pyjamas carrying a Paddington Bear. "Olly what are you doing out of bed?"

" I want Uncle James to read a story."

"You didn't eat your vegetables at dinner. No vegetables, no story," said Bruce firmly. All the adults' eyes fell on the child as his face crumpled.

"Really Bruce, I don't mind," said James, as a tear ran down Olly's cheek.

"Oh let him," said Caro topping up her wine glass, "he loves it."

Bruce sighed. "Okay Olly, but only if you promise me that tomorrow you will eat every vegetable I put on your plate."

"I promise, I promise, I promise" shouted Olly, the tears already forgotten history.

"Come on buddy." James lifted-up the little boy. "Just one story though."

"Night night Olly," said Caro. The boy beamed and kept waving his bear as the pair retreated from the room.

Stefanie felt bewitched by the whole scene. Her life excluded children, and she was jolted by the tenderness that smothered the adults in the little boy's presence. She smiled at Caro. "How do you do it? You work long hours, run your own firm, and have a large family."

"Simple. Staff," said Caro whilst chewing a salami and pickle canapé, Bruce had prepared.

"What about me?" said Bruce feigning a hurt tone.

"You are staff darling. And don't tell me I don't pay you well for it," said Caro with a mischievous grin aimed at Stefanie.

"Bloody charming," said Bruce, slicing into a beefsteak tomato.

"Do you want kids?" said Caro.

Stefanie blinked. She hadn't expected such an abrupt question, so personal, and so early into their relationship. She felt Caro's bulging eyes boring into hers.

"I...I'm not sure, not really." The words sounded lame and insincere even as she was saying them. She had thought about it, but until now, she had not seen a scintilla of interest from anyone she'd dated.

"Well, plenty of time I suppose. You're still young. How old are you?" Caro took another gulp of wine.

Stefanie was unused to being the subject of an inquisition, especially one in which the inquisitor appeared to read her mind.

"Thirty-six. But who's counting?" said Stefanie avoiding eye-contact and reaching for her glass.

"He's good with kids, James. He has five god-children. Jack, Jess, Rosie, Olly, and Eva. You've now met them all," said Caro with an unmistakably mischievous grin.

"Yes. I've yet to meet Eva in a social context," said Stefanie with a stare and a small smile. "But then I think you know that."

"Of course. James tells me everything."

Stefanie smiled and let the silence between them grow. "Everything?" she said finally, unblinking and staring back at Caro.

"You know Stefanie, I've known James longer than anyone else in this world. He is my kid brother. We have always looked out for each other. He visited the family every single day when I was in prison, courtesy of the FCA."

"I had nothing to do with your case, Caro."

"I know that, and I wasn't suggesting you had."

"And you must know that my career would be finished if the FCA found out that James and I were together before the trial." Stefanie sensed a threat lurking in the shadows of their conversation.

"I wouldn't dream of going to the FCA, I-"

"Then, I'm sorry but what are you suggesting?"

Caro sighed lightly. "Simply, that I would do anything for James and he would do the same for me. Nothing will ever get in the way of that."

Stefanie opened her mouth then closed it again. The conversation had turned acidic because Caro seemed threatened by her. And she feared the reverse. She needed to take a step back, to show a concession. She didn't want James in the middle having to choose.

"I think James is very lucky to have you. I have never had anyone so close." Stefanie hoped it sounded like a truce.

"What about your family?"

My father and mother live in a small town in Germany. They dote on my brother and his two children. They live almost next door to each other. Not one of them has ever bothered to visit me in the UK. I am regarded as a deserter, a traitor and worst of all, a barren middle-aged woman who hasn't brought them grandchildren."

Caro's face softened and she made a show of topping up their glasses. "Let's have a toast. To a bright future for us all." Their glasses clinked as James walked back into the room.

"James. How are the new centres going?" asked Caro.

"Good. Filling up quickly."

"Has he taken you to visit one yet?" said Caro.

"Not yet, I've been too busy," said Stefanie.

"You should find time. The children are unbelievable, given what many of them have been through."

"I will, soon. Work has been mad. And I'm not allowed to recruit. My team's budget has been cut."

Caro grunted. "Not like James's lawyer. Mark Phillips always manages to exceed an unlimited budget."

"He did his job," said James, entering the kitchen.

"Not for me, he bloody well didn't. Sorry Stefanie, a point of contention between James and me."

"I think the man likes himself a lot," said Stefanie, adding to the bridge they were building.

"That is something we can all agree on," said Bruce, holding aloft a griddle pan of honeyed chicken. "Corn on the cob, and a couple of salads on the way. I hope you like quinoa and pomegranate, Stefanie."

"I eat everything. The way to this woman's heart is through her stomach. Ask James."

"She imprisons me in the kitchen all the time," added James.

"Join the club," said Bruce.

"Best place for you all. Leave us women to run the world. You've had your chance and blown it," said Caro grinning and winking at Stefanie. They had landed on fertile common ground to journey late into the evening.

Chapter Twenty-Two   Birthday

Cath's dilemma over what to do about Mark nagged away from the moment the alarm woke her. It still hurt. She peered through the curtains, to brooding black clouds. She would fix her face into a smile before she woke the kids. This morning she would wear her sunniest clowning mask for Ralph. She wanted him to remember being eight for the right reasons, so had invited Mark over for supper.

The excitement had started straight out of bed and simply spiralled up and almost over whilst Ralph engulfed a second bowl of some chocolate flavoured cereal; a special treat for his birthday but perhaps with the benefit of hindsight, not the best choice. Trying to calm him down before his big day at school, she had allowed him to open one present; a shiny Fulham Football Club ball. The rest were hidden away till his father arrived and wrote in his birthday card.

Her morning routine was an exercise in juggling children and their demands for food and clothes. Natalia would ferry Miranda to her pre-school session for gifted children and return to help Cath with breakfasts for the twins and Ralph. Cath would then accompany Ralph to school.

Ralph burst out of the front door, a ball of energy, a spinning top of flailing arms and school bags, the broad beaming grin of pure joy. Cath stumbled out a good deal slower; she had never been a morning person and found conversation in general and indeed any noise other than a kettle boiling or the toaster clicking, difficult to bear. Even on a run of the mill day, boisterous kids served as a daily challenge of self-control. Normally she found herself repeating, 'indoor voice please', futile attempts to make the day's dawning more bearable.

The football hung in a string bag from his wrist and he kneed it incessantly as his mother trailed just behind him. It was an eight-minute walk to Our Lady of Peace, a highly lauded junior school, adored by local estate agents and shrewd parents. Mrs Rogers, the stern headmistress with a steely stare was intolerant of lateness and a good deal more. Parents eyed her with a mix of awe, respect and fear.

Despite her best intentions to be a good parent, Cath invariably left home late with only a few minutes to spare before the school bell rang out, proclaiming another frenetic start to the school day. Then the walk turned into an early morning dash. As often as not, Ralph would hear the urgent shrill of the bell and sprint the last two hundred meters. Once over the main road, he was allowed to do the last section on his own nowadays, a concession easily won from his mother.

Ralph wanted to arrive early on his birthday, to show off his present and enjoy a few minutes' kick-about with his class mates. Cath bear-hugged and kissed him goodbye at the usual spot on the corner of Charlwood Road. She would often loiter there along with a couple of other mums to gaze at their adorable offspring as they gambolled and chatted their way to the school gate just over the hump bridge, out of sight. This morning she was a little early for the slovenly mother set, as they laughingly referred to themselves.

As usual, they had pre-arranged a gossip in *Coffee Heaven* on the high street after drop-off. But first she needed to shower and mutate from pyjama-top-track-bottom-wearing-sloth into yummy-mummy. The transformation wasn't getting any easier these days. She tore her gaze away from her adorable boy who had caught up with his best friend, Sam. She rushed homebound, hoping Natalia had cleared up the morning's mess and gotten the twins ready for nursery. She would drop them off on her way to the high street, whilst Natalia left for her English class.

It was just before the school gate that Sam nudged a chatting Ralph and pointed to a woman holding a placard proclaiming "Happy 8th Birthday to Ralph".

"Happy Birthday Ralph!" she exclaimed, "your mum said you'd be surprised. Here's an extra special present for you." Megan bent down, smiled broadly at him, and held out a white plastic carrier bag bearing the initials, 'F.F.C'.

Ralph was a little startled and anxious since he had always been told never to talk to strangers.

"It's a Fulham bag," enthused Sam. Ralph peeked in and drew out a white shirt.

"Wow, that's brilliant!" said Sam, "a Fulham football shirt with your name on it.....and it's got a number eight for your birthday. Lucky!"

Noticing Ralph's coyness, the woman explained, "I'm your Auntie Sally, an old friend of your mum's. We cooked this up together" she laughed. " I have another treat for you. We're going to visit Fulham Football Club this morning. You may get to see all your favourite players. And get out of school work for a couple of hours."

"Craven Cottage. Lucky!" whooped Sam.

"Really," said Ralph, with a small disbelieving smile. Won't Mrs Rogers mind?"

"Don't worry about her. I'll just go and see her now. Come on, let's go in the playground."

Megan guessed Ralph would feel at ease amongst his other friends and with several mothers, chit chatting in the yard. Blue-uniformed children shot around the playground like ricocheting bullets. Ralph was surrounded by half a dozen joshing boys. He was jubilant, showing them his new Fulham jersey and bragging about missing school to visit Fulham.

A couple of the other mothers shouted birthday greetings to Ralph whilst quizzically eyeing up Megan. She went over to introduce herself as Cath's old friend from university and asked where she could locate Mrs Rogers. Each of them wished her luck as the headmistress was renowned for her intransigence over children being absent from school for any reason. Megan smiled and sauntered off confidently into the school building. This was the riskiest part of the entire exercise she had rehearsed over several days. No one had noticed the figure on the corner opposite the school gates, peeking over the top of a magazine.

She relieved herself in the toilet and took a minute to wash her hands, check her wig and wipe her dark-tinted glasses. She breathed deeply and then marched briskly into the playground and smiled at the dwindling group of mums. She told Ralph they had to go straightaway. Mrs Rogers had given him a pass until lunchtime. Ralph's friends watched them scurry out of the playground, arm in arm. He twisted round just as they disappeared out of the gate, grinning triumphantly.

The bell rang as Megan turned the corner. "Come on. We don't want to be late." She stretched out her stride and Ralph bounced alongside. She felt the warmth of his damp delicate hand on her palm and squeezed gently. She looked down on his unrestrained, animated face as he began to chat excitedly about his favourite players. To any passer-by, they looked like a typical south-west London mum ferrying her son along to an early morning appointment, doctor or dentist. She checked the time on her mobile as it pinged into life. She responded to the message confirming they were on schedule.

By the time they had reached her car, parked near the river in a permit and CCTV free zone, Ralph had moved on to team tactics and formations. Megan was hopeful that she would be spared an explanation of the offside rule which seemed to fascinate all boys, both young and old. His innocence had eased her pulse rate a fraction, though her stomach still performed somersaults.

They slid into the car, just out of sight of a row of terraced houses, dark windowed residences of young professionals who'd left for work when the streetlamps were lit. Megan handed Ralph a coke. His face lit up when she held up a large bar of chocolate. He fumbled it with his fragile fingers; more piano playing than goalkeeping, thought Megan. She pressed the ignition, peered in the mirror and took a deep breath, held it, and then blew out. Her heart was motoring. Sitting there, she could barely believe she had agreed to snatch the child. But no-one else could be trusted, and so she felt she had no choice. She owed her life to James. He was trapped by Caro's insistence on this final act of revenge. LifeChance would receive its lifeline, and she could stop lying to overdue creditors.

"We're going to the training ground, not the stadium. That's where the players are now," said Megan.

"Cool," said Ralph through a chocolatey mouth.

She was thankful to be driving in the opposite direction to the stalled traffic choking up Putney High Street, a main artery conveying tankfuls of pollution to the local residents, then over the bridge to the wealthier denizens of the capital. Within minutes she had reached the borders of Wimbledon Common, the scene of her early morning running regime. Today had started out normal: five miles to cleanse mind, body and soul. How early her day had turned abnormal.

She geared up as she exited on to the A3 carriage-way, careful to keep within the speed limit. She was pleased to see that the traffic was flowing smoothly and that Ralph had continued to jabber away. He let Megan know his England team, position by position, if he was the manager. He was convinced his team would be world champions. His dad who liked football agreed. They had season tickets at Fulham.

"What does your daddy do?" Megan asked, eager to escape the world of football for a few moments.

"He works in an office. It's really cool. They have biscuits and hot chocolate all day long."

Having outsmarted the speed cameras, Megan turned off the dual carriageway and descended into suburbia: neat painted semis and gleaming parked cars; spacious un-littered streets, smooth tarmac, brilliant white and yellow markings, street signs with warnings, penalties for unlawful drivers. She spotted a uniformed traffic warden greedily tapping a car registration number into his handheld device, checking for a valid parking permit. A thin woman in a black raincoat with two poodles, dangling as many poop bags. A BT engineer fiddling inside a telecomms cabinet. None of them bothered to look up as she passed them.

A few minutes later, she spotted the discrete sign announcing Fulham Football Club's training facilities. She swung the car into the pristine painted car park, packed with an impressive range of shiny Mercedes, BMW's and Porsches.

Like a poor relation, her puddle-marked Golf squeezed into a tight corner, overshadowed by a polished black Range Rover. As they got out the car, they could see a part of the grounds through the single bar barrier. Hoardings, freshly coated in club black and white paint, obliterated most of their view. But it was enough to turn Ralph into a bouncing rubber ball. As Megan led the way, passing through a narrow gateway, a long arm shot out blocking their way.

"Can I help you ma'am?" said a puny fellow in a grey uniform.

"We're just here to watch the team train for a while. Is it okay to take pictures?" said Megan.

"I regret that is not possible ma'am. Could I see your entry tickets please?" Megan took a step back. It had not occurred to her that a ticket would be required just to watch a bunch of grown men running about a bit and doing a few exercises on a patch of grass.

"No sorry. We must have missed it. Where do we buy them?" said Megan, looking around for the box office.

"You can't," said the unsmiling figure tightening the knot of his black tie. "You have to apply for them from the Club."

"But that's no good. It's his birthday today. He's eight."

The creature started to chuckle. "I wish I had a fiver for every time I've been spun that line. Anyway, makes no difference. No ticket, no entry."

"But he's a season ticket holder. Surely that must count."

"Nope." The guard stepped in front of Megan, legs apart and hands crossed in front of him.

Megan saw tears welling in Ralph's eyes. "Please. Just for a few minutes. We won't take photos."

"No you won't, because you're not getting in and that's all there is to it."

Megan, invariably thorough, was silently berating herself for not checking beforehand. She hated men in civilian uniforms. They were all a bunch of small-minded Jobsworth types whose uniform gave them some miniscule quantum of power over people. Stupid men clothed in stubbornness. She so wanted to smack him and hurl abuse at him. Tears started to roll down Ralph's face. "Look. I'll stay here. Just let the boy in. I'm willing to pay," said Megan reaching into her handbag.

"Madam. Rules is rules and I don't make them. I suggest you take the matter up with the Club." He now wore his smug face. How she wanted to sink her fist into those rotting yellow teeth. She realised it was hopeless to appeal to his better nature. He didn't have one.

"Well done," said Megan yanking a sniffing Ralph away, "You've ruined a little boy's day and lost a fan forever. But one day, he'll be something, not a jumped-up miserable security guard who can't even do up his flies." The man's thin smile collapsed as he looked down and saw the white shirt tail poking out of his trousers.

Back in the car, Megan soothed Ralph with the promise that she knew a secret way in. She made it sound like they were going on an adventure. With a fresh coke in one hand, and switching through the music stations on the radio with the other, Ralph was happy again. Megan drove slowly out and around the perimeter roads of the training ground, one eye on the road, and the other on the high fence and netting above. On her second circuit, she slipped the car into a space, not overlooked by houses where the fence was shrouded under the canopy of trees on either side.

"Stay here for a moment," she said. She got out and fished about in the boot. She reappeared with a short crow-bar, and snuck through the undergrowth to the fence. With one end edged behind the lip a lap-fencing panel, she yanked hard with the other end of the crow-bar. The sound of splintering echoed under the trees. Megan attacked several pine panels, creating a gap wide enough to squeeze through. She returned the car and stowed her wrecking device in the boot.

"Right. Job done. Come on," said Megan.

"Won't we get into trouble?" Ralph must have been watching. Worry was written in his wrinkled forehead.

"Course not. Anyway, we have our getaway car," said Megan smiling. "Just follow me."

They sneaked in through the gap, and peeped out from behind the trunk of a giant London plane tree. In the distance, a group of men she presumed were footballers were running like ants in a quadrant. It meant nothing to her and when she turned to peer down at Ralph, she expected to see a disappointed face. Instead, a face beamed back at her as he started to reel off the names of the players before them.

"This is the best birthday ever," said Ralph.

She scanned the training ground where the players now appeared to be huddled in a group, surrounding a thick set older man with a balding head. "Who's that?"

"That's John Taylor, the manager. Don't you even know that," Ralph teased. "They call him the 'guvnor'."

"So, he's the boss man is he?"

"I s'pose so," said Ralph shrugging his shoulders.

The boy was besotted and could have stayed rooted to the spot for the entire morning. Drizzle turned to a light rain and then into a steady downpour but he didn't budge. The sound of a police-car siren convinced Megan that she had pushed her luck, and they should get moving.

"Come on." She tugged Ralph's sticky warm hand. "We should get going now. I have another treat for you," she said grinning as widely as she could manage. She spotted Jobsworth appearing from the Clubhouse and starting to peer around the ground. They retraced their steps through the wet undergrowth back to the car.

"Where are we going?" said Ralph as she strapped on his seat-belt.

"Well, do you like school dinners?"

Ralph screwed up his face and stuck out his tongue. "Yuk."

Megan smiled at him. Back in the car, she was feeling safer again. "Nor me. So I thought we'd go to McDonalds."

She had expected a cry of joy. She got his frowning face instead. "What's up, don't you like Macs?" said Megan, astonished and wondering if he'd been raised as a vegetarian.

"Mum doesn't let us."

"Ah. Well, she said as a special treat for your birthday, it's okay."

A beam appeared across his face. "I wish it was my birthday every day."

They both giggled as Megan checked the rear mirror for signs of police cars. Then they were off again, away from the training ground and heading to the home of Happy Meals. A few minutes later, Megan pulled into an outlet off the main road. Before getting out of the car, she smoothed down her brunette wig in the mirror, reapplied more bright red lipstick, and reset her dark glasses. They walked hand in hand across the pristine tarmac. As they got closer, the palpable image of a joyful mother and son, may have appeared to a CCTV camera above the entry.

Megan thought Ralph would be mesmerised by the menu options as they stood in line for the counter. The place was buzzing. He surprised her. He would have a chocolate

316

milkshake and a 'Big Mac'. That was what his best friend Sam always had when his dad came to see him.

Back at Ralph's school, pandemonium had broken out. The panic button had been pressed the instant Cath answered her mobile in *Coffee Heaven*. The caller's message was abrupt - 'we have your son and we are taking him out for his birthday. Have a nice day.' Cath later described the female voice to the police as unaccented, possibly young and chilling. Feeling sick but clinging to a hope the call had been a hoax, she had called the school secretary immediately. The standard text message to all parents of absent children was about to be sent out. The morning register listed Ralph as absent.

The next minute, she was racing to school whilst screeching into her smart-phone for Mark's secretary to interrupt his meeting.

"Mark, someone's taken Ralph; he's gone and I don't know where. I-," wailed Cath.

"What do you mean he's gone? He can't have gone!" interrupted Mark.

"I should have taken him all the way to school, but it's his birthday and -"

"Cath, calm down. What's happened?"

She told Mark all she knew. Just saying the words made her feel like she was sliding into a dark void of terror. He listened till her outpouring died. He said not to worry, that there would be a simple explanation, that everything would be fine, that he'd jump in a taxi and meet her at the school. She ran faster and, ever the Catholic when it suited, begged God to bring her son home safe.

Mrs Rogers met her at the school gate. The headmistress had already called the police and logged a call to alert

Wandsworth Local Authority. They were sending a lawyer to attend. Ralph's teacher, Ms Neat, and his best friend Sam, had been summoned for interrogation.

It was break-time and the noise in the playground was deafening. The children parted like the Sea of Galilee as Cath and the headmistress made their way to her office. Moments later, the children were thrilled to see a flashing police car pull up outside. A pair of uniformed officers strode into the school. The cold breeze in the playground hissed with whispers that Sam had been arrested for swearing at his teacher and was going to prison.

Mrs Rogers had squashed seven chairs into her depressing room, functional and forgettable. She was sat with two uniformed police officers, Cath and Mark. A dedicated officer for missing children was en-route, as supposedly was a lawyer from Wandsworth. Ms Neat had taken Sam away to his classroom where she could keep a weather eye on him. He had been quizzed gently but they couldn't fool a smart eight-year-old. He was crying.

A squad car had been sent to Fulham's football stadium, on the north bank of the Thames, and discovered that no stadium tours were taking place that day. Another car was being sent to the club's training ground in Motspur Park, a few miles out of town. Calls had been put out to mums in the playground that morning to try to assemble a facial composite of the woman who had taken Ralph. An alert with preliminary descriptions of them both had been transmitted throughout the Metropolitan Police area for sightings. So far nothing had been seen or heard of them but it was still early. The police officers said there was no need to panic, yet.

The dull routine of questions done, only intermittent exchanges, strangely stilted, punctuated the hot room. No one wanted to talk but no one wanted the silence either. The air was thick with guilt and unspoken accusations. Cath was crucifying herself for not taking Ralph every last yard to the school gate, for letting him have his way when she shouldn't have allowed it, and for not stressing the gravity of 'stranger danger', even though she thought she had. Every nagging second without news felt like a minute, every minute like an hour.

Mark sat beside her, gripping her hand, helping her to fight off a creeping panic. He had strangled his earlier rage. He had ranted at the police that more should be done, and let them know that he was a lawyer. But when challenged by an officer what more meant, he was stumped and simply broke down and wept. But Cath was sure that his accusing eyes raged with fury, against her. She should have deposited Ralph in the playground. She should have listened to Mark and sent Ralph to the private prep school with the bus pick-up from home. She should have let her husband come back home and allowed him to take his son to school on his birthday. He would have been safe. A son needed his father.

Cath heard the door click open and felt a draft of cooler air, followed by a waft of boiled cabbage. In front of her, Mrs Rogers' mouth had gaped open. Cath swivelled her head. Ralph's teacher stood with her hand on his shoulder. She was crying and he was tugging at a strawberry liquorice stick.

Chapter Twenty-Three   Spring

James glanced at his watch a moment after he'd spied Caro perched on a stool at a high table, tapping at her mobile. 9.30pm on the dot. For a change he wasn't late and she was early. The rooftop lounge was buzzing with City suits and dashing cocktail staff. Soul music was playing in the background of the mellow-lit room. A tiny, candle-lit lantern, highlighted remnants on several small plates where Caro sat. Ice melted in a couple of empty cocktail glasses.

"Be with you in a sec," shouted Caro above the din, as James slid into the seat opposite her. He had clear views of Tower Bridge and half of the City skyline, illuminating the dark February evening. A few spirited or drunken souls were braving the outside terrace. He slid his I-pad out of his case as a wordless waiter delivered several plates of tapas and four salt rimmed cocktail glasses, festooned with lime slices and sprigs of mint.

"Are we expecting guests?" said James leaning towards Caro.

She finally put down her mobile, and beamed at him as she picked up a glass. "No. Just left." She started to chomp her way through a couple of boquerones."

"Four cocktails?"

"I'm sure you can get through a couple of mojitos." She grabbed a dripping beef skewer and slid half of it into her mouth.

"I shall do my best. Cheers." James grimaced as the rum hit the back of his throat. He rarely bothered with spirits these days. He drank too fast and the hangovers cost him too much. He glanced around. This was not Caro's typical haunt. Too noisy. Too brash. Too young. "Why are we here?"

"Elysium," spluttered Caro as she devoured more beef. "New clients. They love it here. Insist on coming here every night. Third time this week."

"Hope they're worth it."

"A billion. They signed today. Funds coming next week."

"American?"

"Brazilian. Family office. Third generation. Very professional. Very thorough."

"You've checked them out?" James regretted saying it even as the words spilled from his mouth.

"Course I bloody well checked them out? Do you think I'm a moron? Do you think for one second, I want to go back...there? For Christ's sake James!" The intensity of her fervor surprised him, but not the rest of the room which soaked up the outburst like a splash in a screaming sea. He wondered how long she'd been drinking.

"Sorry. I just-"

"You're in no position to lecture me."

"Sorry."

"You're the one taking stupid risks." Caro gulped at her mojito and glared over the top of her glass, daring him to deny it.

James looked around the room. He knew better than to get into an argument with Caro. He would never win it. She had what he needed. And it seemed to him that for the past week, she had been unavailable. His messages had not been returned. Bruce had been his loyal self, proclaiming that she was working all hours, trying to land a big client whilst setting up a complex series of trades revolving around a commodity he had never heard of before. He couldn't remember whether she'd gone long or short, but something about controlling a third of the market drizzled through his consciousness as he prepared supper for the kids.

"Have you had a good week?" said James retreating to safer ground and reaching for a mini tortilla.

"Best bloody week in our history. That's all. I told you I'd show them." Them were the faceless, nameless City grandees she still blamed for her incarceration. Them and the Weasel. "So, show me the video."

James fired up his I-pad and played the compilation of video footage showing Mark's reactions on the day his son Ralph had gone missing. The first series showed close-ups of the lawyer's stony face as he tore out of his office building, his bulging eyes betraying pure terror, as his safe, sheltered world spiraled beyond his 'square-mile' comprehension. The second set pictured Mark scampering along a street near the boy's school, half walking, half running, staring ahead, damp-eyed, his privileged life hanging by the shoelaces of his *Alfred Dunhill* brogues. The final episode showed Ralph sandwiched between his parents, each hand locked into one of theirs. He was crying and they were trying to console him with encouraging smiles as tears dripped down their cheeks.

Caro grunted as the video ended. "Is that it?"

"There are a few more stills. Here." James presented a gallery of Mark's facial shots, distress etched into every one. "You can see how terrified he was."

"For a few hours. That's all."

James let the comment slide. He knew Caro would never accept that Mark's suffering could ever compete with what she had borne.

"That's what we agreed."

Caro stared back at him. Slowly, she nodded, visibly fatigued. "We did."

"Time to move on, Caro."

She took a slug from a full glass, and wiped her mouth with the back of her hand, and sat up as if to banish tiredness. "I already have. I don't have time for this nonsense any longer. I have a business to rebuild."

And I have a charity to build and I need the money you promised to send us, thought James. He was hoping she would have sent the remaining million pounds by now. Her second tranche of two point five million transferred before Christmas had become one point five million at the last minute, according to Caro because of a short-term liquidity issue. James knew it was nothing of the sort and she knew he knew. It was simply further encouragement to complete his final Weasel assignment and another reminder of how much he relied upon his big sister.

"So," said James popping an olive into his mouth, "it would be really helpful if you could send through the final million now." He blinked. He hated asking for the money but they were walking a financial tightrope with LifeChance, one that was fraying badly according to Megan.

"Of course," said Caro dabbing her forehead with the palm of her hand. "You should have reminded me before."

James let that pass too. "It's become more urgent. We need to pay the main contractor for the last two centres in the current programme." This was not entirely true. They had been paid. Megan had been turning financial cartwheels, diverting cash from WinBet to bridge urgent funding demands. But she feared the venture capitalists would start asking difficult questions about the cash burn rate unless she could return part of the funds transferred by the month end accounts date. She aimed to return some of WinBet's cash by using Caro's million-pound injection into LifeChance.

"How is your on-line business going? Got that magical betting algorithm all sorted?"

"Broadly in line."

"Broadly enough that you don't have to fiddle the books anymore?"

James grimaced. "Well, let's just say we're making progress. You should come for a visit."

"Never. I don't want to have anything to do with the place. You know I don't agree with what you're doing."

"We're preparing to list the company?"

"Already?"

"The market is really hot for this type of story right now."

Caro snorted. "Well you'd better be careful."

"We have advisors pitching at us all the time. A load of them have visited. All of them left impressed."

"How about Stefanie?" asked Caro. "Has she visited?"

"No, not yet."

"Good." Caro threw back her head and drained her cocktail. "Keep her away from it too. She doesn't deserve to be contaminated either."

James smiled to himself as he pronged a griddled prawn from a plate. That was the nearest to a seal of approval for Stefanie, he could expect from Caro. She had never had much time for any of his previous partners. "We are being careful, very careful. We're not over-reaching. Megan's on top of the detailed planning."

Caro signaled to a passing waiter for another round of cocktails. "Just don't get caught, okay? I'd hang around for you, but you can't expect anyone else to. Your so-called friends would drop you like a losing lottery ticket."

James reached across the table and placed a hand on Caro's. "Don't worry. Nothing will happen. And no-one will come between us. We'll always be there for each other."

Caro pointed at him, and in a slightly blurred tone said, "if you fuck it up, I'll fucking kill you."

"Thank you."

"And I'll transfer the funds tomorrow."

"Thank you."

WinBet's main meeting room was filled with the hot air and stench of lawyers who had been parading through it all day as they competed to act as the company's legal advisors for the planned AIM listing. Even though James fully intended to retain Bone, Cumberbatch and Smith, LifeChance's advisors on the original acquisition, a competitive tender was required to keep them honest, or rather cost competitive. James and Megan forced themselves to smile and nod at appropriate intervals to keep the whole pantomime going.

The last legal meeting of the day had been reserved for BCS to show off. James understood why Mark would have insisted he accompany his corporate colleagues at BCS: to emphasise the closeness of his personal relationship with James, the key decision maker. He would be determined to receive credit throughout the firm for introducing an increasingly profitable corporate client.

James hadn't seen his lawyer since the end of the trial. He understood from Eva who exchanged the occasional text with Mark, that he'd buried himself in work. James could empathise with that attempted antidote to remedy personal and professional afflictions. But he knew that cure wouldn't last. Instead, James was hoping his evolving romance with Stefanie would provide the permanent fix.

The session with BCS finished with the usual platitudinous remarks, smiles and handshakes. As his corporate colleagues turned to leave, Mark suggested to James that he stay around for a catch-up, and perhaps a quick tour around the building. He told his colleagues he would see them later. Megan led them to the lift whilst he and James loitered in the windowless corridor, painted a morose grey.

"Sorry," said James, "but I have to dash in a minute. I have to interview some corporate financiers next."

"No problem. I've been buried since the trial. Seems like the FCA is on a prosecution binge."

"Sounds good for business."

"I met with your non-executives. Sorted them out for you." James had already thanked him by email. But Mark was clearly determined to drive home that he had won James's freedom, that he felt a debt was owed, even though he had earned a handsome fee which had been pleasingly paid already.

"Maybe we can catch up properly over dinner some time."

"Sure. That would be good."

"I'll get my assistant to fix a date."

"Good idea." James meant it. He regretted the role he had reluctantly played for Caro but accepted it had been necessary to save LifeChance. "Look, Megan can show you around if you're really interested."

326

"Yes, a quick tour would be good," said Mark checking his watch. "I've never seen inside a betting operation before."

"Here she comes. Megan, would you mind giving Mark the whistle-stop tour."

"Of course. Megan's face flinched. She reset her features and composed a fleeting smile.

"Introduce him to a few people, just in case we give the mandate to BCS," James said with a wink and a smile.

"We'd be honoured to be of assistance again," said Mark in a wheedling voice. The men shook hands and bid their farewells.

Megan suggested they start the tour looking around the ground floor betting shop. As the lift descended, she provided a snapshot of the operation. Mark caught a faint drift of her perfume. It smelt familiar, of a person or event he'd attended recently but he couldn't place it. The matter subsided as the lift doors opened on to the bustle of gamblers, flashing screen images and gaming machines. Mark's mouth fell open at the sheer number of punters circulating around the chrome and glass emporium.

"Shouldn't they be at work? It's the middle of the afternoon."

"I think most of them are. They're tapping away on their mobiles and tablets as they watch or place their bets."

They left the din of the retail space after a few minutes and climbed some back stairs up to the first-floor offices. Mark was introduced to someone referred to as the 'boffin' who kept talking about some algorithm. It could have been a foreign language. All that he recalled later was an open-plan floor, computer screens everywhere, desks in clumps, pot plants, whirring floor-fans, papers stacked on steel filing cabinets, and office paraphernalia littering every available surface.

He was surprised by the contrast of the second floor. He could hear a babble of voices from the lobby, even before Megan pulled open the thick wooden door. Banks of desks and desk-top terminals all looked similar, but newer. But there was no junk anywhere. Everyone wore headset microphones and talked and tapped away on keyboards incessantly. They looked young and hip, which Mark defined as ripped jean-wearing, goatee beard-adorning, body tattoo-decorating and piercings in odd places. And about half the floor was empty of any furniture.

"This is our latest development. It's growing fast." Megan explained the concept behind attracting the older, wealthier punters, whilst Mark listened vaguely and peered at screens. He was introduced to one of the operators who explained in too much detail, the information on her screen about her last client. All the screens looked identical to him. So, he focused on the one thing he could understand and located the name of each customer as he toured around the desks. At one point, he thought he had seen the same name on repeated on a screen.

"Quite possible," explained Megan. A client may end a call and then almost immediately call again to place another bet. They are unlikely to get the same operator the second time."

Mark shook his head. He had a deep desire to accumulate wealth and gambling to him was a sure way to diminish his pile. "They call all day long?"

"And night. We run twenty-four seven, three shifts, eight in the morning till four, the next one till midnight, and then a smaller team overnight."

"Holidays?"

"Even busier. The clients have more time on their hands."

"Amazing. I've never placed a bet in my life."

"Well it's time you did."

Megan led him back to the ground floor and introduced him to the floor manager. "Larry will give you a basic lesson in horse-race betting." She handed him a ten pound 'first-bet voucher' and told him to have some fun. Then made her excuses and left.

He hadn't seriously considered staying but considered it would look rude to not play along, particularly as there was a mandate to tie up for his firm. So, he used his voucher to make an each-way bet on a 33/1 outsider, the aptly named 'Unlucky For Some' running in the 3.55pm race at Cheltenham. He liked the name. He enjoyed watching the race on the big screen, surrounded by men, women, old and young, office and manual workers. He marveled at their slightly muted passion, the urgings, cries of pleasure and groans of pain as the finish line beckoned. His horse came second and a grinning Larry pushed him to a service counter to collect his winnings of thirty-eight pounds.

His luck finally ran out at Kempton Park's 5.05 race. With a rueful smile, he waved goodbye to Larry, threw his scrunched-up losing ticket into an overflowing blue bin, and headed for the exit. As he looked around for a taxi, he spotted several faces he recognised from the second floor of his tour. They formed part of a larger group, chatting and smoking in a biting wintry wind. He thought it odd that they were standing outside still, as Megan had mentioned their shift finished at four. He was curious, so decided to follow them, at a safe distance. He had stalked Eva several times without her knowing. It had given him a thrill.

Within a few minutes, Mark found himself in a pub. It's traditional high ceilings with ornate cornices and capacious varnished wood interior, accommodated a modern afterwork crowd starting their weekend on a Thursday. He settled with a pint of lime and soda at a table adjacent to the troop he had followed and pretended to read some papers. Much of the chatter in between malicious gossip about celebrity stars, seemed to revolve around auditions for acting parts, shared laments for failure, and sympathy for near misses. Then he heard one of the girls griping about WinBet. The firm gave such short notice, and though she had to admit that the money was really good, two or three days per month was not enough. She needed to find another part time job in addition to the waitressing she did. Otherwise she'd have to move out of her flat and back home to her parents' house in Esher. The group made sympathetic groans, agreeing that would be unbearable.

Mark left soon after and wandered back along the road against the on-rushing hordes of commuters heading for tubes and buses, criss-crossing the great metropolis, above and below ground. The same brawl as every other weekday in the pursuit to reach home. His direction was taking him back to the betting shop. He knew he should get back to the office but the pub conversation had twisted his curiosity into suspicion. What he had seen and heard jarred with what he had been told on his tour of the office. The pieces of the puzzle didn't match.

He entered the betting shop warily, looking out for Larry. No sign. It was busier than ever. The screens had turned from horse-racing to football. Gradually he moved to the back, towards the door marked 'No Entry', which led to the stairs he had climbed with Megan. He backed slowly into the swing-door, surveying the activity around him and then slipped through. He stood in the darkness for a few seconds looking up the concrete stairwell. He could hear no sounds. He felt for the cold metal railing and crept up two levels, feeling his heart pounding. Light sneaked out from under the door, which creaked as he opened it a slither. He could see no-one in the lobby. He walked over to the office door. It was locked as he expected, so he put his ear to its smooth wooden surface. He strained to listen but heard nothing. He bent down to check whether he could spot any light but found only darkness. Two minutes later, he was back staring at a screen showing clips of Spanish football, anonymous amongst the punters as they pored over their decisions.

It had been a few weeks since Mark and Thomas had shared a Saturday run: Thomas had been away at a couple of medical conferences and Mark felt he needed to stay around home now that Cath had relented and allowed him back. She had finally insisted that he get out for a run as he was too fidgety and wanted everybody up and about when all they wanted to do was chill out. So, the pair had decided on a long, slow, chatty run, taking in a dirt track on Wimbledon Common which led on to a loop of Richmond Park, and then down to the river near Mortlake brewery, and along the tow path back home to Putney.

Early morning spring showers had cleared and white puffs drifted lazily in a blue sky. The chill they had felt when they started their run with stiffened joints and tight muscles had vanished. A rising sun now warmed the air and their sweating faces as, an hour in the bag, they hit the tow path and headed east. They had settled into a steady pace, breathing evenly, allowing for the usual topical conversations. They had shared the load, taken their turns to rotate through minor injuries, sport, work, family, films and friends.

A steady stream of cyclists and runners were out on the tow path, most heading in the opposite direction out to Richmond, picturesque and ideal for looping back via the park or crossing Chiswick Bridge and returning on the north side. Whenever they passed approaching runners, they would observe the unwritten joggers' code and nod in acknowledgement of a kindred spirit. Following a lull in their chit-chat, they passed a couple of lycra-clad women, thirties, slim and attractive. They traded cordial smiles.

A few seconds later Thomas threw his curved ball, perhaps reading Mark's mind. "That girl you had the fling with - was the sex good? Was it really worth it?" Thomas had turned his head away slightly to the river, already busy with club rowers.

Mark swivelled his head towards him, his front foot clipping a stone jutting out of the damp path, leading him to stumble. "Fuck. Almost went over there." Mark had stopped a few metres behind Thomas who now looked back at him. A silence as ripe as the catkins drooping from the willow trees by the water's edge, briefly filled the distance between them.

"Yes and no in that order," said Mark finally, before starting to run again.

"I'm really glad you and Cath sorted it out."

"Me too."

"You don't see the girl any more then?"

"Course not. Cath would kill me." Mark thought better of sharing the facts that he physically ached for Eva occasionally, that he stalked her sometimes or that they had maintained an intermittent text-based relationship. He had finally weaned himself off texting after catching Cath in the kitchen going through messages on his mobile. His other one had been in his briefcase in his study, and he realised it was foolhardy to run such a risk. Cath had been adamant that any further contact would mean divorce.

"That wouldn't be good for your health."

"Let's pick up the pace for the final section." He'd had enough of talking for a while.

They arrived at the end of the tow path at Putney Embankment, dripping with sweat, lungs burning and panting heavily. They ran through their routine lactic-acid-laced leg-stretches, pushing against the railings to the whooshing from eight-oared shells sweeping past. Then they stuttered like novices on stilts into *Leader's Gardens* to collect their reward of coffee and croissants in the café overlooking the play-ground. Though barely nine o'clock, the swings, slides and climbing frames were jammed with screaming toddlers. Kids darted between the green and blue and yellow plastic structures. Pallid looking parents, mainly fathers in dishevelled weekend clothes, yawned nearby and cast envious eyes towards the cafe's patio, filled with people gorging on weekend newspapers.

They settled at a slatted wooden table, imbibing the fine Spring morning and the children's laughter.

"Still not heard anything from the police, about Ralph?"

"No. Don't expect to now," said Mark, as he chewed his croissant. "Nor the mugging. Though, strangely, my briefcase turned up on our porch afterwards. Everything intact."

"Seriously? That is odd. And no clues?"

"None. I still think some ambitious bastard at work is most likely. Power hungry, wants the top job. I'm in the way."

"Really? That's extreme, not to mention risky."

"Perhaps. But first the photos, then the mugging and afterwards Ralph."

"Well the mugging could have happened to anyone. And the other two events aren't necessarily linked."

333

Mark sighed. "Maybe. Anyway, I've kept my head down at work, excused myself from management meetings, and it seems to have stopped."

"Good. Back to normality."

"Not really. I'm always on the look-out, suspicious of everything." Mark's eyes darted to the playground, alerted by the piercing scream of a child.

"Oops. Someone's taken a tumble," said Thomas swivelling his head, as the sound of bawling reached them.

"Kids. At least they leave you in no doubt what they're thinking or feeling. Us adults, we're a deceptive bunch."

"Speak for yourself," said Thomas with a smile, before draining his cup. "One for the road?"

"Sure." As Thomas went to the counter to order coffee, Mark's thoughts drifted back to his WinBet visit. He kept mulling over the puzzle, persuading himself there was a rational explanation, that he had misheard Megan, or she had got the shift pattern wrong, or that it was usual for part timers to work in the call centre. But the matter wouldn't settle. His mind looped back to his suspicions that something was being fabricated. He should let it go. The law didn't pay him to speculate about the guilt of his client. It paid him to create reasonable doubt in the minds of the jury.

It still burned, the comment from the chair of the firm's Standards and Ethics Committee, that they would give him the benefit of the doubt over the Caroline Noble billing. Bastards. And she still wouldn't respond to his messages. James had said she was busy. Aren't we all. He must be covering for her. When Thomas returned with the coffee, Mark decided to share his suspicions, well aware that he would be breaching client confidentiality.

Thomas listened and interrogated as they sipped their cappuccini. He made Mark backtrack several times, learnt more about LifeChance and its unusual chief executive. He quizzed Mark about the share-dealing trial when he had defended James. Finally, he delivered his verdict.

"You've every right to be sceptical, even though there may be a perfectly innocent explanation," said Thomas. "If you think this LifeChance bloke was probably guilty of insider dealing, then he's capable of getting up to all sorts of things."

As they left the clammer of the park in-mates behind, Mark felt calmer, relieved and resolved. Relief that Thomas had absolved him of paranoia about James and resolved that he would pay another visit to the second floor of WinBet's office.

Chapter Twenty-Four   Leap

The chrome and glass of Bermondsey tube station reminded Stefanie of the bright LifeChance centre she had just visited with James. She stood ahead of him on the right of the packed escalator taking them down to the depths where they would take the Jubilee line to Westminster. Where she had been, whom she had met, and what she'd heard had overwhelmed her momentarily. She had been impressed and disturbed. She felt even more conflicted than before she'd finally agreed to accompany James.

Since James's trial, she had doubled down at work. Professionally, her losing the case had been a blow. She was unused to experiencing colleagues' faux sympathy, catching them whispering together when she walked into the room. Or worse, her boss distancing himself from the decision he took to press ahead with the case. All of which made her even more determined to show them that she was still the best lawyer they had. So even a couple of hours out of the office at the end of an afternoon felt like neglect. She wanted to be there and James wanted her in Bermondsey. He'd been wanting it for several months.

"Are you okay?" said James as they found a small space on the platform. She had been quiet since they'd left the new LifeChance branch. They'd walked through a mish-mash of streets, taking in brick council blocks, tired Victorian terraces, gentrified old warehouses and soaring glass apartment towers. The rain had scrubbed the buildings and roads and drenched the litter. A tramp had been sat on damp cardboard with his mongrel dog outside the station. James had spoken to him, given him ten pounds.

"Fine." She manipulated her mouth into a smile, then looked up to the indicator board, showing a train was due. She was looking forward to the soothing chorus of a Monteverdi piece that James had booked at Westminster. Before James, classical music hadn't been a part of her life. She wondered whether she had really changed James's life, whether he would really care if she disappeared from it. The concert would give her a chance to think, or perhaps switch off for a while. She felt tense and tired. She needed to get to her 'Boxercise' class at seven in the morning. She had just enough time before her first meeting if she picked up breakfast on the go.

A train clattered into the station and they squeezed into the carriage, the air hot and stale. She routinely avoided rush hour, hated the stifling heat, the bad breath and body odour of strangers. As the door closed, sealing them in, she began to count the seconds till the next station arrived with its brief respite of draught when the door opened. By London Bridge, she could already feel the sweat on her forehead and was blowing air upwards from her mouth.

She imagined what it must have been like for some of the children she had met at the new branch, crammed into the backs of lorries or containers as they journeyed to a promised land. Some would have endured days without food or water, locked in darkness, swilling in filth. But even that was better than the fate that some of them endured elsewhere.

She recalled the beaming face of Harmony, a fourteen-year-old girl from Nigeria. Like the other boys and girls being taught in small groups at the learning centre, turned out smartly in their various school uniforms, she had smiled and politely answered her innocent questions. James had warned her not to ask questions about their journeys from their homelands for risk of upsetting them. He would fill her in later. Right now, she was wishing he hadn't.

Harmony had been eleven when she and her mother started out on their journey. Her father had deserted them many years before. Her mother, a teacher herself, had scrimped and saved, and finally with the help of Harmony's grandmother saved enough for the traffickers to take them to England, to a better life. They guaranteed safe passage, a job in the big city and contacts with whom they could lodge for a while on arrival. Somewhere along the line, having been shuttled like cattle from truck to truck, Harmony was forced into a separate lorry from her mother. She had never seen her since. On arrival in the UK, she was taken to a flat somewhere in London and held captive. She was treated as a slave by her 'uncle' and soon after, other men came and paid money to have sex with her. If she refused, she would be beaten and then starved into submission. She had no passport, no idea where she was, and only Pidgin English. Finally, with life so unbearable, she kicked out at a 'client' and escaped onto the streets, where she slept rough for a few nights before being picked up by social services.

Resurfacing at Westminster, Stefanie turned her face up to the warm droplets falling from the evening sky. Big Ben tolled a quarter hour as they turned the corner next to Parliament. They weaved through the homebound commuters, the tourists gawping at the gothic edifice, and a bunch of spirited

338

protesters with placards obliterated by the downpour. They sidled past a crowd with raised selfie sticks surrounding a tour guide with a giant yellow umbrella pointing at Winston Churchill's monument. After the Abbey, they skirted Victoria Tower Gardens tracking the river. She would have liked to stop off at Emmeline Pankhurst's monument but the ensemble performing the four-hundred-year-old 'Monteverdi Vespers of 1610' would be starting soon. They crossed over the road, dodging traffic at Millbank, where the crowds thinned out.

"So, what did you really think of our newest outlet?" said James as he checked his watch again. He'd asked something similar after they had left the place. Her muted response had evidently not satisfied him.

"I thought the children were amazing."

"And the teachers?" suggested James.

"Really impressive, so keen. Are they volunteers?"

"Some but not most. It costs about a quarter of a million a year, running one of those centres."

"Lucky kids," said Stefanie, purposefully not looking at him, but immediately regretting her choice of words.

"Hardly. Given what they've been through."

"I meant having that centre, the opportunity to learn when most don't."

"True. That's why we have to keep growing, opening more centres. There's so much need out there."

"Yes. But you can't keep expanding. There must be a limit You've got to be realistic." She had previously over-ridden her natural aversion to remaining silent on issues that mattered to her. Now she felt like a guilty truant.

James grunted. "So many people have said that to me. Right at the start, nearly everyone said what a wonderful idea but not very practical. Too much prejudice. No one would support it."

"I don't think it's prejudice. I think people just wonder whether it's right to encourage so many migrants. Okay so some are genuine asylum seekers but as I heard today, many are simply economic migrants."

"I don't see anything wrong with that. Why shouldn't people try to improve their lives, improve the lives of their children." He sounded indignant that she should have a different opinion.

"It's just not practical. You can't take in everybody."

"Your country took in a million migrants the other year."

"This is my country now," she corrected. "Germany needs people to work to pay the pensions of those who don't. Merkel encouraged a flood of hopeful migrants from around the world and then slammed the door shut."

"Well at least one million people will have a better life," said James, the pitch of his voice rising.

"And the traffickers continue to get rich on people's misery," returned Stefanie with vehemence.

"So, do you think Harmony, now a grade A student with a bright future, wishes she stayed at home?" He was beginning to sound exasperated.

Stefanie thought for a moment and only the slap of their footsteps on the wet pavement filled the air for a few seconds. "I don't know. But do you? Do you know how she feels about losing her mother, about being raped and enslaved, about being stripped of her culture?"

"So, what's your great solution?" James said with a sneer." We do nothing but wait for the politicians to stop arguing?"

"We already have laws. Without them there would be chaos. All kinds of strife. If people obeyed the laws, traffickers and their evil activities would not exist."

"And the poor would stay poor in their under-developed world, whilst we rape their countries by stealing their doctors and engineers. Yes, that's really fair."

"James, for God's sake, life isn't fair. Grow up!"

James twisted his head to stare at her. He stretched out the length of his stride and they turned the corner in silence. The Georgian terraced houses caged in by iron railings either side of the darkening street, seemed to peer at them with through dark sash windows. They moved swiftly, wordlessly and grimly towards the ghostly St John's ahead. The stone built baroque church with four corner towers loomed over the red brick houses of Smith Square. They sprang up a dozen steps to the pillared portico, still shining white from the rain, and joined a trickle of last-minute arrivals at the entrance of the concert venue. The chattering din began to subside as they squeezed along the tightly packed row, mumbling apologies. They slumped into their seats, seething. They'd had their first serious argument.

Stefanie had still not said a word and they had reached Lambeth Bridge. The concert had soothed James, and the upset he felt at Stefanie's outburst had largely dissipated long before the standing ovation. Something was bothering her. He knew she believed in his mission. He thought a quiet walk back home to his apartment, along the tree-lined south bank of the river would avoid the crowd and melt her mood. The rain had stopped, and the air had freshened. He peered downriver as they ambled across. The sky, a deep purple and silver, appeared to accentuate the brooding glow of the Palace of Westminster. Opposite the phosphorescent blue circle of the London Eye seemed poised to spin away into the night sky. In the distance, countless lit-up tower cranes looked as if they were searching, suspended in mid-air.

At the middle of the bridge, Stefanie stopped abruptly and looked up at a lamp stood on top of a steel lattice-work pylon. "That is beautiful." She sighed as she leant on the balustrade. "I bet they don't make them like that anymore. Too intricate. Not efficient to produce in mass."

James was glad she had made the first move, that they were speaking again. He assumed it was her way of apologising. He joined her by the rail. "You know why this bridge is painted red?" She shook her head. "It's to match the seats in the House of Lords over there," said James pointing.

Stefanie cupped her face in her hands and watched the effervescent trail of a party-boat, the muffled sound of a bass rhythm disappearing into the night. "I think efficiency defines me too much. I'm an efficient worker, an efficient daughter, and an efficient lover." She turned her head askance and made a half smile.

"I love your efficiency." James draped an arm around her shoulder.

"Maybe I'm becoming a machine." She sighed again.

James studied her for a moment. "What's the matter?"

"Next month, I have to go back to Germany, to see my parents. They are having a fortieth anniversary party. Everyone will be there. Everyone I don't want to see."

"You don't have to go."

"I do. My brother will be there with his gloating wife and spoilt kids. School friends I've avoided for decades will be there with their spouses and their tribes of children. I'll be the only one on my own, apart from my parents' widowed friends."

"I'll come with you if you like."

"No. I wouldn't put either of us through that. I'll just be the efficient daughter. Fly in, play my part, smile at the appropriate points, and fly back again in time to be the efficient worker on Monday morning."

James wasn't sure where this was going but getting off at this point was not an option. "You can be efficient and beautiful. You are. LifeChance is. We run it efficiently and it produces beautiful outcomes."

"LifeChance. Everything comes back to LifeChance." She twisted her body around to face him and frowned. "So efficient you could make do without Caro's money?"

"We could still make it work, but it would be much smaller."

"You could never accept that though. You have your vision, and everyone has to fit in with that."

"What do you mean? said James in a squeaky voice.

"Well, look at how you run LifeChance. Like a business taking huge risks. Who ever heard of a charity owning a gambling company?"

"We have to. You know how difficult it is to raise donor funds. We've talked about this. We have to find income another way."

"Because your vision demands it."

"Because there is a massive unmet need. Children who need our help."

"So, you accept Caro's money and do everything she says."

"I don't."

"You do. I watch you."

343

James paused for a beat, his mouth open, his brows knitted. "Are you jealous of my relationship with Caro?"

"No, of course not. I'm jealous of her. She has it all."

"Including a criminal record."

"Which you'll have too if you don't stop."

"Stop what?"

"James. I overheard snippets of your telephone conversation with Megan the other night. You kept saying WinBet's flotation has to happen now or LifeChance cannot grow. And I heard you say whatever it takes, you'll make sure the numbers work."

"A figure of speech. I meant we'd push the management team to make sure the numbers will work."

"And what if they can't? Will you accept LifeChance has to shrink? No, of course you won't. You're so damned determined your vision has to be met. No compromises."

"I've done okay so far."

"And you're still not satisfied. Go on. Admit it. LifeChance will never be big enough for you. You will feel that you are failing no matter what." Her tone softened. "I think you're looking in the wrong place for happiness."

James's eyes blinked several times in astonishment. "So help me. Where should I be looking?"

"Me. Us. You idiot."

"But we already have each other."

"For how long? Where are we heading? What's the point of us?"

James looked bewildered. "I..I-" he stumbled.

"James. I'm almost thirty-seven and I'm in love with a man for the first time in my life. And you're forty-three, and I hope you feel the same way.

"I do. Of course, I do."

344

"So, we should grab our opportunity whilst we can. It may never happen to either of us again."

"You mean you want us to get married?"

"I mean I want us to have a child."

James's head shot backwards. "But I thought you said you didn't want children. That your career was more important."

"I changed my mind."

"When?"

"I don't know. This week, last week, last month. Does it matter?"

"Why?"

"Why?" She almost laughed, sounded incredulous. "Because of you. I never felt I wanted anyone else's child. I want yours, mine, ours."

"Bloody hell." This was huge. James had always believed that the decision to have a child was the most important facing any man or woman, yet one taken without thought so often. It was a commitment for life, a commitment that was broken for all kinds of reasons that he saw too often. There was cruelty, carelessness, selfishness, and of course, fate. His mother would never have left him. Could he really commit, for life?

They stared at each other, speechless. The thought was growing within him, instantly, a seed in the pit of his stomach spreading like a beanstalk throughout his entire body.

"Shit. Yes. Of course. Why not? I mean, I just never thought I'd be any good, you know, at being a father."

"You'd make a brilliant father. I see you with Caro's kids. They adore you."

"Shit. Why not. Yes. Let's bloody do it." And he took her in his arms and hugged her. He sensed he would fall over without her, that he would crash head first into the inky water

345

below. He finally released her, and they kissed. A passing double-decker bus blasted its horn and rumbled on its way.

Mark's second, third, and fourth visits to WinBet had left him in a quandary. The second time he crept up the dark stairwell, he found even the lobby without light. He had decided to confront James about the issue when a corporate colleague working on the WinBet flotation mentioned they were attending pitch presentations from corporate finance firms at the office the following week. On impulse, he said he would like to join them as he'd never sat in on such meetings and it would be a good networking opportunity, a chance to hand out business cards to senior investment bankers. Who knows when one of them might need his services. And it would be a good opportunity to sneak up to the second floor to finally confirm his suspicions.

He hadn't needed to sneak anywhere, as each of the visiting firms was given a tour around the office. He had joined one and listened intently as James informed his guests that the high-roller call-centre was their crown jewels and was growing exponentially. When Mark asked about the hours of operation, James gave a politician's response, that they were working towards a twenty-four seven operation. After the all-day meetings, Mark had spent a pleasurable hour on the ground floor losing a couple of hundred pounds. Larry had made a fuss of him, but never ventured far from the door to the stairwell. He had spotted familiar faces from the second floor leaving and followed them once more to the pub. This time he garnered nothing new from his eaves-dropping.

He went home convincing himself that his suspicions about WinBet were probably groundless, that Megan had merely been guilty of exaggerating to impress her visitors. After all, she was not a lawyer. His craft required meticulous attention to detail and every statement verifiable. Yet his instincts told him something different. He found himself in meetings distracted by a replaying of his visits, his brain engaged with a loop of reanalysis. Like his recurring thoughts on the photographs with Eva, and his obsessive re-imaginings and occasional stalking venture. Like a gambling addict bent on giving up, he would make one final trip to WinBet.

So, on a wet Wednesday lunchtime, the ground floor thick with dripping punters who'd forgotten that showers didn't end with April, Mark slipped unseen, through the back door. The second floor turned out to be ghostly quiet, no sound, no-one in sight. He vanished as quietly as he'd come and reappeared in the body of the noisy high street.

Back in his office, he had gotten as far as picking up the receiver to call James. Then the thought occurred to him, that he ought to prepare his ground better. The lunchtime test had not been a fair one. Horse racing may not have started and the high-roller centre mainly dealt with equine punters. So, he slammed the receiver down in its cradle, and determined that he would pay a visit during the middle of a weekday afternoon. He would get hold of 'The Racing Post' and pick a day loaded with race meetings.

A week later, he slinked down the dark stairwell and back into the betting shop wearing a satisfied smirk. His suspicions had been confirmed. The second floor was as empty as the ground floor was full. He meandered through the avid screen watchers, to the exit and turned for a final look. His eyes met Larry's. He was standing behind a counter, arms crossed, unsmiling, staring at him. He swallowed, smiled faintly and waved fleetingly, before darting into the street, his face blushing.

He guessed Larry had seen him come through the 'No Entry' door. Confirmation came later that afternoon when he received a call from James inviting him to lunch the following week. They already had an appointment fixed for next month. His tone seemed more solicitous that normal. During the brief phone-conversation, James mentioned how impressed his team were with the work Mark's colleagues were doing. The plans for listing were progressing well, even though a small part of the business, the high-rollers' operation had been down-scaled following a dramatic fall-off in business. According to James, a couple of big competitors had set up rival operations. Mark feigned only slight interest and changed the subject, asking whether he had bumped into Caro recently. It rankled him that she had not returned any of his calls or messages. The looks he got from senior colleagues sometimes, suggested the shadow of his accounting error lurked in their suspicious minds. A simple explanatory letter from Caro would clear everything up. James mentioned he would be seeing her for dinner next month, and that they had much to catch up on. The way he emphasised the last part sounded to Mark like James was dangling the prospect of some kind of deal.

His suspicions about WinBet now confirmed, Mark decided he should delve further, in preparation for the lunch with James. The firm could not be associated with any wrongdoing. But he needed to learn more before taking the leap by whispering in the ear of a colleague working on the listing. A lucrative fee would be lost, and so he had to be sure that any skulduggery amounted to illegality. Like his trips stalking Eva, his heart thudded with the same unexpected thrill, a blast of excitement and fear.

348

Chapter Twenty-Five   Raw

Mark felt his chest thumping as he stood under the canopy of a pink cherry blossom tree, one of many lining an expansive residential street of imposing double-fronted properties. He recognised the five-storied, white stuccoed, Georgian house, diagonally opposite him. He had been through its glossy red door on two occasions. And now he had just watched James Tait disappear into its interior, welcomed in by a man in a rainbow patterned pinny with a champagne flute in one hand. Mark recognised him. Bruce Noble, husband to Caroline Noble, his erstwhile client who now ignored him. But seemingly not James Tait, who reported not having seen her for a good while. And during last week's call, he had not mentioned he had plans to meet her until next month. Perhaps, Mark reflected, the arrangement had been made since then.

Mark had now trailed him on four evenings from his Southwark office. He knew his routine from having advised him. So, it had been relatively easy. He had pitched up at Shakespeare Square just before eight, and on each occasion had followed him at a safe distance, along the river for the short walk to his apartment. Till tonight, his outings had been dull and uneventful, on a par with the firm's obligatory quarterly partners' meeting, he'd endured that afternoon. This evening however, he had tracked James over the bridge and down into Blackfriars tube station. He'd hopped on to a Circle

349

Line train just as the doors were closing. The through gangways allowed Mark, hidden behind his newspaper, an uninterrupted view of his paperback-reading quarry.

Mark peered up through the branches at a crimson sky and wondered what he should do now. Twilight was almost past, and there was a chill in the air. He couldn't hang around all evening. He heard a car approaching and so stepped further back into the shadows. The car, a blue BMW, stopped outside number 44. The two back doors opened, and two women smartly dressed and made-up, got out. He recognised the shape of Eva immediately. The other woman took a few seconds longer. As she turned to slam the door, Mark caught a glimpse of her face, front on. It was Megan, James's Operations Director who had shown him around WinBet. As the pair walked arm in arm, shoulder to shoulder and with matching strides up the steps to the front door, it suddenly occurred to him. They must be mother and daughter.

Before he could make any sense of what he'd seen, the lights from another car appeared on the road from behind him. As the BMW moved off, a green Prius slid into its parking space. A few seconds later, a woman's slender legs emerged from the front passenger door. And then a moment later, the rest of the woman, tall, long-dark hair in a skirt-suit. She shut the car door, twisted round and waved at the two women standing at the top of the steps. She joined them just as the front door opened, and they stood in a blaze of light. Just for a couple of seconds, as they exchanged greetings with Bruce, Mark snapped a photo with his mobile, then ducked down behind a car. He heard the front door shut, then slowly stood up again. He peered at the screen and moved his finger-tips to enlarge the image. It confirmed what he had seen but not quite believed. The last time he had seen the third woman was in a court room in Southwark.

Mark remained rooted under the darkness of the canopy, wild thoughts snapping like firecrackers in his mind. A few minutes later, another woman he didn't recognise, hopped out of a minicab and up the steps. He guessed her to be mid-thirties, small, the build of a child, spright and furtive as a thief as she stole up the steps. He hung about for another quarter of an hour, wondering who could be next. When nobody came, he knew straightaway that he had to get back to his office. He could order his thoughts there and check out a few hunches. He saw in the distance, the glow of a yellow light bobbling down the street. He flagged down the black cab and clambered in.

Twenty minutes later, Mark marched into his office. As expected for nine-thirty, the floor was still fully lit, and most of the junior staff at their desks. He collared the assistant who'd helped him with James's case and asked him to retrieve the latest annual return LifeChance had filed with the Charity Commission. Within minutes he had in front of him its list of trustees. Midway down the list he found what he had expected, the name Megan Gilman: sufficient proof for him now, that she was Eva's mother.

He rose from his desk and locked his door. He took a ring of keys from his briefcase and unlocked the grey filing cabinet in which he kept his case files. He pulled out the top section and reached to the back, where he rifled through a hanging file. He withdrew a brown envelope. He returned to his desk, switched on his desk lamp and sat down. Gently, he slid out the photographs. One by one, he inspected the images of Eva and himself, naked and frozen in various positions on the bed. Was he imagining it, or was she peering into the camera?

Thomas's warning about Eva sprang into his mind once more. Had she approached him or had he made the first move before the marathon. He couldn't recall. What motive would she have to harm him anyway, unless of course she was working for someone who had? Why had his colleague, Gordon Cumberbatch, supposedly been sent the photographs? He returned the envelope to its file and locked the cabinet.

He slumped into his chair, heaving a huge sigh. A barrage of unconnected thoughts fired off in his mind. Perhaps WinBet's ownership was somehow at the centre of something illicit. Would the proceeds raised from the planned listing be lining the pockets of those he had seen at Caro's? He picked up the phone and got through to his corporate partner on the WinBet flotation project. He gathered they were working hard on the legal due diligence in preparation for producing the Admission Document for the IPO, a pre-requisite for any company raising capital from a placing of shares with institutional investors on AIM. Mark asked about the reporting accountants and the status of their financial due diligence. His partner advised that their report was almost finished. Finally, he got around to asking how much money was being raised in the public offering and who were the principal recipients. Pantech would receive ten million pounds for part of their shareholding and twenty million was going to LifeChance for a minority of their shareholding. Several of WinBet's management team were cashing in share options for several million pounds. None of LifeChance's board representatives owned shares and none would receive bonuses following the listing. He was getting nowhere.

He went to the staff kitchen and helped himself to a lukewarm coffee from the percolator. It still smelt okay and the caffeine would help him think. He had not known what to expect when he followed James, certainly not the assembly of people he had witnessed gathering at Caroline Noble's. He sensed that he was somehow enmeshed in their web, one he couldn't yet see or comprehend. He took a sip and then caught sight of a fruit bowl on the granite countertop. It reminded him that he had not eaten since lunchtime and he suddenly felt hungry. He picked up a pear and bit into it. Juice dripped down his chin. As his mouth closed in again on the moist flesh, he breathed in its mellow fragrance. An image, then another flashed through his mind. He knew the smell. It was there, when he was mugged and had his briefcase stolen. It was there, in the lift with Megan at WinBet.

He scurried back to his office where he unlocked the filing cabinet once more. He stretched to the back again and took out a piece of paper. On one side, a single paragraph gave a description of the woman who had taken Ralph, compiled mostly from mothers who had seen her at the school gate. Their words were graphically represented overleaf in a composite facial sketch. Mark grimaced. He had to accept that it bore little resemblance to Megan, or the other woman he hadn't recognised arriving at Caro's earlier.

There had to be a link somewhere. Go back to the beginning he told himself. He had been introduced to Caro first, via a call from his senior partner. He hadn't asked how they knew each other. You didn't question SP, you answered him. And you did what he demanded, though they were always sugar-coated as requests. SP had his favourites, candidates he would like to see succeed him. Mark had thought he was one of those. Gordon was another.

Then Caro introduced him to James. He had taken a table at a LifeChance gala dinner. He had paid two thousand pounds for the table. Another thought dawned on him and he went over to his desk, sat down and opened the top drawer. He lifted out an old cheque book, with only the stubs remaining. He flicked through and found the stubs of two cheques made out to the charity, one for two thousand and another for ten thousand pounds. He remembered the glorious week with the family in the Tuscan villa. It felt like a punch to his stomach. Of course. He had never given his personal banking details to Caro. This was the only possible way she could have gotten them. From him. But why?

James had asked him to be his defence lawyer presumably because Caro had recommended him. And he'd done a superb job in winning his case hadn't he? Unless he suddenly thought, he hadn't won it. The prosecution had deliberately lost it. Ms Zuegel was now in their pay. That thought struck him hardest. That his professional ability could be questioned. They had bribed someone to lose the case because ultimately, he couldn't be trusted to win. Why?

He sat pondering for a while before slamming the drawer shut in frustration. The key fell out of its lock to the floor. As he bent to retrieve it, he knocked his head on the desk. He winced and raised his head sharply. And with the pain came the pinhole into the dark box of Caroline Noble's tricks. Of course. Because he had lost Caro's case. He had lost it through no fault of his but he was being blamed for it. Every mishap that had happened to him over the past year or so had been because of that. His appointment as James's lawyer was used to deceive him. That's why he'd been looking in the wrong place. The motive wasn't a contender warning him off leadership of the firm, but a client bent on revenge.

He was shaking with anger and indignation. How dare they play around with my life. And my family's. He would make them pay. But how could he prove any of it? His instinct was

354

that something murky was being concocted at WinBet. If he could expose that, then things would start to unravel at LifeChance, and all sorts of questions would be asked of the promoters. He had no idea how far the web of deceit stretched and who might be implicated. But in his experience, as webs unraveled, and lies surfaced, individuals tore at each other to save their own skins.

The night air was clear and cold, with a full moon and canopy of stars. James and Stefanie had just wandered in from the balcony, carrying cups of camomile tea. They settled on the sofa chewing over the supper at Caro's, an informal celebration to mark Stefanie's moving in with James.

"I really liked Alicia. Such an interesting job," said Stefanie. Alicia was a bespoke jewellery designer. "So nice to be able to work from home pursuing your passion for a living."

"She works alone. Refuses to take on staff."

"She said she has a long waiting list of customers."

"Almost all celebrities or rich Russians or Arabs."

"She mentioned a few, but I 'd never heard of any of them," said Stefanie making a face. The entry-door buzzer sounded.

"Ignore it. It's probably just a hoaxer." James checked his watch - twenty to midnight. The ground floor reception and front entrance closed at eleven. After that, guests had to use a keypad on the wall.

They listened for a few seconds, and the door buzzed again, for a full ten seconds. James sighed and went over to the intercom. "If you don't stop, I'll -"

"James, it's me, Mark. Mark Phillips."

James's head jolted back involuntarily. He remembered his last call with Mark. This had to be trouble. "Hi Mark, erm. It's a bit late."

"I need to see you."

"Okay. Well I can come to your office first thing in the morning."

"No. Now. I need to see you now."

"Can't it wait till tomorrow? I was just going to bed."

"Tomorrow's too late."

He sounded resolute. He was not going to be put off. He had to get rid of Stefanie. He didn't have long. "Okay. Come on up. Apartment Seventeen-Eight."

"I know," said Mark before clicking open the entry door.

James turned around to see Stefanie staring at him, a quizzical frown on her face. He swallowed hard.

"What do you think he wants?" she said. "He sounded a bit mad."

"I don't know, but it's probably not a good idea if he sees you here." James stared at her, his eyes beseeching her not to protest.

"But he'll find out soon enough. We can't stay secret forever."

"Agreed. I know that but if he sees you, I guarantee your work colleagues will know by tomorrow. I think you should be the one to tell them first."

Stefanie nodded several times, slowly. "Okay. That makes sense." She rose with her cup and pecked him on the cheek. "I'll be in the bedroom. Don't be long. We've got a baby to make."

James smiled at her. Now that Stefanie had stopped taking the pill, a frisson had been added to their lovemaking. The immense power to create life was an unexpected aphrodisiac.

356

A minute later, James heard a sharp tap on his door.

"Mark, come in. Take off your coat," said James with a forced smile.

"No. Thank you. This won't take long." Mark stared at him. The door behind him clunked shut.

"Can I get you something? A drink perhaps?"

"No. I'm fine," said Mark scanning the room.

"Take a seat." James gestured towards the sofas, but Mark remained fixed on the spot.

"James. I know about WinBet. I know about your scam."

James could feel the side of his mouth twitching. He had feared something like this since Larry had mentioned seeing Mark creeping out from the back stairwell. "I don't know what you mean."

"Oh, I think you do," said Mark with a sneer of a smile. " I think you know that and a lot more besides."

"Mark, really -"

"The entire high-rollers operation is a complete fabrication. It's a big lie. You've been making up the numbers haven't you, James?"

"Mark, are you okay?"

"Don't fucking patronise me!"

"Mark, please keep your voice down. You'll wake the neighbours."

"Tomorrow," said Mark, his voice just as loud, and now starting to shake, "I'm going to share my concerns with my colleagues, who will no doubt share them with the reporting accountants who will in turn share them with your venture capitalists. It won't take long for an investigation to reveal your lies. The IPO will be pulled and you'll be hauled in for fraud.

357

"Look Mark, calm down." James's eyes flitted to the door leading to the bedrooms. It was ajar a few inches.

"No. I won't fucking calm down, till you admit what you've been doing to me. You and Caroline Noble and your poisonous cabal, ruining my life."

"Mark, if you won't quieten down, I'll have to throw you out."

"Why don't you call the police?" Mark taunted.

James's couldn't stop his mouth twitching, and now he felt the blood in his face. He needed to shut him up before Stefanie heard anything. His eyes caught sight of a bronze figurine set on an alabaster block on his bureau. The twenty-five-year old image of smashing Boris's head with a clock flashed through his mind. How tempting, he thought, but madness.

"I'm not going anywhere till I've finished." spat out Mark, a notch lower. "You used Eva to entrap me. She fixed my drink during the marathon, then slept with me, so you could send the photos to my wife, and colleague."

"That's ridiculous."

"You gave Caroline Noble my bank details, and the funds were deliberately deposited into my personal account."

"Mark, really -"

"Shut up. I'm not finished. Your partner in crime at LifeChance, Megan Gilman, mother of Eva, mugged me with an associate."

"I think you should -"

"And then you snatched my son. How could you sink so low? You bastards, you almost ruined my marriage, you interfered with my family, and threatened to end my career." He stood shaking and his shrill voice soared.

"Mark, that's crazy. Why would I, we, do such terrible things?"

358

"Because Caroline Noble blames me for losing her case, and she owns you all."

"Mark, that's nonsense. Why would I hire you as my lawyer, to protect me from going to jail?"

"To throw me off the scent. Of course, you made sure I couldn't lose by paying off that prosecution bitch. She's on your payroll too. I saw her with you at Caroline Noble's house tonight."

"You're wrong."

"She put a clown into the witness box. Her first witness. She must have known he'd blow it straightaway. So how much are you paying the bitch?" Mark suddenly turned his head to his right, in time to register the furious face of the bitch rushing at him. But no time to stop her right hook landing smack on his nose, or her left following up into his rib cage.

"Bloedes Arschloch! Miststueck!" screamed Stefanie as James leapt forward and hauled her backwards. "How fucking dare you. I knew precisely what I was doing getting that idiot broker to testify. But I've never taken a bribe in my life. I'm not the one defending guilty rich bastards."

Mark peered up from the floor, his hands cupping his nose, blood spilling between his fingers.

"Stefanie. Leave him. Calm down."

"Let me go, you lying bastard. Let me go!"

James released her from his grip and took a step backwards. She turned and spat in his face.

"You lied to me. I was going to have your baby. Or was that just another lie? I bet you've had a fucking vasectomy already!"

"Stefanie. Please. Calm down."

"That doesn't work with me either. Just tell me, look me in the face and tell me what he said is not true." Stefanie glowered at James, her fists clenched in front of her. "Come on. Do it."

James opened his mouth, but nothing came out. He couldn't face lying to her but neither could he admit the truth, not in front of Mark. They stood staring at each other, the seconds stretched by betrayal.

Without a word, Stefanie strode past him, grabbed her handbag from the coffee-table and headed for the door. She yanked it open and slung a set of keys over her shoulder as she disappeared. "I won't be needing these, anymore."

James stood open-mouthed, peering at the open door, the new empty space in his life. He exchanged stares with Mark but neither moved or spoke for a few seconds.

"You might want to use the bathroom," said James pointing to the door through which Stefanie had flown at Mark. "Your face is a mess."

Mark winced as he heaved himself up from the floor. Wordless, he made his way to the bathroom, blood dripping down his chin on to his shirt. A few drops had splattered onto the cream carpet. The least of his worries thought James, but nevertheless sought a wet sponge from the kitchen whilst Mark sorted himself out in the bathroom. Better than doing nothing.

Mark reappeared with tissue stuffed up both nostrils.

"Is it broken?" asked James.

"Don't think so."

"Good. Well, at least that's something."

"So, you and her...?"

"Yes. After the trial...one thing led to another..." James was determined to keep Stefanie away from any trouble she might otherwise face at work.

"I trusted you, James."

360

"I know."

"Are you now at least going to have the decency to admit what's been going on?"

James looked at the bronze figurine, then back at Mark, and smiled. "What would your advice be, if you were my lawyer?"

Mark shook his head and sighed. "Okay, tell me one thing. How were you planning to get the money out of LifeChance?"

"I wasn't. Not a penny for me, or any of the others."

"Not sure the judge will buy that this time," said Mark with a thin smile. He turned and walked to the door.

"Mark. It's all for LifeChance. Please. Don't spoil it."

Mark pulled open the door and left.

James slumped on to the sofa, covered his face with his hands and gently rocked. He needed a few moments. Just a few, and then he'd act. He peered tentatively into tomorrow and the possible abyss: everything running downhill, all that he had constructed over the past five years cratering, him behind bars, Stefanie nowhere. He then recalled being a child, frightened, afraid and alone after his mother never came back. He felt so much better now than he had then. As a kid, he had chosen to climb the hill. He would have that courage again. He would choose a different option to the abyss. Through force of will, he would gouge out another path.

He picked up his mobile and dialed Stefanie's number. It went straight to voicemail. He left a short message pleading with her to call back.

Then he dialed Caro's house. Bruce picked up.

"Hi Bruce. Sorry to call so late."

"No worries. Just clearing up the mess you guys left in the kitchen, ha ha."

"Great dinner. Thanks Bruce."

"I'm sure you didn't call just for that."

"Sorry, no. Has she gone to bed?"

"She's with Olly. He's had a nightmare."

"Sorry to hear that. But I wouldn't bother you if it wasn't urgent."

"Hold on a minute. I'll fetch her.

James listened as Bruce's footsteps echoed on the floor, then padded on the carpet up the stairs. He heard his muffled whisper to Caro, and the rustling as the handset changed hands.

"Caro, we have a problem. A big one."

" Just a minute...I'm listening," said Caro as the sound of a door clicked shut.

James laid out the events of the past half an hour without interruption. He concluded by saying that he would take sole responsibility for the fall-out from WinBet, and that as far as he could tell, Mark was working on a hunch. He had presented no proof to back up any of his accusations. But they knew his hunch would be corroborated once the reporting accountants were directed to scrutinise WinBet's accounts in greater depth.

Caro had every right to rant at him. She had warned him enough times about the risks he was taking on with WinBet. But she didn't raise her voice or rebuke him. He had forgotten Caro was at her coolest, calmest, analytical best at times of crises. She reminded him that they had some important cards left to play with the Weasel. She asserted it was probably best that she dealt them to him. She would call Mark right away and insist on a breakfast meeting tomorrow. He would be too curious not to accept and anyway, he had nothing to lose, and much to win.

"Have you spoken to Megan yet?" asked Caro.

"I'll do that now. Call me back when you've spoken to Mark. We can agree on the detailed script for your session tomorrow." Immediately, the line went dead.

Mark called Stefanie again and left a second message on her voicemail, before trying Megan. He heard her pick up and apologise to Alicia. She had just gotten to sleep, but his first few words acted as a lightning rod. He repeated what he had told Caro, and what they had agreed.

"What about Stefanie?" she asked as soon as he'd finished.

"I've been trying to reach her. She's not returned my calls."

"Maybe if I try?"

"Okay, you could try."

"You know, I'm sure she wouldn't say anything."

"I know that, but I just need to speak with her."

"You two are good for each other."

"I know."

"You need to fight for her."

"I know that too."

"She has to feel you will do anything to get her back."

"I would. I would do anything." James exhaled deeply. "What would you like me to do?"

"Go into the office. Check over all the legal documents relating to WinBet, and make sure your signature is not on any of them. I'm pretty certain I kept you out of it, but worth checking."

"Anything else?"

"Just act normal. I'll be in after Caro's meeting with Mark. I'll be listening in the next room."

"Good luck. I'll let you know if I manage to get hold of Stefanie."

He called Stefanie again and left a third message. This time he ended it by saying he loved her, that whatever happened, he would still love her and that if she gave him a chance, he would never be anything but honest with her in the future, and that he didn't want to think about a future without her, and please, please call back.

Then he called Caro from the landline, and together they plotted how they would ensnare the Weasel one last time, and forever, in a trap he had made himself.

Chapter Twenty-Six   Confession

Caro was waiting for Mark as he stepped out of the lift on the top floor of WoMan's offices. Unlike the modern building's other floors, this level aimed to inspire clients and visitors with a spirit of Britain's buccaneering age of brilliance. The walls were lined with original oil paintings from the Victorian era, images from the Industrial Revolution. Velvet flock wallpaper in ruby red depicting birds in trees, lined the corridor. A patterned carpet in delicate pink and gray ran down the middle of the dark wood parquet floor. Tiffany lamps on walnut oval tables provided subdued lighting.

"Thank you, for coming in," said Caro extending her hand.

"Interesting greeting on the ground floor. Hardly a welcome." Mark gripped her hand for a moment and returned her gaze.

"New security arrangements. Blame our head of Compliance. Can't be too careful about bugging these days, he says." Mark had been thoroughly frisked, his briefcase searched and his body subjected to a scanner.

"Well, I gather you're an expert in such matters these days," said Mark with a sneer."

Caro smiled. "Good to see you haven't lost your sense of humour. Now please, after you. It's the second door on the right."

Mark walked along the corridor and turned through a doorway from where the aroma of toast was escaping. The room was dominated by a vast marble fire-place under a carved mirror and crammed with over-stuffed furniture: three mustard button-backed armchairs, a couple of dark blue ottomans, a sofa in forest green covered in chintz cushions, and an imposing mahogany library chair in tan leather. A carved oak writing desk lay under siege from framed period photographs, pieces of china and a tall crystal vase sprouting red, yellow and pink carnations. A burly man in livery stood next to a giant mahogany sideboard with side cabinets. Blue and white pheasant tableware, a silver coffee pot and a china teapot laid upon a lace tablecloth, covered its surface.

"Thank you Eamonn. I can handle everything from here," said Caro. The man nodded, glanced at Mark, and walked slowly out of the room. "What can I get you? Coffee, tea?"

"Coffee. Black. Please." The door clicked shut. "He doesn't say much."

"Eamonn? He's mute. Amazing hearing. And very strong. Help yourself to a muffin, or a danish. There's toast as well, and we can rustle up some eggs if you'd like."

"Just coffee is fine."

Caro poured them both coffee and grabbed a croissant for herself. "Please, take a seat." She indicated one of the armchairs and selected the slightly raised library chair opposite. She set her cup on a small round occasional table, and bit into her croissant whilst looking at Mark.

"So, where's the letter you promised me last night?" said Mark. Caro had lured him to the meeting with a pledge to give him a letter clarifying how she had mistakenly deposited money into his personal account, rather than his company's.

366

Caro made him wait until she had finished chewing. This was her throne room, not his. This was the place she brought her favoured clients, or new ones when she was about to clinch their funding commitment. The Americans loved it, viewed it as quintessentially English. Finally, she reached over to a black file on the burr walnut coffee table separating them. She extracted a sheet of paper and slid the letter across the table. "Let me know if you'd like me to amend anything."

Mark grasped the letter he had been seeking for several months and scanned the page. "It will do," he said, and shunted the paper back across the table. "It just needs your signature."

"All in good time. First, we should talk about James and LifeChance."

"I told you last night. I'm going to inform my colleagues about my suspicions, and no doubt a thorough investigation will follow. Who knows what will be revealed," said Mark with a contemptuous curl of his mouth.

"Why would you do that?"

"Why? Because I'm pretty sure some kind of fraudulent activity has been going on."

"But you're not sure. And even if you were to be proven right, tell me who has lost out because of it."

"The venture capital shareholders of course. And future shareholders if the flotation were allowed to proceed."

"Well you can forget that. You see, I already know there won't be a flotation. Apparently current trading has taken a turn for the worse."

"That still leaves the current shareholders."

"The largest of which is LifeChance."

"Pantech Ventures invested twenty million pounds in WinBet."

"And to date they have not lost any money."

"If, as I suspect, the financials have been fabricated, then it is only a matter of time before they realise a loss."

"So, you'd be doing this to save an incredibly wealthy venture capital firm a few million pounds?"

"I'm doing this because the law has been broken. There has to be consequences. This is about fairness."

Caro snorted. "You make a living from defending guilty rich people all the time. They pay you vast sums of money to evade the might of the law. How fair is that?"

"I resent that. Under the law, everyone is innocent till proven guilty. You know that."

"I know one thing. I was guilty of a technical breach of law, which I told you. Yet you, against my better judgement, advised me to fight for my innocence."

"There were reasonable grounds, mitigating circumstances."

"Because of you, I spent months in prison, separated from my family. Half my employees had to be laid off and the business almost failed."

"And that is why you and your cronies jointly conducted an extended vendetta against me. You started off by poisoning me-"

"Slight exaggeration-"

"You besmirched my reputation amongst my colleagues."

"A misunderstanding-"

You entrapped me!"

"You entrapped yourself."

"You mugged me."

"You got everything back-"

"And you even stooped to kidnap my son."

"He was taken out for a surprise birthday treat."

"My wife almost divorced me!" screamed Mark.

"But she hasn't. Not yet at least."

"I'm going to bring you all down, starting with your partner in crime, James Tait."

"So finally, you admit it. This is not about the law at all. It is simply about revenge."

"Yes. And you should know all about that."

"Okay. Well let me just examine where your revenge will lead. Firstly, let me make clear. I have no involvement with LifeChance other than as an arms-length donor. James is responsible for the charity and all its dealings involving WinBet. No one else at the charity has signed anything or can be implicated in any wrongdoing. So, yes, you may stand a chance of bringing down James, as you delightfully put it. No one else. LifeChance itself perhaps. Would that be a proud moment?

"Not my problem."

"Though I'm not sure a large venture capital firm will want to be seen suing a charity. Better to go after the 'big boys' who advised on the deal - the accountants and the lawyers. That includes your firm. Not sure what your colleagues will think of that."

"Rubbish. You're bluffing."

"You have no proof of anything."

"People start talking when the shit hits the fan."

"Not my people. Not James, not Megan, not Eva. Never."

"Well we'll see about that," said Mark rising from his chair.

"Sit down. I'm not finished."

"I am."

"Do you want this letter signed?"

Mark hesitated. "You're not going to sign it."

"I am. I made a promise."

Mark sat down again, tentatively, perched on the edge of his chair, and watched as Caro got out her pen, and scribbled her signature on the letter.

"I'll just get you an envelope." Caro rose and went over to a small writing desk, by the window, partially hidden by voluminous rich red damask curtains. Half-drawn festoon blinds blocked out the early morning sun. She withdrew a large brown envelope from one drawer, and a small white envelope and a postcard from the other.

"How is your family doing now everything has settled down?" said Caro with her back to Mark.

"Fine. Just fine."

"We might not like one another, but we might as well be civil," said Caro, as she returned to her seat. She laid on the table, the postcard of Mark's happy family on vacation that he had sent her whilst she languished in prison. "I'd like to return this to you?

"Why?" He seemed genuinely puzzled.

"To remind you." She picked up the letter, folded it and inserted it into the small envelope. "I prefer a win-win to a lose-lose, don't you?" she continued before licking the seal.

"What do you mean?" said Mark, a frown appearing on his forehead.

"Well take a peek at this." Caro handed him the large brown envelope.

Mark's look of puzzlement changed to horror as the photograph slipped out onto the table. Even in the subdued lamp-lit room, he recognised his naked image in his hotel bedroom.

"Does your wife know that your order-in habits extend beyond pizza?"

Mark's eyes were bulging and his cheeks reddening as he screamed. "You bitch! You won't get away with this." His eyes bounced between Caro and the photo of him riding a bored-looking woman doggy style, on his hotel bed. He inserted it roughly back into the envelope.

"Does she know about the interesting websites you liked to visit on those lonely nights in the hotel. I have a USB stick of your laptop's memory. It's quite educational - Secret Affair, Pornhub, Local Shags, Come Dogging-"

"Shut up, shut up!" Mark shouted as he jumped out of his chair, his fists clenched, and teeth bared.

"That's fine Eamonn. Everything is okay" said Caro as the door opened. "Mr Phillips was just helping himself to another coffee."

The door clicked shut, and Mark made his way over to the sideboard. With an unsteady hand, he helped himself to a fresh cup of coffee. "This is blackmail."

Caro sighed. "Permit me to postulate a possible scenario." She waited until he had sat down, taken a bitter mouthful of coffee, and fixed his eyes on hers.

"You go back to your office with the letter, and WoMan Investments as a new corporate client. Your colleagues' joy at you introducing another new client, and guilt over their whispered suspicions, puts you back in the race to become senior partner. WinBet's trading slows but does not collapse. The flotation is postponed pending an uptick in trading, which never quite arrives. Meanwhile any fictitious accounting which may or may not have occurred is gradually unwound. The auditors sign off the accounts. No-one is any the wiser. Pantech begins to accept that their judgement may have been faulty, that the J-curve forecasts they bought into, will never be achieved. Eventually they accept an offer by the company to buy back their shares at a discount. They lose maybe half their money, less than one half per cent of their fund size. You go back to your family, your wife and children, safe in the knowledge that your secret life remains secret. How does that sound to you?"

Mark sat frozen with his arms folded and his face set like granite. The sonorous ticking of a grandfather clock filled the void, acting as mediator. "If, I say if, I were to agree, why should I trust you?"

"Because I have to trust you. You can make your allegations at any time."

"I can't. They lose their currency unless I act now. People will ask why I didn't say something before. I'd be implicated in your web."

Caro sat back in her chair, looked at the ornate ceiling momentarily, then reached into her jacket pocket. "Take a look in the back pouches," she said, reaching over to hand Mark her black leather flip wallet. He opened out the wallet and fished out a small photograph, showing Caro with Bruce and the children.

"That's your family."

"Part of it. Now look in the pouch on the other side."

Mark withdrew another photo, this one faded and yellowing, showing two young children, holding hands and grinning into the camera. "Is that you and-?"

"James? Yes. I was six and he was four. He's my family too. You see, I would do anything for my family. Anything I had to, to protect them." Caro's steely-eyed gaze bore into Mark. "You're a family man. You should understand that."

He shifted in his seat, and rubbed his forehead with his finger-tips, obscuring his face. "How do I know that the

372

photograph, and possibly others in your possession, will never come to light?"

"I promise to destroy them." She was careful not to say when that might be. "I don't care what you do with your private life. You can screw around with whom or whatever you like.

"It was just the once. I was drunk."

"That's of no interest to me."

"And what about all the vile acts you've subjected me to. Am I supposed to just forget those?"

"No. No more than I can forget the life I lost in prison and the damage it caused."

"Easy for you, now you've had your revenge."

Caro laughed bitterly. "Don't kid yourself that I think we're even. If it wasn't for James, you'd still be enjoying my wrath in its creative forms. He stopped me. He made me realise that nothing truly lasting can be built from revenge. It just makes you angrier and hungrier for more revenge."

Mark exhaled deeply, threw the wallet onto the table, then stared at his hands. "I need some time to think it over."

"No. We have a deal or we don't before you leave this room." Caro sensed that Mark was teetering towards acceptance but fearful that given more time to reflect, his hunger for revenge would overpower reason.

"But what if your lawyer friend Ms. Zeugel betrays you. I'd be forced to speak out then, if only to protect myself."

"Maybe. Then our deal would be off."

"That wouldn't be fair."

Caro shrugged. "I think you have to trust me that I can handle Stefanie." She was now gambling blind, for at that moment, she had no idea how Stefanie would react. She picked up the white envelope from the table and waited for

Mark to look at her. For a few seconds again, all they could hear was the clock's muted bass ticking.

"Okay."

"We have a deal?" Caro stood up and held out the white envelope.

"You'll become a client of the firm?" said Mark, grabbing the brown envelope as he stood up.

"Yes. Set up a meeting later this week if you like."

"You'll answer my calls this time?"

Caro smiled. "I promise."

They shook hands firmly, unblinking eyes lingering, as if the intensity somehow made their deal more unbreakable.

It was just after seven when Megan rang the buzzer to Stefanie's flat. The queue at the station for coffee had cost her a couple of minutes. Caro would already be meeting with Mark Phillips. At least that meeting had been arranged. She hoped Stefanie would be there and would let her in. James had elicited no response when he arrived around one in the morning.

She buzzed again, this time for longer. Getting no answer, she went out into the road and peered up at Stefanie's apartment. She was sure she saw a flicker from the window blinds. She went back to the buzzer and firmly pressed again until finally she heard a mangled voice from the intercom. She caught the last two words.

"...go away."

"Please Stefanie. I have to talk to you. James doesn't know I'm here. I've brought breakfast." She waited for a few seconds, then pressed again.

"...don't want to see anyone."

"Just a few minutes, I promise. Then I'll go." Megan waited. Just as she was about to press again, she heard a click. She yanked open the opaque glass front door and entered the lobby, choosing the stairs to the second floor.

The door was off the latch, so Megan made her way in to the apartment, and through to the lounge. Unlike the last time she had been there, the flat seemed airless, bare and empty. She wondered how much of her stuff, Stefanie had already moved to James's place. She found Stefanie in a baggy T-shirt and shorts, crouched over in an armchair.

"Breakfast," Megan announced, trying to sound upbeat, whilst dangling the take-out bag in mid-air. "Latté and lemon muffins."

Stefanie did her best to reciprocate with a smile, but her reddened and moist eyes told the truth. "Thanks," she said wiping her nose with a piece of tissue torn from a loo roll on the floor.

Megan parked herself on the sofa next to Stefanie and laid out the bag's contents on the coffee table. "Did you manage to get much sleep?"

"Some. Enough." The bags beneath her eyes told a different story.

"Are you working today?"

"Of course. I have a busy day. This can't take long."

"Right, well, ...help yourself," said Megan before taking her first sip of coffee.

"You know, you didn't need to come. I won't say anything."

"I know that."

"So, why are you here?"

"I was worried about you. I am worried about you, and James. I spoke to him last night. He was crying over you."

375

Stefanie reached for another piece of tissue, as a tear escaped. "How can I possibly stay with a man I can't trust?"

"But you can," insisted Megan. "He only didn't tell you anything to protect you."

"How convenient. That way you have a licence to lie forever."

"He hasn't lied to you."

Stefanie snorted. "Oh, so remaining silent about fraudulent activity is okay is it? He even kidnapped that awful man's son. He-"

"No-one kidnapped anyone. I, not James, took Mark Phillips's son out for a birthday treat for a few hours. He thought his mother had arranged it. He had a lovely time. Okay, so his father thought he had been kidnapped."

"And his mother. What about her?"

"Okay," said Megan with a sigh, "I regret that but, it couldn't be avoided. Caro insisted."

"And if Caro insists, everyone jumps."

"No. Not anymore. James had a huge argument with her about it. Look, she has been determined to get her revenge on Phillips. His arrogance ruined her life. James had to do what she asked because otherwise LifeChance would have suffered, badly. We needed her support. We had no option."

"And it will always be the case. I've watched him. He is so driven to save the world with his charity that he'll keep breaking the law. He'll never be satisfied."

"Perhaps, if you-"

"How can I do my job, a job that I love, and stay with someone who routinely breaks the law I spend my life upholding?" said Stefanie, tears now streaming down both sides of her face. "Tell me."

Megan reached out and enclosed one of Stefanie's hands. "I think you need to ask him to stop."

"Oh right. And he'll do it just like that."

"I think he will...for you. And I will back you up. As Caro will. Because we agree with you. He will never be satisfied with the size of LifeChance. His vision is unrealistic, too ambitious. He is putting the whole thing in jeopardy."

"It's too late. That odious lawyer, Phillips will expose James and he'll be lucky to escape prison."

"I don't think that will happen."

Stefanie frowned with a look of disbelief. "Come on. Really?"

"Really. I'll be open with you. Caro is meeting with him now. He is an ambitious man, and desperate for his marriage to stay intact. Caro can help him. And she has some damaging photographs of him, with a prostitute, which he will want to bury."

"That's bribery."

"I think it's more a final negotiation. After this, no more dirty tricks. No more false accounting."

"But it's bound to leak out at some point."

"Not if we're careful. We'll cancel WinBet's flotation and gradually unwind the accounting issue. We'll have to tread water for several years with LifeChance, till we build the donor base. Caro has agreed with me to continue supporting it."

"And James has agreed to that?"

Megan took a deep breath. "We haven't spoken to him yet. We need your help. We think he'll only listen to you."

"Why me, the person he's been deluding for months?"

"Because he loves you, because you are the only person who can bring him true happiness, give him what he desperately needs."

"There are plenty of other women out there."

"I've seen him with other women, over the years. None have them have come remotely close to knowing him. Since being with you, I've never seen him happier."

"I'm not sure I really know him. You know him far better."

"I've known him for much longer but I can't give him what he wants, what he needs."

"I'm not sure I really know what he wants."

"Let me show you." Megan released Stefanie's hand and dug into a pocket. She held a small red box with scuffed edges and a rusty hinge on the palm of her hand. "Go on, take it."

Stefanie opened the box. A vintage ruby and diamond engagement ring was mounted on a soiled creamy velvet bed.

"Take a proper look," said Megan as Stefanie peered at the ring.

Stefanie withdrew the tarnished yellow gold ring, very gently, and rotated it between her fingers and thumbs. "It looks very old."

"It belonged to James's mother. He asked me to get Alicia to restore it. He was planning on presenting it to you on your birthday. He told me you were planning a family. I'd never seen him so overjoyed."

"It's beautiful. He told me about his mother but I had no idea she was engaged."

"Secretly. And not for long."

"I knew she never got married. All very sad."

"He told you how his mother died?"

"Yes. Run over by a car."

"And how he blames himself for her death?"

"He does?" Stefanie frowned. "I know he still has nightmares about it."

"They were playing a game. He ran into the road and the next thing he remembered was hurtling through the air. She pushed him out of the way of the car. She sacrificed herself. That's what mothers do."

Stefanie put the ring back in the box and handed it back to Megan. "You were a young mother."

"Yes. Foolish. But I don't regret having Eva for one moment. Nothing else in life compares."

Stefanie looked down, studying her bitten finger nails. "Do you think I'm too old, to start now?

"No. And I think James would be a great father."

"You didn't stay with Eva's father?"

"He died."

"I'm sorry."

"Don't be. I wasn't. He was a drunkard, a gambler and a womaniser."

"But not a fraudster."

"He was violent too. If it wasn't for James, I wouldn't be here. He saved my life. Maybe Eva's too."

"What do you mean?"

Megan blinked. She hadn't considered that James had never told Stefanie how they had first met. However, she was certain that he would not have revealed precisely how Boris had died. "Did he tell you about his time just out of university when he worked for a private investigations firm."

"I think he may have mentioned it."

"Well, that's how we met. He was in the right place at the right time for me." Megan went on to provide a potted account of the day that James had intervened when she was convinced Boris would have killed her. She skimmed over what had

379

happened to Boris after James had struck him, implying that he had fled the house before being discovered dead a few days later. "The police autopsy concluded he had died from hypothermia having fallen unconscious after hitting his head."

"So, James saved your life then, and you've been saving his skin ever since." Stefanie finally smiled.

"He's always been like an older brother to me. We look out for each other."

"My older brother is ghastly."

"James has always been kind. Headstrong, yes. Driven, totally. Idealistic, probably too much. But he cares about the right things. He cares so much about you. And you can save him from himself. By having a baby together, his mother's legacy can continue. He might be able to forgive himself finally."

"Maybe. I don't know. I need to think."

"Of course. Take your time."

"I'm not sure I can. I'm almost thirty-seven."

Chapter Twenty-Seven   Legacy

James finally had time to survey the room. Fifteen hundred people crammed into the Park Lane hotel's ballroom, festooned with helium-filled silver and black balloons. Twinkling white fairy lights spread across the entirety of one wall, like stars in the night-sky. Large digital screens flashed regular updates on bidding for the silent auction lots. Bowl-shaped chandeliers cast low lights on a sea of circular tables, from which centrepiece arrays of pink and white carnations and roses with green foliage sprang. Crushes of silver cutlery, side plates, napkins, glasses, bottles of wine and water, and tablet devices crowned pristine white linen. Liveried servers weaved between tables, serving up bread rolls with silver tongs from woven grass baskets to the gala dinner guests, their appetites fuelled by the pre-dinner champagne cocktail reception. Whilst their stomachs groaned under ball gowns and dinner jackets, the guests' necks craned in the direction of the podium where the speeches had begun.

He could see Caro's table. She had pulled out the stops, cajoling many of her contacts to host tables for the privilege of handing over five thousand pounds, and donating prizes for the live charity auction, later in the evening. Their invitees were expected to bid aggressively, to raise several hundred thousand pounds for LifeChance. She was back to her best, driving her business hard, and winning new clients and even a few old ones back. Her sleeveless black gown hid the extra weight that bothered her. She'd had a gym constructed in the basement at home and finally listened to Bruce and hired a personal trainer. She was one of his more frustrating clients. On one side of her sat a charming Chilean whose name James had already forgotten having met him over cocktails. On the other, he could make out the benign smiling face of Bruce, sporting a lurid orange and yellow MCC bow-tie. Now that Olly was sleeping through the night again, Bruce had the energy to throw himself into his latest hobby, growing organic vegetables.

He looked to his left and caught sight of Eva, stunning in a glittering moonlight and gold dress, which revealed just enough. A diamond cluster necklace and matching pendant earrings dripped from her, courtesy of her companion, who appeared to be whispering something amusing in her ear. Alexander showered her in presents for her birthday and had lasted a record number of months. It helped that he was a Russian oligarch's son, Harrow educated and with access to his father's jet for extravagant weekends on the continent. It also helped that he had become a LifeChance donor, had an indecent sense of humour, and worked the same long hours as Eva at Gladwyn Morson. James liked him even more because he worshipped his god-daughter. She had recently been promoted, and now with a higher salary and his and her mother's help, was about to purchase her first property: a two bedroom flat in Tooting for three quarters of a million pounds.

His eyes slid to the adjacent table where Mark was refilling his wife's wine glass. He had met Cath before dinner quaffing champagne, when she'd volunteered that she had escaped her four children and she was going to make the most of the evening. She was bubbly and delightful and pretty. They

382

discovered a shared interest in spy fiction, which came to an abrupt end when Mark interrupted by introducing a doctor friend who was training with him to run the London marathon again. Mark dragged his wife away to meet someone called Gordon, a work partner who had pitched up with a minor celebrity on his arm. Meanwhile, the doctor friend bored on about training schedules, and then golf. James nodded with feigned interest, and at the same time puzzled over how Cath's marriage to Mark worked. He and Mark had talked over a lunch he had arranged several months ago. He had apologised to him, and now he felt once again, they had a professional, bordering on cordial relationship. He could put up with Mark's pomposity and views always expressed as expert opinions. Mark was back in the running to be senior partner of his firm once more. James couldn't help wondering if he had learned anything over the past year and a half, a period in which he himself had been forced to evaluate so much.

On the next table, tiny Alicia sat next to the bulk of Akhtar. On her other side, was a space which would soon be occupied by the person on the podium making a speech. Megan, managing director of LifeChance stood in front of a microphone, delivering lines rehearsed and co-written with James. Hitherto, he had been up there, talking about his vision, about the positive contribution that refugees bring to society, and introducing the film telling the remarkable success stories of the children educated by LifeChance. Megan, in a royal-blue, full length chiffon dress looked and sounded polished. The congregation was quiet, hanging on her words. He remembered having to talk over an indecent amount of murmuring until some benevolent soul took it upon themselves to shush the audience. So this was a poignant moment for him even though he was glad to have moved on.

Back to investment banking but forward to a new firm, a boutique advisory outfit assembled with old colleagues. They were busy, which was excellent news for LifeChance as he had arranged to donate a third of his profit share each year to the charity.

LifeChance had changed since he had stepped aside six months ago. He was just a trustee on the board, now chaired by Roger. Shahid had died of a heart attack before getting the knighthood he'd always craved. He could see Roger on a table near the podium, next up after Megan, to encourage the assembled gathering to dig dip into their pockets. Ramesh was still on board but planning a move to San Francisco to be part of a tech start-up. Yet most of the change had been instigated beneath the board by Megan. Most of the top team of executives were new. Fund raising and marketing had been boosted, led by inspirational social media campaigns drawing regular donations, small and large from tens of thousands of people. James had to admit that Megan had built a good management team and delegated effectively, something he struggled with, always wanting to control everything tightly. But then, the charity was no longer running the risks he had undertaken to drive income growth to fund ambitious expansion plans. Megan had sacrificed growth for stability and strong foundations. She had miraculously transfigured sand into stone.

She had begun to unwind WinBet's false accounting, and without any hint of discovery, the auditors had signed off the accounts. A wry smile appeared on James's face as he spotted the ruddy faced audit partner, his face sweaty and his body bursting out of an old tuxedo. On the same table, he recognised two partners from Pantech, the venture capital firm. Megan had excelled there too. She had explained that

WinBet's trading performance had slowed significantly because of intense competition in high-rollers' phone-line services, necessitating a deferment of the planned flotation. The following month, she revealed to them that after much analysis over an extended period, they finally had to accept that the guru's miraculous football betting algorithm was flawed. It functioned no better than the lower risk, balanced-book approach used by the rest of the industry. The linchpin to the company's sustainable competitive advantage was broken. A spectacular story of high-tech driven, explosive growth had become nothing but a spectre. Every investor in the world could see that fiction whilst they craved facts. Megan cheered the Pantech executives with news that their innovative retail format was trading well ahead of plan, and proposed a new strategy based around a roll-out of new outlets in the same format. But she knew before she presented her well thought through plan, that they would lose interest. They were click not brick investors. A roll-out would take too long, use up a lot of capital and even then, growth would not be spectacular. Without agreement on strategy, the business would simply flat-line.

Over a period of six months, with James advising in the background, she had manoeuvred the conversation with Pantech to parting company with them as shareholders. They waited patiently for the venture capitalists to make the first move, improving their bargaining position. They ultimately agreed to use some of the cash still sitting in WinBet's bank accounts since the original investment, to buy back Pantech's shares. They accepted just ten million pounds for a stake that had cost them twenty million just a year earlier. And they accepted it cordially, secure in the knowledge that other investments in their fund would bring them their lucrative rewards, and that a loss of ten million pounds in one investment would barely register with their investor base. So, the two venture capital executives and their wives and friends sat at a table, feeling very good about themselves, supporting such a worthwhile cause as LifeChance.

The aroma of salmon starters arrayed on plates silently delivered by light-footed servers, drifted into James's reflections, minutely before he felt the edge of Stefanie's ring digging into his finger, and the hiss of her whisper in his ear.

"Stand up. Stand up," she murmured. "She wants you to go up."

"Who? What?"

"Megan, up on the podium."

His frowning face, a daze of confusion, gave way to open-mouthed gawping. This wasn't in the script they had crafted together. He saw that everyone on his table was looking at him, expectantly. He felt Stefanie release his hand under the table and peck him on the cheek. He shunted his chair backwards and climbed out, looking first at Megan then glancing down at Stefanie. Her silver-grey off-the shoulder gown showed off her slender shoulders and failed to mask her plump stomach. Maternity leave beckoned in six weeks. He'd already learned much from the mother of their unborn child, not least to reinvest in this life, and to accept that his own mother would not have wished him to spend it atoning for her death. She had simply loved him more than herself. He squeezed past Stefanie, careful not to push against her chair, and zig-zagged his way to the podium to the increasing buzz of the room.

With his musings, he had missed much of Megan's eulogy, praising him for founding LifeChance and driving it forward to help thousands of refugee children. He joined Megan on the stage, unsure what he was supposed to do or say next.

"Okay everyone," announced Megan, "we all look back on key moments which became major turning points and changed us and the course of our lives. I'd like to share with you all, a short video that goes some way to revealing the inspiration behind LifeChance." He felt Megan's hand on the back of his shoulder, encouraging him to turn around to watch the large screen. She returned his look of bewilderment with a broad smile. He wasn't comforted.

The film started with footage of a walk through a dusty, shanty town. Next came the sound of voices he did not understand or faces he did not recognise. And then the camera zoomed in on two figures standing behind a make-shift stall of brightly coloured fruit and vegetables. He recognised the woman almost instantly, and by deduction, the girl standing shyly next to her. As they began to speak, their translated words skipped along the foot of the screen. The woman was thanking him for saving the life of her child. She was now almost a teenager, a bright and lively girl, who helped her mother look after her three younger siblings. The girl, Duaa, thanked him with a dazzling grin, and a promise that one day she would be a doctor and help people just like he did.

James felt his bottom lip quivering and his eyes moistening. He plucked the silk white handkerchief from his top pocket and made a mental note to thank Stefanie for insisting upon this last-minute adornment. The film ended and as Megan turned him around to face the audience, he saw several young people he recognised, graduates from the LifeChance programme, standing up and clapping. Others joined in, and soon enough like a roaring tsunami, the entire congregation united in the ovation.

After several attempts, Megan managed to hush the crowd. "Please, one last thing, then I'll get off." She turned to face James. "We wanted to present you with something, something to remind you of us, and also everything you have achieved. So, knowing you have just moved into a new office, and seeing how you cling on to your deal tombstones, we thought we'd go one better."

James felt a light tapping in the middle of his back and swivelled round. The grinning face of Duaa, and her mother gripping a one-foot high acrylic tombstone greeted him. His shock, snatched by a photographer hired for the event, disintegrated into a twin-armed clinch, lubricated by salty tears. Over the mother's shoulder, he spotted Stefanie standing and applauding as the room exploded with more cheering.

He took an internal snap-shot of the moment. He glimpsed a fleeting image of his mother, smiling down at him. "God, I hope she can see this. Don't let me forget this moment," he thought. They finally ended their embrace and James accepted the LifeChance tombstone. It told his story in numbers - not money, but people: the thousands of children educated since the start; the hundreds who had gone on to university, and more who had graduated from the program and into training or jobs, and the tens of centres opened and the hundreds of people employed full or part-time by the charity.

A rousing chorus of "speech, speech" ricocheted around the ballroom. There was no escape. Later, he couldn't remember what he said to the audience. It had all become a bit blurred. He thanked a lot of people. He remembered thanking Megan and Caro in particular. And Stefanie, of course. And he recalled, roughly, how he had finished because he always ended with the same plea.

"We live in an era governed by endless rules and regulations, the fairness of which depends upon the hand each of us was dealt at birth. We all need rules to live by for society to function, but even more, we need shared values to lead us to do the right thing. What happens elsewhere matters here. We're all connected. Everyone deserves the opportunity to shine, and education is key to that. As Cicero once said, 'to not to know what happened before you were born is to remain forever a child'. Through LifeChance, our practical deeds of love will be returned with interest by these children as they become the adults of tomorrow making the world a better place."

Three months and five days later, Saskia was born, to be joined by a brother, Jordan, the following year. Their shy faces were centre stage on the wedding photograph on James's desk, taken at St. Bride's. He held Saskia, and Stefanie held Jordan. A support cast of extended families and friends, led by Caro and Megan grinned back at the camera, frozen in time, captured for his lifetime.

Acknowledgements

Writing this novel involved a lot of people, including some who may be unaware of the help they afforded me.

Thanks to my lovely wife Lynwen Gibbons for doing all the things for me that I should have been doing whilst I scribbled away in my study.

Thanks to stalwart friends Kevin Gilmartin, Paul McNeil, Ruth McIntosh, Kevin Reynolds and Lynwen, whose reading of earlier drafts greatly shaped the telling.

Thanks to Stuart Anderson for his brilliant cover design which magically transformed the manuscript into a real book.

Thanks to lecturers at Roehampton University's Creative Writing department, particularly Judith Bryan, Leone Ross and James Smythe, for their knowledge, guidance and enthusiasm. Thanks also to my many classmates for their constructive kicking during editing workshops – you know who you are!

Thanks to Stephen Pollard for the many shared lung-busting miles, banter and occasional pain-free interludes which gave birth to some rich ideas.

Thanks to my family for putting up with me.

Thank you for taking the time to read my novel. If you have enjoyed it, please do me the great favour of posting an enthusiastic review onto Amazon.

Printed in Great
Britain
by Amazon

31260735R00236